Legends of the Spectral Realms

by D.J.Ebenal

www.heartlandchronicles.com

G

Copyright ©by Darcy John Ebenal

Published in 2008 by GoldenTree Books

P.O. Box 3592 Castlegar

BC Canada V1N 2Z1

D.J. Ebenal

Legends of the Spectral Realms: Love

ISBN: 978-0-9809388-0-7
0-980-9388-0-5

Acknowledgements

Julie Catherine Vigna has been the final authority of all things excellent about this novel. When you realize how good it turned out blame her. Without her, none of this would have happened.

Trevor Strand has been a constant encouragement through the years it took to develop this project.

Candice Lucey, for the insightful critique that helped achieve excellence.

Pat Parish, not only for the amazing cover illustration, but for the renewed competitive camaraderie that prods me on to raise the bar just one more notch, and the unwavering encouragement that makes it possible.

And for Don Ross and Jerri Parish for being his support net - work, because Heaven knows guys like us need all the help we can get.

Everyone else who believes dreams come true.

ஐௐ

The Dark Forest

By DJ Ebenal

I remember the first day I saw him. Jarel was a young man then, and I younger still. But his slender muscles had already lost their soft boyishness in return for the lean stamina of a woodsman. His eyes were a brilliant gray, gentle yet keen, with such a piercing way about them I was sure he could see right through me. But his smile was permanent, as if put there to disarm the often shocking reaction to his gaze. And his smile was genuine, warm and inviting, painted onto a face that knew both grief and wariness but never bitterness.

Never that.

He was tall and striking in the gray tunic, his brown and green cloak and his tan leggings. He wore the colors of the forest. I knew he could blend into that place seamlessly. He'd have to, to traverse those paths. But in this memory he stood out in stark contrast to the place, perched a few paces from the edge of its angry boundary with a stag slung across his shoulders and his feet planted wide apart as if posing for an adoring audience.

I was still too young to know what it was that caused such a strong effect on the older girls and young women tending the fields around me. With guarded looks towards Jarel's victorious emergence from that dark place, exchanging knowing glances with each other, they seemed to agree upon some implicit conclusion that caused the colour to rise in their cheeks. But I was not beyond the awe he inspired, and stared openly at one who had just appeared out of legend and myth.

He seemed to come to some decision and began to stride towards us. The authority in his step, not to be mistaken with the haughtiness of so many of our young men, was a genuine strength that drew the respect from his elders and his peers. Yet he appeared humble enough, finding balance so early in life when it escapes so many others altogether.

Of course I did not realize any of this at the time. I pieced these things together over the years as I watched how people in our castle reacted to him. All I can say about that first impression was that as I watched him my awe blossomed into adoration, a childish idolization of a hero to our people.

"Our castle." Later wisdom of age would bring a clearer picture that excluded any right I may have had in claiming any kind of ownership of Keeper Fortress. But I had not yet felt the sting of the slaver's whip, thinking it instead an honor to be allowed to help in the fields. I hadn't noticed the significance between the upper table and the lower ones, or the silk frills the noble girls wore, compared to the rough spun tunic that itched so unbearably on my scrawny shoulders. I thought only that those girls were pretty, that those tables were there by chance. If anything, I pitied the others for not having the happy childhood I had, trusting my momma to supply the final answers to life's most elusive mysteries.

And Jarel, whatever conclusions he had drawn, walked fearlessly up to the gates and past the soldiers standing on guard. They did not salute with their weapons as he tromped by them. But I noticed the nods of respect, and how they let him by without so much as a question to hinder his passage. And then he was gone and I went back to work, thinking of nothing else for the rest of the day.

That afternoon we were brought into the great hall, my momma and I, herded together with the other slaves. I saw him immediately from across the hall. He was seated at the foot of the high table, already in deep conversation with those four closest to him. The nobles seemed enthralled by every word he spoke, leaning towards him like eager children. And he catered to them with his words, with his simple charm, with manners that defied his profession as a woodsman.

There was the stag, a great mass of roasted meat served up on a single platter in the center of the high table. The stag's head and antlers had been removed and my eyes went to the vacant place on the wall where I knew it would appear in time. I was disappointed not to see it there already. But I knew some things took time if they were to be done properly.

And my hungry child's mind couldn't gravitate far from that steaming carcass for long. "Are we going to taste deer meat, momma?" I asked her. Looking up from where I held her hand, I could see her shocked expression before she smoothed her features over.

"Hush, now child. Wait and see." I could understand that, so I looked back at the splendid animal and saw that I had caught Jarel's eye.

He sat there staring at me, almost as if he'd heard my question, although that was certainly impossible. And then he turned back to entertaining his hosts. I kept watching him for some sign that he had indeed heard me all the way from across the hall. And when Breanne bent down to retrieve his tankard, he motioned for her to bend closer and whispered into her ear. Breanne was a stoic young serving girl who spoke very little and laughed even less. She nodded and relayed those words to our lord at the far end of the table.

Lord Tyrone flushed with anger for a split second, but when he glanced at Jarel his expression shifted to show pleasure. "Of course!" he exclaimed with upraised hands. And then his voice lowered again so that I couldn't hear what was said.

Later that evening, once the nobles and Jarel had been served their meal, other servants came forward with the slaves' fare. A child's portion of cooked meat was placed in front of me. I looked up at my momma for guidance. She watched me, eyes wide with excitement, as another serving was placed before her. "Go ahead, Leena. It's yours."

That night, as the field workers were on their way to bed, Breanne confessed to us that it had been Jarel who had requested we receive a share of the stag.

That had me wondering. And from the talk at the inn in the weeks that followed, I wondered how many other people had experienced something like that.

"It's no wonder the boy is odd.' This came from Banter, a bearded, great muscled man who sat with his axe leaning against his table. He sat facing the common crowd – the tradesmen and farmers, slaves and serfs who had all come to share a word and a tankard of ale after a long day of toil.

One would wonder what a slave girl as young as I was doing in such a place. Keeper Fortress was small and isolated, nestled on the edge of the world. Huddled in the shadow of the great Dark Forest, a vast empty sea of pastureland spread out from the castle south, west, and east. We were like family, all of us.

And momma had passed me off to papa for a bit of a respite. He had taken me by my hand, down to the tavern, where I sat watch - ing and listening from the safety of his lap and his enveloping arms.

"I don't dare go near that forest, and I'm a woodcutter!" Banter glanced at his axe as if to remind himself of his own trade. "Look at me! No stronger man is there at Keeper Fortress." None disput - ed that. "What common sense that lad must lack, striding in and out of that place like he owns it."

"Jarel doesn't spend his nights in the castle," alleged Mable, one of the serving wenches, while she poured ale from a clay jug.

"And he won't have none of us, neither," Aerial, another one of the servants added.

My papa covered my ears with his hands. "Hush, Aerial. There are children."

Aerial looked absolutely shamed. "My apologies, Kenneth." Papa took his hands away. Then she looked at me. "My apologies, Leena." She looked as though she might cry.

"But it's true!" Banter cut in before I could say anything.

I got up off my papa's knee and went over to Aerial.

"Keeper Fortress is as it has always been since as far back as I can remember," Banter continued. There were nods of agreement all around as I put my arms around Aerial's waist and hugged the sadness out of her. She was awkward at first, but then she felt the happiness and put her free hand on my head as a way to embrace me back. I loved that woman.

"And now this stranger shows up, defying the forest by bringing a stag to our lord's table, and just like that, Lord Tyrone wel- comes him into our home. I should say our good lord showed sense that day. But the way the boy treats him in return!"

"He treats him with a goodly portion of respect, I'd say," Rily, our butcher admitted.

More nods accompanied me back to my father.

"But he treats every one of us with the same measure of respect he credits our lord." Banter gestured towards me. "I bet even young Leena here has been awarded this stranger's favor at some time."

"Don't be silly," Mable scolded.

But Banter persisted. "Tell us, little one. Has he?"

"Leave her be, you're frightening her," Mable reproached him.

Uncomfortable with being the center of attention among so many grownups, I blushed and bowed my head.

"It's okay, Leena," my papa reassured me as he placed a hand lightly on my shoulder. "You're not in trouble."

"It is as I say?" Banter asked, as gently as he could.

I thought about the feast carefully before I looked up and nod-ded.

"You see!" Banter cried, pointing at me with both hands while chatter broke out through the entire crowd.

"The woodsman is neither slave nor noble, but slave to slaves and noble to nobles!"

"There is no place in this world for such a man." Immediately, the room fell silent. A man sat in the corner of the room. His hair was short, his beard was of matching length. His tunic was dark brown, cut off at the shoulders, frayed on the edges. He wore a leather belt with a short sword tucked into it. But the weapon was without a scabbard, rusted and chipped along its edges. His leg-gings were dark, his boots rough and worn. The man was thin and mean looking, angry and dirty, but at the same time exuded confi-dence and intelligence. He appeared to be a soldier newly returned from battle, but by the faint smell that emanated from him I knew he had recently returned from the road, and most probably, the stable.

His eyes, large brown evil orbs, swung out at the rest of us and I think we collectively leaned away from him so as to keep our distance. "The woodsman is frail in the head. No doubt he's lived in isolation for so long that at the mere sight of you people he craves your good spirits, lest you drive him out of your midst.

"And then what would he have? The Dark Forest – he'd be all alone again in that place, and we all know how evil that place is!"

That brought nods and exclamations of assent. But as the crowd broke up I kept watching the stranger, and I realized that he never seemed to look anyone directly in the eye. Of course, he was good at pretending; but a child notices such details.

I also noticed that the more I stared at him the more uncomfort - able he grew. He fidgeted and his eyes began darting around the room, as though he was desperately looking for me, but couldn't find me. And he appeared to be growing very afraid.

Well! This only made the sport worth while. Such an evil man for saying such nasty things about my… about my Jarel! I thought. He deserves to be afraid, and of a young child, at that. I'll show him! I pushed from my papa's lap and took a step towards the stranger – and it was suddenly as if he grew afraid for his very life. Everything in the room faded until there was just me and him and the evil words he had spoken.

But then my father's hand grasped me by the shoulder and we were back in the inn again. No one else had noticed the stranger's reaction to me, and my father was rising to his feet.

"Come, Leena. It's time for us to go."

I stared at the man as long as I could before my father dragged me out of the inn. And even afterwards Jarel kept coming around, walking in and out of the forest with not a care in the world, entering then re-entering our lives, just as blithe as can be.

The time came, as it inevitably would. It wasn't pushed. It wasn't forced. And it wasn't feigned. Yet circumstance smiled upon me when Jarel stood across the castle courtyard looking directly at me. I confess I had grown old enough by then to feel my heart flutter. Jarel smiled and strode across the courtyard, and I had to hold my hand to my bosom in hopes it would prevent my pound - ing heart from bursting through my chest.

"You aren't going to the feast, my lord?" I asked. I had almost grown into a young woman by then, old enough to know my place but young enough to keep dreaming. Jarel, on the other hand, seemed not to have changed at all. One would have thought that at least his clothes would have become ripped and soiled over the years. But it seemed to me that I stared up at the young face of the same man I'd first seen marching free of the forest with a stag on his shoulders. He had grown a beard, though, and yet somehow I was convinced this was simply a ploy to convince people that he was, in fact, aging.

"I am no lord." He was as close to angry as he would ever come, and I was shamed. But then a smile returned to his face and he stepped forward as if to comfort me. Something halted his movement though, and he looked back at the great hall from which he'd come. "No. I must return to the forest, ere it gets too late. I have chores to attend to."

"Chores? You?" I couldn't believe it. Despite his denial, such a regal man as he must be a nobleman. Perhaps he owned a castle of his own hidden deep in the forest. Surely he could simply com - mand and people would follow.

He smiled. That smile again; it couldn't help but affect me. Then he came forward until we almost touched, and he held his hands out to me, palms up. I looked from him to his hands, then back again. "Go ahead," he urged. "Touch them."

I placed my fingertips against his hands. And I frowned. Then I ran my fingers over the surface of his palms. There was nothing sexual in my exploration. Such things hadn't yet begun to enter my mind, but I was curious and amazed and fascinated. His hands were covered in calluses and scars that left deep ridges across the natural lines I expected to find.

"Bow string and glass cuts," he explained with a shrug and pulled his hands away. "Did you feel the calluses?"

How could I not?

"Do you know what they're from?"

I'm sure he had the answer, but I nodded anyway and said, "hard work." To a peasant or a slave, it didn't matter what we did. If we worked, we had hands like that.

My answer obviously pleased him more than his intended response. "Thank you for showing me your hands." Thank you for letting me touch you, you mean – silly girl.

"Thank you for not finding them too hideous to touch."

That left me grinning like an idiot.

He shrugged. "The nobles are disgusted when they see them."

"Tell them it's from sword work." Nobles might be soft, but they can fight, I'll give them that.

He took a step back and his gaze swept over the forest behind me. "Close enough to the truth, that is."

I gazed into the forest, trying to see what he saw. "Do you have to fight when you go in there?"

His eyes blazed. "Only when I win."

"What do you fight, then?"

He grinned and I could not tell if he was joking or not. "Angrymen. Good bye, young Leena. Fare you well, until our next talk."

I could only blink and stare up at him. He said we were going to talk again!

And he strode through the gates.

I watched him go, thinking of our first encounter, thinking how blessed fortunate I was to come to feast late for a change. My appetite forgotten, I watched him take those confident, unwavering steps towards the forbidden shadows of the Dark Forest. The fearless manner in which he looked neither right nor left, (and most certainly never backwards) made me believe what he said about always winning whatever terrible battles must rage inside that place.

I saw Jarel often after that, and we spoke frequently. He departed and reappeared at the castle with such regularity that his visits became quite commonplace, which frequently left the castle on its head with grins and giggles and welcoming arms as often as with disappointment.

His comings and goings became natural though, as did our brief lingering together. But he considered all in the castle his equal, and many other people longed for his company, at the high table and in the common room in the inn. Jarel was a busy man.

He kept that outrageous beard. As the years passed, I found his whiskers so comical that I often laughed when I first saw him. "Does it get cold in the forest at night, woodsman?" I would manage to choke out through tears of mirth. "A young woman would help more than that scratchy beard!"

Never once did I realize – all right, never did I once acknowledge – that I was such a young woman. I could look him directly in the eyes now, equal with his own height. But my body was slim and hard, like that of a young boy's, though my breasts would be full enough if I ever had children. And my hair, although it was long and black as midnight silk when it was wet, was frizzled and flat, and dirty a good portion of the time. My lord earned my loyalty for letting me keep it long and free of lice.

Lord Tyrone was a good man. Surely things would have been different if we'd not been so isolated. But here, on the periphery of the Dark Forest, with naught but servants and slaves for company, he'd come to be included in our family and made sure we were happy. And for me, happiness consisted of my hair and the woodsman, Jarel. I was glad he could see it. I even flipped it coquettishly out of my face and over my shoulders, flaunted it before this scruffy, beautiful man.

He grinned, as he did so often. "I'll cut my beard when you cut your hair, woman."

That left my knees quivering. He called me woman! (I was a flighty young robin back then. I'm flighty still, if a bit of a stiff old crow now. But at least I'd long come to accept the effect he had on me. And I knew Jarel could see what he did to me. As the inhabitants of the castle teased me about it – endlessly – I was sure I'd given myself away a long, long time ago.) I glanced down at my chest, then back at him. "It took you long enough to notice! I thought you'd gone blind!"

My declaration finally brought the reaction I was looking for. (And once I'd discovered I could make the great Jarel blush, I sought endlessly, day and night, for ways to make it so.) I smiled, gave a quick tug on his beard and swayed my hips as I resumed my work in the fields.

To his credit, I noticed he kept his eyes elsewhere, blushing furiously as he stammered unsuccessfully for something to say, then finally simply shook his head and walked on.

"Shave your beard!" I shouted after him.

He held up his hand and continued walking towards the castle. Part of me was glad he didn't turn around with a reply; that man could talk honey from a bee. But part of me was really curious about what he might have said.

Of course everyone else had a similar relationship with Jarel. He had this aura, a way about him that clearly attracted people, always smiling, always courteous. He was always simply there for one and all, except when he just wasn't there.

Fate must have favored me back then. Looking back at it now does not diminish my good fortune in managing to find time alone with our celebrity woodsman. Despite the funny beard, the times I could exchange a few words with him were the moments I cherished most. I inhaled them like a drowning woman would air, holding them inside me until I would burst for want of another gasp.

And I found occasions, though times were changing.

In our youth we'd teased and taunted each other about the angrymen. As a child I had discovered one in our inn, and chased the awful creature from our castle. But now they were showing up more frequently. They could be seen walking down the road, trudging through our fields with cargo on their backs, almost like frightening snails. They came to our gates and it was to our soldier's good credit that they were stopped there. But unfortunately, the men constantly let these vagabonds through. The angrymen seemed always to have coin and they brought trade, and Lord Tyrone was glad for their company. And cheerless company it was!

For myself, I despised the wicked men openly, and was left alone for my trouble. Jarel was clearly incapable of such emotion, but I knew he did not like them any more than I did. I remember once I was standing by the stable well, with a water bucket in my hands, taking advantage of an opportunity to let my eyes linger on Jarel while he conversed nearby with some friends. His back was to me, but I could see the others facing me well enough to piece together much of what he was saying. The experience was well worth it, and I was content just to stand there and gaze at this breathtaking man.

But then along came one of these angrymen, acting haughty and glaring about with unblinking, hateful eyes. He stalked right up to the little group, spreading his angry, mean filth before him, and stared into Jarel's face with such a look of contempt, I thought he would spit upon my beloved right then and there.

12

I knew exactly when Jarel stopped talking and stared back. For a moment a look of abject horror crossed the angryman's face, and then he lowered his eyes and hung his head. Just as the other angryman in the inn had done when I stared him down as a child, this one assumed the same cornered animal posture. He looked just as frightened, although the knowledge of his own fear seemed to fuel this man's bitterness. With visible effort, he stood his ground and kept his tone low and friendly, talking to the others as though Jarel was invisible.

No one else seemed to notice the angryman's peculiar behavior. They were enthralled with the man's smooth-as-silk tongue, which elicited nervous chuckles, then outright laughter from his listeners, all of course, except Jarel.

Jarel watched in silence, never taking his eyes from the man. He stood his vigil until the angryman had deftly drawn the crowd away from him and led them back into the inn, and then word - lessly spun on his heel and stepped towards me.

Caught in the act of ogling, I did not have time to be coy and look away. But something I saw in Jarel's expression made me put aside our ongoing game of flirtation and grow serious. He looked at me intently, not wholly surprised by my depth of under - standing.

"You see them." It was not a question.

I bobbed my head in assent. "Filthy creatures, every one of them. I can recognize them from afar now."

Jarel nodded as he propped a boot up on the ledge of the well and draped his arms over his bent knee while he contemplated this. His eyes narrowed thoughtfully, and then his gaze returned to the door of the inn, the door that thing had disappeared through.

"They aren't human, are they?" Something that repulsive could never be human.

He turned and gazed at me.

"Why can't any of the others see them for what they are?"

He started to reply, then caught the words before he spoke. He paused and then said, carefully, "People don't want to see what is there before them. They want what's before them to be what they see."

I saw the sense of that. "That must not make us very sensible people."

He grunted and nodded his head. He looked back at the inn.

"That really bothers you, doesn't it?"

Jarel looked back at me. "That? No, not really. People will be who they are. It's those angrymen I could do without." Again his eyes slid back to where the angryman was entertaining his friends.

"Angrymen?" I asked.

"That's what they're called. Distasteful creatures, with no good in them; the world would do well to be rid of every one of them."

"Then you weren't joking when you talked of fighting them in the forest."

This time his eyes swung around to meet mine and stayed there. "What do you think makes the Dark Forest so dark?" His voice was flat, but I could hear the underlying vehemence. "Truthfully, if the angrymen had their way, the whole world would be covered by that forbidden place."

I believed him. "I believe you."

In the process of straightening up, he paused. Something flick- ered behind his eyes as he stared keenly into mine. "Thank you, Leena. Not many others would."

He looked troubled, so I reached out and touched the underside of his hand tenderly. "Thank you for these scars, Jarel."

It was hard to read his expression, but our hands lingered for a moment. Then he chortled, chucked me under the chin and said, "It's not all me, you know!"

And then the moment was gone.

℠℥

Matters between us didn't become clear to me until later that year during the harvest. Every available hand was laboring out in the fields, scattered far apart, right up to the very edge of the Dark Forest. Our backs bent wearily under the hot sun and our harsh toiling brought sweat and blood as much as tears. Harvest was never a pleasurable time.

The formidable power of the forest drew our attention; that is, as much as could be spared from the sickles we wielded. It was an evil place that was too colossal to ignore for long. It stretched along the perimeter of the fields in a perfectly straight line, restrained from spilling over its boundaries by people much braver than we. Even where our own fields ended and the wild ones began, it was obvious where the forest's dominion ended. It was like a line had been drawn across the earth; and on one side of the line was the domain of evil, while on the other side was the realm of man.

Despite the fact that I was aware of Jarel's ability to walk this line and exist on either side of it, thoughts of the angrymen kept my eyes downcast as much as the next person.

It was that same fear, that same instinctive wisdom that occu-pied our minds constantly, struggling to keep the fear at bay. I had been so determined not to give voice to it that I had not spo-ken to the others of what Jarel had said about the angrymen, keeping the knowledge to myself. And to be honest, part of my silence was because I acknowledged how ridiculous our beliefs

were, too. Life at the castle was not an easy one, and to be perceived as an oddity among my peers was something I dared not
do.

There was shouting from the castle and I turned to see smoke
billowing menacingly. At the northern gate, the two guards that
usually stood watch were crumpled upon the ground, cast aside
like worn out rag dolls. A woman screamed in terror, the terrible
sound rising from her throat cut off abruptly. I heard the clash of
metal on metal and realized that no smithy ever made a noise like
that.

My eyes widened in shock as I understood what was happening,
and one thought flooded my mind. Jarel.

I dropped my sickle and my bundle of wheat; turned, and fled
towards the forest as fast as my legs would carry me. The others
had grasped what was happening too; I could tell from the edge
of hysteria in their voices as they shouted for me to come back. I
shrugged off their warnings. My fear of the forest did not deter
me, not for a second. My thoughts were on Jarel, and so I continued to run.

As soon as I committed myself to that first step into its awaiting
death, the forest reached out to tear at me. Had I been in my right
mind, I would have screamed in horror. Had I been sane, I would
have immediately turned and fled back out into the open. The forest was alive in its wrath, clawing at my eyes, tripping up my
feet, and entangling my clothes, grasping at me from all sides
with barren, claw-like branches.

Inevitably I tripped. With my eyes pinched shut I hit the
ground. The force of the fall knocked the wind out of me, and I
massaged one of my wrists gingerly, certain that it was sprained.
But my fear and pain was not great enough to shake me of my
need to find Jarel. I lay there panting, hearing the blood pounding
in my ears, growling, get up, you stupid girl, through clenched
teeth. I held my breath, noticing how quiet and still it was.

Surprisingly, the trees seemed to have backed off, for as I lay there I realized that the branches weren't attacking me anymore. Eventually the pain subsided enough that I could open my eyes and look around. I was surprised to find myself lying on a carpet of brown needles and rotting leaves. I couldn't see very far though, because a bleak, gray shadow cast an eerie gloom all around me. I used my good hand to push myself to my knees, gasping for breath. The trees were gnarled and ancient; thick twisted trunks with a multitude of ominous, outstretched branches that looked as frightening up close as they did from the fields.

The fields!

I forced myself back to my feet and stumbled further into the Dark Forest.

Everything was different in the forest. Out in the fields all was flat, but here the ground was over-run with huge ravines and sink-holes. It was a labyrinth, a silent, endless, deadly labyrinth. In some places, the ground simply vanished under my feet without warning. The first time that happened, I was walking along the ledge of one of these ravines. Suddenly I found myself scram-bling frantically in the air, and it was only by chance I managed to seize a tree root and cling to it before I had fallen too far. I hung suspended for a moment, too surprised and too relieved to remember why I was hanging there under a tree against a dirt cliff. But then I thought of Jarel, and a silent urging rose from within me, giving me renewed strength.

I let go of the tree and slid to the bottom of the ravine.

A gnawing hunger eventually drew my attention. It grew until it was all I could think of. In the distance I heard running water, and supposed that if I filled my stomach with it I wouldn't feel so hungry. But something inside me cringed at the idea of going so far off course. I didn't know where I was. And I was here to find Jarel, not to feed my sudden hunger or slake my thirst. That seemed logical enough for me, so I continued to search for Jarel.

Presently, I stumbled upon a clearing, not realizing how dark the forest was until I actually stood facing open sunlight once again. I hadn't noticed how deathly silent it was either, until I heard sounds of merriment and saw finely-dressed courtiers lounging about on a grassy knoll in the center of the clearing. And I hadn't truly realized just how hungry I was, how utterly famished, until I saw the food. And such food it was! Set out on several low tables, the fare was plentiful and exquisite, making even my heart reach out to it. I could think of nothing more than to sample that spread, to fill my mouth with its tantalizing flavors, my stomach with its nourishment.

As I was about to step into the light, I hesitated, remembering Jarel. I recalled that I was in a forest I had been terrified of my whole life. And I remembered that my home had just been attacked by evil people, possibly even angrymen. What was I doing?

I did not know these people. I did not know this court. And I did not know that food. But I did know Jarel, and my heart reached out to him once more. I turned from the feast and trekked through the thickest part of the forest I could find, allowing the bushes to tear at my arms and legs as penitence for my weakness. Eventually the awful hunger pangs subsided.

And then I found something else. A path. I laughed and cried at the same time and eagerly fell upon it to kiss it. But then I remembered it was just a path, and I had no desire to taste dirt. So I regained my feet, wiped off most of the leaves and soil from my dress, and set to work freeing my hair from a crow's nest worth of forest.

This took longer than I expected, but I managed to comb out most of the knots before I reminded myself that I must still look a fright, with tears and soil smeared all over my face. I laughed at myself, sprained wrist and all, then picked a direction and set out once more. I took perhaps three or four steps before I again thought of Jarel, cursed at my vanity and spun on my heel, marching off in the opposite direction.

The light began to fail long after exhaustion had taken hold of my limbs. But I trudged on, resolute now in my determination. Still, I was only human, and as I began to worry about where I might spend the night, I came across another clearing. It lay directly in my path, basking in the fading rays of the brilliant, golden sunlight.

I smiled, thinking it would be such a relief to be out from the gloom of the forest, even for a few moments. Yet my smile faded when my weary eyes beheld the vision of a lady standing there in all her white finery. She was tall and blonde; beautiful, with hands that had obviously never touched a day's work. Even as my heart fell I felt a rebellious tug of possessiveness, thinking that I now knew the real reason Jarel spent so much time in the forest.

But when she turned and gazed at me all my childishness receded, and I immediately felt safe and welcome. Beside her was a bed of deep satin cushions. The bed was surrounded with tall wooden walls, one of which was detached and opened like a giant door, and I knew it would keep me safe from the terrors of the night and the forest. The woman beckoned me towards it, promising she would keep watch over me as I slept, providing me with even more security in this malevolent place.

I stopped and stared in disbelief. Had word of my arrival spread through the forest? Were these what we called the enchanted people? This incredibly beautiful woman was so much like Jarel I did not doubt that they were kin. Were they welcoming me in his name while they sought him out?

I had no answer. And I so longed to fall into the solitude and the respite she offered, to give in to my exhaustion and put off finding Jarel until the morning.

But Jarel had a right to know what had happened. He might still be able to help, to do something, or at the very least, to warn someone.

I hardened my resolve once again and tromped into the clearing, ignoring the woman with her fine, low-cut dress and her noble lace, determined not even to glance in her direction. Instead, I stalked past her. But what a sight I must have looked to one so accustomed to finery! However, this only strengthened my deter-mination, and I cringed only slightly as I entered the shadows on the far side of the clearing.

Half a dozen paces through the trees I pulled up short. I had found him. Jarel knelt on the ground in front of a cabin, rocking back and forth, wailing in anguish as though struck by some terri-ble blow, keening like a child. He pulled at his beard and hair and pounded the ground with his fists. He stopped when I entered the clearing that surrounded what was apparently his home and squinted up at me through his tears.

At once I knew that he knew what had taken place.

"You could have done something!" I screamed at him, suddenly furious enough to fight the intruders myself. I hurled myself at him, determined to pummel him then and there. But he grabbed both my hands, winced when I did and let go of my injured wrist, dragging me to my knees before him.

"There was nothing I could have done!" he shouted at me through my rage. "They would have taken me as well!"

"You knew!" I cried. "You knew and you did nothing!"

"They did it to themselves!" Jarel exclaimed. "The people let them in! Gave them a home! They drank at their board, laughed at their inn! They traded their money with them, opened their arms to them! Don't you see? They opened their hearts to them!"

I paused in my attack and stared at Jarel. There was more than just terror here, more than simply fear. Righteous anger burned next to helplessness, and I was overcome with witnessing such fierce emotion.

I calmed and slumped down in front of him, stunned by his words.

"They opened their hearts to them!" he cried again and I thought he would go back to tearing at the earth. But he seemed to grow comforted by my presence, so he quieted, and finally he spoke softly. "Angrymen only have the power that you give them."

Angrymen! The castle really had been attacked by angrymen. "Then all is lost," I admitted, tears already welling up from within me.

With supreme sorrow, Jarel held his arms out to me and I fell into his embrace. We held each other and cried together for some time, there in the forest in front of his cabin.

When our tears finally ran dry and the living silence of the forest restored our hearts, when the blessed discovery of his loving embrace grew uncomfortable and awkward for the need to stretch sore muscles, we wordlessly helped each other to our feet.

And my life inside the Dark Forest began.

ஐஇ

I spent the night on a small cot inside a small cabin, but lay awake wondering about my fate, worrying about the future, and cowering from the shadows of swaying trees through the windows. I was relieved to see Jarel appear at the door with the first light of dawn. He'd disappeared after feeding me a simple woodsman's fare of roast duck, wild nuts, and water, and I had not seen him again until now.

He looked haggard and disheveled, and by the knowing look in his eye I surmised he was thinking much the same about me. "You haven't slept a wink," he said.

As tempting as it was, I thought better of playing the languishing maid, so I threw the covers off and swung my legs out of bed. "Neither have you," I retorted. I brushed what I could of the wrinkles of my peasant dress and quickly ran my hands through my hair. Slipping into my soiled leather shoes I turned to face my host with my hands on my hips. "What now?" I asked.

He made an effort not to laugh. In light of yesterday's tragedy, Jarel restrained his mirth to a quizzical expression and a slight twitching of his lips. But rather than humiliate me, as had been our prior custom, he now held a hand out to me, reaching out over the threshold as if he dared not cross it himself.

"We must be wed," he said simply. It was not a proposal. Our time spent huddled in each other's arms had been enough for both of us to know the course our lives would take.

Although a grieving embrace was as far as we'd taken our relationship, both Jarel and I saw things differently than the others at Keeper Fortress. For them it was about the destination, the goal. For us it was the journey. I did not begrudge him his lack of romance, but took his hand in my own grimy grip and stepped out into the gray dawn.

"The trees seem less forbidding in the light," I commented, looking around the clearing.

"They're not," he said, turning to watch my face. "They only look that way." Then he led me down the path towards them.

Holding his hand, I was less inclined to be afraid. Yet my feet dragged, if only a little, and I followed a step behind, resisting his pull. "You don't seem to be afraid of them," I remarked. "Like those other people, those nobles in the clearings between here and the castle, your people."

He stopped and looked at me. His face did not show surprise, but only enormous curiosity and wonder, a wonder I could not fathom. "And you still made it through… " his voice trailed off.

"What is it, Jarel?"

"I tell you the truth. Those clearings are not there now. We can go back and look for them, if you wish. But the forest has claimed them, or they've given themselves up to the forest once again. We are quite alone here."

"Then this forest really is enchanted?" I wasn't really surprised.

He nodded. "But it only has the power that you give to it."

"Like the angrymen."

He resumed walking. "Just like the angrymen."

I caught up to him with a few hurried strides and fell into step beside him. We went hand in hand into the forest, and I was not afraid.

Our way led from the path at a dark place, where the shadows were thick and the dawn barely penetrated through the malevolent branches overhead. The trees, though, seemed benign to our pres-ence and left us alone as we navigated our way among them. Perhaps I only imagined them attacking me yesterday afternoon, when I had first fled from the invasion of Keeper Fortress. Yet the realization did not dampen my resentment towards them, my indifference to their apparent benevolence. As if to spite them in my new-found courage, I raised my nose at them and followed Jarel as he threaded his way through them, stepping where he stepped, following in his footsteps exactly.

Eventually the sunlight reached us even amongst these massive, still monsters, because we stepped out on the edge of a pond and sunbeams streamed down upon the water. In the middle of the pond was a tiny island with a clump of beautiful long stemmed flowers, their petals a vivid scarlet and golden-yellow.

A profound peace drifted over the water and reached us where we stood, welcoming us. The peaceful solitude of the pond was at odds with the dark forest and its frightful shadows, its horrendously twisted boughs that looked more like the bony hands of some ancient grasping crow. I felt as though I was intruding, and turned to go, but when I reached for Jarel's arm, he took my hand once again and shook his head.

"This is where we belong," he said in a hushed whisper, as if he himself could scarcely believe his own words. "Come. Let us go out into it and become even more unsightly than we already are."

I stared at him. He looked fine. He was as clean and as presentable as always, if perhaps a little disheveled than usual. I was not put off by his words. There was no one here but us. Rather, I was encouraged at the prospect of having a bath, and eyed the pond with renewed interest.

Jarel chuckled and then stepped into the pond, boots and all. I cried out with surprise, but he did not let go of my hand, and I was dragged in behind him. I could have laughed and dived in to the water with sheer pleasure, so glorious did it feel. But there was something so serene, something holy about the place, and I was loath to disturb the tranquility that reached out from the water and enveloped me. Instead, I waded further into the pond, which was no deeper than my waist, and Jarel led me to the island where the beautiful plants grew.

We climbed out of the water, dropped to our knees and rested, dripping wet, while the tranquility seeped into our very bones. I felt refreshed, rejuvenated. And all of my discordant feelings for the dark forest were replaced with simple detachment. This was what was important, this feeling of cleanliness, of purity. It didn't matter that all around me were foreboding sentinels that somehow felt wrong, out of place. Let the enchantment of the forest continue to exist. It no longer held its power over me. I had found an enchantment within an enchantment, and it would change my whole life.

Eventually, Jarel spoke. "As this place is our witness, our hearts are one."

I wasn't sure if I was intended to repeat his words, but I did, and I meant them with all my heart. He raised a knife that I had - n't been aware that he'd had, and I nodded silently. I knew this ritual. Such ceremonies were commonplace in the fields, outside the reach of the forest.

He cut his hand, across the palm. It wasn't a deep cut, just enough so that a bead of blood formed in the gash. But it made me wince, although I was not afraid when it was my turn. Jarel seemed not to feel any pain, but merely made a fist with his hand and lowered his head. Then he passed the knife over to me, and I took it.

"Now, as this sacred place is our witness, let our bodies be joined as our hearts already are," I intoned. And I ran the knife across my own hand. I scarcely felt the cut, but the wound was bleeding.

Jarel reached for my hand and I took his, and we clasped our hands together so that the blood from each would mix and become one. He guided my hand over the flowers in front of us, and we kept our hands locked together until some of the mixed blood fell amongst the leaves.

Satisfied, Jarel released my hand. He was grinning hugely, and in the face of the terrible tragedy of yesterday it was good to see some of his old self return. I smiled back at him. Leaning for - ward, I kissed his lips ever so gently, and he kissed me back. Then I straightened and looked at his smiling face.

He turned to tend to our wounds, but when I saw that he was going to tear the sleeve from his tunic, I stopped him. "Oh don't, Jarel. Let me take a piece from my dress, instead. It's a damned impractical thing here in the forest, anyway."

He watched as I used the knife to rip a length from the bottom of my rough spun dress. "I know a thing about making clothes," he said. He seemed awkward since being married, as though he didn't know what to do now that we'd come this far. But if I knew one thing about Jarel, it was that he'd be able to figure it out sooner or later.

"I'm sure you do," I observed as I nodded at his own clothes, which were so much finer than my own. "Where did you learn that, by the way?"

He shrugged. "I've visited some of the enchanted clearings myself, on occasion."

After I wound a length of cloth around my own hand, I cut off the excess and handed it to him. "I believe I have some spare clothing we can alter, back at the cabin somewhere," he continued as he wound the bandage over his hand. "I dare say it might be a bit scandalous, you dressed like a man all the time."

I harrumphed at that. "Not as scandalous as the remains of a dress that keeps getting shorter because we keep cutting lengths off of it," I retorted.

That made him grin, and I was delighted to see my old Jarel reappear.

"Come. Show me these clothes," I said, tugging at his hand. "I wouldn't want to give you any more ideas … well, not here, anyway. Not in this sacred place."

He grinned again as we lowered ourselves into the water. "Is that why you're in such a hurry to leave?"

I refused to meet his eyes, or answer his question. But I did hasten, and forced him to do the same.

We didn't get much done that day.

It was good for the heart, though, to spend so much time laughing and holding each other closely. It was a day of emotion, of expressing all our emotions. And we each found a closeness with the other that we would carry with us always, a closeness that allowed us to say anything to each other, to speak honestly whatever was on our minds.

It was a beautiful beginning.

ഇരു

Our life together was a simple one, and filled with work – con - tinuous work, from sunup to sundown. But it was also full of wonders and memories that would outlast the dark memories of the forest. Jarel taught me the secrets of the land, how to exist as one with nature, how to nurture our surroundings while harvest - ing from the land.

And he taught me the ways of the forest, of this forest in partic - ular. In those early years I never wandered very far from our clearing unless Jarel was with me. But he insisted the forest could do me no harm unless I wished it. I never saw the mysterious noble people again, and of the clearings they had inhabited there was no sign, or at least, none that I could see from my short exer - tions into the haunted realm.

It had been perhaps a month since I had fled from the castle. I can't say that my mind never returned to my old home, because it did. But I must confess that it never lingered very long on Keeper Fortress before my mind fled to a more comforting refuge. Life with Jarel was blissful; a dream come true, and I desperately feared that my time with him would come to an end someday . I was afraid that either whatever had attacked my friends and fami - ly and had seized them as trophies – or worse – might return; or that Lord Tyrone had somehow managed to repel the attackers and was now looking for me.

I had been but a mere slave girl, born into Lord Tyrone's house- hold. I was merely one of his possessions. In my mind I enter - tained the notion that Jarel was more nobleman than commoner , obviously a freeman. Perhaps my beloved husband had a secret treasure somewhere, gold or gems hidden in a cave or hollow tree trunk. Maybe Jarel could buy my freedom and we could be married in the presence of our people, just as we had been in the presence of that sacred pond.

But I saw him less and less in the first days of our marriage, and became despondent, thinking sometimes that I had escaped from being Lord Tyrone's slave only to become Jarel's. And then when I did see Jarel he was distracted, obsessed with his own thoughts. He would spend hours by the fire, staring moodily into its embers, muttering under his breath. Often he would spring to his feet and rush out the door at all hours of the night, seemingly forgetting all about his new wife and the tender day and night he'd first spent with her.

I was confused and disheartened. I was lonely and homesick. It seemed that the woodsman I had been in love with for so long had turned into a man I didn't know anymore. And now I was alone, a prisoner in our cabin, too afraid to leave and find myself back in that dreadful forest. Besides, Jarel was my husband. Where would I go? What else could I do but remain where I was and make the best of it?

Then one day he showed up at our door, smiling at me affectionately. I paused in my chores and stared at him in confusion. The light behind him silhouetted his head and shoulders and suddenly he seemed to be every inch the man he used to be.

"I've been distracted since you got here," he said. "And for that I am terribly sorry. I have no excuse for the way I've been behaving."

"Why?" That was all I wanted to know.

"Keeper Fortress. I've been trying to find out what happened to Keeper Fortress."

"I thought you knew."

He shook his head. "I knew only that the angrymen attacked from the inside out. But I didn't know what had happened to our people."

Our people. They weren't really our people at all. They were my people. But I loved him for saying it, nonetheless, and I wait - ed for him to continue.

"They are still alive, most of them, anyway. The angrymen have taken them as slaves and now live off of their labor."

He opened his arms, and I sighed and moved into them willing - ly, holding him close, allowing my relief to be evident.

"That's not all I've been doing," he admitted to me after a moment. "There is a cave not far from here. I do much of my work there and use this place only for sleeping, mostly. I was going to move camp there entirely, but then you showed up and I was distracted. But I'm finished now. I want to take you there."

"I don't want to live in a cave," I confessed, clinging to my hus - band still.

He laughed, and it was a rich honest laugh, the one I had come to love. "Have you ever been in one?"

I had to admit that I had not.

"Every cave is different, and this one has high ceilings with walls that sparkle under torchlight."

So he did have a treasure. "The sun enters it from above so there is light, but there is only one entrance that animals can get into and I've blocked that off."

"I still don't want to live in a cave."

He held me at arms' length. "You won't. You'll never have to go in there if you don't want to."

I was confused, and by the look on my face, he could tell.

But instead of laughing at me, he grinned and held me by the shoulders. "Come," he urged. "Come and see." Then he led me from the cabin, through the forest, to a brand new cabin that was nearly three times the size of the one we'd been living in!

"I wanted to make it perfect before I told you about it," he con - fessed. "I only now finished it. I hope you like it." He searched my face eagerly for my approval.

I could only gaze at him, open-mouthed in wonder , but my eyes were drawn to the cabin. It was a regular house, like a merchant' s house might look, like the kind I'd heard about in the cities to the south. It even had windows and doors, and everything! It was built against a great cliff, and I suspected the cave entrance was somewhere in the back. I could see the openings in the clif f Jarel had talked about. A charming waterfall cascaded down the cliff to the right of the house, ending where a little bit of a pond formed and a creek bubbled off into the forest. But the forest – and this was the best part – the forest didn't come right up to the clif fs! There was a wide field of tall grass, totally free of the dark enchantment that surrounded us. The field was green and friendly, and it swayed dreamily in the gentle wind.

I looked back at Jarel and hesitated, longing evident in my eyes, as if asking permission to explore, and he laughed outright. "Go ahead, Leena! It's your cabin!"

Then I whooped for joy, and ran across the grass and through the front door of my brand new home!

I would have thought that with the completion of the house, Jarel would have ceased his fussing. But although he had returned to his usual self, to the man I had come to cherish and love above all others, our quiet life inside this enchanted forest was anything but ordinary. And Jarel seemed to be very content with its singu - larity.

At night was when I noticed it the most. The malevolent spirits that rested in the trees by day seemed to waken and be released from their ghastly tree-bark prisons. The darkness was a complete and total darkness, the kind where you could hold your hand up to your face and yet never see it. And complete darkness was maddening; it got under your skin and festered; it pounded in your temples in a cadence that left you believing that you were as mad as the forest.

But there was something else. Yes the evil was there, the evil I saw in the angrymen, there was no denying that. But there was also a profound goodness that would often rise up out of nowhere and would never appear in the same place twice. Like the unfor-gettable serenity of the pool of water, this life force of nature would blossom and flourish for no more than a night, often only a few hours. Hues of blue, green, red and yellow, glowing like northern lights but materializing upon the ground, would twilight the forest floor with wonder.

The first time I saw this marvel I was standing at the window, glaring out at the trees. The sun had long since set but the moon was full and bright, and I could easily see the beastly things undulating in the wind. I had been chopping firewood all day long; and even though my hands were raw from bursting blisters and my back ached from the strain, I never seemed to have enough firewood.

In truth, we always had more firewood than we could ever hope to use. But Jarel understood my feelings and supported me, shar-ing my distaste for the bewitched forest we lived in.

Then the mysterious lights began, rising up out of the ground like mist. I could see the silhouettes of people dancing amid the lights, and cried out in surprise when I heard the rhythmic tempo of the beautiful lutes.

I must have moved towards the door, because suddenly Jarel's hand was there, grasping my arm and I felt as though I was wak-ing from a trance. I turned to him and he shook his head. "If you go," he said sadly, "you'll never come back."

I was dismayed and looked back at the captivating goodness before us, a goodness I was sure promised so much more. "But how could something so pure and beautiful do me harm?"

"It's not that it would seek to harm you. It's that what you see before you is only a shimmer of what there is. This beauty will fade again beneath the bitterness of the forest and you will go with it, too enthralled to leave it behind."

I turned to look at him, seeking the truth of his words.

The sad look in his eyes told me he was not jesting. "Yes, it will feel like home for you. And once you've seen that magical place you will never be able to look away. My place is here, and if you go I will be alone again."

"I would never leave you," I told him fiercely. Yet part of my heart still longed to go out and explore that beautiful light, that wonderful music, those enchanting people.

"Look at them," Jarel whispered. "Feel their pull on your heart. The closer you get, the stronger the call will be."

I did as he bid and stared out the window, immersing my senses in the glorious feeling of their presence, of their celebrations. And then, realizing that I would never be satisfied with remaining here as long as I was under their mesmerizing spell, I stepped back from the window, quietly closed the shutters, and blocked the sensations out.

Alone with my beloved, with the light from the lamps and the fire, and the faint murmur of the waterfall, it was a long time before I managed to put those sensations behind me, a long time in my lover's arms before I felt a total return to my senses.

He took me to bed and stayed with me until he was sure I was approaching sleep. But when he moved, that ridiculous beard tickled me, and I stirred and awoke. I lay quietly, waiting.

In the shadows of our bedchamber he didn't see me watch him dress. And I was curious when he left without making a sound, taking our only candle with him. So I rose and followed him, with no light to guide my way. But to my surprise, he did not go out amongst those wonderful, enticing enchantments.

Instead he went to the fire, to the chair he kept there.

From where I watched in the shadows, I could see Jarel pinch out the candle with his fingers and lean forward to stare deeply into the fire. For a few moments he remained motionless; then he began muttering absently, lost in thought, probably not even real-izing he was speaking aloud.

He wasn't going near the front door. He seemed to be trying to shut the memory away, as I had tried. I was saddened somehow, disappointed. But I think my heart grieved for him, too. What must it be like to live so close to such a heavenly place, in the midst of such divine company, only to have to spend his days here, in a dark forest filled with evil trees, fighting a passion he could never give in to?

I vowed then that I would stand fast at Jarel's side. I would spend my life with him, in this place, caught between night and day, never allowed to fully enter either. But no matter, this man was my husband, and I loved him deeply. More than life. More than enchantments.

With that thought I crept back into bed, careful not to disturb his contemplations.

ഈരു

Jarel kept a forge in the back of the cave.

For all my stubbornness, I eventually got over my fear of the place. It soared into the air over our heads, allowing light in and smoke out, as he had promised. But it was also a shallow cave, nearly as wide as our house, and all open spaces were cleared of loose rock to use as ledges for his work.

Along with his other, considerable skills, the multitude of things considered necessary to live alone and isolated from trade, Jarel was also a glass-smith. He loved to melt down crystals he gath-ered from the cave, which he made into bottles.

I could never figure out why he spent so much of his time mak-ing something that seemed so useless, so one day I resolved to get over my distaste for the cave and sought him out to ask him about his fascination for bottle-making.

He was hard at work over a billowing flame, balancing molten glass on the end of a long pole. He was spinning the pole and the glass was setting. A bottle was forming around the outside of a beehive-shaped mold.

"Jarel!" I called, for I knew I had to raise my voice in order to penetrate through his thoughts. "Jarel!"

He was startled, and the bottle at the end of his stick dipped dangerously close to the fire. But he righted his concentration just in time and saved his work. "Why are you bothering me woman?" Although his tone was brusque, there was no malice in his response; the twinkle in his eyes showed me he was teasing me.

"Why do you waste your life building bottles?"

He was silent and I suspected he was gathering his thoughts for some witty banter. But instead he answered, "To bring together fire and water, earth and air; what could be nobler than that?"

"But surely you can bring the elements together some other way, in some way that won't waste so much of your time."

He pulled the pole from the fire, staring at it with a critical eye. "I shall show you, wife. And you will see for yourself what is so amazing about what I do here."

I rolled my eyes and left him alone.

He came into the house some half an hour later with a bottle in his hands. A purple light glowed from within, illuminating the entirety of the bottle and casting a magical hue over his hands and chest. Silently, and with great care, Jarel set the bottle gently on a ledge in the kitchen. Then, only after he knew it was safe, he sighed and stepped back to gauge my reaction.

Wow! I should have known; enchanted forest, mystical forces, unexplained lights… lone woodsman. And now, glowing bottles. But I hadn't guessed the significance. My eyes widened as I stared at the bottle, at the mysterious purple flame illuminating it from within.

Jarel looked from me to the bottle, then back to me. He waited for me to speak, and when I didn't – couldn't, said, "Exactly!" And then he was off, to retrieve another. He came back with an orange bottle, and set this one in the window near the front of the house.

I stared at it in amazement as he passed me; then as he placed it carefully in the windowsill, asked, "is it safe there?"

He nodded. "Safe enough. I doubt you would knock it over. Let the trees look at it and tremble!"

I grinned, and he returned with yet another one, a bottle that shone with the light of a silver moon. This one brought tears to my eyes, it was so beautiful, and by the reverence on Jarel's face, I knew this particular one was different.

"This one goes near the fire," he whispered. And he placed it on the mantle with the care shown a newborn infant.

"How many of those do you have?" I asked.

Disappointment and something else – regret? – flashed across Jarel's face as he replied, "This is it. The chance to find a new light comes often, but rarely comes to pass … for one reason or another."

"That's why you have so many other bottles."

He nodded. "It seems wrong to put the light into an old bottle. Each flame deserves its own bottle and the old ones feel like they've been used."

I stepped forward, knowing better than to ask how he'd accomplished this amazing feat. I laid my head against his chest and put my arms around him, my heart bursting with love. Mollified, he hugged me back. "Make as many bottles as you like," I whispered.

"Thank you, Leena, I will." I knew he meant, "Thank you Leena, but I was going to anyway." We both chuckled.

⁊

One time I was walking through the forest, axe in hand, humming softly to myself and in utter disregard for the forest around me. The blue sky shone through in patches. Green leaves overhead were pierced with the golden light of the sun, and even though I was in this haunted place, I was completely at ease.

I guess that's how they were able to sneak up on me. Three of them. Angrymen. They lunged at me all at once, one from behind, who pinned my arms to my sides in a bear hug; and one from the side, while the other appeared in front of me, smirking evilly as I reared my head and flailed and kicked at the air, to no avail.

"Well, what has we caughts us today, brothers?" one of them hissed.

I went still and stared at him, panic and fear making my heart thud in my chest. But then I remembered my youth, and the words Jarel had said so often, it only has the power that you give to it, and the fear melted instantly. With a calm anger, I bore imaginary holes into my assailant's face, and he screamed in very real pain before he turned and fled into the forest. My head swiveled around to the angryman at my side, who had been eye-ing my axe, an idle finger stroking the edge appreciatively.

His eyes lifted towards mine, then widened in terror, and he stumbled backwards, tripped and fell to the forest floor. I contin-ued to stare at him until he finally tore his eyes from mine and scrambled to his feet to flee wildly into the forest.

There was still an angryman imprisoning my arms. I tried to turn my head, but he was smarter than the others and refused to look me in the eyes. He heaved upwards and hoisted me off the ground in a ferocious, malicious embrace.

I cried out as he forced the wind from me; then, unable to move, tried to picture his face in my mind's eye. The image came quickly, almost unbidden, and I immediately bore down on it with my angry glare.

The angryman screamed in agony, as if he were burning from the inside, and dropped me. Quickly regaining my footing, I swung my axe with as much force as I could as I veered around to face him. But the angryman was already darting into the forest, and my axe barely clipped his shoulder in passing.

Still, it had been enough to cause the miserable creature to stumble, and as he ran from view I brought the axe up to find a smear of blood on its edge. (I never did clean the blood off.) My heart was still thumping with excitement when I returned home to Jarel and showed him my trophy, almost babbling in my rush to tell him of my victorious encounter with the angrymen.

"There is nothing in the forest that can do you harm," he pro-nounced proudly. "Only that which would take you from me."

"Even so, I am careful," I replied as I leaned into him and kissed him lightly through his itchy beard. How ridiculous that thing looked on him! "The only lights I acknowledge now are those that have come to us, not those that would seek to enchant or imprison us with their magic and spells."

The silver flame shimmering in the bottle on the mantle seemed to dance when I nodded in its direction.

𝕰𝕺𝕽

My new authority over the angrymen was never tested more than the day I saw one step out from the forest.

I was out collecting truffles with our truffle-hunting pig, Jarel. I'd named the creature as a way of rebuking Jarel for not shaving his beard. But Jarel, dear man, had turned the tables on me and made a big show out of welcoming the young piglet into our home, as one might welcome a favorite dog. I wasn't sure why all the fuss, but pig Jarel seemed ecstatic with the attention that bearded Jarel shoveled in his direction. So the pig grew up a welcome member of our household, and proved to be a fine truffle hunter.

We had wandered near the edge of the forest. I had even sighted Keeper Fortress through the trees, so I knew where I was, although the signs in the woods would have pointed out the direction to our cabin clearly enough if it had been necessary. I called Jarel the pig to my side and crouched low to observe what had once been my home.

What I saw saddened me profoundly, and will distress me forever. The slaves were toiling in the fields, pulling up weeds and rocks that seemed to rematerialize in the soil every year. The slaves looked wretched, and I could scarcely recognize some of their faces, so changed with years of brutality they were. They looked thoroughly miserable, malnourished, beaten.

An angryman was patrolling with a long, menacing whip in his hand. Every now and again he would shout a curse and lash out

with his switch, snapping it cruelly, and one of my dear companions would cringe with pain.

None dared look at their captor, but kept their eyes downcast.

I had seen enough. Quietly, I backed up into the forest with
Jarel the pig in tow, and we retreated to our truffle hunting, deep
in the forest where none would see us.

I happened upon a beaten track that led out of the forest and
into the fields. It was a new path, one I had never seen before. It
must have been made since my flight into Jarel's world, I mused.
I assumed it had been constructed by the angrymen.

I stopped, and from where I stood amid the shadows of the dark
forest, I could see where the path began. Jarel the pig got impatient and went off on his own to look for truffles and I let him go,
convinced I could call him back if need be. So much like the
other Jarel was he, that I determined the animal should spend less
time with humans and more time with his own kind, even if I had
to go out to market and bring an animal back myself.

I can't say just why I stood there, waiting. But it wasn't long
before the air began to shimmer near the beginning of the path,
like heat waves on a dusty road. But in this case, the waves
moved inwards, towards a single point. They intensified, and suddenly an angryman stepped out of the apex, and the glistening
waves dissolved behind him.

I stood my ground. Of course I stood my ground. No matter
how much I'd been startled by his appearance, I knew the truth
now. There was only one way to drive an angryman away. So I
stood and stared at him as he sauntered down the path.

My intent focus drew his gaze towards me and he abruptly
stopped. Then his hideous face contorted as he leered at me.
"Little woman," he cooed. "So alone and by herself." He cocked
his head to the side, as if willing me to fear him. "So unprotected

out here in this nasty forest!" He took a few menacing steps towards me, daring me to fear him.

I did not. It was a contest of wills, and I refused to give ground to this angryman. "Flee!" I spat, matching anger for anger. "Be afraid, and flee!" I drew myself up to my full height and stabbed him with my eyes.

"Why should I... " The angryman faltered. "... be afraid of you?" My eyes bored into his, but before I had a chance to retort, he turned a ghostly pallor and escaped down the path towards the castle, undoubtedly towards easier prey.

I sighed with relief and sank down to the forest floor, shivering in the aftermath of the confrontation. Breathing deeply, I tried to gather my wits. Gradually my heartbeats slowed, my apprehension eased, and I felt the tension lift from my shoulders. I felt like crying. The vile force of the fear and terror the angryman had used flooded over me before I remembered that the real danger had passed, and I had truly driven the alien creature away.

Jarel the pig reappeared, attracted to the truffles I carried in a cloth sack. I was comforted by his presence and scratched his head absently. We sat silently there together for a time while I rested, then I rose to my feet and began the slow journey back through the Dark Forest to my home. Jarel the pig followed close on my heels.

I had emerged victorious. The forest was mine after that. I roamed it at will, from sunup until sundown, alone or with Jarel, and as often with Jarel the pig. It mattered little. If I happened across mystical or heavenly wonders I simply ignored them and continued with my own business. My lack of reverence must have seemed outrageous to these angelic creatures! And when I encountered angrymen or other dark presences lurking in my domain I faced them head on with a confidence that could not be swayed, and the depraved creatures fled from my presence.

But sadly, Keeper Fortress remained out of our reach. We left the forest often, to go to market or travel abroad. But whenever we returned to our own beloved world, our refuge, we found my people in deep bondage, slaving miserably over labors that mat - tered very little in the huge expanse of the universe.

Oh how we longed to go to them, to set them free! But we knew the fear angrymen could instill in humankind. We knew the influ - ence they possessed over human thoughts and actions. Against an encounter with one angryman, we had little doubt of the outcome. But against a mob of very human slaves viciously driven by nightmarish masters, there was also no doubt what would ensue.

So we left them alone, although we grieved in our hearts. And in the steady rhythm of changing seasons, years passed. Our bonds in marriage deepened with the years. We were truly as one. We cherished our days together, and many a night was spent whispering secrets to each other in the dark.

And so it must have been hard for Jarel when I woke up one morning, chilled to the bone and feverish. He tried to lie, to reas - sure me that I'd be all right. He was a woodsman, after all, and a good one at that. The secrets of the forest were his to pluck, and he would make me well again in no time. But after days of searching for the right remedies, my fever worsened and it become hard for me to breathe.

As the days progressed, the malady spread to my throat and then into my chest. I suspected that I was dying, even though Jarel insisted that wasn't true. And I'm sure he didn't think he was lying, that he truly believed he could cure me. But whenever I tried to ask him how bad my condition was, he would stubborn - ly refuse to give me an answer.

I hated lying in that bed, feeling useless and alone while Jarel was out there, feeling helpless and fretting about me. So when I awoke abruptly to sweat-soaked sheets, I sat up. It was night, and an inky blackness enveloped the forest.

Determined despite the chills sweeping through me, leaving me shivering, I groped through the darkness until my hand touched a clean, warm blanket. I wrapped it around myself and padded softly down the darkened hallway to the great room in the center of our house.

Jarel was leaning over the fire, as was his custom. His brow was furrowed and he seemed distant, distracted, torn with worry. Muttering frantically from deep within his long, scraggly beard, his words seemed chaotic, disjointed. They made less sense than they usually did. And his hands! My beloved's hands were so close to the fire I could not help but cry out in alarm.

He jumped at my interruption. "You should be abed!" he tried to scold me, but was too worried about me to be angry.

I ran to him, albeit somewhat unsteadily, and he straightened as I approached. I clutched his wrists and turned his hands so we could both see the fresh burns upon the palms.

"I was distracted," he confessed. "I was worried about you. I did not realize I was so close to the fire." In the light of the wood fire and that of the silver glowing bottle, Jarel was beautiful, like some kind of fierce wood elf from a story book.

I could only stare at him, my heart full. This magnificent being was my husband, and I loved him dearly. For what seemed an eternity I gazed at my beloved, my illness forgotten.

Jarel's face reflected my feelings, and for a time we simply stood there, enveloped in the reflection of love we witnessed in each other's eyes. Then Jarel sighed and grinned at me. "I should see to these," he said wryly, "they hurt." His grin was infectious. He chucked me under the chin. "You, to bed." Then he left through the front door, into the night.

I stood, wavering, at the open door for a moment. Then I reached for my boots and crept after him through the darkness, my blanket still wrapped around me like a shawl. If it took all the strength I possessed, I needed to follow my husband tonight.

After spending half my life in the forest, I could move through it as silently as he. And it wasn't after all really night, but early morning, the time when dawn first touched the sky with grey, and all seems to be embraced with both shadow and light.

I had no fear of being seen. And although fever wracked my every step, I knew Jarel well enough to realize he was too preoc- cupied with his own misgivings to watch me until I was tucked soundly in bed. Besides, I could hide in the shadows. Keeping low in the open field, skirting from one tree to the next in the for- est, I kept him in sight as he trudged through the underbrush. He kept his wounded hands away from as much brush as possible, which slowed him down a little. So as ill as I was, I had little trouble keeping up.

He reached the sacred pond where we had been wed, and seemed almost relieved when he sank into the water, not pausing to remove his boots or his clothes. As on the day of our marriage, Jarel made his way across to the island, fully clothed, keeping his hands below the surface of the water for as long as possible. And as I watched from behind a nearby tree I felt a great sorrow for my husband for what he must be suffering because of my ailment.

It took most of my concentration just to remain silent. I so wanted to rasp and cough, but it was difficult enough to remain unseen and unheard.

Jarel climbed onto the island and sank to his knees, just as we had the first day I came here. Curious, I watched, wondering what on earth he could be up to. Was he going to cut himself again? But no, he simply reached out his hands towards the flowers and began to speak softly as if he was staring into the fire back at home.

At first nothing happened. But then the island itself began to stir. The flowers, their petals and their stems, began to sway as though caught up in a gentle breeze. Yet there was no wind, the pond showed no ripples upon its surface, nor did the leaves stir from the branches overhead.

Yet these flowers moved. And then their petals turned towards Jarel's upraised hands. Tiny golden specks of light appeared from amongst the flowers, like fireflies, though infinitely more beautiful than anything I had ever seen, except perhaps for the magical bottles and their spectacular flames of light. The specks rose into the air, circling about Jarel and his hands. It was as if Jarel was greeting them, drawing strength from their presence.

My throat itched with the need to cough. And I was poised on the balls of my feet to flee into the forest in an instant; ready to leave my beloved to his secrets.

I remained, though, and watched, fascinated as the lights coalesced about his hands. He smiled with such an intense look of relief that I wept for joy at the sight. When his burns began to glow with that golden light I finally turned and crept back into the forest.

I understood now.

Somehow, despite my condition, I made it back to the cabin undetected. The effort had left me exhausted and weak, yet my head was full of wonder, and a deep love for Jarel. I did not feel betrayed that he had kept this secret from me. Rather, I felt honored that he had allowed me into his life as much as he had.

I fell asleep smiling and slept better than I had for a long time.

When I awoke Jarel's clothes had dried by the fire and he was in his workshop, concentrating on creating another bottle.

"Leena! Leena! Come and see this! You'll not want to miss it!" Usually so kind and considerate while I was slumbering, Jarel's voice penetrated my sleep and jarred me awake with the energy of his excitement.

"What is it?" Since the night I'd followed Jarel to the pond my fever had worsened, as had the cough and pain in my lungs. I doubt my voice had the strength to carry far enough to be heard. But he heard me, as he always had.

"Come see!" he cried, bounding into our room and lifting me into his arms with the blankets still draped around me.

I smiled and tried to cuddle into my husband without touching his prickly beard, and he carried me into the great room.

A fog was spilling across the ceiling.

"Close the window, Jarel."

"Hush, wife. It is the fog I've brought you to see."

I sighed, much more dramatically than I intended, and settled down to watch the mysterious fog thicken in my home. Then the strangest thing began to happen. Tiny lights, much like the golden ones I'd seen appeared in the fog, like miniature torches. They would twinkle for a moment, and then extinguish. And another torch would emerge somewhere else.

And not just golden lights. Silver ones soon became visible as well, and mixed with the golden radiance. I looked over at the sil - ver bottle, half expecting the flame that burned inside it to have floated to the ceiling to join the other lights. But it remained where it was. In my feverish state, I even imagined that the little flame seemed ecstatic to be in the presence of the others, and glowed all the brighter because of them.

When I looked back, the lights had changed again. This time, the seven colors of the rainbow shone amidst the glittering gold and silver lights. The sight took my breath away. I was enraptured by it, awed by the marvel of what I was witnessing. Then something occurred to me and I looked at Jarel uncertainly.

"Should I be looking away?"

"No," he replied, equally awed by the honor of our being allowed to view this otherworldly enchantment. "These beings have no desire to cause harm. It is us that pull at their heart - strings. We lure them, as though we were the enchanted ones."

I gazed at them, wondering what it was that Jarel wasn't telling me, until, exhausted, I fell asleep in his arms.

My sickness worsened. It got so bad I shook all the time and needed constant care. Jarel was there through it all, sitting up by my bedside every hour of the day, attuned to every flicker of my eyelids or variation in my breathing.

The fever made me hallucinate, and I passed in and out of dreams without ever being certain if I was awake or sleeping. I was walking a fine line between two worlds. But the latter was a troubled world, fraught with war, where love and hate existed next to each other as traumatically as squares on a chess board. And while different, the borders of the wondrous world I lived in were drawn just as swiftly, and were just as stark.

Then I would awaken, and I would feel the forest, feel the evil presence that blanketed the trees. And I would feel the shifting forces of heaven, of something of such unsurpassed beauty that it would cause me to cry out, "Oh Jarel!"

And he would be there, holding my hand, mopping my brow with a damp cloth. "Don't fight it, love," he would murmur. "Let it all go. It's time."

The meaning of his words escaped me. Not once did I consider he meant that it was time to die. But after hearing his voice I would slip back into my dream-like state, and re-enter the mes - merizing world of angels and demons.

The glowing bottles Jarel created were brought in and placed around the room. They appeared to drive back the evil forces of the forest, defying them with the same steadfastness I had learned to use to repulse the angrymen. And in my delusional state, I could swear that I saw other apparitions in the room, graceful translucent forms of light and color, bending silently over my troubled countenance to soothe and encourage me. They would offer a kind word to Jarel, and touch his shoulder sympathetically before vanishing or dwindling in size until they were mere pin-pricks of light, then whisk themselves away through some crack in the floor or walls.

One blonde girl, as thin as a wisp and taller than even Jarel, was clad in what seemed to be a flowing red costume, and was as transparent as a ghost. She spoke to Jarel anxiously and with compassion.

Jarel sat there looking up at her, nodding, hanging on to every word. Yet while he did not speak aloud, it seemed to me he was communicating with her in a language beyond human speech, even beyond the ways of the world I knew.

Jarel's eyes were somber, and as I lay there watching him, I saw something in his face, the indistinct shape of his jaw under his beard, the shade of his eyes and hair, that bore a distinct resemblance to the angelic, immortal creature before him.

I struggled to move, but was so weak I could scarcely turn my head. Even the slightest moan took too much effort. But my beloved was so attuned to me that he heard, and they both turned towards me. It seemed as though my thoughts had reached their ears with perfect clarity.

She turned to Jarel and nodded solemnly, and again I heard the words. It's time. Don't you think? Past time. Let her go. Then the faerie-like being turned, and gracefully, incredibly, vanished through the wall.

"Jarel," I managed to croak. My rational mind was fighting with the hallucinations, but I needed to know. I needed to see my husband's face. He leaned over and gently took my hand in both of his. Although I knew he understood me without words, he waited for me to speak. "Shave your beard," I pleaded. "Let me see you one last time."

"Don't speak like that," he entreated.

I only looked up at him, letting my emotions speak the words I could not.

Finally Jarel gave a small sigh and nodded. "All right." He caressed my cheek lightly, lovingly. "Rest now," he whispered, his voice thick with grief.

And I did.

I awoke with more clarity than I had experienced for ages. My body felt cold, although it bothered me not at all. My fever, while it seemed to have worsened, seemed somehow distant, like it mat-tered less. Jarel sat by my bed, his face shaven and smooth. And somehow I understood that my time was close.

I looked at my husband, my beloved; saw his clean, beardless, handsome face. Without the whiskers that had hidden it from my eyes for so long, Jarel looked young, as young as the day we met, though it was plain to see that he was terribly wrought with grief and worry and lack of sleep.

"I do not need sleep the way you do, Leena, not the way you think, anyway." So he really could understand my thoughts. He only smiled, as if to say, not really. And then he spoke. "I only see the heart of the matter, precisely as you do."

I tensed, a little afraid I was hallucinating again, and of what this all meant.

But Jarel simply leaned over me and took my hand. All of a sudden, all around my bedside, the angelic, translucent forms materialized. And from the three bottles my husband had created and nurtured, the tiny flames spiraled upwards and hovered around my bedposts, where they were somehow transformed into tiny beings no larger than a hand-span. They had the prettiest, most delicate wings, one set a glistening silver, one a full, rich purple, the other brilliant orange, just like the light they radiated inside their bottles. I giggled uncontrollably when I saw them. I've gone mad, I thought! My fever has finally driven me over the edge! I could not stop laughing, albeit somewhat weakly.

The silver ethereal being could take it no longer. She flew over to me and landed on my chest so she could look me in the eye . I stopped my crazy laughter and tried to look at her, although it seemed my eyes crossed with the effort.

She had dark auburn hair, almost brown, and wore a sleek miniature tunic and trousers that glowed with the same translu - cent color as her wings. She had tiny wooden shoes on her feet.

She held me with her reprimanding gaze for a few moments longer while she read my face and saw the pain there. And it seemed that her heart broke with what she saw, and she stepped closer and put her tiny hands on my face; one on my mouth and the other close to my ear, as if she was hugging me. "It's okay," the little being said, quite clearly and audibly. I could see her wings ruffling, stirred by an invisible breeze. "Let go, little sister . Just let go."

My eyes flickered towards Jarel, imploring him to explain. What is going on?

Jarel waved the tiny sprite away with a gentle swish of his hand. She harrumphed softly before ascending to land on his shoulder, watching me closely from her perch.

"The story begins," he said. "In a world not so far from the sur - face realm; with a tragic war that divided this world's peoples between what is good and what is wrong. All have heard this story, for it is truth built into our very hearts from the time before we were born. And the surface realm witnessed this other world being torn apart."

"But there is yet another world that lies between the two; and the terrible war carried over from the heavens into the realm of fire, the most magical and wondrous of the five realms. The fire realm fights this war amongst itself, and although darkness was first to lay claim to our world, it is known that light has a power darkness can never conquer."

Jarel had said, our world. In spite of my fever, he now had my full attention.

He reached into his tunic and pulled out a small pouch that he emptied into his hand. Seven stones of light, one for each color of the rainbow, glowed luminously in his palm. I had never seen such a magical phenomenon, and gazed in wonder at the face of my husband, a face that miraculously never seemed to age.

"This continent has an abundance of stone like this," he continued, "and it is our most powerful and revered secret. It is what houses the fire realm; and the trees' roots touch these stones, bringing a part of our home to these forests. Those who wish to live in peace from this war, beings of evil and light both, seek refuge within forests like this one. So far removed from any other race, here we are free to reshape the shadows and light in deep, hidden places, and not be troubled by humankind or other races that exist within the surface realm."

"Most of this forest was a sanctuary for the peaceful Aigelendai and the Tenleness," he waved at the wraith-like beings around him. "To the faeries. But then there was a mighty victory for the warriors of light within the fire realm, and a great host of wicked Aigelendai were driven to this realm also. This whole country was changed as a result, and none of it more than the forests that border its perimeter."

Jarel leaned forward in his earnestness, and the tiny silver sprite shifted to a more comfortable spot on his shoulder. "Many of us chose to leave the fire realm altogether, to leave the forests and our homes rather than stay and fight. So we took human form." He pointed to himself. "And so we left the forest."

Jarel paused and gazed intently into my eyes before continuing.

"But there was one couple who knew that the world of mankind was a terrible place, that their infant girl would grow up embit - tered and disillusioned by the wrongs of humanity. They could not take her with them, take her from her home, from her her - itage. So on the eve of the invasion, they fled to Keeper Fortress, to a place on the outskirts of their enchanted forest to save their daughter. It was their hope that one day she might grow up to make her own choice; to remain in the world of humankind, or to return to what was left of her once-beautiful home."

"There was a slave woman in that household, who wept with the midwife over a stillborn babe. It was late at night and the two had removed themselves to a far corner of the castle, so as not to dis - turb the others with the woman's labor pains. No one saw these two Aigelendai, grief-stricken as they were, follow the waves of grief, so much the color of their own, with their tiny baby in her young mother's arms."

"They were cautious in their approach, and their kind and hum - ble spirits were obvious and went far to comforting the grieving mother. The astonished midwife was sworn to secrecy and the two Aigelendai took human form, growing in size and losing the color of their spirit; their wings faded until they were unde - tectable. The sleeping infant was caught in the transformation also, and placed gently in the grieving mother's arms. Stunned by this course of events, the slave woman nonetheless put the baby to her teat, and the young one suckled contentedly."

"The Aigelendai mother wept, and her husband endeavored to comfort his grief-stricken wife. But the slave woman was over - joyed to have an infant at her breast; and the midwife took the stillborn, wrapped it in coarse linen, said her farewells to the two otherworldly travelers, and took the body away for burial.

"Both women were weeping now, and the Aigelendai-"

"- The Aigelendai mother – her name was Cateline," interjected the silver-winged faerie.

Jarel half-turned his head, frowning slightly at the interruption, then turned his attention back to me. I listened closely, mesmerized, while he continued his story.

"– Cateline stepped forward and embraced the slave woman; then transformed into her more natural form, shrinking in size and developing vivid green wings, until she was nothing more than a dazzling green speck hovering before the slave woman's eyes.

He fixed his eyes on mine again, as if to emphasize his next words. I was transfixed.

"Then she left, and your father followed your mother out, before he, too, transmuted into a midnight-blue flame of light and flew into the night, away from the Dark Forest."

When Jarel finished his incredible story he sat back and raised his hands into the air, palms up. "There is no pain for us, no day, no night. What humankind sees as physical, are merely light and shadow to us. For us, the world is a blur of music and sound, of cascading sunlight and running water, of the life inside the trees, in their veins, and the all-prevailing beauty of emotion. Those are all the physical confines there really are, and we exist inside that place."

"But you, my wife, oh loveliest of all, you have lived the life of a human, not knowing of the release our ethereal bodies are blessed with from sickness or death. You've lived your whole life with the burden of having to use voice to create sound, never able to hear the splendor that nature conveys all the time, all around us."

"And yet, how beautiful your music is! It is perfect. You are refined through suffering, and your soul sings out to us with such a symphony of purity that you call to all Aigelendai within this forest. Without awareness, you sway many evil ones to turn from their ways; and because of you, many who are good live perpetually in sight, as you do, to let their light torment the Dark Forest. Oh, how the angrymen cringe when they see you coming, cowering so that they may stay invisible to your human eyes!"

Jarel spoke softly now, and I strained to hear his words.

"I could not live if I could not be a part of your life somehow. I saw how an angrymen, a dark Tenlenesse, told stories of how a child-changeling had tormented one of them within your inn. And I knew that all Aigelendai have such power when they take human form. So I disguised myself as a woodsman and entered your world, to be close to your spirit that sang so mournfully, yet so… "

"… Words escape me," I whispered.

My beloved looked deeply into my eyes. "And you came to me," he continued softly. "The angrymen surely would have destroyed you had you stayed; and even the good Tenlenesse of the forest rose up from their hidden realm to try to soothe you in your need, so great was their love for you. But you resisted them, and came to me instead. You came to me."

I was too weak to respond. I had no idea that Jarel felt so strongly about me. The energy of his presence had often left me speechless, but now I felt a heaviness from within that robbed me of all desire to speak. I sighed and closed my eyes, so weary from my illness that I was unable to keep them open any longer.

"Now love," he said, bending close to my side and taking my hand once again. "Let go. Shed your human shell and be free. You've done your time in this world, you've inspired us all and taught us what is worth fighting for. Your call has been a war-cry since the moment of your first blister upon your young hands. Your first taste of the slaver's whip was a call to arms that changed all our colors to fury. Now let it go, dear heart, with the knowledge that your light will burn in this forest as brightly as a star, as brightly as these stones in my hand." He held them up for me to see. "Brighter even than these.

"Illness will never touch you again, I promise. And you'll never know the sickness of our kind, what was wrought on us long ago. Let go, knowing that you bring the cure of humanity."

I nodded, or tried to. I was so parched, so weary, so hot, so uncomfortable. It was time. I couldn't hold on even if I had desired. So I closed my eyes and in my mind I simply let go of everything and fell back. And when I finally opened my eyes again, Jarel was grinning down at me from a giant's giant head, with a ridiculously disproportionate nose.

I felt absolutely exuberant. I allowed a feeling of freshness to radiate from me, and it seemed that I was enveloped in a golden flame that somehow did not burn my skin. I pushed myself from my pillow, a pillow that reeked of sweat, of sickness, and of death. And wings, I had wings! My wings! They flexed and undulated of their own accord. They too were engulfed in a blaze of gold. From the tip of my toes to the top of my head, from one outstretched butterfly wing to the next, I guessed that I was per - haps the size of my human body's smallest fingernail.

And I felt like I could grow smaller still. I felt like I had stepped into an entirely different world, with completely different rules. But I couldn't think too much about that right now. For now, this was enough. I must have been human for too long; this level of release was all I could deal with. The world sang, as Jarel had promised. I was surrounded by sound, even though the room had been deathly quiet earlier. But this sound was in harmony with itself. No note clashed with any other. And the ominous presence emanating from the forest made me feel like I was on an island amidst an ocean tempest. But what was that to me, espe - cially now? I was the island, its shores I took with me wherever I went.

It was all so glorious!

The silver Aigelendai, who had claimed to be my sister, came to me then and embraced me, drawing me up to a bigger size, though not so large that our wings faded. And Jarel was suddenly there, beside us, the same size as us. His color was fascinating, a blend of silver and green, with a touch of onyx around the edges.

At my quizzical expression he said, "I must confess. I was born amongst the angrymen. When I saw the sacrifice your parents made to keep you so close to the Spectral trees – " to my unspo - ken question he replied, " – the trees that touch the glowing stones." I nodded and he continued. "I could not stay among them, so I put myself under the care of the Aigelendai at the pond."

And so my renewal was complete.

If life in the forest was interesting before … but that is another story.

These days I spend much of my time in a bottle of my own, glowing as brightly as I can with a brilliant golden light, while Jarel carries me, laughing, through the forest. The Tenlenesse and Aigelendai, good and evil, see our light, for I would not be who I am without Jarel in my life, and all are drawn to it. Whether it is used for ill or health is something they must decide for them - selves.

I bide my time as I explore my new life as an Aigelendai. And I will continue to inspire all with what I have learned of true humanity. In time, when our numbers are strong, we'll drive the angrymen completely out of this forest, into the flames of the fire.

And then we'll rise up and overthrow Keeper Fortress, to liber - ate my other family.

The Siren's Heart

By DJ Ebenal

Kallen clutched his side. With each breath came a sharp pain
from his ribs. Tears of frustration threatened to fall into the sky
underneath him, but bitter disappointment kept his despair locked
tight. Even his wings, the steady constant beat of them against the
open air, were growing weary. Starting at the very tips of his
feathers, the ache was spreading towards his shoulder blades. Yet
try as he might, they carried him no higher, struggling constantly
just to maintain altitude. But even this was a losing battle.

Kallen never thought he would see the day when his wings
would fail him. Like giant dove wings, angel's wings sent by
Almighty from Above, they'd held true from the time when, as a
child, he had first been tossed into the air to glide, laughing, all
the way to the ground. "Again! Again!" the young Kallen had

clamored. The older Trilians had merely shrugged and said, "Lift yourself up."

He had. And now those words were becoming Kallen's mantra. "Lift yourself up. Lift yourself up." But with each beat of his wings, he knew he was falling instead.

Beneath him, far below and beyond a thin dusting of cloud, the ocean spread out forever like some perverted version of the sky. If he fell into that, all would be lost. His wings, drenched with water, would weigh him down – he would sink to his death. He would drown, far from home, unable to warn his family of the Ikiling clan and their movement into his family's territory in the skies above Mishard.

Kallen was not a quitter though, and while strength still remained in his body he fought on, driving his wings downward with forceful determination as he clenched his teeth and grimaced in pain. The pain in his ribs was growing worse. And there was no place to rest.

Kallen squeezed his eyes shut. He had no alternative; he had to go on. If he turned back now the Ikiling would overtake him. And after what they'd just done to him he had no illusions about what they would do to him the next time.

Then he felt it. His wings, exhausted beyond measure, lost a finger-width of altitude.

His eyes snapped open in alarm.

The only reason why the Ikiling let him escape at all was because they knew this would inevitably happen. There was nothing out here, nothing in either the sky or the water .

He dropped again.

Worried now, tears of despair finally fell. The burning in his ribs was spreading. All Kallen could do was continue to labor onwards, gasping for breath and fighting with all his might to keep the rise and fall of his wings at a steady, strong rhythm.

He began to plunge a little farther each time now. The water was rising up to meet him at an alarming rate.

And then he saw it. Not sure if it was real, blurry through the tears and the pain, an outcropping of rock peaked out from the water. Only a speck on the horizon, Kallen's hopes went out to it and he lifted into the air a few feet.

He laughed, although the sound came out as a moan; and then steadied for the trek ahead and forced his wings to keep him air - borne until he reached it.

A few long agonizing minutes later, when the tiny island failed to grow any bigger, Kallen realized that he must be farther away than he had first thought. He knew there was no possible way he could accomplish such a distance, and the strength seemed to flee from him. Tired and winded, Kallen glided in the air, all the while dropping swiftly towards his death.

But then he remembered his family, what it was to be a Trilian, and what it meant to be a Thoroughblood Trilian. His was the family that held true to the convictions of the first Trilian. His was the family that had left behind their home and the hypocrisy of their kind to seek out the blessing of Almighty in the air realm during the rending of Mishard. And his was the family that had grown large and prospered in the floating islands above The Island.

Kallen would not give up on them so easily, especially now, when the Ikiling tribe of Trilians was invading his territory. Bloodthirsty since the time when the Thoroughbloods had first exposed the true heart of the Trilian nation, the Ikiling were at last moving to take their revenge, and only Kallen knew of their movements.

He growled through gritted teeth and fought onwards with his failing strength. Each beat of his wings carried him closer and closer to the rocks far below. But each beat of his wings told him in an increasingly louder voice, It is too far.

Still, Kallen began to see it as a matter of pride to make it as far as possible, to crash as close to that island as he could. If he must fail, then let it be a small failure rather than a large one. So he coaxed his wings forward, beyond all limits, beyond all reason.

He landed abruptly, with a mighty splash that dragged him under the ocean waters. Kallen choked, and struggled to force his weakening limbs back to the surface long enough to gasp a mouthful of air before his wings dragged him under again.

In another time and place, he would swim. He was a fine swim - mer, and his wings could be manipulated like flippers to propel him through the water. But this time, already exhausted, they were simply dead weight. Kallen was being dragged even further underwater.

He opened his eyes to determine his fate, and noticed that the island he had seen was now but a stone's throw away. It was actually the tip of a much larger mountain that grew out of the ocean floor, whose slope was underneath him.

Hope returned once again, even though he knew he had only moments before he drowned. But, resolutely, Kallen kicked out towards the island. His lungs burned with the effort but he forced his legs and his wings to carry him forward. Finally, scrambling with his hands to pull him up through the water towards the light, he managed to break the surface just when he thought he must let go of his breath and give up. He had made it to the mountain.

Kallen crawled a few paces out of the water and collapsed.

෫෨ඏ

A cold wet touch upon his cheek. He moaned and his eyes flick - ered, although he lacked the strength to open them. The touch was withdrawn, and an instant later he heard a splash.

Oblivion returned.

A putrid stench made him flinch and fight to turn his head away; the movement was slow in coming, and Kallen groaned his displeasure at the foul odor that forced him to awaken. "Uhhg!" He lifted his head and opened his eyes.

A pile of rancid seaweed had been placed by his nose. The bright sun hurt his eyes and his lips were parched. The rest of him was chilled though, and Kallen knew immediately that he had a fever. Gingerly he eased himself into a sitting position and wrapped his wings around his shoulders for warmth. A soft intake of breath from behind him startled Kallen, and when he turned around, it was his turn to gasp.

A mermaid rested on the edge of the island, which was no wider than the length of his body. From the waist down she had the tail of a fish. She sat with her back towards him, staring over her shoulder with wide, intelligent eyes. Her exquisite face was framed by long blonde hair that appeared to be tinged with green. Her arms were crossed in front of her, and Kallen quickly real- ized she was covering her exposed breasts. He just as rapidly rec - ognized that the lovely creature sitting before him was a Siren.

"This is awkward," he said, offering her a tentative smile. Sirens and Trilians were by nature ancient enemies. And here they were, the two of them, within striking distance, and he was with - out either a weapon or the strength to fight.

The Siren seemed to sense his meaning, and made as if to plunge into the water.

"No, wait!" Kallen pleaded, his hand outstretched towards her.

She froze and faced him once again.

"You wouldn't have anything to eat, would you?" Kallen didn't expect her to speak the same language as he, but hoped that his friendly manner was enough to disarm the Siren and quell some of her fears. He held his hand to his mouth and motioned as though he were eating. "You know, food?"

Her eyes narrowed and she glanced down at the seaweed between them. Then she looked at him again and then back at the seaweed.

Kallen's heart sank as he understood her gestures, and some of what he was feeling must have shown in his expression, for she giggled.

For about a hundred years Sirens had been viewed as demons by the proud Trilians. For one reason or another, Trilians had found an excuse to label all of the nineteen other sub-races as demons, for only Trilian had remained faithful to Almighty during their transformation from humanity. The Sirens had been embittered by the Trilians' hypocrisy, and the war that had raged between them had been bloody, if not brief.

The Sirens had dragged to their deaths any Trilian they caught near the water, and for their part, the winged men had speared schools of the swimming targets from the sky, tracking them from the air and following them to their lairs.

At some point each species figured out how to avoid the other, and an unspoken truce had existed since then. The sky was the sky and the water was the water. Each race had its own world to explore, and problems enough in their own realm without complicating matters further.

But that had been before the Thoroughblood clan had broken away from the Ikilings and the rest of the Trilian tribes. Kallen and his family had forsaken the warmongering hatred, the diplomacies and the condemnation that seemed to have replaced the noble love for Almighty and all his creatures.

61

Yet listening to this Siren laugh so freely, Kallen realized that there was no way for her to know that. To her he was just another butcher with wings. He sighed and grew sad and instantly she became silent while she watched.

She nodded towards the seaweed one more time. "There is your food, wingman. It tastes horrible. But it will restore your strength and take away your chill. Consider it medicine."

He stared at her and she smiled.

"You know my language!"

"No. You know mine."

"Perhaps it wasn't so long ago that our two races were friends."

She glared at him. "Yes, wingman. It was that long ago. But perhaps the many other races interact with each other and with men, with dragons and with immortals. And perhaps we share a common language that was proposed at the Council Of The Rending."

He nodded. She'd tried to rebuke him but instead she'd given him the answer. The Council Of The Rending was a council that had been made after the spectral realms had been created. Those races present when the spectral stones exploded into the rest of Mishard had gathered together under a banner of truce to decide what was the best way to survive in this new world.

This was when the Thoroughbloods had stood up and asked to be counted amongst those peoples that strove to do what was right in the eyes of Almighty. They had been in the mists when all the world changed. They, out of all the other Trilians, were the ones with the most experience with the other races. So it was they who accepted the truth about their distant cousins. They were not demons.

"My father was at that council," he admitted.

"Then where is your spear?" she asked with a nod. She took him for a noble, a warrior caste.

Kallen shrugged. "I don't carry a spear."

Her eyes widened.

"I carry a sword, a long sword I usually keep in a sheath on my back, between my wings. But it was ripped from me in a fight with the Trilians you have so much reason to hate. Where is your spear?"

She was silent, then looked away, out across the endless waters. "I don't carry a spear either. I too am a warrior, though. I am a spear sister and will remain one until the time of my death. There is nothing I can do about that. But I grew weary of killing and left my people to wander the open waters alone."

"With no weapon?"

She shrugged. "There is nothing I can't out-swim. Do you not know what a spear sister is? I can swim up waterfalls, if I want."

He shook his head. "No. I did not know what a spear sister was."

"No. How could you?"

He picked up a piece of the seaweed and placed it in his mouth. Then he spat it out.

She laughed. "You must eat it, wingman, if you want to recover."

He grimaced, but the next piece he forced himself to chew and swallow. "Aaahg!" He retched, to her ongoing amusement. To take his mind off his discomfort, Kallen looked at the Siren and asked, "What do they call you?"

"I am Malekie Triskamorn, spear sister of the Alergeere Pod, though I have broken from my school to swim alone against the ocean currents. You?"

"I am Kallen Thoroughblood. We are a renegade family that has declared war on the other Trilians."

"That is hard."

"It is," Kallen agreed. "But we have prospered. No one could have known that the sky realm was such a great place. We chose exile but we went into a land of promise and plenty. Now the Thoroughbloods are more numerous than all the other Trilians combined. It is our legacy Almighty has chosen to continue." He looked at her as she kept her back to him. "Why have you left your clan?"

She frowned thoughtfully for a moment.

"To seek a way of peace and to find the currents of Almighty that have been forgotten by my kind," she said at last, shrugging her shoulders.

"Then you too will be blessed."

"Thank you, wingman. That is kind of you to say."

Kallen returned her smile.

ഇൻ

Kallen was stranded on the little island for many days. His fever, though not severe, robbed him of his strength to fly. And his broken rib, for broken he was sure it was, made it too painful to lift his wings for any length of time. He should have been mis - erable there, stranded out in the open under the elements, but his wings gave him all the shelter he needed against the cold rains that swept the island at night.

And the rains collected in a shallow on the island, providing Kallen with enough water to satisfy his thirst. The seaweed Malekie brought him became less fetid the more of it he ate. And he was never alone for very long. As the days grew, so did his friendship with the insurgent Siren. One day, while they sat

64

together, she with her back to him as usual, he asked, "I've been wondering ... how do you ... I mean, when do you ... ?"

Her eyes narrowed. "I've been wondering when that would come up," she said.

"How is it that mermaids can seduce a sailor to his death when a mermaid doesn't have the body for it?" he finally managed to ask diplomatically.

She placed a hand on her hip, where the human body ended and the fish scales began. "Watch carefully," she instructed him. Then she pushed the scales down to expose a bit of her leg. The scales rolled up under her touch. After a moment, she unrolled them once again.

"How far can you roll your tail up?"

"All the way to my feet, I'd imagine."

"You have feet?" Kallen blurted the words out and then blushed profusely.

Malekie laughed at his discomfort. "Yes, wingman. I have feet." She paused. "I can't remember the last time I've seen them, though. And they aren't like human feet." She flapped her tail against the water. "See those points in the fin on either end? Those are connected to my toes. Even if I did roll my tail up, I'd still have flippers on the ends of my feet."

"You could trim those, couldn't you?"

"I guess I could, if I really wanted to. But it would make swim - ming really awkward, cutting off the tip of my tail like that." Then she looked at him. "I am a spear sister , though. I may not carry a spear, but a sister I remain. My tail is my pride, my strength. All Sirens forsake their legs for the ocean currents, but for a spear sister it is so much more than that."

"I feel that way about my wings," Kallen admitted.

Next time she came to visit him she wore a covering made from seaweed. "I thought it was appropriate," she admitted, "consider-ing how you are so interested in my body."

He laughed, but realized he couldn't dispute what she said. His eyes widened when he realized this, almost reeling with the implications that could have.

And to Malekie's credit, she didn't dive back into the ocean and leave him to his fate. Instead, she placed a new supply of sea-weed on the rocks in front of her and pulled herself onto the island. She sat with her fin in the water and looked at him for a long time, realizing her feelings for him as well.

Finally, she turned away to watch the ocean, as was her custom. Only this time, Kallen walked over and sat down beside her, their shoulders touching. Then he draped his wing across her shoulders and over the front of her torso in a soft, downy embrace.

They stayed like that for a long time, each enjoying the pres-ence of the other, the gentle touch, the companionship.

"How's your rib?" she asked at length.

"It hurts."

The relaxed silence stretched onwards again.

"That's really comfortable," she finally admitted, referring to the feathers draped across her.

"I know."

Malekie pretended to be offended and tried to push him over. But Kallen was well braced and she only succeeded in losing her own balance. Yet he held her upright in his wing's embrace, then pulled her towards him until her arms were around his neck and their lips were pressed together.

ॐ

The sun was setting. Half submerged behind the endless ocean, half adrift in the endless sky, it set both ablaze with light and fire, casting reflections against the waves and the clouds, turning them all to brilliant shades of red and orange. Kallen and Malekie sat with his wing wrapped around her, as was their custom. They held hands and watched the golden sunset in silence, each simply content to be touching the other.

It had been some time since they'd first met. Neither of them was counting days, but Kallen had done the impossible and grown accustomed to a diet of a variety of seaweed and raw fish she brought back for him.

He'd never felt this way before about anyone. And he told her that – often. For her part, Malekie tried not to think about the impossibility of their being together. She was simply swept away by his passion, by his conviction that they were meant for each other. And she returned his affection, drawn to his strength and his optimism even as he dwelt on that tiny island of stone.

"How is your rib?" she finally asked, cutting through the silence.

"It hurts."

"You always say that."

In truth, he barely noticed his broken rib anymore. He knew if he set off into the air he would aggravate the wound. But he also knew the real reason he played up his injury was because he was putting off leaving. He had a family, an entire clan of friends and loved ones who must be worried sick about him. And all he could think of was Malekie, about the dreaded day he would have to leave her, would have to say good bye. He shook the dark thoughts out of his mind and squeezed her hand to remind himself that she was still at his side. The sunset never looked so beautiful, and was made all the more so because it might be one of the last he could spend with her.

"It hurts," he said again.

She put her head on his shoulder and embraced his arm with her free hand. She understood. "I love you, Kallen."

There was a long silence and then, "I love you, Malekie."

"Strange."

"I know. But it had to happen sometime, to someone, some - where."

"But why us, why now, on this rock?"

"We are the fortunate ones, I guess. Almighty has blessed us."

"I guess."

&)C&

One day while Malekie was away foraging through the ocean, Kallen suddenly realized how constraining his tiny island had become. He paced in circles while he stretched his wings. The ache in his side was only a small discomfort. And he longed to feel the wind in his face, to feel his muscles in his back flex as he climbed into the air, to dive and soar and glide once again.

And so he leapt from the island and glided out over the ocean. He almost laughed at the sheer pleasure of feeling the wind beneath his wings, but he was too determined to race into the sky to waste the breath. He climbed in widening circles around the island, keeping it in the center of his flight path. And he kept climbing until his wings had their fill of the exertion.

Then he did laugh, high above the ocean, amongst the clouds. And he allowed himself the luxury of soaring on the currents. Ever so slightly, he began to drop back towards the island, and his circles became smaller as he slowly descended.

He saw her long before she saw him. She was sitting in the cen - ter of the island with her tail drawn up before her and her arms resting on where her knees would be if they weren't encased in a

68

fish tail. Her head was on her arms. His gliding took him to the surface of the ocean, and he stayed just above the water, flapping his wings as he circled around and watched her.

And still she did not look up.

"Icky!" he called to her, exhilarated by his flight. He turned and shot straight towards her, panicked and thinking she was hurt.

Malekie looked up at him and there were tears in her eyes. She rose to her feet – or rather, stood on her tail – and waited for him to land before her. The flutter of his wings as he plummeted and stopped caused her to lose her balance, and he dived forward to steady her before she could fall.

Wordlessly, she wrapped her arms around him and sobbed into his shoulder.

Feeling awkward, Kallen held his beloved in his arms while she cried, unable to understand what was wrong, but eventually she pulled away. "You left me!" she cried. "You flew away!"

"If you love a bird you let it go," he said sagely. "If it comes back to you it's yours forever."

"How can that be? Can you live on this rock forever? Can I? Out here in the middle of nowhere, where we are vulnerable to attack from sea or sky?"

"There is no one out here but us" Kallen replied soothingly. "You said it yourself. The Sirens stay closer to land, and the Trilians, the ones we need to worry about, are out there closer to land, fighting with the Sirens and everyone else."

"What about your people?" Malekie demanded. "What of your father? Will you go on letting them think you are dead? If you do you are not the man I thought you were. And will you not tell them about the threat to their territory from the other Trilians? If you won't do that, then you are not the man I love, but someone pretending to be him."

Kallen looked away. He had been trying not to think about that. "I'll come back."

"You won't! How will you find me? This island is just a speck, a drop in the ocean. And you have nothing to mark your bearings with. You'll never find it again and you'll kill yourself trying, like you nearly did the last time. Only this time I won't be there to nurse you back to health. And you'll die. I'll never see you again! And I'll be alone again!" She threw her arms around him a second time, holding on in a tight embrace as though her arms alone held him to the ground.

Kallen knew not what to say to her, not for a long time. But then a thought occurred to him, and he dared to hope. "You can come with me."

She let go of him and laughed bitterly. Tears stung her eyes.

He gestured towards the ocean. "Please, Malekie, sit and let me tell you about the sky realm."

She glanced at the edge of the island and back at Kallen. "I need your help," she replied. "When you weren't here I rolled my scales up so I could walk. I thought I'd be able to – I don't know what I was thinking. But I sat down and put my tail back in place as soon as I got here. I can't get back without exposing myself. And I'm not going to do that."

He raised an eyebrow and blessed her with a roguish, crooked grin.

She laughed, her natural humour restored, and smacked his arm; then held her arms out to him. "Lift me up," Malekie demanded.

Kallen lifted her into his arms. "Some day," was all he whispered as he waded into the ocean.

She simply locked his eyes with her gaze.

He eased himself into the water, keeping her in his arms, and she stretched out and ducked her head below the surface. Kallen watched as gills opened up along her jawbone and her chest rose as she inhaled a breath of water. What a remarkable creature, he thought to himself, amazed at the perfection he saw in her, the seamless way she meshed with the water.

She looked at him from beneath the ripples and sat up. Water streamed off her face and wove rivulets through her hair. Blinking through the dampness of her lashes, she gently touched his adams apple. Then she touched his second one. Every Trilian was possessed with two, giving them the ability to call out through the air in complicated birdsong. Kallen was also a product of perfection, she was reminding him. Although they were different, they were the same.

His wings stirred the water around them, half in and half out. In that time and in that place a part of both of their worlds.

"Tell me about the air realm, then," Malekie urged.

"The spectral stones have created islands in the sky."

She nodded. "They've created giant air bubbles under water, too; air bubbles and other things with fire."

"We have the fire too. But the land, the islands – if you have a solid piece of spectral stone, you can use it to help push the islands around. It takes a lot of work, but if there are enough Trilians and enough stones, it can be done. We've done it. We've pushed some of the bigger islands together, or closer together, anyway."

"That doesn't ... " Malekie began, but Kallen gently laid his finger over her lips and continued.

"Some of these islands have springs in them. They have ponds and waterfalls that flow between them."

"How does all the water circulate?" Malekie asked.

"The mists. You don't have mists, do you?"

71

She nodded. "A type of mist. It's the membrane that separates the ocean from the air inside the underwater air pockets."

"It does the same thing up there. I think the water is spectral water, turns to mist and is recycled back into the spectral stones inside the islands, before it melts off and bubbles back into the water."

"So I would be a prisoner in the sky, then?"

Kallen frowned thoughtfully. "I hadn't thought about it like that."

"It sounds wonderful. There's just one problem. How would we get there?"

ഇൽ

Kallen wouldn't leave her. So they stayed on the tiny, nameless island in the middle of the vast seas of water and sky. The days came and went and their love for each other grew with a convic - tion that they were meant to be together. Together they were strong enough to face anything, which was a good thing, because they knew a Siren and a Trilian together could be forced to face anything. And one night that strength was finally put to the test.

It was dark out. Kallen was asleep amidst a cushion of billow - ing feathers. Malekie had lain in his arms for a time, but as was her custom, had returned to the ocean to sleep through the darker hours of the night.

A gale of warm wind rose up out of nowhere and struck the lit - tle island with such force that Kallen was instantly awake, staring with bewilderment into complete darkness. A moment later a swell of water surged over him, leaving him sputtering and coughing as he sought to recover from the unexpected flood. Then the rain hit with a mighty roar, and Kallen was blinking and knuckling the water from his eyes.

He tried to look around, but all was in darkness. And then lightning struck, illuminating the skies in a fearsome storm. "Malekie!" Kallen shouted.

Another wave washed over him, but he held on to the island with his hands, barely had time to draw a shuddering breath before it submerged him. "Icky!" he called out in desperation. Thunder rolled over him, drowning out his words.

But then he felt the brush of cold scales against his arm, and she was there, clinging to him. "You'll drown in this!" Malekie shouted through the rain.

He nodded, realizing too late that she couldn't see him agreeing with her. "I can still lift off!" he shouted back. "We can make it! The oils in my feathers are fresh enough to put up with the rain, if I can just get above it!"

"What if you can't?"

"I can still coast back into the water if I don't make it, and you'll be safe!"

"But you'll drown – and I'll have to watch you! I can't do it!" Malekie protested, shaking her head vigorously.

"You'll have to do that anyway if we stay here and do nothing!"

There was a long pause, and then Malekie shivered and whispered, "all right!" She was already groping through the darkness for his embrace.

Kallen lifted her in his arms and leapt into the air. His wings left a mighty spray as they fought free of the raging storm. A wave struck a wing in a down stroke, threatening to topple them both back into the water.

But he kept his balance and struggled upwards.

The warm air made it easier. Strong winds tossed them about, first one way, then another, like invisible waves themselves. But these were waves Kallen knew how to ride. And he did not care where they were going, as long as it was up. Malekie was terri- fied and wept against his chest. But she would not be separated from her lover, and no matter what might happen, she did not regret her choice.

Kallen fought the storm throughout the night, gaining altitude that only he could feel – and luckily for them both, his strength held out. Though it raged in all its ferocity, when dawn approached, Kallen saw they were just below the clouds that car- ried the storm.

Keeping his eyes heavenward, he climbed through the storm clouds and rose above them to a calm blue sea with golden sun- light spilling all around them. Neither Kallen nor Malekie were the worse for being soaking wet; and indeed, both were used to that.

"I tried to breathe through my gills," Malekie said, smiling. Her relief and gratitude at being out of the gale was obvious.

Kallen looked down at her tenderly, studying her beautiful face. "Did it work?"

She laughed and shook her head. "Only a little."

He smiled and managed to get his bearing from the sun. Then he turned them around in the air and nodded. "That's the way home."

They flew silently through the clouds and golden sunlight. Kallen was saving his strength and Malekie was gazing in silent awe at the world he was showing her. "It's beautiful," she said at last. "So bright, it hurts my eyes."

"I'm sorry. I hadn't thought about that," frowned Kallen. "It's darker on the ocean floor, isn't it?"

She nodded. "Twilight is where the Sirens live. Utter darkness drives us closer to the surface. But when the sun rises we dive again."

"You've spent much time in the sun with me," he contended.

Malekie simply shrugged. "I love you. Where else would I be? Besides, I think I'm getting used to it."

Kallen nodded. "That wouldn't surprise me. We're both descended from humans."

"Don't remind me."

He looked down at her, and Malekie flushed. "Sorry," she said, "Some of my Siren upbringing coming through."

"Is it true — the stories, I mean? That Siren women seduce human sailors into the water and then drown them?"

"You have to understand that I've turned away from such wicked practices, and to even talk about them is an offense to me" Malekie avowed.

"Sorry, Icky. I didn't — "

"That's okay, love. I just wanted you to know my opinion of the practice, that's all."

"So it is true," Kallen replied.

"It is." Malekie nodded. "Surface dwellers are viewed much the same way as sky dwellers. Only they clean out our oceans with no thought of replacing what they take. They pollute, they destroy. They invent ways of doing evil to the oceans and justify it by measuring the weight of their purses." She shuddered, gulped a little and then continued.

"So Sirens cater to that selfishness, that greed, by feeding the human lust. They roll their tails into their legs and entice the humans into the water. What goes on between them before the human drowns is unspeakable. But many of my spear sisters claimed lives this way. They are at war. In war there are no rules. And amongst the Sirens there is no decency."

"Have you ever taken lives this way?"

She looked away, a painful expression in her eyes. "Yes and no. The more a tail is used the stronger it gets. I would not weaken my strength by putting a man between my legs. But I have lured many men to their deaths by the beauty of my breasts alone."

"And yet I have never seen them, though I've seen your back many times, and your thigh once."

"I told you, love. I turned from those ways to follow the guid - ance of Almighty. Someday, though."

Kallen looked down at her, his expression serious. "Is that a promise?"

She nodded and grew silent again as she watched him carry her through the clouds.

෪ාൂ

Throughout the day they stayed silent. The only sounds were the steady beating of Kallen's wings and the distant rush of wind. While he kept his eyes on the sky before him, Malekie kept hers locked on his face.

At first he was steadfast and secure. But as the day wore on Kallen gradually became pained, worried. He kept his thoughts to himself, though, saving all his strength for the flight ahead. But he could hide nothing from her. By the look in his eyes and the tightening lines on his face, Malekie knew things were growing bad as they crossed a vast expanse of open space.

But suddenly, in a rush, the worry melted from Kallen's face. He looked down at Malekie and smiled. "I know where we are now," he said. "I was attacked below and behind us. That's where my rib was broken. That storm carried us high, really high. We're fortunate."

"How do you know where we are?" Malekie thought he was teasing her, although she suspected the look of relief in is face was genuine enough.

Kallen nodded ahead of them. "See those clouds?" he asked.

She turned her head to look at the thin, wispy clouds above and before them, perhaps two, maybe three leagues away.

"Those are spectral stone clouds," Kallen said. "They never move."

Malekie stared at him and arched her brow. "I don't believe you," she retorted.

Kallen only smiled. "There's more," he promised. Then he renewed his efforts and lifted them even higher into the air. The exertion brought sweat to his brow and soon had him gasping for breath.

"Pace yourself, Kallen! You won't survive a fall to the ocean!"

"Peace, love," Kallen replied soothingly. "All is well." Though the labor was difficult, he was smiling. "You'll see."

Something about the look in his eye kept her in suspense and Malekie watched the approaching clouds carefully. She finally had to admit he was right when he said they didn't move. But nothing could have prepared her for what she saw once they finally reached them.

The clouds held water inside them like giant bowls filled to the rim. She laughed when she saw it, laughed until tears streamed from her face. The clouds were long and narrow, joining together in some places to form channels. Others were close enough she could imagine jumping across the empty spaces between them.

Kallen came to a stop beside the closest pool and eased her into the water.

"It's warm!" she cried.

"That's the spectral fire." He tapped the edge of the pond, where the water met the mist. "I wasn't joking when I said these were stone." To prove it he hoisted himself onto the ledge and stopped beating his wings.

Malekie laughed and clapped her hands in delight. "We're suspended in the air!"

He only shrugged. "You can't tell me you don't have spectral stones in the ocean."

"I guess you're right," Malekie agreed, "but I've never seen them do anything like this."

Kallen smiled and swung his feet into the pond. Then he eased himself into the water as if entering a hot bath. "I needed that," he sighed contentedly.

"You should sleep," Malekie urged.

"I will. And I don't dare go further until the sun sets. We're too vulnerable, unarmed and burdened down. Too many predators live in the air realm for us to travel further in safety."

"What about the water?" Malekie asked. Kallen glanced around before replying.

"These pools? These are safe enough," he said. "No one has any use for them. The effort to fly up here is hardly worth it. And none can see us from below. Just don't fall out when I'm asleep," he warned. He looked so weary as he spoke. "I might not be able to catch you in time. And it is a long way down."

Malekie giggled, swam forward, and kissed him. "I won't," she promised. Then she turned and streaked to the opposite end of the cloud, leaving a wake behind her. Kallen could hear her silvery laugh before she plummeted below the surface. In a few moments she resurfaced in front of him, her gills pumping while she laughed and threw her arms around him.

He propped his wings over the edge of the stone cloud and embraced her. The last thing he remembered before passing into a dreamless, exhausted sleep was kissing the top of her head and murmuring, "We are meant to be."

Malekie mumbled her agreement, her head buried deep within his embrace, but by the stillness of him she knew Kallen hadn't heard. It was a long time before she carefully untangled herself from his grasp and set out to relieve muscles cramped from being out of the water for so long.

ജ്ഞ

When Kallen opened his eyes, it was to find Malekie staring at him. She had a grin on her face, hovering with her head and shoulders out of the water while the rest of her stayed submerged. He'd never seen anything so beautiful as her, the way the setting sun reflected off of her golden hair, the way her pearly white skin seemed to shine with the water she was always in.

He was about to tell her that, too. But when he stirred, Kallen winced at the cramped muscles in his wings. He eased himself off of the ledge and flexed his wings, stretching them out as far as they could go and holding them there until the cramps started to subside.

Malekie's eyes flickered around them, mesmerized. The sun was setting and all was awash with brilliant orange. "I'd never imag-ined such color," she breathed, "such light."

"Do your eyes hurt?"

She shrugged it off. "I think I'm getting used to it, like you said."

"Surely there must be color like this down in the ocean?"

"Only around the spectral stones, it's true. The colors and the life … But up here — it's everywhere!" Her eyes were round with amazement.

79

Kallen smiled. "It's not all that different than where you're from, Icky. The sky realm floats in the sky the way the sea realm floats in the oceans. Most of it out there is just open air, empty space. Nothing can live out there without falling into the ocean."

Malekie returned his smile. "It's like that under the ocean. Most of it is empty water, where anything living just floats to the sur-face."

She went back to looking at the clouds and he went back to watching her.

Presently he spoke again. "Are you hungry?" he asked.

She shrugged. "I'm alive and I'm still with you."

"Did you sleep?"

"Couldn't. It was too bright out. And besides, I can sleep in your arms tonight."

That was true, Kallen supposed.

He wrapped his arms around her and lifted her out of the water.

"What are you doing?" Malekie asked with a giggle as she wig-gled in his grasp.

Kallen turned her over so she was face down, facing the water, then placed her bottom half back into the pond. "Try this with me? I dreamt of it while I slept." He held her sides and she grasped his hands.

Then she nodded, realizing what he had in mind. And with a surge of strength, she pushed through the water, diving back under the surface while he stayed above with his wings extended, gliding through the air.

Faster and faster they went, both flying and swimming, as one. And then their propulsion began to lift her out of the water, and she laughed as her gills closed, feeling the sensation of flying for herself. Then he lifted her more comfortably into his arms and she draped her own arms around his neck.

They sailed into the darkening sky, leaving the stone clouds behind for the deeper regions within the sky realm.

As the sun dipped towards the ocean horizon far, far below, the sky seemed to come alive with light. Stars sparkled into being, too numerous to count. And each one was awe-inspiring to Malekie. Although she'd seen stars enough from the ocean sur-face, up here they seemed more vivid somehow, more alive. And as the night continued to deepen, northern lights came alive with the colors of the spectral stones, stealing the breath from her as she watched them flicker and dance across the heavens.

Kallen glanced over his shoulder. "It is a good night for stars," he commented, unimpressed, but with a smile on his face. "I am glad you were able to see them."

Malekie only turned her look of awe towards him for a moment before turning back to watch the heavens.

She did not sleep that night, although she promised she would. Comfortable and safe in his arms, part of her recognized the impossibility of what they were doing and wanted to savor every moment as though it was her last.

He seemed remarkably casual about the whole thing, but Kallen wasn't fooling her. There was a reason why they traveled at night. A Trilian caught in the air by an enemy was one thing. A Trilian caught with a Siren, a demon, was quite another. An enemy could expect a quick, honorable death, but one carrying a Siren in his arms … Malekie had heard the stories about Trilian puritans and they had made her shudder.

And Kallen was taking her home, to them.

But Malekie trusted him. Kallen had proclaimed that his family, the Thoroughbloods, no longer belonged to or followed the cor-rupt ways of the rest of the Trilian race. In any event, she reasoned, it was too late to turn back now. She forced herself to study the stars and the northern lights and tried to ignore the ris - ing apprehension in her stomach.

They flew on in silence. The tense look in Kallen's eyes and the quiet, rhythmic beating of his wings, the way they were slowly descending, gliding for long intervals between each pump of his wings, told Malekie that he was being as quiet as he could. All she could do was trust him now, trust and hope for the best.

೫೦೧

She must have dozed off, for the next thing she knew he was landing on solid ground. She came awake instantly, stirring in his arms. "We made it?" she asked quietly.

"We made it, love." He took a few steps forward, then sank to his knees and lowered her into a pool of water.

That brought her fully awake, the unexpected delight of it. In the distance, she could hear running water, a waterfall! Kallen's boasts had not been a lie. Yet still, Malekie felt a surge of sudden panic, and reached up to grab his ripped and stained tunic.

Kallen took her hand in his and sat down at the edge of the pool. The light was too dim yet to see, but Malekie knew the way into his arms and jumped out of the water to sit down between his legs. She put an arm around his neck and lovingly caressed his face with her other hand. All the while the fear grew. "Don't leave me," she whispered urgently. "Please don't leave me. Not tonight."

He'd never seen her so afraid, and so took her in his arms and kissed her, reassuring her in the way words could not.

Dawn was only a short time away, and it found them sleeping in each other's arms, enveloped in his wings for warmth, upon a green pasture with his feet and her tail dangling in a pool of water. They were on an island, yet floating in the sky. To the left was a smaller island, miraculously floating in the air only a dozen paces or so above a pool of water. It was covered with thick foliage, vines and trees and thorn bushes. But from the center of it a spring gushed forth from the green flora to splash into the pond Malekie and Kallen lay beside. At the far end of their bigger island was another waterfall that cascaded through the sky from a third island floating far overhead. It was an enigmatic mystery, shrouded in a mist that revealed only a faint outline of its bottom.

The island they were on was likewise surrounded by mist. As the sun lifted, droplets suspended within the mist sent there by spray from the water or rain from the sky, reflected the sunlight-like prisms, casting a myriad of miniature rainbows across the exotic landscape.

Stiff and sore from their journey, exhausted from their emotional and physical trauma, and famished from lack of food, the couple nonetheless stirred and sat up somewhat gingerly. Malekie looked around, and although she was so close to the water, the first thing she noticed was not the mist, nor the aberrations of floating rock, nor even the waterfalls, so impressive a sight to see. No, the first thing Malekie noticed was the mansion resting on the other side of the island, a great big hideous thing, built of stone and wood and perched on the edge of the island amongst and atop a jagged stone precipice some half a league away from her.

Her eyes widened at the sight and she shuddered in fear before she plunged into the very depths of the water, to leave a confused Kallen to rise to his feet and wonder what had happened.

His relatives found him there, searching the bottom of the pool fruitlessly. His clothes were in tatters, his feathers askew, patches of them missing. His hair was filthy and his face had a wild, haunted look, as though he was used to being hunted. And his eyes seemed so desperate, so longing; it appeared to all that Kallen had lost his sanity.

"Kallen?" his father inquired, softly, hesitantly. He and the rest of the members of his household had crept up around Kallen quietly, giving him room. They were excited he was alive, brought to a hushed awe by the miracle of seeing him standing in their midst. But was changed somehow. Something was very different, as if much of the Trilian standing before them was a stranger, while their beloved family member was still there, only much diminished.

Noticing them for the first time, Kallen spun to face his father. "Kasan." He looked at his brother standing next to their father. "Flaveldon." Then he turned to the rest of them, his cousins and aunts, his mother in tears at the sight of her lost son returned. It was a large family; Kallen himself was of the third generation. The elders, those that had survived to see the day of their sunsets, were still at the mansion, too burdened by the weight of their wings to make the trip across the plateau. But he knew they were watching from the windows of their house, and his eyes went up to greet them while he extended his hands towards his kin.

Grateful beyond words, they rushed at him, shouting and cheering, pounding on his back and squeezing him in hugs or pumping his hands enthusiastically.

Malekie watched from across the pool, from the underside of the waterfall. Her face was barely out of the water, lest she be seen. But she knew she was well hidden behind the downpour of all this water. In the spray, her gills had opened up and she put a hand to one of them, feeling it breathe in the dampness that landed there.

With Kallen's back to her, she could see his wings, his proud wings glittering in the morning light, multicolored under the drops of water that hung suspended in the spectral mists, as though he wore a patchwork cloak made from heavenly material sent from Almighty Himself. So proud and regal he looked, so refined and noble were his people, dressed royally, with fierce and hungry weapons by their sides. The women were beautiful,

84

all subtle curves and full lips with brightly shining, intelligent eyes. The men were tall and proud, muscular, their features kind. The lot of them looked like angels, Malekie mused, and this, their place, must be heaven.

How could such a place be for her? She could not fly. She was covered with the filth of seaweed just to hide her nakedness. Fierce she may be, but regal certainly not. She was not from a family like this. Sirens are born much the same as humans. But they spend the first years of their life inside an egg, the way drag-ons do. Delicate and transparent as a fish egg, there are a great many infants born in one moment to live in such a bubble. But Malekie's earliest memories were not kind, as she watched her brothers and sisters and herself being abandoned by her parents, and any and all that could have called her family.

Her spear sisters had chosen her simply because she was the best swimmer, the fastest, the strongest. It was through her prowess with the spear that she had earned the right to call anoth-er family. And here Kallen was, accepted by this great host of angels simply on the merits of his birth alone.

He knew not what he had done by bringing her to such a place. And even had she known, Malekie wasn't sure if she would have stayed behind in the cold oceans of Mishard.

But then Kallen turned and peered into the waters again. Their eyes met, though she knew he could not see her through the froth. And the sadness, the pleading, the love she saw there convinced her she would go out to him, to be revealed in all her filth, her hideousness, if he asked.

As if he had heard her, he waded into the pool and held his hands out towards the water. He was facing away from her, but she knew his heart was calling out for her to come to him. And so she drew in a deep breath, as much through her gills as through her lungs, and plunged into the water. As she fought the currents of the waterfall, she determined to go through with any ordeal she must, pushing all doubt and fear aside. The moment could not have been more frightening for her than if she dove blindly off the ledge of this sky island, out into the vast emptiness of space.

Kallen sank to his knees, much to the wonder of his family. Surely their son had truly lost his mind. His hands dipped beneath the surface of the water. His wings spread out to the sides to give Malekie some privacy, and then she was there in his arms, covering her gills with her hands as water dripped from her face.

He tenderly brushed the damp, greenish-blonde hair from her face and smiled gently as his arms, as well as his wings, embraced her.

"My gills," she whispered quietly. "They'll see my gills."

"You're more concerned about your gills than you are about your breasts," Kallen teased her.

Malekie glanced down at her chest. The seaweed bikini was still intact.

"I wouldn't be, if I was uncovered," she rejoined.

That brought smiles from both of them. "Someday," they said in unison, forgetting for a precious moment where they were and what they were about to do.

"Do you want me to fetch you a scarf?" Kallen asked.

She stared at him. She wasn't sure what that was, but surmised it was some kind of covering. She shook her head. "They'll close in a moment. Please Kallen, hide me here until they do?"

He nodded ever so slightly, then kissed her on the forehead. "Thank you for doing this," he murmured.

Malekie let all her fear and nervousness bubble back to the surface and trembled in way of an answer.

He kissed her again, then pulled a hand away from a gill. "It's nearly closed," he said before lightly kissing her gill. She trembled and he brushed the water away from the outside of the gill. The slit on her cheekbone closed, and Kallen turned her head to look at the other one. It was gone.

"Perfect," he declared, holding her chin in his hands and gazing earnestly into her eyes. "Everything about you is perfect."

Malekie searched his eyes, and witnessed the truth she found there.

Then he was taking her by the shoulder and turning to face the mass that had gathered to witness their son's insanity. He held her tight as she lifted out of the water, the strength of her tail keeping her in constant motion as she tread the water he stood knee deep in. The effort was little, but it amplified the fact that she was not human, and certainly not Trilian.

A collective gasp went up from the crowd, which visibly recoiled at the sight of her. But now that Malekie was here, secure in Kallen's arms, the pride in her came rolling to the sur - face, challenging them to prove they were not the hypocrites that the Trilian race was. The Thoroughbloods had claimed she was no demon. But did they have it in their hearts to welcome her as their guest long enough for Kallen and her to find a place where they could be together?

Conflicting emotions, from shock to horror, to fascination, to admiration showed on their faces. They stared at Malekie with wide, unbelieving eyes, and none of them wanted to be the first to speak.

Fear started to erode her courage, and she looked at Kallen for strength.

He had been watching her with a smile on his face, which widened into a confident grin when she looked up at him some - what shakily.

"This Siren has saved my life," he said loud enough for the entire assembly to hear. His eyes, though, never left her as he continued to speak. "She has forsaken the ways of her people to seek out the will of Almighty. She is alone and unattached from the wars of the surface realm. Her name is Malekie and I have chosen her to be my wife, and she has chosen me to be her hus - band." He looked up at the crowd, trying to gauge their reactions.

An uproar of commotion spilled from them, ranging from con - fusion to anger to outright rejection. His mother moaned and sank to her knees as her wings covered her head. One of the cousin's cousins, a young blonde woman, cried out in agony, then spun on her heel and thrust her way through the crowd as she stormed away in fury. Her brothers went with her, shooting Kallen hateful looks as they followed their sister.

But two of the Trilians stepped forward, Flaveldon, Kallen's older brother, and Kasan, his father. It was on them that Malekie focused her attention, tuning the others out completely. She could go no closer to the shore without being carried, and they seemed willing to wade in to greet her, but one look at their regal footwear and she reached for Kallen to lift her into his arms. He obliged — of course he would — and carried her to the shore, where he set her down carefully before his father and brother. Standing there, balancing on feet buried within the membrane of her tail, Malekie was hard pressed to maintain her equilibrium; but Kallen gallantly steadied her with his firm, comforting grasp.

"Welcome," Flaveldon said as he moved toward Malekie and embraced her. He held her at arms' length for deeper inspection, then winked and glanced at Kallen. "She's quite a catch," he grinned.

That brought a smile to her face and a giggle to her lips.

Then Flaveldon was handing the teetering siren-mermaid off to his father. Kasan's face bespoke great wisdom, deep lines were etched across his sun-baked face, and his knowing eyes were able to quickly examine problems from every angle. He knew what was being done today must not be taken lightly. And he had already correctly guessed the reactions this union must cause from every one of his people, people who ultimately were his responsibility. Yet there was kindness as well, and a genuine smile graced his lips. "Daughter," was all he said as he hugged her, accepting fully who and what she was. He pulled away and held her upright as he looked into her astonished eyes. All he did was nod at her, but it seemed to Malekie that this man understood every fear she had. "You're a brave girl." Then he turned and regarded his son. "You'd better get her back in the water before she dries out."

She rolled her eyes. She hated it when her scales were dry. The itching was unbearable.

Kallen lifted her up into his arms and carried her into the pond, where she let the water cover her face. She stared up at him while her gills opened, then blew him a kiss and swam out of his arms.

Kallen turned and walked back to the shore to be led away by his father and the crowd. Flaveldon and a few others remained, and Malekie could not help but flee to her refuge behind the waterfall once again. Yet as she watched, she knew they were not offended by her shyness. Instead, they walked along the edge of the pond until Flaveldon chose a spot and had them all sit down to wait for the Siren's re-emergence. She swallowed her fear and plunged back into the water.

When she resurfaced, she was holding her hands over her gills and hovered with just her neck above the water as she peered timidly at the Trilians sitting on the bank.

"Why are you holding your chin like that?" Flaveldon asked.

"I have gills. I am self conscious about them."

Flaveldon accepted this with a nod of his head. "I would be too." The girl sitting next to him thought his words cruel and hit him on the shoulder, but Malekie liked his honesty. The strange-ness of the situation assured that there would be more than one awkward moment shared between them. And she liked being defended; even if it wasn't needed.

Flaveldon saw her look at the other girl and remembered his manners. "This is Tacanaly. We call her Tacky for short." The girl shrugged as a way of accepting the fate of her name.

"Kallen does the same with my name," she told the Trilian. "He calls me Icky."

Tacanaly smiled. "It must be a family thing."

Maleckie returned the smile.

"And this youngster here-" Flaveldon reached over Tacanaly's shoulders and tousled a younger Trilian's hair. The boy seemed to revel in the rough affection, drawing approval from Tacanaly. "-is Keefer." He pointed at the older lady. "Mallsen. And the one sitting next to me is Shae." Shae was a curious Trilian, and by his manner and the two swords jutting out over his shoulders, Malekie supposed that he was a warrior.

"Kallen is my best friend," Shae explained.

Malekie noticed there were no older Trilians here, and she said as much.

Flaveldon shrugged. "They were pretty relieved to see Kallen again. I'm sure you'll see one of them soon."

She didn't believe him but this time she kept the words to her - self.

Flaveldon seemed able to read her face, however, and hastened to reassure her. "Trilians are nothing if not political," he said, "but our hearts are in the right place. You'll see."

Just then Malekie spotted Kallen flying through the air, and all her negative thoughts were immediately banished from her mind; she had eyes only for him.

His brother grinned to see the reaction and cast a fairly similar gaze towards Tacanaly. Kallen landed beside them and knelt on the grass to lean over the water.

"Your clothes are new," Malekie said, admiring the new clothes he wore.

"Well, according to the women, I'm still as filthy as I could get. They can't understand that just because I was away from the house for so long, I'd stay clean?"

"Imagine that," was all she said. "It must be a woman's touch."

He smiled and leaned a little closer. He took one of her hands, still covering the gills on her chin, and peeked beneath it. "You can take your hands away now. They've closed."

She did what he said, shyly, of course. But he sat back on his heels and let her swim all the way to the shore.

"What's it like, having gills?" Tacanaly asked.

"What's it like having two voice boxes?" she asked in return.

Tacanaly had no answer for that. But eventually, she admitted, "We have a lot in common."

"That's what Kallen and I think," she agreed with a rise of her eyebrows.

"Come," Kallen cut in. He took her by the hand and guided her out of the water. "There is someone who would like to meet you." Then he scooped her into his arms and lifted her clean into the air.

"That's so romantic!" Tacanaly exclaimed.

"That's so romantic!" her brother mocked. Tacanaly threw him a disgusted look and then ignored him.

The Trilians rose to their feet.

"Why don't you ever do that for me?" Tacanalay complained to Flaveldon.

"You're too heavy," he answered without pausing to consider his words. She smacked him in the shoulder again, a little more forcefully this time.

"Your wings make you too heavy?" he answered again, all too serious.

"Grow some muscles," Kallen told his older brother. "You'll be glad you did." Then he was lifting into the air and soaring towards the house.

"There must be some benefits to carrying your girlfriend in your arms everywhere you go," Mallson admitted somewhat enviously, watching them fly away.

Tacanalay gave Flaveldon a look as if to say, "Mallson gets it, why don't you?" Then they were flying after Kallen and Malekie.

℘℧

The mansion was unlike anything she'd seen before. Malekie had never been near a surface dwelling, but this was even unlike the buildings of humans. Mermaids often lived in giant air bubbles caused by the ever-wondrous spectral stones. But these were as different from those as sky was from water.

There were no stairs, and many, many floors with balconies everywhere. There were peaked roofs but more flat roofs with trap doors. As many doors and windows dotted the dwelling as possible; and Malekie thought perhaps the thing would fall over, there were so many holes in it. But the closer they flew, the more noticeable the great stone pillars became, holding the mansion together as it sat on the edge of the sky island.

Kallen took her to a door on the ground floor, knocked once then opened the large wooden, peaked paneling. At once they were in a cavernous room. The lighting was poor. What lights there were came from sky blue stones glowing from pedestals around the perimeter of the room. The effect was like seeing portals open up to a cloudless sky.

There was something very soothing about the room; safe, aesthetic. The furniture was sparse, and the room had a high ceiling that allowed Kallen to stretch his wings to their full height. What few pieces of furniture there were — a four-post bed, a desk and chair, a settee and a bookshelf — were made from gray stone, and there were no coverings or cushions on the rock slate that passed for a bed. Malekie thought little of this oddity. Sirens also had little use for such possessions, and she remembered the way Kallen's wings had offered all the comfort he'd needed in his sojourn on their island.

A Trilian sat hunched over the desk. Malekie could not tell if it was a man or a woman, but it had long grey hair that hung down its back and over its wings. The wings, instead of being folded and upright, ready for flight, drooped, their membranes hanging limp down the back of the chair and onto the floor like some immense, heavy cape covered with feathers.

Kallen saw her gaze as he eased Malekie down, and leaned forward to whisper into her ear. "We can do that, wrap them around us like a cloak, if we want to."

"I've never seen you do that before." She needed his hand to steady herself as she balanced on unsteady feet sheathed inside the tail of a fish.

"It is burdensome and the muscles in the back grow sore. It's not a natural state until we grow old. But Trilians don't usually see old age, not on the surface, not with their demon crusades."

Malekie simply nodded.

"Flasator!" Kallen called across the space to the elder. He waited during the long pause that followed, and when he received no response, he shouted, "Aunt Flasator!"

"There's no need to shout, Kallen. I'm not deaf, just busy." Slowly the Trilian pushed herself to her feet and turned slowly to face them. "So I'm old, am I?"

Kallen blushed and stammered incoherently, caught off balance.

"That's all right, young man." She dragged her wings towards them, each step carrying with it a heavy weight. "I just like to see you squirm." She grinned.

Just then the others caught up to them and piled into the room behind them.

Malekie stared at the elder's wings, as Flasator inspected her tail in return.

"So it is true," she said after a lengthy silence. Everything Flasator said was careful and slow, well thought out before the crux of the matter broached.

Malekie tottered unsteadily on her fin and grabbed at Kallen's arm. Flasator smiled, as if Malekie had given her answer enough. She motioned for Kallen to lift the Siren back into his arms, then turned to drag herself across the room again.

Malekie turned to Kallen's relatives. "Flaveldon, help your aunt," she ordered. Immediately she realized she'd spoken out of place, without thinking, but she could relate to the difficulties the old woman was having and hated to see any creature suffer.

Flaveldon looked as though he'd been slapped in the face and he rocked back on his heels. But the elder only laughed, her rich voice echoing across the chamber with multiple sounds, both voices sounding like a choir as they worked together to form different notes at the same time.

"It's all right, Flaveldon. Our ways are not the ways of our brethren down on the surface. I'd be honored if you'd help carry my wings."

Flaveldon glanced at Tacanaly and both of them jumped together to lift Flasator's wings from the floor.

As she led the Siren back to the stone couch, Flasator
explained, "Trilians are all about strength and honor. There is no
greater symbol of either than our wings. For a Trilian to admit he
needs help lifting his wings is to admit he no longer has any
strength or honor."

"But that's not true," Malekie cut in stubbornly.

"Such is the way of a corrupt society. There are many things
that are wrong with what they do. But at one time Trilians were
thought to be physical angels created from the pendulums of time
by Almighty himself. Our little clan is out here to try to get that
nobility and piety back. There's no room for burdensome traditions, I'm afraid."

Kallen sat her down on the couch as Flasator eased herself
down on the other side and faced her guest.

"You make it sound like a bad thing," he said to his aunt.

Flasator glanced at Kallen standing over them. "I'm old, sweet-
ling. All I have are my traditions."

"You have us, Auntie," Flaveldon reminded her.

Her smile was genuine as she patted her nephew's hand resting
on the back of the couch. "Thank you, dear. I'd almost forgotten
that. Now leave, all of you. I would talk to the Siren alone." As
the others obeyed, Flasator stared up at Kallen. "You too, brave
one. You may have come back from the dead with a miracle in
your arms. But cross me and you'll wish you were back on that
rock."

Her threat only brought a smile to Kallen's face. "Yes, Auntie,"
he said dutifully, in a very small, very timid voice that had to be
mocking her. He kissed Malekie's cheek and whispered, "Careful,

she bites." Then he turned and followed his brother and their friends out.

"Forgive my bluntness, Malekie. But once your wings no longer carry you, you start to get right to the point."

Malekie nodded.

"You are kind, too kind to be a spear sister."

Malekie was both taken aback and insulted by the statement, and knew her expression gave her emotions away.

"Don't act so surprised," Flasator said. "I know a thing or two about the spear sisters. I wasn't old forever, and I spent much time on the surface hunting the women below the water line, and being hunted in turn."

Malekie nodded. "Not much has changed. But those are my sisters, my family. It is hard for me to listen to you speak of them that way."

"I know it must be. But you left your family and Kallen has boasted of your status amongst them. You must have left for a reason."

"Tradition and corruption," she admitted. "It was the same for me as for your family. I wanted to find love. I knew of Almighty and I was tired of turning my back to him."

"So now you seek to join my family."

Malekie frowned for a moment before she replied. "I hadn't thought of it like that. There was only Kallen when we fell in love, not Kallen and his people. He was ready to stay with me down there. But the surface is no place for us, not with the wars."

"There is a place. There are always places," Flasator pointed out.

Malekie shrugged. "We don't know where they are."

Flasator leaned towards Malekie. "Trilians are the reason for that, the only reason for that, the only people you need to blame. Keeping the races separate is the single utmost goal Trilians have. Do you know why? They are afraid of the abominations that would be born if the races were to intermix."

Malekie hadn't thought of that either. But by the expression on this Trilian's face, it was the only thing she'd thought of since finding out her nephew was going to attempt to marry a Siren.

Flasator dragged herself to her feet and over to the end table. She pulled something from a drawer and turned around slowly to face Malekie's bewildered look. She then tossed a linen garment to Malekie and made her way slowly back to the couch.

Malekie held the garment up to examine it and realized it was actually two garments, a snow white robe and a matching tunic.

"No one's expecting you to shed your scales," Flasator said as she repositioned her wings on the couch and sat down. "But you can't go around wearing nothing but seaweed. And there will come a day when you will want your feet, if only for the marriage bed."

Malekie nodded.

"The robe should work if you're not quite ready to go back into the water."

"You approve, then?"

Flasator eyed Malekie shrewdly and then nodded. "I do."

Malekie threw herself at Flasator, embracing her with a warm, enthusiastic hug.

"Welcome to the family," Flasator said with a smile, returning the embrace. "Now take that seaweed thing off. It's getting my wings dirty."

Malekie pulled away, beaming. "Yes ma'am."

The entire assembly of Trilians arranged themselves around the edge of the pool Malekie had come to know as her home. Flaveldon, Tacanaly, Flasator, Mallson... even those who had first opposed the union had come around and accepted what was about to happen.

As different as Malekie was, her love for Kallen had been enough to ride out the hard time she'd gone through adjusting to life in the air realm. Every moment had been focused on this one day, this one event. Every second she'd been up here in the clouds she'd anticipated this. That was enough to lighten the burden. Her love for Kallen had made everyone and everything seem so new, so refreshing.

It was rare to be around so many people all at the same time. Generally, Sirens were a distrustful, aloof group, even when Malekie had lived with them – the relationships she experienced with her own kind were not like the warm and friendly camaraderie Malekie shared with these Thoroughbloods. It was rare to find a Siren in closed waters like this; the limited space was often claustrophobic. Muscles not continually worked would stiffen and cramp. Water would be stale and miserable to breathe, hard on the fin. But here there was not one but two waterfalls Malekie could exercise in, and both were of different intensity. The large waterfall was powerful, fast, potent. It allowed her to throw herself at it, racing the current, fighting to gain purchase higher in the air. The second waterfall was much smaller and slower. It was to this one Malekie went when she wanted to swim for a great distance. If she paced herself she could stay between the two islands for hours on end. And as for food, there was nothing difficult about adjusting to the new diet. The Trilians had all manner of different islands they had cultivated. Meat was fresh and plentiful – and cooked. And the vegetables! So many different types of salad had she sampled since arriving here: Malekie had known that the surface realm had variety, but she had no idea this many types of plants could even exist.

As for her more basic needs, the Trilians had set up a lavatory close enough to the water that she could reach it, but far enough away that it wouldn't pollute the precious water supply. If Malekie wanted to be alone, she could utilize the smaller of the two waterfall islands, the one closest to the pool. It was covered with thick thorn bushes and rough boulders. The creek came from a spring in the center of the island. And with some patient labor and a few cuts and scrapes, she had rearranged the boulders to form a bit of den with a roof of thorns. And she could hide behind the larger of the two waterfalls, as she had when she first arrived here. The Trilians had built a large stone gazebo on top of the larger waterfall island, which was almost half the size as of the main one. The stream came from the base of the gazebo, and she had discovered this was the best place to visit with the Thoroughblood family.

ФШШ

Kallen had sent a few of the more powerful Trilians back to the surface. The reason why had remained a secret from Malekie until they returned with full water bags. Kallen had been excited at their arrival, and Malekie thought he was crazy the way he flew to the Trilians and bombarded them with questions that she could not quite hear from where she watched. He wasn't silenced until one of his cousins finally gave him one of the bags and he peeked inside. What Kallen saw there made him beam with even more excitement, so much so that it brought him past the point of being able to speak. Instead, bag of water in hand, he flew to Malekie and sat down on the shore with his feet in the water, grinning hugely.

"Don't the rain and the spectral stones give us all the water we could ever use?" she asked him. "What's so important that you had to send to the surface realm?"

To answer, Kallen bent low and kissed her on the lips, long and full. When he came up for air, he lowered the bag into the water and carefully upended it. A few dozen tiny bright fish scattered into the water.

Malekie cried out in wonder, clapped her hands together and disappeared under the surface with a flick of her tail.

Kallen laughed to see her delight and watched while the other bags were lowered into the pond and various exotic fish were released.

It was a good long time before Malekie surfaced, glowing with joy. She even forgot to cover her gills as she proclaimed, 'You know they'll have to be fed!"

Kallen nodded. "I thought about that. So we brought back some food. I don't know if you'll want to feed them yourself, sneak the food into the water, or just dump it in all at once."

Malekie reached out and took the sack of food from his hands. She gave him a look as if to say, "I can take it from here." Then she swam to the small waterfall, gazed lovingly at her betrothed, then launched herself up the waterfall and into the dense thorn bushes where the creek bubbled out – all the while keeping the sack of fish food dry in one hand. She reappeared a few moments later, to slide head first off of the cliff and dive into the pool of water below her.

"I can never get over how much like a fish she is," Mallsen admitted to his friend.

"She can't get over how much like a bird you are," Kallen retorted.

Mallsen grew quiet as he considered this. "I never thought about that," he finally said.

"Neither did she."

ॐ

And now, here they were, assembled as witnesses to the day she'd dreamt of for so long.

Kallen's father, Kasan, stood on the shore, positioned between the couple. Malekie knew that he was speaking words, but she did not hear them. All Malekie could focus on was Kallen's face, his eyes, his smile. She became aware that something was being asked of her, and she blankly glanced at Kasan, smiled and nodded her head before turning back to stare at her beloved again.

But when Kasan looked at her and said, very clearly, "I now pronounce you husband and wife. You may kiss the bride," Malekie was fully aware of what was happening around her. She grabbed Kallen and pulled him into the water, immediately sinking with him to the bottom of the pool.

From where the crowd stood on shore, a great applause went up, with excited acclamations about the great day that was dawning, a time of peace between Trilians and Sirens. But eventually, their cheers and their boasts subsided as the guests became concerned about what was happening under the surface. All they could see was Kallen's back and the outstretched wings hovering over him, hiding him and his bride from view.

"They've sure been down there a long time," Tacanaly voiced what everyone was thinking.

"She must be breathing for him," Mallsen pointed out.

"Either that, or she's drowning him," Flaveldon said.

That brought a round of nervous laughter as everyone peered anxiously into the pool. Thankfully, a few moments later the couple resurfaced. Malekie's gills were blazing when she and Kallen emerged, grinning and laughing as, with no small measure of relief, the crowd cheered them a second time.

Kasan motioned towards his eldest son, who solemnly stepped towards the couple carrying a package wrapped in white linen. It was long, and judging by his somber manner, obviously held some great ceremonial significance. When Kallen saw it he began to weep, but at Maleckie's inquisitive gaze, he merely shook his head and wiped the tears from his face.

Flaveldon bowed towards his father, who reached out and unwrapped the linen. A golden staff shone in the afternoon sun, and Malekie looked on with increasing interest. Then, as more and more of the linen was withdrawn, she cried out in surprise and delight. For in Flaveldon's hands rested a spear, a beautifully crafted golden spear, whose weight Malekie was just itching to hold.

She covered her mouth with a trembling hand as Kasan picked the weapon up and held it out to her. No words were needed; his expression told her everything. Overcome with emotion, Malekie too began to cry, and with shaking hands reached out and touched the weapon tentatively. Then, unable to contain herself any longer, and growing bold with her eagerness, Malekie grasped the spear in the firm, sure hands of a warrior.

"Welcome to the family," Kassan said quietly. Malekie turned to him, her heart filled with gratitude, and they embraced as father and daughter.

For a third time a cheer went up from the spectators.

₧₨

"Why doesn't she ever come out of the water?" Heleopatra, Kallen's mother, stood in their immense kitchen, her arms folded stubbornly across her breasts, wings half extended like some avenging angel, with a scowl to match. "I'm tired of this. She has feet. Let her use them," she demanded peevishly.

Kallen was growing impatient. "She is awkward out of the water," he replied with a sigh.

"Like a fish out of water," Flaveldon grinned.

Heleopatra leveled her scowl at her oldest son. "Not quite. Trilians have wings but we also have feet. We use them, see." She stamped her foot on the stone floor. "Just like Sirens, but apparently, this one's too good for her feet." Her voice dripped with sarcasm.

"Malekie did not use her feet in the surface and water realms," Kallen pointed out. "She was renowned as a spear sister, and her greatness came from not using her feet."

Heleopatra rolled her eyes. "She's not in the water realm now, is she?"

"It takes time, Mother. Give it to her, please."

"It takes time, Mother," she mimicked Kallen. Frowning, she challenged, "How much time does the woman need? Isn't she even a little bit curious to know how the rest of us live?"

"She's been in the skies," Kallen argued, "just about every day, when she's not swimming in the waterfalls."

"But not in the house!" Heleopatra retorted.

"Would you be willing to trim your wings if you lived in the water realm?" he asked.

"I don't live in the water realm! That's exactly my point! And if she's going to live here, she's got to adjust to life here."

"She has, mother," Kallen insisted. "As well as she can."

"She hasn't!" Kallen's mother disagreed. "Her strength down there is her weakness up here! There's so much more she could have, so much she could experience! We could even give her a room in the house, on the ground floor ... "

"Malekie has a room, mother; three, actually. And she is quite happy with them."

Heleopatra closed her eyes in frustration and focused on calm-ing her breath. "It is selfish to refuse to ever come out of them," she finally managed to choke.

Kallen knew he was getting close to that point when he could no longer talk to his mother civilly, but he shrugged and said any-way, "You don't understand, do you, Mother? You can't imagine what it would be like to not be able to use gills you don't have."

She lifted her chin into the air and pointed to her throat, where the two voice boxes would have been had she been male. "I can imagine all I need!" she reminded him. "But even my voices need a break from singing once in a while."

Kallen saw the truth in her words and nodded. "I'll talk to her about that," he conceded.

"You do that." Heleopatra responded, unwilling to give an inch.

At the pool, Kallen sat cross-legged on the ledge. He gazed into the water, tracking Malekie as she schooled with the fish. It seemed to him that she could communicate with them on some primitive level. If she wanted, she could be ignored by them, or her very presence could frighten them to the far end of the pool. But she could also call them to her, or choose to school with one or more types at any time. She would swim along just inches behind a school, only to turn and have them follow her for a few paces. Interacting with them was a game that could entertain her, and often a Trilian audience, for hours. Now, with a hidden signal to the colorful creatures, Malekie broke off from the group and swam to the surface, smiling as she rose out of the water with gills glowing.

"Mother invites you to the mansion," Kallen announced.

Malekie spoke lightly, keeping her smile in place. "Does she, now?" She wasn't blind; she knew Kallen's mother bore some resentment towards her. But neither would Malekie allow

Heleopatra to dampen her experience of being in love with the woman's son.

"She would like you to walk," Kallen said, eyeing Malekie warily.

"I'm not walking."

"But — "

Malekie held up her hand to stop him. "I'm not walking that distance. That would ruin my tail. I'll wear the robe Flasator gave me. She probably foresaw this day."

"Most of the Old Ones do," Kallen agreed. "Where is the robe? I'll get it."

Malekie waved towards the island covered in thorns. "It's in there," she said.

He stared at the island for a moment, then sighed and resigned himself to the task.

"I can get it," she told him.

"No," Kallen assured her. "I like it in there, it's just that my clothes will get wet."

"Oh, poor baby!" Malekie teased him.

Kallen looked at her and then grinned. "I'm thinking about Mother," he laughed.

"Don't stay, then. I'm a big girl."

He nodded and launched into the air.

Malekie watched with her arms crossed, admiring her husband as he set down in the creek above the waterfall and stooped low, his wings dipping into the water. He disappeared into their private haven and returned a few moments later with the robe in his hand.

"You keep adding things," Kallen said. Malekie was always adding 'things' to their place, it was just that he wasn't always around to see the changes. He almost seemed hurt that he wasn't involved in the latest renovation, but said, "It looks good." She was building a cave out of all that stone, continually deepening the channel of water, but leaving a ledge he could rest under, next to the water, away from all the thorns. It was their place, their private retreat, a place where they could spend the night together and be alone, away from their family.

Malekie smiled her understanding. "I'll tell you next time I'm going to work on it," she said.

"I'd like to help," he admitted. "It's just that with this war … "

"I know Kallen. That's why I thought you wouldn't mind if I went ahead with it."

He shook himself to banish his momentary sadness, and bowed formally before Malekie. "Anyway, Mother awaits," he grinned. He held his arms out to her.

She glanced around to assure herself they were alone, then stripped out of the white tunic. Kallen grinned. Someday had come and gone, and he still appreciated everything about her. She lifted herself out of the water with her arms held in the air. He took his cue and draped the robe over her arms and neck, careful not to let it touch the water.

"It's hard to swim with this thing on," Malekie confessed. "The robe gets in the way."

In response, Kallen scooped her into his arms and carefully placed her on the ground. "Problem solved," he said.

"Shallow end?" she asked as she pointed to the far side of the pool. "Please."

He was happy to oblige and had her there in a heartbeat. Malekie hiked the robe up to her waist and sat down in the knee deep water, staring at her tail. She took a few moments to splash water over it. Then, knowing there was no longer any excuse to put it off, she pushed at the membrane where tail met skin. The scales rolled into two lines that started at her waist and ran down the outside of her legs, all the way to her ankles.

She was modest and discreet, even though they were alone. One just never knew who might be watching out here in the open. As the tail retracted, she pulled her robe down to hide her nakedness, edging herself out of the water when it was appropriate to do so.

Malekie hated going without her tail. But since she and Kallen had been married, she'd been happy to shed its confining embrace for his. Plus, stretching her legs was a daily activity, as it was for all Sirens. With a lifetime of practice behind her, the tail was hidden faster than Kallen would have thought possible. His face registered his surprise.

"I've never seen you put it away that fast before," he declared.

She grinned. "We've always been under the roses."

He returned her grin fondly and nodded his head. "Now I know. Things will be different, now," he said as he lifted her gently into his arms.

"That's what you think." She draped her arms around his neck then kissed him soundly on the cheek. "The mother-in-law awaits."

Kallen chuckled and shot into the air.

Malekie's feet hurt; her knees, unaccustomed to being apart for so long, began to ache before he even set her down. He was careful, sympathetic to his beloved's awkwardness, knowing how much of a sacrifice she was making. Malekie took a step toward the large common room before her, and was thankful for the sunlight and the colors streaming through the open windows. At least she'd have the beauty of the air realm for comfort. That was something.

She clung to that good thought, tried to wrap it around her , imagined it was the robe she wore. She drew a steadying breath and stepped hesitantly into the room. Kallen remained outside, knowing instinctively that this meeting was for the women only.

Kallen's mother stood by the sink, chopping vegetables with a huge knife. Another Trilian woman named Sasha stood with a similar knife across from Heleopatra, chopping filleted fish and scooping the pieces into a large pot of boiling water.

Malekie swallowed uncertainly and took another wobbly step into the kitchen. A rustle of wings made her glance over her shoulder in time to see Kallen disappearing over the railing. "Malekie!" the voice was Mallsen's, friendly and warm, inviting.

Malekie turned around with a genuine smile on her face and stretched out her arms in greeting. "Malsen!"

Mallsen crossed the room to assist her, and Malekie accepted, realizing she would be better able walk with help, since she only had flipper-like feet at the moment, and virtually no coordination in her biped state.

The other ladies stared at her, openly scorning her as if she were some kind of a freak. But Mallsen squeezed her hand reas - suringly, and Malekie was able to keep her smile.

"We didn't hear you land," Heleopatra said, putting her knife down. "We're glad you could join us."

Before Malekie could respond, Sasha gestured at the massacred fish in front of her. "This doesn't offend you, I hope."

"No," Malekie said with a shake of her head. "I'm just curious though, as to where you got them from."

Sasha's eyes glittered as she gave Malekie a tight-lipped smile and turned back to her work. Over the rise and fall of her knife she said, "On another island. Different Trilians have claim to different islands, different resources. It's private property. You wouldn't be allowed."

"Sasha!" Heleopatra reproved her, although her voice was tinged with mockery and a hint of a grin flickered across her face.

Malekie's eyes narrowed and glanced around. She may be on land, she thought, but she was still a spear sister, and in no way did she need to be afraid of these women. She took another step towards them, her feet awkward and off-balance. Where Malekie knew much in the way of embraces, things like walking meant little to her, and she knew the strength in her legs outmatched that of these women who spent so much time out of the water. Her muscles rippled with each step she took, and the confident smile on her face despite her handicap caused them to regard Malekie with a grudging respect.

"Forgive us, Malekie," Heleopatra said, her words and expression genuine this time. "Trilian women parry with words rather than swords."

Malekie acknowledged this with a slight nod of her head. The wary look in her eyes never changed, however. "Siren women never use words," she asserted. "Just spears and really short daggers. Little daggers about this long." She released her grip on Mallsen and held her fingers about three inches apart to emphasize her words. "With a curve in them like this." She drew a ninety degree arc in the air in front of her.

Sasha's eyes widened with the imagery. She could see the scars on Malekie's shoulders that testified to the validity of the Siren's claim. "Why so short?" she asked, curiosity overcoming her resentment.

"We fight up close," Malekie explained. "Under the water a strike is robbed of its strength, so we rely on getting as close to our enemy as we can. The knives are designed to destroy the gills. You see," she continued, "Sirens don't kill each other. To live on the surface and be forced to walk is worse than death to a

109

Siren, and the worst humiliation there is to a spear sister. A spear sister is the greatest of warriors amongst her people, revered for her ability to kill and lure surface dwellers into the waters."

"Surface dwellers and Trilians," Heleopatra reminded her, turning back to her vegetables.

Malekie nodded. "To all air dwellers, especially. Your men are completely inept at defending themselves once they are within a Siren's arms. Their wings, especially, are vulnerable to breakage."

The women knew there was nothing they could respond to that, and suddenly they did not want to mince cruel words with Malekie. They had forgotten Kallen's stories about her. But she was obviously a great warrior, one without fear, and each one of those scars was well earned. Where they had left their people to find a gentler existence, one without persecution, Malekie had left hers because she was sick of doing the persecuting.

"Is there a chair or something where I can sit?" Malekie asked quietly. "Carrying my weight for a long time on my flippers makes my feet tingle."

"Of course, anything." Mallsen jumped into motion, making sure Malekie was secure with both hands placed on the counter before she ran to the far end of the kitchen and picked up a tall, wooden stool. Malekie smiled when she saw it. Mallsen put it down in front of her with a warm smile. "Anything else?"

Malekie eased herself onto the stool with a grateful sigh. "No, thank you Mallsen."

Mallsen patted her shoulder, her face flushed with pleasure, then leaned against the counter across from her.

Malekie turned to Sasha, who was still preparing her fish stew. "Is your lake stocked?" she asked her.

"How do you know it is a lake?" Sasha countered somewhat belligerently.

"I know a great many things about your lake." Malekie nodded towards the meat in front of the Trilian. "Well fed, and with natural foods." She reached out a hand towards one of the pieces of meat. "May I?"

Sasha intercepted with her knife, although she was careful not to seem threatening. "We all might live under the same roof," she said, "but our clan is made of families within this family. The mist ensures our privacy and the resources within those mists assures our wealth, our ability to trade with each other."

Malekie nodded her understanding. "And you do not want me to know what those resources are," she stated flatly.

Sasha blinked at her frankness, while Kallen's mother watched their exchange carefully from over her shoulder.

"I understand that," Malekie nodded. She withdrew her hand and the room was filled with a heavy silence. "It must put you at great advantage to know what Kallen is interested in," Malekie commented.

Sasha sniffed angrily. "I don't see it like that."

"Well, tell me then. Do Trilians marry for politics, or for love?"

Sasha turned on Malekie with anger in her eyes, although she kept her voice low. She had been the cousin of Kallen's cousins who had stormed off when he'd announced his intention to marry the Siren. She had been proposed to Kallen before he had gone missing. "They are supposed to marry for love," she spat out.

"Then be grateful," Malekie replied, "for it seems you and your family have a double advantage now."

Heleopatra laughed with a slight trace of bitterness. "She's got you there, Sasha."

"That's a good point," Sasha conceded. She returned to her work and pushed the bucket at her feet in Malekie's direction. "For your kind words, and to stay fair," she said.

Malekie stared at Sasha, then peered into the bucket. Her eyes widened and she pushed herself out from the stool and sat down on the floor beside the bucket. The waste from the fish had been placed inside it, their heads and innards, their bones and tails.

Sasha watched her inspect the contents. Malekie picked up a fish head, inspecting its gills and under its eyes. Then she held up a skeleton and sniffed the bones. She selected a tail and rubbed some of its scales between her fingers. After a while it became clear that Malekie was simply appreciating the catch because they were fish and had come from the water. Even so, she wore a pained expression on her face, a look almost of sorrow. But it wasn't because she grieved for the animals, but rather that she envied them.

"So can I assume you are interested in my family's island?" Sasha asked.

"You can assume I'm interested in any island with a lake this big, or any island with a waterfall on it. You could have assumed that without letting me look at this. She pushed the bucket back towards Sasha. "Thank you for sharing so much of yourself with me."

She shrugged. "Trilians take pride in their honesty."

She caught Heliopatra roll her eyes when Sasha said this but Malekie nodded and dragged herself back onto her stool. "Sirens are similar." She glanced across the counter at Malsen. "The expressions on our faces tell all," she divulged.

"We've noticed," Sasha commented dryly.

ↄↃ

Malekie pulled away from her husband's embrace and sat up with her back to him. They were in their cave, surrounded on three and a half sides by a stone shelf, with water at their feet and an impenetrable blanket of thorns over their heads. The water was warm and inviting, and the twilight sky enshrouded them in a comforting blanket of shadows. But the Siren's eyes were well accustomed to shadows and Kallen could read every nuance of her movements, and needed little light to know something was on her mind.

"What is it?"

She took a moment to collect her thoughts as she rubbed the scales of her tail back into her thighs and over her knees, though she kept her legs free. He realized she was stalling for time and gave it to her patiently, knowing that when she turned around to look at him he would know what was on her mind, even if she said nothing.

"They were so cruel!"

Kallen knew what she was talking about. "Icky, Mother was expecting me to marry Sasha. Sasha was expecting to marry me, though there was little enough love between us."

Malekie nodded. "I know all this," she said.

"But what you didn't know is that, unlike Sirens, who just run away from each other when they have a problem, Trilians share the same nest." He wasn't being cruel when he said this, but Kallen knew his words had stung nonetheless.

Malekie turned and looked at him. Her big brown eyes implored him to understand. "Sirens only gather for war. Even our children are abandoned, left to hatch on their own and picked up as slaves by any older Siren that would have them. Husbands – what are they? Family?" She shrugged. "I thought what we had was family. And it's wonderful, and good. But that... " She pointed towards the mansion. "That isn't what we have."

"Fish have the whole ocean to scatter to, but birds need to perch sometime. And in case you haven't noticed, Icky, there aren't very many branches this high up."

"So you share. And I'm to be held in your beak like some kind of prize for the nest to fight over."

Kallen blinked at her, confused.

"Sasha has a lake."

Kallen knew what that would mean to his wife. The pond and her two waterfalls would seem awfully small after a while.

"It's about half a league long, a quarter of that deep and it does- n't have any waterfalls on it. It has bugs, though, insects. And a lot of marsh and a lot of mud. It might even have a beaver on it, or a few otters."

"I've been there," Kallen admitted.

"Why didn't you tell me about it?" Malekie demanded to know.

He shrugged. "Because it's not mine. And I know what it would do to you, how that knowledge would torture you."

"Do you have an island?" she asked.

He shook his head. "This one is my father's island. He taxes the others and they submit to his rule. Each of theirs is a place where they can be left alone. I have a small one, a place I found. But it is tiny, though full of iron. We smelt the ore on one of the other ones. There is no water on it."

"Why don't they just live on their own islands?"

He held up his empty hands and shrugged. "Tradition. It is our way. On the surface Trilians had to nest together for protection, and for pride. We could do great things when many of us were in one place. We are still trying to live like that here."

"But here is not there."

"What is it you want, Icky?" Kallen asked her, concerned by her obvious agitation.

"All the water islands moved together, where they are connected together by waterfalls, every one of them."

"Impossible."

"Why?"

"No one has that much money."

"Why not? Why can't you buy them all? Trade with the surface, for spectral stone."

"No one would ever agree to giving up their privacy like that. And we trade with the surface for the stone, but it is we who buy them, and at great price."

"What about the stone clouds, the ones with water in them? Couldn't you bring those down to us?"

"Too dangerous, I don't have an army to fight off the dragons and the Rames and all the other demons out there."

"I need that water, Kallen," Malekie pleaded.

"I believe you."

"So what am I supposed to do then," she demanded. "Just live in this little fish bowl as the trophy on your table?"

"Icky, please, keep your voice down."

Malekie didn't realize she'd been shouting, but they were con-stantly afraid their voices would carry to the mansion, so she low-ered her eyes. "There's something else." She smoothed the rest of her tail into place and slipped into the water. Once her tail was covered, she turned and looked at him. To him, she was perfect, a beautiful stunning woman silhouetted by the little light they had. He could feel his desire for her stirring again, but was mindful she needed to talk, and so contented himself to simply be in her presence.

"I am beautiful to you."

It was not a question. Even in the gloom she could read his expression. A blind woman could read his expression.

She opened her gills and pointed at them, at the line of her jaw bone.

In the deepening night he could not see them. But he under - stood her point.

"Siren children must hatch from eggs." It was a declaration meant to shock Kallen out of his love for her. But he had an admission of his own, something that to Trilians was just as hideous.

"I think all twenty species lay eggs," he confessed to her. "As far as I can tell. It's like Almighty knew the difficulties the child would have, so he gives them a time of peace and security, when their bellies are full and they don't realize how cruel the world they've been born into really is. The Thoroughbloods consider it a second pregnancy and cherish the eggs, keeping them always around the other people, where there is laughter and joy."

"Sirens abandon theirs to the ocean floor, to let them die. We only give birth to them to get the filthy things out of our bodies. A great many of them don't hatch. And a great many of them are laid." Malekie was almost in tears, infuriated as she fought to keep her voice hushed.

Kallen grew quiet, thoughtful. "I did not know that," he said finally, sadness evident in his voice.

"What kind of children would we have, Kallen? What kind of monsters would I birth?"

Kallen had no answer. But he did know such a thing, if it was even possible, would be considered hideous, an unspeakable evil that would best be destroyed quietly and compassionately, for its own sake. Yet wasn't such an attitude the very reason why the Thoroughbloods had left the other Trilians? He rubbed his face with his hands and leaned back into the comfort of his wings. He hadn't thought of any of this, of the cruel reality. All he knew was that he was in love and that it was right. Nothing else seemed to matter at the time.

But it mattered now.

"I could push an island back towards the place where we met. You could have your ocean and I could have my sky."

"If you can't bring the islands together how do you expect to bring the different realms together?"

"They exist together within the mists."

"This isn't the mists." Malekie's voice was bitter now. "And you know we wouldn't survive if we left."

"I don't know what to say, Icky," he said sadly.

In response, she slipped into the water and was gone. Kallen watched her go, heartbroken, saw the outline of her as she plunged off of the edge of his island and heard the distant splash she made as she dove into the bigger one. The darkness was complete now, and Kallen was at a loss. He lay there, unmoving, hoping the answers would come to him. Then he began to pray, to call out to Almighty, at first silently and then aloud. His soul was in anguish, and he revealed it all to his beloved creator, who had done so much for them already. Kallen was grateful for the time Almighty had given them. The months he and Malekie had spent together were the happiest Kallen had experienced in his entire life. But could he be greedy in his desire for more? He had no answer for that, and it seemed that none was forthcoming as he lost track of time, wrapped in the warmth and the darkness in his and Icky's private alcove.

ഇൻൽ

"Kallen. Kallen." He was confused. Her voice had pulled him out of a troubled and sorrowful sleep, but it sounded elated, frenzied even. "Kallen!" He opened his eyes. Their alcove was cast in a rich purplish glow, as though the amethyst light from a rainbow had been poured out over the little room. He looked over at Malekie. She was grinning, her face shining in the light that poured from between her fingers to bask her in unnatural radiance. "I found it under the rocks at the bottom of the pool!"

He looked askance at her. Spectral stone was not uncommon here in the air realm. It was the reason why the air realm even existed, what tied these land masses to the sky and kept them suspended high above the other realms. But to possess a stone was uncommon enough to consider having one a real treasure. However, legend cautioned that if an island lost enough of its spectral core, it would plummet into the earth far below. Still, there was no harm in Malekie holding the stone, Kallen supposed, as long as she never took it from these islands. Malekie knew the special significance of the spectral stone, but to discover one still stirred such joy in her that Kallen waited for her to reveal the rest of her treasure, for there surely was more.

"I was out there in the dark, thinking in the small waterfall," Malekie began. "And I realized that what we have is amazing, Kallen. We've been through so much, seen so many hardships together. And our love for each other only grows with each trial we face. Your people have their faults, even if they aren't like the rest of the Trilians. But your people have just begun their journey into the sky realm. I am Malekie Thoroughblood of the sky realm. But I know not what the sky realm is, how big it is, how far it stretches, how rich it is. For all we know, there could be an ocean bigger than the ones on Mishard out here somewhere, floating in a giant cloud, just waiting for us to discover."

Kallen nodded. He agreed with her. "But there are so many predators up here, so many dragons and subspecies."

Malekie shrugged her shoulders and thrust her chin out. "That doesn't matter," she replied. "Love is all that matters. And I realized that whatever the cost, our love will prove strong enough to pay it." She swam up to him and kissed him, the stone still clutched tightly in her hands. "I'll clip my fin tomorrow," she whispered softly into his ear.

"Are you sure?"

"I am trapped in this little fish bowl until I do. At least then I'll be able to walk across this island."

"What are you going to do with that?" Kallen asked, with a nod towards the spectral stone.

Malekie gazed at the ceiling of their little cave, to the thorns overhead. "How hard would it be to build a real ceiling, one that could keep out the rain?" she asked.

"Not hard, if you know how to fly."

"But can you do it in secret?"

Kallen glanced at her quickly.

She looked back at him. "Everyone thinks this is just a small, useless island covered in thorns," Malekie explained. When he nodded she added, "And they have little interest in it, especially when they get soaking wet just coming in here."

"And risk getting their wings caught in the thorns," Kallen added. He'd talked to people about this, and it was a major con - cern.

"Can you see the stone walls we've built?"

He shook his head. "No. Everything is covered in the thorn bushes."

"I want to keep this stone here, to remind us of our love." Malekie had a remote look in her eyes, as though dreaming of something she would not name. Whatever it was, her smile remained. "This place is mine," she declared.

ಇ⊃೧ಜ

A fierce winter wind blew snow and ice through the skies in great gusts, but from Malekie's pool of water in the sky all was warm and mild, as it always was. Still, vapor rose from the water a little more than usual, and the mists in the air often wafted away to expose the darkened sky above, allowing the blizzard to pelt down into the tepid climate of her home. At first Malekie thought the island would plummet once the mists that supported it drifted away, but she soon realized that the spectral stones bestowed more than enough of their mysterious abilities to keep the island securely in place.

But nothing could take away the worry Malekie was feeling for Kallen. Snow blanketed the ground and saturated the pool as it merged with the warm water, enough to keep her gills open even as she perched on the edge of the pool, but Malekie's only thoughts were of her husband.

Kallen had gone out with a company of Trilians to bring back another island floating to the south-east. It was a fairly large find, situated lower in the atmosphere and empty but flat. The Trilians hoped to dig another pool of water into it, extending Malekie's waterway. She was beyond excited at the possibility of expanding her terrain, even though she had to trade some smaller pieces of the spectral stone to obtain the island. But now, looking at the blizzard and feeling the cold winds, she wasn't sure it was worth it.

The Trilians would be snowbound. The labor to lift them higher into the air in the frigid winds, the heavy burden of wet snow on their wings, and the simple discomfort of the cold temperatures would be enough to prevent the Trilians from traveling very far this night. They would be huddled under their wings, using the great plumage of their feathers to keep dry, while the sky island they would wait out the storm on would be enough to keep them warm.

Still, Malekie worried about them being so far away, so exposed and alone out there in the dark. Never once did she consider that she was the one that was alone until a sudden plume of light erupted in the sky before it faded back into darkness.

Malekie dared not take her eyes from the spot, and slipped silently into the water. All remained peaceful beneath the surface. But the storm and falling rain muffled any noise from above.

She was still a spear sister, Malekie thought. Whatever was out there, whatever had caused that light, she doubted it could con-tend with one of the strongest Sirens of her time. Thinking imme-diately of arming herself, she sped towards the base of the small-er waterfall that led to her own sanctuary, lunging up and over the cascade within seconds.

Another spiral of fire exploded into the sky behind her, so bright that it illuminated the thorns above her head.

Yet rather than taking refuge in her tiny cave, she retrieved the spear Kallen's father had given her, then slipped silently into the larger pool of water.

Hidden deep within the murky waters under the raging water-fall, Malekie knew she was safe. But her breath caught in her gills and her eyes widened with foreboding when a third burst of fire, for fire it truly must have been, cut through the darkness, peeling back the mists and the storm.

Malekie kept to the bottom of the pool and swam noiselessly away from its edge to keep a better eye on the clouds that were quickly tapering back into darkness.

Another fire bolt burst around the sky island. The mists flared into a brilliant orange sunset glow, and the island reverberated with silent ferocity. The water temperature changed a fraction of a degree; the difference was minute, but enough for Malekie to feel fear.

A Siren has great tolerance for diverse temperatures. From arc-tic ice to tropical beaches, as long as water is present, a child of the oceans can be found swimming in it. And yet there was no greater horror Malekie could think of than to be boiled alive in the very water that sustained her. And whatever was out there now, whatever was causing such violent flames, could very well accomplish exactly what she feared.

A hideous dragon landed on the edge of the island, perching there like a gargantuan, malevolent bird. But while its features held a birdlike quality, its appearance was more lizard-like, hideous. Landing amid a great flurry of wings that brought fur - ther darkness to her already gloomy view, Malekie saw that its eyes, blinking like a cat's, but huge and reptilian, gave off a frightful yellow luminosity, and its tail whipped about its body to skim the surface of the pool.

Malekie froze, drawing slow, even breaths. If this demon could see in the dark, then surely she was fully exposed. But she did not underestimate the depths of shadows that clung to the bottom of her hiding place.

The dragon's head twisted to the right, towards the waterfall. Then its neck coiled and reared back and its chest puffed up, and Malekie knew in that horrible instant what was to come next. The wave of fire was dazzling enough that she winced from its angry glare. Then the brightness subsided and the pain started. Boiling water flooded into her hiding place. Her skin burned and her gills seared, sending flames of agony all the way into her lungs. Malekie screamed in pain, the breath erupting from her in a burst of bubbles. Involuntarily, her gills slammed shut, her body des - perately trying to prevent the anguish from spreading.

She struggled to hold her breath, knowing that if she breathed through her nose or mouth she'd drown. Yet Malekie's instincts and training, her very identity, kept her hand steady and her thoughts focused. The only movement from the bottom of the pool was the slight adjusting of her hand on her spear. Her eyes remained fast on the creature above her, searching, always search- ing for an opportunity to strike.

The dragon's gaze shifted towards the other waterfall. It tilted its head back and its chest heaved, and suddenly the burning water no longer seemed to matter.

She was vengeance unleashed. She burst from the water, sucking air into her lungs as she soared into the air. The dragon's attention shifted to her, eyes growing wide with surprise, and then time seemed to slow as Malekie screamed her battle cry and unloosed her own fury.

Her spear sailed straight and true. Even as the flames erupted from the dragon's enormous mouth, her weapon plunged into its left eye and embedded itself deep into the monster's brain.

Malekie collapsed back into the water as the beast stumbled. The flame discharged low and missed her private sanctuary. The dragon howled it's fury, and spewed a huge blast of fire that surged over her pool before darkness and silence settled in the sky once again.

§⊃Q₿

Kallen set off before the others, setting his teeth against the biting cold and forcing the frigid air through his soaking wings.

"Kallen, wait!" one of his companions shouted from the safety of the island. "It's too cold!" But he ignored the warning, marshalling his strength instead for the flight ahead, and before long, he was gasping for breath, leaving clouds of steam to mark his trail through the heavens.

All he could think about was his wife. Exposed and alone, Malekie would be vulnerable. Too many Trilians had agreed to help them bring the sky islands together. It was astonishing how readily they had put aside their petty squabbles. The Thoroughblood clan had instantly recognized the wisdom and strength they would achieve with a network of defendable islands. Malekie was right when she said perhaps the Trilians had only begun to explore the sky realm; and they had jumped at the opportunity to take a stand of might amongst the other races that harbored refuge amongst the stars.

Kallen smiled as he remembered how easy it had been to bend the others to Malekie's desire. The Thoroughbloods were not racist; they had proven that by the way they had accepted the needs of one they now considered their own; one who, although so different, they had come to love as an equal. To be imprisoned amongst the clouds, with no wings to set her free — they could only imagine how hard it must be for her. Malekie had proven her strength and loyalty to Kallen, and so to them, so they in turn had felt obliged to do the same for her.

And we left her alone, like the fools we are, Kallen berated himself.

Kallen had to remind himself that his beloved Siren was a big girl and could take care of herself. But this damn storm had snuck up on them so swiftly that it had left even him feeling exposed and vulnerable, and he could fly!

He saw the island from afar. The mists were diminished this day, probably driven away by the rain. Kallen could see the underside of the great piece of land floating so incredibly by itself out in the open air, and his heart soared to be so close to his beloved. And then, just as rapidly it plummeted into the pit of his stomach as dread seized his spine with its malicious claws.

Even from this distance he could see part of the dragon's carcass, its tail and one leg hanging limply over the edge of the sky-island. It was obviously quite dead, considering it's unnatural pose. But the horror was that the dragon was on the edge of Malekie's home.

Eyes wide with terror, Kallen forced himself onward and upward, reminded fleetingly of other journeys through the sky that had demanded such physical exertion of his muscles and his will. Generally Kallen's thoughts were accompanied by an aware - ness of a miracle greater than simply his home — the miracle that

124

made this place his home, a love that should by rights never be, yet was. And now, Kallen didn't know what he would ever do without Malekie. Perhaps he would become a wanderer, take to the skies or the surface realm, in a hopeless attempt to find peace.

But even as his mind envisioned his heart's exile, Kallen's reasoning banished the terrible thoughts. She is alive, he told himself. His wings beat against the air like a hammer against an anvil. The creature is dead! She is victorious! But his silent assurances did little to lift the trepidation that had settled around him like a cloud of poison vapors.

He crested the edge of the island, his eyes still wild with horror. In a moment he took in the body of the filthy dragon, with its head buried in the water, its wings splayed out across the surface in death. It was a large creature. Though not as mighty as some, it was by far no fledgling. What had she done, he wondered, drowned it? But the inky filth that had poisoned her little pool of water made Kallen shudder with repulsion. The beast had bled to death, by a wound he could not see.

Then he saw her. His beautiful, beloved wife was laying on her back, gasping for air. Her breath came in short, shallow pants.

Kallen rushed to her side, leaping up and over the body of the fallen dragon without so much as touching the foul thing. His eyes were only for Malekie as he settled on his knees on the soft grass beside her. His wings, as if to match his heart, drooped to the ground and his hands stretched out to touch her. But although they shook with the desire to hold her, Kallen forced them away.

The part of Malekie's flesh that was human was red and blistering, as though it had been scalded. Kallen glanced at the dragon's corpse and understood the beast must have scorched the pool before it died. Then his glance was drawn back to Malekie, the dragon already forgotten. He could see her gills, though she was long since dry. They were closed, but unlike other times when Malekie had been on land, they were invisible now. Two white lines, like knife scars, marked their presence, and Kallen couldn't imagine what that ordeal must have been like for her. Her tail scales were white and flaking off. Through the membrane, he could see her thighs, and a glance at her fin told him he could see her toes exposed as well. The fin, once a matter of supreme pride for Malekie, had already been clipped so that she could walk among the Trilians. But now it was all but ruined. It was shredded and had been boiled. Most of it was missing, torn now, nearly to the tips of her human feet.

Kallen's lips quivered as he watched his wife, heartbroken at seeing the condition she was in. "Malekie," he whispered urgently, unsure what he would do if she didn't answer.

Her eyes flickered open, but although she struggled, she was unable to speak between her pained gasps. Her eyes seemed to plead with him to end her torment; to throw her off the edge of the sky island. Kallen was bereft. Never had he seen Malekie robbed of such strength before. The hopelessness and terror he saw in her face left him shaking his head with a despair that matched her own. "Water?" was all he asked, still too afraid to touch her burnt body.

Eyes still wide with horror and pain, she managed a slight nod of her head. her gasps for air seemed to be growing desperate.

"Okay," he whispered. With utmost care and gentleness, he lifted her into his arms.

When he touched Malekie, such a scream of pain erupted from her that Kallen was afraid he had killed her. He wept as he rose into the air, thankful to be away from the putrid foulness of what had once been her home.

A moment later he hovered above the waterfall and then sank into the waist-deep water of the third island. The stone gathering place was empty. Kallen found a bit of relief in that knowledge as he tenderly lowered his wife into the spring. She'd been looking up at him, but when her face submerged and her gills opened, a look of anguish crossed her features and Malekie closed her eyes to stop him from seeing it.

She lay there panting for a time, her gills inflamed, and then gradually her body grew heavy in his arms. Thinking that she had died for sure this time, Kallen began to remove his hands from her, but her own immediately grasped his wrists and held him to her. Kallen nodded, understanding that she was only resting, and he helped roll her face down into the water so that she could sleep easier.

The others found them that way, Malekie sleeping like a dead man with her face in the water, Kallen holding her motionless in the current, with his feathers floating in the water around them. There was no quick expulsion of giddiness, no terrible surprise. They had all seen the body of the dragon below, the ruin of the pool that had once been Malekie's home. Although it was not the Trilian custom to dwell overly on death, Kallen's friends and family respectfully surrounded the couple, eyes cast down in sor-row, silence settling about them as the mists grew thick once again.

Heleopatra, spoke up first, shaking herself out of her silent reprieve. "Be gone with you!" she scolded the others, "Life goes on! We have work to do!"

As the Thoroughbloods moved to depart into the mists, Flaveldon looked at Shae and said, "The manor was all but empty when the attack came."

The other nodded angrily. "We have grown sloppy."

But his words did not dismiss Flaveldon's meaning. "She killed it, by herself, Shae," he pointed out. "One thrust of her spear, and it was enough."

"But at what price?" Shae asked. His eyes never left Kallen and Malekie.

Flaveldon laid a hand on his friend's shoulder. "With the price any one of us would have paid. But tell me, my friend, how many of us could have done it?"

Kallen heard this, and his eyes rose to look at his two friends standing partially concealed in the mist.

They nodded their well-wishes to him and then left also, leaving Kallen in blessed privacy once again. Although his hands remained steady, his composure finally crumbled. Kallen bowed his head and wept brokenly, letting the keening of his voices carry through the mists and across the sky realm in a symphony of sorrow and anguish.

℘✺℘

Malekie's condition went from bad to worse. While the Trilians could never know the physiology of a mermaid, her human symptoms, those similarities she shared with her family, were all too easy to read – and they weren't good. Her skin was beginning to heal, but something terrible had happened to her ability to breathe, something that left her gasping for air when she wasn't floating face down in water. And she simply refused to use her legs. Malekie's cure came in the water, with the water. And the closer she remained to it, the better off she seemed.

And even with the constant support of her family, Malekie's tail was not improving. Her muscles eventually screamed at her to swim, yet her scorched lungs failed to give her the breath she needed. What she needed was colder water, currents, and the open spaces of the ocean. Malekie needed to be set free.

She was in constant fear, and every time she looked at the sky Malekie was reminded of how vulnerable, how helpless she was. Here Malekie had no means to defend herself, no natural defenses to call upon. In the state she was in now, should another dragon happen upon this place, there was naught she could do about it, and Malekie knew it.

She said little about any of this, even to Kallen. But he knew. The mermaid's inability to hide her expressions would have been enough. But the natural bond a woman shares with her husband shouted out loud enough for him to hear clear across the other side of the island. She loved Kallen, and she did not begrudge him who or what he was. If anything, the realization only made her fonder of her sky-man. But there was no place in this world for a Siren and a Trilian to remain together safely.

Their kin talked of her in awed whispers. She was a matron saint to them; a martyr and a warrior and a woman and a wife. She had become their sister, their lover, their aunt. They did not see Malekie as she saw herself, cast out upon the world to live if she could, exiled from her own kind. She was their heroine, with strength to kill a dragon by herself. Had the Thoroughbloods been like the paganistic sub-races they'd left behind, they would have worshiped her as a goddess. Instead they adored her as the treasure of their people.

Malekie, however, saw herself as a disgrace, the weakest link. With people as proud of bearing as these – free to roam the skies and sing in the choirs of angels, to defend their territory with righteous claymores in hand, and quote poetry to each other upon the clouds – to such people, how could a simple fish out of water ever hope to compare?

Kallen would have been able to argue if Malekie had used actual words. He might have been able to make her see the truth, make her see what she had come to mean to him and his people. He could have even begged for forgiveness on behalf of his people for leaving her stranded and exposed. But she never spoke of it. So close to a lingering death that stole the breath from her, Malekie now relied on the voice of silence and the expressions of her kind to convey the hopelessness growing inside her.

And despite all the power she gave him, all Kallen could do was look back at her, his face filled with anguish and loss.

She would smile weakly, and kiss his face ever so gently before going back to the grossly inadequate spring of water above the waterfall that had once been her playground and was now her prison.

It didn't matter that the pool below was becoming clear once again. It didn't matter that the dead fish had been removed and replaced with new ones. And it didn't matter that the dragon's head, along with Malekie's spear, were mounted in a place of honor within the manor house. When Kallen finally lowered her body into the newly restored pool of water, Malekie immediately sank to the very bottom, to lay despondently amongst the stones and bask in the shielded light of the spectral stones she kept hid - den down there.

Their marriage chamber, the island overgrown with rose bushes, remained in a state of neglect. The thorns eventually grew to cover the passage into their cave. Kallen watched the ruin dispas - sionately, his only desire being to see his wife healed and happy once again.

One time, he even slipped into the pool and dove to the bottom. Malekie liked that, happy to see her husband. She caressed his face as she cried tears that went unnoticed in the pond water. Kallen pressed his lips against hers gently, and she closed her eyes, savoring the memory of the time when she would breathe for him. She even blew air into his mouth a few times, in an attempt to resurrect the feeling of happier days.

But the shallow breaths that entered his lungs left Kallen scram - bling towards the surface. Malekie watched him go, crying help - lessly as she unconsciously pressed herself tight against the bot - tom of the pool in her need to find deeper water.

Kallen broke the surface gasping for air, frustrated and bitter with his failed attempt to reach through to his wife.

෨෮ය

Early one afternoon, he could not take it any longer. Standing on the edge of her pool and watching Malekie's still form, he simply could not bear the anguish she was in one more second. He stepped into the pool and sank immediately to the bottom.

Malekie looked at him inquiringly, her expression asking the words she could not speak; what are you doing down here?

He held his hand out to her, standing commandingly above her as his wings billowed out in the current of the two waterfalls. Take my hand, his own face said. She reached out and took it, knowing he could not hold his breath long enough to argue, and he swam with her back to the surface.

They were both gasping and struggling, but they swam together with their heads above the surface until they reached the edge of the pool, and Kallen pulled himself back onto dry ground. He turned around and reached out for her, and all of a sudden Malekie understood.

If she'd had the breath, she would have argued. She would have told him many things in that moment that would have convinced him to let her stay. But the look he gave her spoke the silent truth that rang through the heavens as resolutely as a thunderclap.

This time the tears were visible on her face as Malekie rose out of the water and into his arms. Wordlessly he turned and stepped from the edge of their father's sky island.

"Kallen and Malekie are leaving!" someone exclaimed in the distance behind them.

Kallen did not turn around, and Malekie did not take her gaze from her husband's face.

A cry broke out from amongst the Trilians, and with their multiple voices, they raised a great din of protest in their wake. But in the next moment their voices were silenced, and as Kallen looked over his shoulder, he tried not to choke on a sob.

His brother, his sister, his friend, his father, his mother, his aunt, his cousins and their cousins, all of them had taken wing in pursuit, in tribute. For Kallen had taken their sister and their friend, their cousin and their cousins' cousin. He had taken from them their heroine and their martyr, their aunt and their daughter. And they would see her set free.

They flew through the rest of the day, and it was an easy flight. They spiraled towards the surface in a gentle pattern that would not harm Malekie or aggravate her injuries further. With this many Trilians protecting her, bearing swords and great bows, the younger ones armed with lighter daggers or short spears, she could not help but feel safe. Malekie was sure that in the ocean she could find what she needed to recover, a little at a time.

She had no voice to give to those who had so many, no way to express to them her love and thanks for all they had given her. But they all got the picture, hovering close enough to clasp her hand and offer some sentiment she could take with her back into the water realm. Each one of them approached the couple, often holding Malekie's hand for a long time while they cried together. Even Sasha shared a laugh with her, chuckling at private jokes only the two women understood. And although Kallen knew of the friction they had experienced in the past, the tears on Sasha's face were steady and constant enough that he did not try to rob her of her time with Malekie. He merely clung to his wife all the more, desperate to hold on to every moment with her he could.

Eventually they reached the ocean and the land. They landed in a small bay revealed by the full moon overhead. A calm breeze wafted through the trees and through their hair. The beach was deserted and the water was still.

The Trilians stepped away from Kallen and Malekie, giving them privacy in their final moments together.

Malekie cupped his face in her hand with a look of acute sad - ness that was mixed with gratitude and anticipation of her impending freedom. Kallen was setting her free, and she would find her strength once again. Never again would she be content to live her life caged in small ponds. Malekie was a spear sister, and without the pursuit of a spear sister's strengths, she would die. But Kallen was her love, her life. Malekie had happily sacrificed all to be with him; and she would sacrifice it all again to spend one more night with her beloved. But it was a choice that was not hers to make, a life she was not fated to lead.

Tears coursed down Kallen's face as she told him all of this in her silent way. He felt utterly broken, defeated, the will to live ebbing from his veins. He wanted nothing more than to hold her close to his heart forever, to be by her side until they grew old and his wings would no longer hold their weight and her fin had grown long and ornamental, a tribute to both her beauty and her peace. But Malekie was a spear sister, and her fin would never grow long. The currents she longed to fight would always rip the excess membranes away, trimming her muscles with a warrior's beauty, a warrior's pride, and above all, a warrior's freedom.

And so, with this sentiment painted across his face and over his broken heart, Kallen lowered his wife into the water. The light of the moon did not penetrate the surface of the ocean. Malekie was immediately hidden and safe after having spent so much time being exposed.

There was a moment when all she did was lie in his arms, and it seemed to Kallen that her chest rose as though she was taking the first full breath of air since the attack. He was sure of it. Her body changed then. Her shoulders squared, her fin began to undulate with the currents, and slowly she took his hand in her own and guided it over her body, to those places she wished him to remember. And then she was gone, with a suddenness that was astonishing. So quickly, with a mere flick of her tail, Malekie had vanished from his arms, from his life, returned at last to the safety of her own realm.

Kallen lifted his head and let his voices embrace the sorrow and loss, and his grief and heartbreak filled the night with a lament that Mishard had never heard the likes of before or since. His keening was long and loud and musical, heart-rending in its beauty, unforgettable in its expression of love. But his cries eventually faded into silence, into a stunned and grieving silence shared by their family.

There was a ripple of movement in the water behind him, so slight that Kallen wondered if he had imagined it. He started to turn his face, but Malekie's voice whispered from the darkness, bringing him up short.

"We will always have our place, my love." She sounded so confident, so sure, Kallen could only wonder at how quickly returning to her own element had changed her. "We will always have a place for us to be together," she repeated.

"Our island," he said, thinking of the time when they first met.

"Our island," she echoed. "And all are welcome if they come in peace. But if they don't … then let them contend with the strength of both the spear sisters and the Thoroughbloods combined," Malekie forewarned.

Then there was a splash in the water and Kallen knew that this time she was gone.

Such strength, such confidence, in such a short period of time. Kallen shook his head in amazement. His wife was free once again, and as her parting gift, she had given him hope, as impossible as that might seem. But as she believed, so then also would he.

They departed soon after that. Kallen, filled with a hope and determination that he would see his wife again, was first to leave the ocean for the skies. The others followed his lead, keeping low to the surface in search of warmer winds to lift them higher.

They found them while dawn was still well away. This was of much relief to the Thoroughbloods, who carried no illusions about the outcome they'd find if they were to linger on the sur-face for long. Spiraling in tight circles to remain within the updrafts, then spreading out in a long line of great white-winged bodies so they all might fly in the same thermals, the Thoroughbloods talked and laughed and cried as they shared their memories of Malekie.

They saw many other winged creatures close to the surface realm; birds, mostly, flocked past them, sometimes in droves. But more dangerous creatures took notice of their passing as well. A band of Rames, heavily armed, emerged from a cloud and froze in midair. The fearsome creatures were grossly outnumbered by the Trilians, who stared at these distant relatives. Unsure of their intentions, the Rames remained where they were, but the Trilians did not once break the rhythm of their wings to give pursuit. The two groups simply watched each other until they were well out of range, and then the Rames turned around and returned to their cloud cover again.

Nearing the end of the day, when the surface would already be cast in the darkness of night, they saw a dragon, a small thing – a hatchling perhaps. But it was too far away for anyone to be sure. It spied them too, and filled with the impudence of inexperience and youth, it charged at them, roaring profanities in the language that only dragons spoke.

Kasan, who had been armed for such an occasion since the attack on his home, rolled his eyes and drew an arrow from his bow. "Archers!" he shouted to his people.

Those who carried bows flew to his side and hovered above or below him. Each removed an arrow from their quiver, and togeth-er they notched their bows.

"Draw!" Kasan cried.

They all trained their weapons on the vicious creature, prepared to strike.

Suddenly, a golden dragon plunged from out of nowhere and grasped the smaller one from above in one of its mighty talons.

"Hold!" Kasan shouted, fearful of striking such a noble crea‐ture. The archers were relieved to lower their weapons.

The golden dragon was perhaps ten times the size of the small‐er, darker one, and was easily able to halt its flight towards the Trilians. It took a firm hold of the hatchling and tossed the crea‐ture to the side. For a moment, the hatchling flew wildly out of control, but finally righted itself and roared fearlessly at its supe‐rior, rashly daring to challenge the might of a golden dragon. The golden dragon spewed a font of fire towards the hatchling, which could have incinerated it with a single blast. As it was, the flames simply came between the smaller creature and the Trilians, mak‐ing the golden dragon's message amply clear.

The hatchling howled its frustration, then turned and flew in the other direction.

The golden dragon watched it go from over its shoulder, then turned and regarded the Trilians. It seemed to smile sadly and then nodded as a sign of respect. Kasan returned the nod and then the dragon was climbing into the clouds far above them.

৪০৩৪

Life returned to normal for the Thoroughbloods, or as normal as possible. The sun still set and still rose, Kallen's mining opera‐tions and trade went on, just as before. But the pool of water behind the manor house was empty. Kallen returned there often, to try to recapture the essence of his wife.

He would sit for long stretches in the noise of the waterfalls, perched on the edge of the island, watching the clouds pass, obscuring the view of the surface. Hour after hour he would sit, too wrapped up in his own thoughts to mingle with the other

Trilians. They kept their distance, casting sad, knowing glances his way. And he grieved and grieved and grieved.

And still his heart would not be comforted.

One evening Kallen turned and gazed at their sanctuary, the small island that had been their own. By now the thorns were ten - drils dragging in the creek. The entrance to their cave had been completely covered. As unbearable as it had been to go near the place while Malekie was injured, it had been even more awful to contemplate returning to the cave after she was gone. But now it seemed Kallen would find no rest from his grief until he did, until he was able to completely let Malekie go.

He would go back to the cave and grieve, Kallen decided. And then he would have the thorn bushes removed completely so as to ensure the place could never again be used as a Siren's lair. He would eradicate all traces of their time together there. And then, maybe then, Kallen could finally get on with his life, empty though it was.

At first he tried to move the thorns by hand, but received only tearing pain and blood for his efforts. He drew his sword and hacked at the opening, and every swipe of his sword brought down tendrils of rose bushes, which fell away to float down the waterfall to the larger pool below.

The opening appeared, just the way Kallen had remembered it, and he had to fight the tears it brought to his eyes. Bitterly , he bent his head and drooped his wings as he ducked into the cave, kneeling into the water. Memories rushed back to fill his thoughts, and for one tragic moment Kallen's life was full of meaning once again. But then he remembered that it was only a recollection, an illusion that could never again be held in his arms.

He made his way to the ledge by the water 's side, the place that had once been his bed, and sat with his back to the wall while his wings cocooned him. All was in darkness, and but for the water gurgling up from the center of this small island, there was only silence.

So empty was life without Malekie. This cave, this place; all of it had become a vast arena, and Kallen a gladiator hopelessly out-matched by the passage of time. He could not hope to recover from his loss. Coming here had been a mistake, he realized, but now that Kallen was here he knew it would be at least a few days before he left again.

Defeated, his defenses crumbled and Kallen began to weep into the silence, heartsick and unashamed, knowing that he was more alone now than he had ever been in his life.

A curious sound reached through Kallen's billowing shield of feathers. It had lasted only a moment, but enough to bring his head up and silence his tears. He strained to hear, yet could hear nothing through the barrier of his wings. Kallen opened his wings to his sides and peered around the cave, seeking the location of the intruder.

At first there was nothing, but then a soft glow filled the cave, and Kallen realized that the spectral stones Malekie kept hidden beneath the surface were slowly rising to the top of the water. Kallen's eyes grew wide as he watched. What in Almighty's blue sky is going on, he wondered. Yet he kept his voices to himself, lest whatever wonder was materializing cease to be.

The features of a child's face appeared below the surface, illu-minated by the light. And then the child was looking at him. Long lashes and curious eyes peered up at Kallen. She held a yellow spectral stone in her hand. Only her head appeared above the water, but it was enough – definitely enough – to tell Kallen this girl-child was Malekie's, for the creature had gills that inhaled and exhaled slowly as she observed the Trilian.

She swam forward and placed the stone on the ledge between them. "For comfort," the child said. "Mother always said the light is a comfort. May it bring you comfort as well."

Kallen was shocked to the core, as if he was seeing an appari -
tion. He stuttered, "you speak my ... how is this ... how did you
... . What is going on?"

"Mother is gone," the child explained compassionately. "Not for
many days has she been here. But we remember her, remember
her kind words spoken beneath the surface, her love that kept us
safe and warm."

A stirring from Kallen's side snapped his head around, and this
time he truly gasped. An infant, this one fully out of the water,
had crept up beside Kallen and was imitating him, the way he sat
with his arms on his knees, though the child had to settle for his
arms on his tail. He gazed up at Kallen and Kallen stared back,
not at the child's face, but at the set of wings that cocooned the
infant, wings identical to Kallen's own, although smaller, propor-
tioned for the child.

"You spent all this time in the cave by your selves?" Kallen
asked, ashamed and still feeling a little in shock.

His daughter shrugged casually. "Mother left us food." The fact
of their situation seemed of little consequence to her, and her
simple gesture tugged at Kallen's heart.

Kallen remembered that Malekie had spoken of Siren children,
explained how they were abandoned while still in their eggs. But
they were also his children, and he had found them in time to
spare them harm. Kallen began to laugh as tears of joy streamed
down his face.

The children shied away from his scandalous reaction, so he
forced himself to calm down so as not to frighten them further.
He reached an inviting arm towards the boy and another to the
girl. "Forgive my silliness," he said. Kallen spoke soothingly,
coaxing them from their apprehension. "I am... well, I am your
father."

Both children took a moment to process this information, and then his daughter smiled and his son shuffled over to perch beside his father. Kallen's heart swelled, and he put an arm around his son. His daughter disappeared below the surface however, leaving Kallen to wonder if he had frightened her away.

Keeping one eye on the pool uneasily, Kallen talked to his son, a child with the tail and gills of a Siren, but the wings and voices of a Trilian. His efforts were met with grateful smiles and an easy acceptance that was shared by all Siren children.

Presently Kallen's daughter re-emerged. Then Kallen's eyes opened wide and his jaw gaped with wonder and awe, and Malekie's words came back to him as nine more children clam-ored out of the water to be embraced by their father's wings.

Avenger of Light

D.J. Ebenal

"I hate her!" Priscilla raged, throwing down her needlepoint. Without another word, she stormed from her mother's sitting room. She was ashamed of the way she was acting, but the tears she shed were hot with anger, her teeth and fists clenched with rage.

She flung open the tall wooden doors that led to the outer para - pet, to the stunned surprise of the two guards who snapped to attention as she fled past them. Yet the empty act of defiance seemed hollow in her ears, compared to the years of regret and misunderstanding that stretched between her and Rose, her older sister.

A long time ago the two of them had not been so different. As children they would laugh and play together, playing the role of royal children with their silks and doilies and china dolls and ponies. But where Priscilla had grown up to have blonde hair with fair, soft features, Rose's hair was raven black. She too was beautiful, if you found her on a good day. It was said Rose looked like a dark enchantress; and that both ladies would fetch a fair husband at court, with a dowry that would give the unions a respectable place amongst royalty.

But that was where the similarities ended.

Bitter tears stung her cheeks and she stared helplessly out across her father's fields from the heights of the castle walls. Priscilla was of the age when she should marry; and though she knew it would not be for love, this had still not stopped her young heart from blooming.

His name was Kinan, Baron Kinan now. He'd been a minor lordling of an unimportant house that bordered her father's lands, and as children they would keep each other company while their fathers went hunting together in the woods. Many generations ago the Barony of Tresville had been cleared of all its forests to make room for the fields Priscilla was scrutinizing now. It had been a wise move for her family, and they had become rich and powerful from the tribute those fields collected. But Kinan's father's estate, the lands of Lebinath, took most of its wealth from its coal mines.

It was a dirty, dangerous job, notorious for causing many deaths and injuries. But Lord Lebinath was a kind man who treated his servants with respect and paid them well, so none begrudged the work. For three generations his estate had been home to one of the best hunting grounds in the kingdom. And for three generations neither plow nor axe had been allowed near the borders of that forestland.

Priscilla and Kinan had spent many summers together while their parents tramped through that forest. But Kinan's father was a famous host to other royal parties as well, much more powerful lords and even the king. This notoriety had earned him many favors at court, and one of those favors had been the extension of his lands to the south.

Kinan was the youngest of Lord Lebinath's two sons. So it was Kinan who went to govern those new lands, new hunting grounds for the Royals, while his older brother Michael stayed behind as heir and co-regent to his father's original holdings.

With Kinan's rise in society came the Royals' renewed interest in finding him a suitable match. Suitable. The word stuck in Priscilla's mind like a bone in her throat. Suitable indeed. What better match could her father think of for this new lord than to marry the man to his household and become a suitable heir to the Tresville barony? Not only would Lord Tresville inherit exclusive rights to the Lebinath hunting grounds, but he would also have a son to step in and take his chair, while Lord Lebinath could keep his eldest son close to home to rule his own lands.

The Barony of Tresville would grow and not be weakened by the union; and to show the Lebinath clan the seriousness of the proposal, her dear father had decided to offer Rose as his wife. She was the eldest daughter, and no matter about all else, her future husband would inherit the Tresville fields.

Priscilla did not resent her father. He was a baron and a man. He lived in a world of commerce and trade, war and hunting. She lived in a world of needlework and gossip, of playing hostess, and of sharing and shouldering the grief that ignorant men with their willful ways caused the other ladies. Yet she kept her love for Kinan close to her heart, and went through the motions of excusing her endless list of suitors.

"A lady knows how to behave in front of her guests."

Brought out of her musing by the rebuke, Priscilla spun around to face her accuser.

Lady Nimway stood there, smirking at the irony of her words. She was an older woman with graying hair, but if anything, her beauty had only increased with age. She was as shapely in her golden years as she had been in her youth. Her mind was as sharp and her tongue as quick-witted as Priscilla's own. She seemed slightly uncomfortable under Priscilla's scrutiny, but held her ground until Priscilla lowered her own eyes.

"Forgive me, my lady. I spoke out of place. You have been a good friend these many years," she whispered.

Nimway laughed, and the sound was cold with sarcasm. "All the baronesses say that of me."

"I am not a baroness," Priscilla reminded the older lady as she turned back to her father's fields. "I will never be a baroness." Her sister would inherit that title.

"Never is a long time, Lady Priscilla. Perhaps you should consider how unfortunate life can be for some of us." Nimway sidled over to stand beside Priscilla and gazed over the Tresville estates. "All this, as far as the eye can see, will one day be Kinan Lebinath's. He is destined to marry one of your father's daughters, it seems."

The lump in Priscilla's throat swelled at the bitter words. "The eldest," she choked.

Nimway turned and faced Priscilla. "The eldest living daughter!"

Priscilla's eyes widened in comprehension as she turned towards Nimway.

"Such things can be arranged."

"She is my sister!" Priscilla hissed. Despite all the pain and heartache Priscilla had borne at the hands of her sibling, loyalty kept her tone fierce.

Nimway turned back to the fields. "Ever since I've known the two of you I have watched as Rose was pampered and groomed to become the lady of a house. You were never excluded but it was Rose whom the tutors came to school. Yet while you sat vicariously learning all that you could learn from lessons meant for her, she dilly-dallied, day-dreamed, and even ran away to hide in your father's fields until the entire staff was sent out to find her. Then, laughing, she would come in from her play, barefoot and dirtied while you, young Priscilla, played with dolls at the feet of the noble ladies, who fawned over you like they would a china doll."

"Then, when you were older, almost young women, Rose grew moody, uncontrollable, irrational. She was selfish and willful and disdained authority. I once caught her sneaking out of her tower window – her tower! She was barefoot and garbed in a man's leggings, claiming she could climb better that way. She knew she was in trouble, yet there was a grin on her face that told me exactly what she thought of any punishment that could be exacted on her."

"You Priscilla, on the other hand, entertained the children of other households, growing popular amongst the court, always being well-liked and held in high esteem. You had suitors then, though they hardly realized it themselves. None would contend with your friend Kinan for your attention though – and yet none wanted anything to do with your spiteful sister."

Lady Nimway glanced briefly at the fields beyond Priscilla, then her eyes bore into hers as she said, slowly and clearly, "Then you became women and one of you became a lady."

"Don't say such things." Priscilla begged, fascinated by Lady Nimway's words but wracked with guilt to hear her sister talked about in such a way… she was torn between dread fascination and forbidden willfulness.

"The other one became a witch," Lady Nimway continued, her eyes holding Priscilla's own as if she were the one bewitched. She shrugged delicately. "Albeit a rather powerless one. The voices began. The madness took hold. Screaming in the night, erratic emotions; why, she can scarcely dine with us at your table now without ruining the event with her theatrics!

"The woman can not live up to her obligations as a lady of the house, let alone as a wife," Lady Nimway declared. "Your father only chooses her over you because she is first-born, and it would be a slight to Lord Lebinath to offer his son anything but inheritance to his lands."

Priscilla was silent for a long time. "I must think on your words," she finally said.

Lady Nimway patted Priscilla hand. "Think long before you decide girl, one way or another."

Lady Feonna, Baroness of Tresville, sat clenching her needlework in her hands as she fought for composure. Her proficiency in the role of wife of a lord, and her adeptness in fulfilling her duties as lady over her husband's lands paled in comparison with the undeniable fact that she could not control her own daughters.

One was as unruly and emotional as the other. Yet where the younger girl had reason for her rebellion, mainly because of the actions of her sister, the elder 's behavior could only be excused within her own mind. And what a dark mind it was becoming!

Lady Feonna forced herself to exhale, to steady her shaking hands and control the rage that was building so quickly beneath her calm exterior. Emotions would benefit her little here, she knew. If she did not find an answer, then an answer would find her; and one thing Feonna knew about being of the nobility was that if an answer sought you out, it definitely was not the one you were hoping for.

She was about to return to her needlework in the silence of the empty room when Dalia, stewardess of the castle, came in and discreetly bowed her head. "Mistress."

Relieved by the distraction, Feonna lowered her needlework and looked warmly at her loyal servant.

"Dinner is served, my lady," she said, giving a slight curtsy and keeping her head down so as not to look at Feonna directly. Though the stewardess may have her odd moments, Lady Feonna thought to herself, she had never found a more loyal servant –

ever. She rose to her feet and placed the needlework on the chair behind her, smoothing out her dress with a graceful, fluid motion.

"How is my daughter?" Lady Feonna asked.

Dalia glanced at Lady Feonna before turning her eyes back to the floor. "Lady Rose is well, lady, as well as can be."

"Will she be attending tonight?"

Dalia was thoughtful for a moment. "I believe so. Will that be all, Ma'am?"

"Make it so, Dalia." When her maid seemed not to hear her, Feonna repeated, "Dalia, Rose is to be in attendance this night. It is my wish to dine with my daughter." Before something happens to her.

"Yes, My Lady," Dalia finally answered. She turned and left to summon the others.

Feonna could only shake her head. Dalia was an odd one, there was no denying that. Never could tell what was going on in that one's head. She shook her head slightly and followed her stew - ardess into one of the smaller dining halls.

Tonight was not a banquet night. The servants and the field hands would eat without them this night. Tonight the table had only room for six. Her Lord husband, Jason Tresville stood in a far corner of the room, a tankard of ale grasped tightly in his hand. He talked and laughed loudly, his thick brown beard hiding his face; and Feonna knew without chastising him that his glass was mostly full. As heir to a barony, he had learned many lessons on the value of statecraft. And as a baron Jason had been forced to learn many more lessons about politics, and about allies and enemies.

He had no fear of the man standing in front of him, though. Raptly hanging onto every word that spilled from Jason's mouth, Lord Cignifred Albony was a lesser lord, a much lesser lord of some holdings far to the south and east of the Tresville lands. And it was no secret that his wife, Lady Nimway, had deftly maneuvered their position into a very favorable standing with the other nobles. The two had grown wealthy as merchants, owning fleets, and soldiers to escort freight across the face of Hansurn and well into the other kingdoms of the Island.

Lord Albony seemed grateful for Lord Tresville's display of bravado. And Jason seemed glad to give it, though perhaps only Rose could tell for sure.

The young lady glided through the hall with the grace of a feline. She seemed on edge, jumpy, but in relatively good spirits. She looked at her father and his guest as she edged into her seat next to the head of the table, then glanced up at her mother, who moved smoothly and gracefully to take the place across from her, on her husband's right.

"She browbeats him," Rose said bluntly.

"That's enough."

"He's grateful for even the chance to watch father's display."

"I said, enough, Rose." Her voice never lost its pleasantry, but both women knew what could happen if Lady Feonna command-ed something to be so.

Rose gave her a small smile. "Father is getting better at the act." It was said quietly, so as not to be overheard.

Feonna returned the smile. "He is, isn't he?"

They shared the silent moment privately before Lady Nimway and Priscilla made their entrance at the far end of the room.

Priscilla looked composed and respectable. Her tears had been dried, the puffiness in her eyes had subsided. She wore a gracious smile on her face, a smile that was icy cold, yet deceptively sin-cere. Lady Nimway looked absolutely stunning beside her, radiating beauty and grace as she all but floated into the room. Together they looked the picture of royalty.

Rose's eyes narrowed as she eyed the two women at length, and finally Lady Nimway's surface of calm began to crack.

"That's enough, Rose," Feonna warned as she reached a hand across the table to her elder daughter. "For once, can we please have a civil meal together?"

Rose looked at her mother. "It may be our last."

"You've heard?"

Rose glanced from her mother to her sister, than back to her mother again. "I've heard," she said with absolute calm. "These walls chant secrets for those willing to listen."

The smile on Feonna's face was pained. "I grow weary of this, child. Please, as your mother, I'm asking you for just one meal. Just one."

Rose glanced over her mother's shoulder. "The men come," she said, disregarding her mother's plea.

Feonna schooled her expression and then quietly expelled a burst of air. "So it begins, then," she murmured.

Rose inclined her head towards her mother and the other women sat down to dine. Divine Providence, it would seem, put Lady Nimway beside Rose, and to watch the child one would think she was sitting next to a coiled snake. Yet Lady Nimway gave no out-ward show of feeling slighted by the heiress of Tresville. Rather, she seemed relieved that Rose kept her eyes averted. The meaning behind this baffling behavior escaped Lady Feonna, so she turned to her youngest child to see Priscilla staring down at the empty plate before her.

Another mystery, Lady Feonna sighed to herself as she sipped delicately from her wineglass. One that Rose apparently under-stood, however; her mind was racing as she observed every nuance of her sister's face. "Have you heard word from Kinan Lebinath?" Rose asked politely. It was no small secret how Priscilla felt about their neighbor.

"I have," Priscilla answered. Not once did her eyes move from her plate. "He has been awarded the Redoff pasture-lands to the south."

"The abandoned fields? How marvelous!" Rose clapped her hands together softly in delight.

"And the southern edge of the forest."

"Oh. I hadn't heard that." Rose frowned slightly as her mind digested this information.

Just then their father and Lord Albony sat down.

"Oh," Rose said again, still processing her sister's words. "Oh no!"

"Oh yes!" her father shouted. "And what a great day it is for the house of Tresville!" He put one hand on Rose's shoulder and another on his wife's. "Do you think he'll accept?"

Priscilla lunged to her feet and stormed from the room.

Rose pulled away from her father's touch and stared at the empty dining chair in front of her. "It is well known Priscilla has feelings for Lord Lebinath," she said quietly.

"And what of that? I'd think she'd be happy to have him living under the same roof!"

"There is no chance I have pieced this together wrong? Just this once?" Rose asked, looking hopefully first at her mother and then at Lady Nimway.

Lady Feonna glanced at the woman for support, but this time Lady Nimway wisely kept her mouth closed and simply shrugged helplessly.

That was all the confirmation Rose needed. "If Kinan is to marry into this household," she announced, "his wedding bed should be moved to Priscilla's tower."

The baron slapped his daughter in the mouth. Her head snapped around and her gaze settled on Lady Nimway. She was unflinching, refusing to cry out. Lady Nimway seemed to wither as Lord Tresville bellowed, "There will be no such talk of dishonoring my daughters! Such filth, that you would declare deeds of incest at the table in front of our honored guests!"

It was Feonna who placed a hand on Jason's fist and said, gently, "All the child was saying was that if anyone should marry the boy it should be Priscilla. Rose has no love for him and Priscilla has enough love for both of them."

"That's all I'd ever say!" Rose screeched as she burst to her feet with such force that she knocked the chair over behind her. Her father reached out to seize her shoulder, but she broke free of his grip and thrust his hand away from her. Then she turned and stormed away from the table in the opposite direction from the one Priscilla had taken.

"I should never have paid for her to take those knife lessons," the baron mused as he watched her leave, thinking of how easily she had maneuvered away from his grasp.

"It is customary, my lord," Lady Nimway interceded, her tone conciliatory. "What would happen if the castle were taken, and she ransomed?"

"How hard is it to fall on your own blade?" He turned back to the table to shrug at Lord Albony.

"I believe there can be a great deal of damage done to the enemy before it comes to that, Lord."

Jason ignored her. "Be thankful you don't have children, Cignifred."

Lord Albony glanced at his wife, as if looking for the correct response. "To be honest, I don't give it much thought, one way or another."

"I should go to her," Lady Feonna said, rising from the table.

"Why Rose?" her husband accused. "Why not Priscilla?"

"Because Priscilla is not heiress of your estates. Because Priscilla isn't forced to marry a man she doesn't love! Because Priscilla isn't marrying the man her sister loves! Because Priscilla doesn't have – ." She caught herself before the words were out of her mouth.

Still, it was as if a huge thunderclap had sounded in the room, so silent was everyone in its aftermath.

"Go to her," her husband said quietly, suddenly calm and understanding. "Do what you can do."

℘☍

She found Rose in the lower level of her tower, pacing around and around. It was obvious she was both livid and nervous, and also more than a little afraid. She seemed so much like a trapped animal, eyes wide with terror, that Lady Feonna could not help but take pity on her daughter.

"Rose. What is it?"

"These walls!" Rose shouted without ceasing her furious pac - ing. "They breathe! They writhe! They whisper secrets of murder! Of my murder!"

"No one wants to murder you, child."

"No one! Do you not think Priscilla would benefit from my death? Do you not think all of Tresville would be glad to see the lady witch thrown off the parapets of this haunted castle!" Rose glared at her mother as she made yet another circuit of the room. "Mother, I swear to you there is something happening down in the

152

basement! Something is being done that shouldn't be done! It brings this castle to life!"

Lady Feonna sighed. This again. "No child," she insisted, her tone low and soothing. "There is nothing downstairs that should not be there."

"You lie! You are all liars!"

"Rose Chantell!" Her mother's voice rang out sharply.

Rose ceased her pacing and whirled to face her mother. Her words were quiet but her eyes, shrewd and piercing, were icy. "Do you not know about that assassination plot? Lady Nimway started it."

"No child!" Lady Feonna stared at her daughter with surprise. "I haven't heard of any plot."

"But at dinner you asked me if I'd heard?"

"I was talking about your marriage to House Lebinath!"

Rose started pacing again, murmuring to herself and eyeing the walls with mad fascination. "That's all it is, isn't it? One house marrying another house."

Lady Feonna nodded. "In time, your sister will come to see that as well." She eyed her young daughter warily. "There is the marriage bed obligation, of course. But Priscilla will still have the same Kinan that she's always had."

Rose glared at her. "That's precisely the point, mother. She wants more than what she has."

"More than that which is her right to take."

"Reason enough to take my life!" Rose retorted. A look of pure anguish crossed her exquisite features and she shivered.

Lady Feonna's voice rose, her alarm apparent. "Rose!" she asked. "What are you doing?"

"The walls, mother. Can't you see the walls?"

"Yes, I see them just fine." Lady Feonna was puzzled.

"They're closing in, whispering evil." Rose's breath came in short gasps. "They're alive!" She stopped pacing and her face went deathly white. "Oh no," she mumbled. "No. I'm sorry! I didn't mean to tell her! No, no don't!" she begged. Rose screamed and clapped her hands over her ears as she crumpled into a ball on the floor.

Lady Feonna rushed to her daughter and put her arm around her as if to ward off her invisible attacker. With the other she lifted Rose's chin so they could look each other in the eyes. The girl was clearly terrified. "We'll find a cure for this," Lady Feonna promised. "You will get better, you'll see."

Rose nodded, beginning to regain some of her composure. "Lord Lebinath needs his bride to be in working order," she said bitterly.

"Be that as it may, "Lady Feonna swore, "enough is enough. We have the means. Let us find a cure at last – for our daughter, not just our heiress."

Rose nodded and held on tightly to her mother, as the terror of that which only she could see continued.

They scoured the kingdom. No expense was too great, no chance for a cure too slim. And in the end, the Baron and Baroness of Tresville found three healers whose boasts reached their ears the loudest. The Lord and Lady decided upon the most reputable healer first and sent for him, answering his outrageous demands as they catered to him.

Mifrey Ontuon arrived at the castle full of pomp and pride. He was a tall, lanky man with brown hair, clean-shaven but possessing an unkind face. His skin was powdered to create the appearance that he was much more pale; and he eyed the royal family of

Tresville with disdain, as if they were the lowliest of peasants and he a mighty king.

"It took you long enough to get here," Jason Tresville grumbled.

Feonna grabbed his hand, "Hush, husband," she murmured into his ear. "Let us not anger our guest."

The healer's eyes narrowed covetously. "The roads are dusty this time of year. I dare not parch my throat or catch some awful disease."

Lord Tresville merely nodded. "I suppose you would like to see our daughter, then?"

"Ah yes. The heiress. I suppose I should. See to it my things are unpacked and my servants are put in their rooms."

Lady Feonna waved to Dalia and the stewardess jumped forward with three other servants. "This way, Sir Ontuon." She nodded her head slightly towards the healer. "Please."

"Just Mifrey, my lady," the healer said magnanimously, extending his arm out to her, which she gracefully accepted. "All awards I've earned myself. I'm no sir, having been given something from birth."

"Of course," Lady Feonna replied, glancing at her husband, who glared balefully at the healer's back. Neither was sure whether or not they had just been insulted; but they led Mifrey to Rose's tower politely enough, filling the empty space with idle chat.

Mifrey Ontuon was as rude as he'd been when they'd first met, but the lord and his lady were so grateful for the healer's help that they were determined to overlook any slight. This Mifrey seemed to expect, to demand even.

But when they lead him up the spiral stairs to where Rose sat upon a chair, staring idly out into the open fields, his demeanor changed immediately, at once becoming brisk and professional.

155

"I see," he said, striding towards the lady Rose. He touched her cheek and she recoiled, glaring up at him. "Very advanced, a very advanced case," he mused.

"Who is this?" Rose demanded, rising swiftly to her feet. "And why have you brought him to my chambers like this?"

"He is to prepare you for your wedding," her father replied, his chest puffing up in arrogance.

"Hush, Jason," Feonna soothed. "Must you word it like that?"

Rose scowled at the intruder. "So, this is to be my healer? Can you take away my hallucinations, healer man? Can you stop the terror and the hauntings that plague me incessantly?"

Mifrey bowed. "I can only try, my lady. It will be a long gradual struggle. But it can be done, I believe." He looked thoughtfully at Rose's parents. "I wish I had been summoned sooner, though. Her condition is very advanced."

Lord Tresville inclined his head slightly towards Mifrey. "You said that," he pointed out.

"There's no more to be said, so I'll get to it, then." The healer clapped his hands together. "I'll need a private room with a table in it," he said. "Have my servants fetch my leeches."

"Leeches!" Lady Feonna protested.

The healer glanced from one to the other. "It must be done!" he insisted. "Her blood is bad, poisons the mind and gives her waking nightmares. If we drain enough of the blood we'll purge the poisons from her body and the sickness will go away."

"I want to do it," Rose said quickly. "Please. Just fix me."

"The room then, with the table?"

"This way," Lady Feonna said, leading them from the tower.

⬡⬡⬡

156

Mifrey insisted on privacy while he worked, so Rose's parents retired to the central castle to await the results. It was some time before the healer reappeared, and he seemed pleased with himself, smug even, as if he had accomplished something terribly complicated and had gotten away with it.

"That's a good sign," Lord Tresville muttered to his wife.

"Perhaps." In a louder voice, she called out to the healer. "Well Mister Ontuon! What is the diagnosis?"

Mifrey remained silent until he was close enough that he had no need to shout to be heard. When he finally stood before Lord and Lady Tresville, mopping the sweat from his brow, he replied, "It is as I fear, my lady. I shall need to continue treating her in this fashion for some time."

"Even while I was administering the leeches I couldn't help noticing your daughter was having another one of her hallucinations. The treatment itself can be a bit unnerving. But with these waking nightmares, these dark visions, Lady Rose had quite a time maintaining herself."

"Thank you, Mifrey," Lord Tresville said. "We'll see our daughter now."

"Oh no, my lord!" Mifrey waved his hands frantically before him. "I'm afraid the leeches have put her in a terrible state! The Lady Rose must take her rest and calm down a bit! I would advise you instead to send up a pitcher of wine and some choice fruits. Let her re-hydrate after losing so much blood."

Jason Tresville glared at him, but it was Lady Feonna who answered. "It will be done as you say, Mifrey. Is there anything else you'll need?"

He shook his head. "Not where your daughter is concerned. I cannot help her more until tomorrow. She's lost too much blood to undergo another treatment now."

"As you wish," Lady Tresville replied. "I'll have refreshments sent to your rooms."

He nodded. "That would be preferable. Thank you." Mifrey spun on his heel, beckoned to one of their servants, and demand- ed the lad show him to his rooms.

The serving boy looked askance at his Lord and Lady. But when his Lord merely nodded, he turned and caught up with the healer just as he was leaving the hall.

Lady Feonna turned to her husband once they were alone. "And so it begins," she sighed.

"Let's hope it is worth it," was all Jason would say, still glaring at the empty door the healer had disappeared through. "That man gives me a twitch."

Lord and Lady Tresville only saw their daughter in the morn- ings, before her 'treatment'. Afterwards Rose was indisposed in her tower, sometimes needing to be carried up the stairs by one of the servants. When they did see her Rose was quiet, withdrawn, her eyes downcast.

Once Lord Tresville asked Rose directly how the treatments were going.

Her only reply was, "I've sworn not to talk about it. Master Ontuon does not want his secrets to be revealed."

"Master, now, is it?" Jason bristled, incensed. "Master over the heiress of the Tresville Barony!" Lady Feonna put a hand on her husband's arm, yet he would not be quieted. "The man rises high- er every day."

Rose kept her eyes lowered. "Yes father. He does," she said before returning to her brooding silence.

Day after day this pattern continued. Rose's behavior was grad- ually worsening, until she would barely respond to her parents other than with one or two words, keeping her eyes downcast as if to cover inestimable shame.

Then one day, Lady Feonna had had enough. She arose early, determined to find out what was happening to Rose, and crept from her husband's side to dress in silence before disappearing into the castle.

Jason lay still, feigning sleep, grateful they were finally going to get some long sought-after answers.

Lady Feonna found Mifrey Ontuon's workchamber abandoned at this time of day. There was nothing here but the table. Even the jar of leeches had been removed. Disappointed but still deter-mined, she crept away before being discovered and passed the time idly with her daughter until Rose sulked away to her next treatment.

Then she followed. Not daring to trust Dalia with such an important task, Lady Feonna spied the pair as they passed through the castle to the treatment room. The doors were locked behind them. Lady Tresville lost sight of them for a few minutes while she maneuvered herself inconspicuously around the servants, and when she finally crept up to the doors and put her eye to the key-hole, she was aghast at the sight before her.

Her daughter was lying on the table, her legs spreadeagle and her face pointed towards the ceiling, horror and shame written there. She was completely naked, and her clothes lay in a heap on the floor. Rose's already pale face was a ghastly white. Her veins showed over her body as jagged white lines. Her lips were pale blue.

Mifrey Ontuon was leering at her daughter, grinning perversely as he took his time applying one leech here, another there. He was in no hurry. His leeches were just for show.

Feonna howled in anger and pounded her fist against the doors.

Rose flinched, but refused to move, such terror did she have of the leeches draining the blood from her.

Mifrey Ontuon, however, jumped at the outburst and shouted back. "I demand absolute privacy! Away with you, or this woman's madness will ravage her!"

Lady Feonna carried a master key. A second later the doors burst open and the outraged Lady Tresville charged in, shaking her fist at the healer. "Out! Out! You lecher! Pervert! Coward! Get out of my castle, get off of my lands! Do it now, quickly, before my husband sees what you have done and has you flogged, or worse! Let me never see your face again!"

In the face of her ire, there was nothing Mifrey could say.

"Now!" Lady Feonna screamed.

"Yes, Milady," the healer mumbled before he turned and fled from the room.

Rose lay perfectly still. A single tear escaped from her eye and rolled slowly down her pallid cheek.

Feonna crossed to kneel beside her daughter. "Is there anything I can do?" she whispered.

"The leeches, get them off!" Rose said through clenched teeth.

"Of course, dear."

As each leech was removed it was cast to the floor in disgust. And once they were all taken from her, Rose shakily sat up and gathered her clothes. Lady Feonna could see she was light head-ed, but her daughter maneuvered skillfully with the evident profi-ciency of someone having long endured such treatment.

When Rose had shrugged back into her dress Feonna exclaimed, "Oh Rose, I am so sorry!"

Rose looked at her mother dispassionately. "That is all right, Mother," she replied sadly. "Tresville needs its heiress. We will try again." Then she turned her back to Lady Feonna, gesturing for her to come forward and tie the back of her dress closed.

℘℘℘

"All hope is not lost," Lady Feonna said to Lady Nimway. Tears had been shed in bitter disappointment, but those tears had come to an end as the resolve to find a cure set in.

Lady Rose had gradually come around to being herself again, although she was as haunted by her phantoms as she had always been. She asserted that they mocked her, having been witness to the degradation Rose had suffered. She alleged they were scorning her for her parents' efforts to find a way to banish them forever, claiming there was no cure for Rose – nothing but madness, endless,
continual madness; and they drove her towards that madness relentlessly.

"There are other healers in this country," Lady Feonna continued as Lady Nimway patted her hand in reassurance. "There is one headed here at this moment, prepared to offer a diagnosis for Rose's affliction, and to provide her with suitable treatment even as we speak."

"Oh, my poor Feonna," Lady Nimway cooed. "Do not get your hopes up too much, my dear. It is enough that your daughter merely survives, that she continues to fight this madness, for madness is what it is."

"I know, Lady Nimway," Lady Feonna replied. "But this healer is said to be very good. His name is Chansan Eelop. He comes from the northern shores of Mendersat. Have you heard of him?"

Nimway brightened. "I have indeed. Oh, he is very good. If anyone can help your daughter, he can."

"I hope so, Lady Nimway. I truly hope so."

Less than a fortnight later the man arrived and took up residence as Lady Rose's full-time attendant. Yet for all his hustle
and bustle, all his endless preparations, he did very little to
actively help his charge. Alas, he did not even see Rose until he
had been settled comfortably in his quarters.

Chansan Eelop was a squat, obese man, who waddled when he
walked, and sweated endlessly while muttering under his breath.
He was a man of motion, continually monitoring an unguent boiling in the fire while preparing ingredients for a salve, running
back and forth between the two, only to begin a third task, to the
ruin of the other two, which burned in the pot and staled in the
air. He ate constantly. A glutton with no equal, Chansan main-
tained that it was necessary to sustain his weight for his health,
swearing that the excess food kept him mentally alert.

When he was at last brought before Lady Rose of Tresville, she
simply stared at her new healer with revulsion. Chansan chortled,
amused, and shuffled over to pat her on the shoulder. "That's a
good girl, Lady Rose! I have good news. Let me just check to
make sure." He placed his finger under one eye and pressed down
on her skin. "Look up." She did as she was told. "Now side to
side." Again, Rose obeyed. "Open your mouth. Stick out your
tongue. Say, 'ahhh'."

"Aaaahhh."

Chansan stepped back and fingered his chin thoughtfully.
"Mmmm, it is as I thought," he finally said. He gestured to Rose.
"Lift up your skirts, please."

"I beg your pardon!" Lady Feonna squealed.

"I'm sorry, Lady. I understand how inappropriate this may
seem. But I would like to examine Lady Rose's knee."

"My knee?" Rose asked, frowning in confusion as she stared
down at the top of the healer's head.

He nodded. "There seems to be a deficiency in your blood. I want to see if there are any white patches in your joints and none are under more strain than your knees."

Rose harrumphed and looked over at her mother as she hesitantly raised the hem of her dress.

Chansan Eelop bent over and poked at one of Rose's knees. Rose flinched at the touch, then giggled as he continued prodding. "Go on to one foot, please," he instructed her. "Now bend your knee. Yes, just like that." He stood up straight and gestured to Rose. "That's enough for now. You may lower your dress. My apologies for the improperness, My Lady. All in the name of medicine, you understand."

Rose glanced at her mother, then back at the healer. "That's quite all right," she said. "I assure you, I understand."

Chansan seemed not to hear her. "I have good news, Lady Rose. Your joints are fine. Whatever plagues you afflicts your mind only. We seem to have caught it early enough."

"That's good news," Lady Feonna said, coming forward and squeezing her daughter's arm. "That is good news, daughter."

"Yes mother. I suppose it is."

"You have a deficiency of vitamins in your diet," the healer declared. "For whatever reason, your metabolism is digesting the food faster than it should; and you are suffering these hallucinations because of a lack of nutrition."

"That makes no sense," Rose protested.

"Trust me, my lady," Chansan replied, "nothing about science makes much sense."

"I eat fine," Rose insisted.

"Of course you do. And therein lies the problem."

"Problem?" Lady Feonna asked.

"Your daughter, Her Ladyship here," Chansan motioned towards Rose, pointing at her slim form, "is starving herself to look like this. She must not do this, not if she wishes to maintain her sanity in the face of these strange hauntings she moans about." He turned to Rose. "You must eat, Lady Rose," he urged her. "Eat and eat and eat. Eat everything, as much as you can, all the time. Do not look so glum. It is perhaps possible you and I have the same ailment of the mind, the same vitamin deficiency. And look at me! I have recovered and climbed to a quite respected position within the kingdom. All is not lost, I assure you, but you must eat."

So eat she did.

The apparitions laughed at her, mocking Rose's gluttony while they tormented her with their usual maddening gibbering. Their tormenting often reduced her to tears, as Rose became more and more self-conscious about her weight and her clothing became too tight to wear. The voices and hallucinations became so ghast-ly, so vivid, so continual, that many a night Rose refused to return to her tower at all, retreating instead to a small recess in the wall, or to the servant's kitchen, or to a pile of clean straw in the sta-bles. She went wherever she could go, hoping against hope that the voices couldn't find her in time to deprive her of a few moments' rest.

"What is happening to my daughter?" Lady Feonna asked Chansan one day as Rose sauntered by with a turkey drumstick clutched in her fist. She was indeed gaining weight, having to borrow clothes from her father's wardrobe and alter what dresses she could.

"The plague of the mind, it is purging," the healer answered. "Envision a stew. You cook it and all the nutrients float to the surface. That is what is happening now. The impurities just seem worse because she is beginning to win free of them."

164

Lady Feonna stared at Chansan as though he himself were mad. But she kept her opinion to herself, and worried after her daughter.

One day, perhaps around midday when everyone in the castle was up and about, a scream erupted from the direction of Rose's tower. Lady Feonna dropped her cup of tea, which shattered on the floor. She flew towards Rose's room, hand clasped to her breast and her heart in her mouth as she ran. Even Lady Priscilla looked concerned as she caught up with her mother at a junction in the hallways.

"What is it, mother?" she asked breathlessly.

"I do not know, child."

"I'm afraid, mother. She's never been this bad before."

"I know."

The guards had opened the doors before them, so Feonna and Priscilla were able to make their way unhindered to Rose's viewing room. There, they stopped short, staring in anguish and horror at their beloved Rose.

She was passed out in a heap in the middle of the floor. Curled into the fetal position, even in sleep Rose shuddered with horror, as if she was being physically prodded. She flinched and cowered from her invisible tormentors. Her hands were clenched tightly over her ears and she was covered with vomit. A plate lay shattered in pieces on the floor beside her, half-eaten food strewn carelessly about.

The sight of any lady reduced to such a condition was too much for either Lady Feonna or Priscilla to bear. Priscilla turned and sharply ordered the guards out, commanding them to fetch Dalia, while Lady Feonna knelt beside her poor daughter.

"Rose," she whispered. There was no reply. "Rose, darling." She placed a hand gently on Rose's face. Her daughter flinched instinctively and awoke with a start. She flushed to have her mother and sister see her so, and averted her face from them and groaned as she sat up.

"Oh … are they gone, mother?" Rose rubbed her brow, her eyes darting about anxiously. "They are so … Are they gone?"

"I do not know, Rose. I cannot see them as you do."

Rose glanced around the room. "They are gone," she said, "for now. They are content to reduce me to this." She looked down at her ruined dress. Words escaped her.

Finally, Chansan arrived, huffing and muttering about the exertion up the stairs. "No wonder the child does not recover. She is forced to climb those stairs every day!"

Lady Feonna glared at the healer. "Mister Eelop, your services are no longer needed."

"Mother, are you sure?"

"Hush child. I'm sure." Lady Feonna's voice was calm but firm.

"But My Lady," Chansan protested, "the deficiency — "

"The deficiency will remain with or without your help," she responded tightly. "Please, Priscilla here will help see you on your way."

Priscilla offered the healer a tight-lipped smile that did not reach her eyes, and motioned for him to lead the way out of the room.

When Lady Feonna was alone with Rose once more, she whispered, "We'll find a cure, my daughter. I promise."

"Thank you mother." Rose labored to her feet and reached unsteadily towards the older woman. "Help me out of this mess, will you?" she implored her mother.

☙❧

They found another healer and sent a messenger out to him. He scorned them in his reply, insulted that he'd been the third healer they'd tried rather than the first. He refused them, declaring he would only cure their daughter if they made compensations for the insult they'd given him.

They paid. Of course they paid. And so Tyson Wind-Talker moved from the Plains of Elgerath into Castle Tresville. He was tall and muscular, wore a leather tunic cut off at the shoulders, hinting at the tattoos that covered the rest of his torso. He wore a matching pair of leather leggings, simple, though finely crafted, designed for riding the horses of the plains. Yet for all his barbarianism, Tyson Wind-Talker was well mannered and well versed. His education was obvious, as was his pride.

"It is all about strength!" he declared after he'd given Rose a cursory examination. "She needs strength of the mind! In the Plains we go without sleep for days on end. And that is what you shall do here. You have nightmares, do you not? Terrible nightmares that do not end once you waken?" He did not wait for Rose to answer, but declared, "We shall drive the nightmares away from you. Without sleep the nightmares can not exist. Go long enough and you will forget the nightmares, but more importantly, the nightmares will forget you."

To their desperate ears it sounded like hope.

And so that very night Rose began her regimen of sleeplessness.

It was a miserable experience, one that left her wits dulled and her mind on edge. Bitter hallucinations that were growing worse every day continued to haunt Rose, piercing her frayed nerves until everywhere she went she was jittery. Yet day after day she clung to the hope that if she slept not a wink, eventually the nightmares would fade, as the healer claimed.

One day Rose found herself out on the parapets, studying the fields and watching the workers toil in the dust. While it was a warm summer day, the breeze was not kind up on the heights, and it seemed to Rose that the fields were wilting under the heat. Even so, it was good to be up high, in the fresh air . Her anesthetized mind woodenly accepted the heat. Her life had become so numb, so hazy, she was growing used to the sensation of mild confusion.

Suddenly the world tilted at a bizarre angle and Rose pitched forward. The sounds of shouting soldiers and hammering feet brought her out of her daze to partial consciousness. Her face hurt where she'd pitched and fallen against the crenel of the battle - ment, but the weight of her body was teetering precariously on the ledge.

Rough hands grasped her around the waist and dragged her back from the edge. Safely back on her feet, Rose looked up into the face of her savior. And screamed. The vision of her hauntings had taken flesh in front of her very eyes. But it was hideous; where the face should be was only a dark gray skull, whose vacant eye- sockets stared at her from their dark void. The jawbone, creaking eerily as it dipped and nodded, seemed to leer at her with such audacity that Rose screamed again and again.

"Do you think we would let you fall to your death, Lady of Tresville? What would be the fun in that? Where would we go, then, where we could find sport quite like you?"

Rose moaned and shook her head from side to side in a desper - ate attempt to free herself of the nightmare.

The skeleton cackled as it seized her in its bony hands.

Abruptly the laughter ceased, and when Rose hesitantly opened her eyes, it was to see her mother standing next to them. The vision of the skeleton was gone, replaced by a flesh and blood soldier, and by the panic in his eyes, he was a very confused sol - dier.

"She swooned and passed out, ma'am. Most of her was already over the edge by the time I got to her. And when I placed her back on her feet, she just started screaming," the soldier said anxiously.

"Thank you, Ridney, it's all right," Lady Feonna reassured him with a small pat on the shoulder. "It is not your fault." She stared at her daughter. "This is getting out of hand."

"Yes, My Lady," Ridney dared to answer. He released Rose and took a hesitant step away from her. "If that will be all, Lady Feonna?"

Feonna nodded at him. "Of course. Go. You've done well this day, Ridney."

"Thank you, My Lady. But that screaming, that terrible screaming... " he glanced at Rose and inclined his head slightly. "My Lady." Then he turned and fled the parapets.

"And you, young lady," Feonna announced as she moved forward to take her daughter's arm. "You are off to bed."

"But mother, my visions?"

"Have they ever been so stark and bleak as they have been this day?"

"No, mother."

"Then you are not forgetting about your nightmares. And your nightmares are not forgetting about you."

"You are right, mother." She leaned against her mother's arm for support and allowed Lady Feonna to guide her. "What would I do without you, mother?"

Feonna shook her head. "Let's not think about that right now, daughter. You must get better. I will tell the healer we no longer need his services."

Grateful, Lady Rose was escorted to her tower and helped to her bedchamber, where she passed into an exhausted, dreamless sleep. For that brief time not even the ravings of her ravaged mind could wake Rose, and she slumbered peacefully.

Her family knew such respite would be brief, however, and they sent out runners to scour the lands for healers they might have missed. But rather than send for the most pompous, most reputed men or women in the kingdom or its lands beyond, they sent for reports of any and all healers who might be able to help. The Tresville Barony had little to lose at this point, all they wished for were positive results.

One by one, days, weeks, even months later, the messengers returned having had little success. Conscious of their duty to bring back healers that might work, they stayed and watched them at their work. And one by one the messengers discovered that these people could not help Lady Rose Tresville.

But one runner, the last to return, stayed much longer than the others; stayed away, in fact, until the castle inhabitants began to worry. Normally no one would think twice about this messenger's absence, but now all their hopes rested on this one man, and the waiting seemed interminable. When he finally returned, some two months after the others, he strode directly to the great hall without cleansing himself of the dusty road, coming straight from the stable where he had left his exhausted mount.

He was ushered into the room immediately. Lady Feonna and Lord Jason were on the edge of their seats as they anxiously watched him approach.

Weary of his travels, stinking of the road, of his horse, of stables and back alleys, the messenger clearly seemed nervous as he came to stand before his Lord and Lady. He exhaled to give himself time to collect his thoughts, then looked stone-faced at the Tresvilles.

"Well Thomas, what is it man?" Jason Tresville demanded. He gripped the edges of his chair, his fingers white with apprehension.

"I do not know, My Lord," the messenger said bluntly. "I have found a man who seems indifferent to rank or wealth. He has been amongst the poor and downtrodden along the eastern fringe of the Horim Mountain Desert Region."

Lord and Lady Tresville cringed visibly. The place was well reputed for its sickness and poverty.

"That is not all," the messenger continued. "While a lone man could never hope to change all of that filth, this one makes a difference, and what he does lasts the test of time. I myself have traveled to that wretched place, have seen the hospitals and the doctors he has trained. I have seen the gardens and the community programs this healer has implemented. I have seen the aqueducts he's had built, the schools he's helped to organize. The people there are now beginning to help themselves. Incredibly, although it will take time, it seems this healer has actually begun to heal the Horim Fringe."

Thomas took a huge breath after this lengthy speech, and looked expectantly at the royal couple.

The Tresvilles were amazed into speechlessness. They stared at each other. Could such a feat be accomplished?

"How long was this healer in the Fringe?" asked Lady Feonna.

"Ten years, as near as I can tell, My Lady. I could not find out where he was before then, and the healer himself would not tell me."

"You spoke with this man!" Lord Jason barked. "What is his price?"

"Well, nothing, My Lord. He seemed reluctant to travel so far to help one single person. And although I tried to convince him he would be well-compensated for his time and travels, he would not hear of it. He said to me, 'What is worth one man's life for the price of another's? Too many people are dying in the great cities of central Hansurn for one spoiled Royal to be of any concern to me.'"

"And what did you say to him?" Lady Feonna asked, her voice dangerously calm.

"I said you would do anything within your extensive power as Baron and Baroness."

"And he said?" Now Lady Feonna too gripped the edge of her chair.

Thomas cleared his throat nervously. "He asked for her symptoms. I told him of her visions as well as I could. He nodded and declared he knew what had ailed her, but to be sure, he asked how much did she eat."

"Not this again," Feonna moaned.

"I said she ate very little, mostly nuts and vegetables, some fruits, but that she disdained meat and loathed eggs. Then he asked me how much she slept. I said a few hours a night, at the most – when she's not been exhausted by some other crack-pot healer. And then he asked me the most peculiar question, I shall never forget it. He said, 'Does she see right to the heart of every matter?' 'Why yes, My Lord,' I answered. And he looked at me and smiled, ma'am. He actually smiled and said, 'She must be very tall and thin and beautiful, with very fair skin and light hair.' 'All of that, My Lord,' I answered him. 'Except that she has black hair, as black as night.' And then he laughed, loud and long as if I had told a magnificent joke. 'Of course she does!' he finally managed through his tears. 'Of course she does!'"

Thomas cleared his throat again and waited.

"So is he coming to help?" Feonna snapped.

The messenger paled a little and shook his head. "No, My Lady," he replied cautiously. "He says too many lives are at stake."

172

Feonna snarled her frustration and pounded her fist upon the arm of her wooden throne. "He knows what's wrong with her, he knows what she eats and how she sleeps. He could even guess at what she looks like! But the one man who can help refuses to, while all those supposed healers were of no help at all, but came taking advantage of our hospitality!"

"It would seem so, My Lady," Thomas nodded. "But he sent me back with a message and made me swear not to break the seal, or to let another break it except for you, Lady, or your husband, the Baron."

"Well now, why didn't you say so earlier? Let's have it, man, let's have it," the Baron demanded, thrusting his hand towards the messenger.

Thomas fished through his pockets and pulled out a small scroll, sealed with wax and marked with a single tear drop pierced with a sword. When the baron spied the mark he quoted, "War with sorrow."

"Or suffering, or grief, or pain," Feonna added, looking over his shoulder. "That is this strange man's insignia."

They shared a glance and then Baron Jason broke the seal and unrolled the parchment.

To the Nobles of House Tresville,

I have little doubt in my mind as to what causes
your daughter's ailment. The cure is lengthy, yet
she will find it gentle and soothing in the face of
the horrors that face her in that place.

"In that place! What does he mean in this place!" the baron bit off the words angrily. "Does he dare believe we are somehow at fault?"

"Hush, husband. Read the message."

Fault lies not in any one man, nor in any group of the living, but rather in the fate of one great woman. Many things I dare not explain, for fear of making matters worse for her, or for you, who must live with her the way she is.

So let me simply declare this: I know of your secret source of power, your wealth. I know of the smithies you must keep in the roots of your castle, of the mines you keep down there and of the priceless glowing stones those mines must yield to you. And you forge with this stone, this strange, malleable stone, heating it with flame and cooling it with water. And the steam rises up to leach into the rest of the castle, to penetrate the gardens and the fields around the castle, where vegetables are plucked and cattle is kept. This steam must seep into your water supply and make its way into your lungs and the lungs of your servants, and most importantly in the lungs of your daughter Rose.

I do not pass judgment, only point out cause. Your daughter is simply allergic to this hidden industry you guard so secretly. For all who participate in the trade of the stones keep the utmost secrecy. Yet to one who knows what to look for your daughter is a telltale sign and gives you away.

I also know your family has a fascination with forests, one forest in particular. For this forest has roots that touch the same stone you command and the trees would have a familiarity to you that you can not place.

There is much more I know about you that even you do not know yourself. Your messenger, the good Thomas, is very knowledgeable, though he knows not what knowledge he possesses.

In light of this, I would not blame you if you sent assassins after me. But let me assure you I am a very hard man to find if I so wish it. And I have very many friends whose notice escapes the likes of Nobles, so isolated as they are in their castles and with their wealth. Do not seek to do me harm. The secrets I have gleaned about you I will keep, and disclose only what is needed in order to help your daughter.

Which brings me to the heart of the matter. If you would wish it, let the child come to me and I will be happy to assist in all that I can. Let her walk bare-foot along the path so she may feel the earth between her toes. Let her run her hands through the wheat fields, and let her walk by a creek so she may hear the music the water makes upon the rocks. Let her drink of the water, or swim in it if that is her desire. Let her take her rest where she would, and find the paths that best suit her. Then, and only then will I be able to help your daughter, for what trou-bles her is not a sickness of the body, but of the soul. So let her soul bask in the sunlight and play in the rain. Let it know once more what it is to be set free.

The Baron and Baroness stared at each other, and then at Thomas. He shuffled his feet and looked at a distant point on the wall. Neither had read the message out loud, and apparently the messenger was quite oblivious about what it was they did in the catacombs beneath their feet.

"We have no choice," the baron said with finality. "We must do as he asks."

Lady Feonna nodded, a mixture of relief and worry painted upon her face. How many others know? The question burned in her mind, yet she dared not utter the words in the presence of their servants.

By the look in his eyes she knew the baron was wondering the same thing.

Despite their concern, or perhaps because of it, there seemed to be only one course of action the Tresvilles could take. In unison they said, "we'll send her to him immediately."

୫୬ୠ

The very next day, just before dawn, a very keyed up Lady Rose Tresville set out from her castle with an entourage of hand - picked servants and bodyguards. Her parents understood the essence of the therapy this healer had recommended, so they had allowed her to oversee every detail of the journey to her own heart's content.

The sun found her striding down a dirt road with a light pack upon her shoulders. She was much relieved to be away from the court; and to have put her back to the dreadful life that so shad - owed her there. She had been given the chance to walk away if even for a while from the mysterious industry whose presence she had suspected for some time; and mostly to escape the tormentors whose existence everyone so stubbornly denied were destroying her mind.

But Rose couldn't blame all her woes on her parents. These were her nightmares, and this was her life. If it hadn' t been for their loving support, she and her sister Priscilla would have been married off the moment they'd reached the appropriate age. Instead, she'd been allowed to experience an independence that was unheard of among the other daughters of the nobility. No, this was her problem; these were her hallucinations.

Still, she could swear the way her body ached from the last thrashing she had received from House Tresville's ghosts that the phantoms weren't entirely within her own mind.

176

They had put her in a miserable state the night before. Wailing and screaming throughout the night, they were punishing Rose for leaving, punishing her for seeking a power over her tormentors. Yet even with such a beating, they were careful not to leave any identifiable marks which might support the theory that she was not mad – and this uplifted Rose's spirits rather than pulling them down.

With the other healers she had been mocked, spat upon by her tormentors. She had been jeered and taunted. But with this new healer, whoever he was, it was different. Rose had detected fear behind the blows the apparitions had rained down upon her. She had detected unease behind the lies they spat at her from between clenched teeth. Rose was their prisoner; this was true. But there was a line that these wisps of vapor and smoke never crossed – they never left any evidence that they were in fact real, not to anyone else, anyway.

And so Rose had accepted this new rebuke, this new chastise-ment. And although she had not yet dared challenge them to cross that line, she rallied at the thought that on the new day she would leave this accursed castle and these cowardly phantoms, who had nothing better to do than to torment one lone maiden. She would experience life outside the castle, and she would finally find help.

So now, travelling into the unknown with her troops behind her, Lady Rose Tresville had two prevailing thoughts: on the one hand she was exuberant, exultant. She was excited beyond reason, to the point where she was giddy, unable to contain the mirth that threatened to bubble through her trained lady's exterior. On the other hand, the torment of her phantoms had left a dreadful scar upon her soul. Rose had known only disappointment and torture for so long that she wondered how this experience could possibly be any different. Having known doubt and worry and torment, having resided in a house of fear and disbelief all her life, Rose feared this little jaunt into the wilderness could not possibly begin to equip her to fight the enemies that lived inside her mind and inside the castle. Either way, real or imaginary, Rose had to continue to face them alone. And what could one mere maid do in the face of all that evil, those who had been her masters for so very long?

So it was with a heavy heart that she trudged down the empty road. Sensible people were abed while she, Rose, mad out of her head, had waited impatiently until she could wait no longer, and had ordered her ensemble to make ready to leave. Of course, her phantom tormentors had raged even louder, but by then she was rousing her servants and men-at-arms from their slumber, and her tormentors were forced to subside lest someone suspect she wasn't actually crazy.

Which only made Rose more infuriated. But her servants had heard her screams during the night. Her household had recognized her cries of torment, and the rebellious outcries of hope. This night had been different from her usual rantings. It had been intense, like the crescendo of a thunderstorm, and made those who loved Lady Rose flinch at the sounds. It left Priscilla swearing she would never have her sister assassinated, then praying on her knees the elder daughter of House Tresville would find help this night.

When Rose took to the hallways, fully dressed with tears in her eyes, her family did not begrudge her early rise. Hope united the Barony of Tresville as the people stood at the gates and watched Rose set her spirit to the road in front of her. She dared not look back, lest she see the vast army of phantoms as well as her family and friends, her servants and her trusted body guards. Resolutely she marched down the road; and already she was feeling her muscles cramp and feet ache.

At first she flinched around every bend and corner. Her mind could not process that her tormentors were trapped in the castle. Once she thought she saw one of them, loafing in the woods as if in some kind of a trance. Rose stubbornly ignored it, and apparently the phantom took no interest in her either.

Rose was elated. Could it be that the apparitions amongst the trees and under the moon did not know of Rose? If she pretended not to see these remarkably human-like creatures, then they could not know that she saw them and would leave her alone.

She reasoned then that her tormentors, those shades that existed within the castle, had to stay there, although the reason for that escaped her. And that meant Rose was free, free at last to explore so much of the world that had always intrigued her.

Despite being in a slightly weakened state, Rose heightened her pace along the wide track that led through the forest. Such was her father's love for hunting that he had allowed a small parcel of trees to grow in the middle of a furrowed field in front of the cas-tle. Lord Tresville had wanted to showcase the field at the front of the castle, so it had been allowed to grow wild. Rose couldn't see the moon through the trees, and when she did, the view was not nearly satisfying enough. She swore to herself she would watch the thing set from the edge of the forest, with nothing but open fields to see her on her way.

And so it was that her entourage finally caught up to Rose, who was leaning casually against the last tree before the open expanse. She wore the traveling clothes of a peasant so as not to attract attention. A straw hat with a wide brim kept the sun out of her face and off of her hair. The light travel pack she insisted on car-rying was slung over her shoulder and her head was lowered, lis-tening to the night and the sounds of her servants laboring after her.

"Lady Rose!" one of them called out. "Whatever are you doing?"

Rose was in pain. The fresh night air was different than from the warm candles and incense burners in her tower. The rigid pace she'd set was more strenuous than her life as a lady. But despite her discomfort, Rose knew the pain would pass. She raised her head and smiled wanly. The smile was lost in the darkness, but her servants heard the mix of weariness and excitement in her voice. "Waiting for the sun to rise, Penelope."

Immediately, her servants set about making themselves comfortable, taking out sleeping rolls and utensils for a fire.

"No," Rose said quickly, rushing out amongst them. "Not anywhere near the trees." She glanced over at them, afraid that she'd revealed her secret to the shades lingering there. A few turned to regard her, and a wave of muttering swept through the shadows under the bows. A gentle wind seemed to pick up within the glen, and the leaves rattled. Rose glanced fearfully at her servants to see if they had heard the wind also. They had.

From out of the ground itself came a slow groan, an angry, vengeful sound that raised goosebumps over Rose's entire body. The hair on the back of her neck stood on end and her eyes widened with terror. "Stop her!" that sound droned.

A great gust of wind picked up amongst the trees, blustering raucously through the leaves in a violent rush.

"Did anybody hear that?!" Rose shouted out over the din.

"Hear what, my lady?" one of the guards called back to her. His sword was half out of his sheath as the unnatural gale grew increasingly louder around them.

Rose glanced back towards the castle. Her eyes widened and she screamed. At the far end of the road a huge column of black smoke was swarming out of the gate. Shrouded by the smoke was an army of wraiths armed for battle. Men, women, and even children, they looked almost too tormented themselves to be tormentors. They appeared weary and angry, vengeful and malevolent – but all were obviously intent on stopping Rose from leaving.

She screamed again to see them pour out of the castle, recognizing some of them immediately. But there were many more spirits than Rose had ever seen before, so many more than she had ever imagined.

"My Lady!" Galadin, captain of her bodyguard, grabbed her by the shoulders.

His touch awakened Rose's senses. She won herself free of his grasp and sprinted out into the fields, thankful that her peasant's garb would not hinder her as one of her fancy lady's dresses would have.

She dared not look over her shoulder, gripped by terror as she was. But Rose's servants, chosen for their loyalty and sympathy towards her situation, looked first at her and then towards each other as the ferocity of the windstorm seemed to increase. The army of evil phantoms swept past the servants in a billowing cloud; and as they were overtaken, it seemed that a mist suddenly engulfed them to blot out the light of the moon.

Rose felt the spirits coming and screamed again. A bony, out-stretched hand reached out to grasp her shoulder and she flinched, recoiling. Suddenly, the cloud swirled backwards into the forest, retreated into the castle, and was gone.

Rose collapsed. Shivering uncontrollably, she began to weep. Galadin gently lifted her into his arms and carried her into the sea of wheat fields and moonlight, her servants following with both sadness and resolution in their eyes.

More than a few were filled with wonder, having witnessed the phantom wind, and seen the moon blotted out by the malevolent darkness. They looked at their mistress not with pity as if she were mad, but with amazement and awe, as though Lady Rose Tresville was charmed.

ಬಃಂಜಃ

She must have slept, then, for when Rose awoke, the sun was already high in the sky, and insects were buzzing in the air. There were some farmers in the distant fields, laboring in the heat behind ox and plow. But for their quiet little sojourn Rose's group had been left alone, either by the vigilance of Galadin and the servants, or by accident. Whichever the case, Rose opened her eyes, alarmed to find herself on a sleeping roll.

She sat up and groaned. Aching muscles screamed in protest and she flinched as she stretched her arms over her head.

"It is best to loosen them up, miss," one of her guards offered. She glanced over at him, standing far enough to give her some privacy, but close enough to keep an eye on her.

She clambered to her feet, placed her hat on her head, and wandered over to him. "What time is it?" she asked.

"Midday, as close as I can tell, My Lady." The guard's name was Tremel. He was a kind, soft-spoken man with a wife and two children, who lived in the outlying buildings of the castle. Tremel's temperament was deceiving, though. Loathe to practice his javelin and shield, if he were goaded enough, his temper would flare, and Tremel would become one of the greatest warriors in her father's household. That in itself had been reason enough for Jason Tresville to assign the man as Rose's bodyguard.

But Tremel had also been one of the men Rose had requested to be considered as a candidate as well. Tremel may or may not have believed Rose's claims of being tormented by ghosts or creatures only she could see; but he never judged her. He treated her as was due a lady of her station, even when they had been younger and his main concentration was on pleasing his father and mother.

Rose had asked him then why he treated her so kindly and Tremel had answered, "What if you were mine own sister, My Lady? Not to say you'd be born out of your station, or me out of mine, 'cause we're not. And we've got differences to be mindful of, and I am. But it seems to me, My Lady, that when we cut right through the titles and the 'My Lady's,' and we do away with the castle and the little hut that is my home, you're just a girl getting beat up by a bunch of bullies. And I'm just a boy who's to be a guard one day, a protector."

"Only this thing I can't protect you from. I can only stand here and watch, and real or in your head, makes no difference, My Lady. They still hurt you; and pardon my presumption, it still seems to me that you need a protector."

"And so you'll protect me anyway you can," Rose said to the adult version of that boy, standing so stiffly and dutifully in front of her with his face turned northward.

He looked at her, assuming correctly that she was thinking of the past. "Yes, My Lady. Anyway, that seems right and proper."

"Well I think it's right and proper that you help me find some - thing to eat."

"We can go ask the farmers for food. They'd be happy to part with their portions for the day, if you'd ask for it."

Rose rolled her eyes. "They'd be happy to sell them to me, you mean."

"They are still your father's vassals," Tremel objected. "They would be obligated to give you whatever you asked for."

"I wouldn't think of asking it of them." Rose eyed all the gear lying on the ground around them. "Where did everyone else go?"

Tremel pointed towards the east. "Wellsworth, My Lady, in search of food."

She took the guard by the arm and guided him towards the north instead. "I have food in my pack."

He was silent as he walked with her. "You do not want to be amongst people," he observed presently. Rose took no offense at his blunt words; that was just Tremel's way.

"No. And it's not just that." She stopped them and stood quietly, surrounded by the sea of fields. "Listen. Do you hear anything?"

Tremel stood in the stillness, straining his ears to hear. "No my lady. Not a thing," he said.

Rose grinned. "Neither do I." Then she turned and headed towards her healer in the north, Tremel collecting himself quickly and running to catch up with her.

ഇൽ

The others found their partially set-up camp abandoned, and were quick to guess that Tremel and Lady Rose had started north already. They gathered their belongings and hurried after her. None were concerned for her safety. Tremel had been left behind for a reason. Rose's entourage knew that had the pair gone in a different direction, there would have been a message left for them. Considering there was none, they left the Tresville fields behind and soon drew near some wild pastures edging the banks of a narrow, meandering river.

Apparently the land was uncultivated, for although it was gentle and rich for farmland, there were copses of trees growing up around the river, and a great assortment of stones strewn through-out the fields. Lady Rose's band of trusted companions, eleven of them in all, were laughing and joking amongst themselves, when suddenly they stopped short at the sight of their lady.

Rose had discarded her boots and stockings, and had cast down her pack. She sat with one foot dangling in the water, the other drawn up unceremoniously in front of her. Her back leaned casually against a tree, a piece of grass clamped firmly between her lips, and she held a fishing pole in her hands. Rose's hat was still perched upon her head but her black hair hung loose, draped over her shoulder and cascading down her tunic.

Rose looked more at ease here than she had ever been, sitting all alone upon the banks of the River Shrine. She was purposely ignoring her entourage, although the effort left her grinning while she fought to hold on to that piece of grass with her teeth.

"It's been said this piece of land has been left undeveloped out of respect for the dead that lie here," she remarked finally, to no one in particular.

No one answered, no one stirred. They were amazed at how relaxed their lady seemed to be.

Without turning, Rose continued. "River Shrine, the living shrine of some long ago mighty battle, is said to have ghosts haunt its shores, ghosts that will live here until they've been buried." She looked over at her people. "This borders the edge of my father's barony. What lies on the other side belongs to Lord Keltrapid. I'm sure my father would be willing to buy his share of the river for me. We could build an outpost right on the bank, with a bridge and a road. We could farm the fields on either side and build a road to go with the bridge. And we could collect a tax, nothing too rude, mind you, just enough to remind Lord Keltrapid and my father to be mindful that this is a cemetery. And we could recover the bones as we find them and give them a proper burial, with a monument on either side of the bridge so all who pass this way would remember the battle that was fought and the losses incurred by both sides."

"Most people would be afraid of the ghosts, my lady," Galadin pointed out.

Rose gazed out across the water. "Most people are afraid of disturbing the harmony of their own minds. All I want to do is find tranquility from mine. Helping a few ghosts put to rest their own torments seems a small price to pay if they will share a corner of this peaceful place with me."

Galadin sighed. "Let us go see this healer first, see what he has to say."

"Of course." Rose tossed her piece of grass into the river and lay her fishing pole down beside her. Then she climbed to her feet and retorted, "it was his idea that I get away from the castle in the first place!"

All at once a fish took the bait and jerked the fishing pole into the water. Laughing with delight, Rose jumped in after it.

Her servants hesitated, but then there was a great scramble to free themselves of burdens and weapons; and then they too cannonballed into the river, dresses and Tresville uniforms and all. Rose recovered her fishing pole just in time to notice their invasion, and laughed until her sides hurt as her people splashed merrily in the water around her.

Just then, Tremel came into view with an armload of firewood. He took one look at the antics of his captain and the men and their willful disregard for discipline, and rolled his eyes. Without a word, he dumped the firewood on the ground and set out to retrieve another armload.

By the time everyone was finished frolicking in the water, Tremel had a fire going, and was roasting enough fresh fish to satisfy everyone's appetites.

It was only a few hours past midday and the sun was still high; but Rose decided they should stay here this night, that they would enjoy the company of the troubled spirits who shared this site. In the evening the group held a solemn ceremony to remember those that had died in this place. Their sacrifices had not been in vain, nor were they to be forgotten. But their deaths had made Hansurn a better place and Rose empathized with the pain that she felt emanating from the sacred ground here.

There were no troubled ghosts disturbing Rose or her entourage that night. They slept peacefully and securely. A few left the next morning swearing that they had been watched over, protected. And no one could think of having experienced a more restful camp, ever.

೫೨೦೫

That first day set the tone for the rest of the trip. When they came across cities, Rose chose to skirt around them, insisting that they pay for everything and be a burden to no one. There were enough men-at-arms in their group to deter any unwelcome mis - chief, and enough serving girls who were clearly castle-bred that no one could question her authenticity.

And Rose herself, despite her lack of appropriate court apparel, was a lady. No one could dispute that. Nor could anyone ar gue that she was a model of finery and impeccable manners – when she wanted to be. Yet neither could one argue that despite her mysterious madness Rose appeared to be fine: in fact, more than fine. She was vibrant and witty, always in the hub of conversation at the inns and taverns they stayed at along the way; laughing and smiling, never rude or haughty as many Nobles were, and she never distanced herself from her people.

Rose did much, actually, to strengthen the popularity of the Baron. Having his daughter dine or sleep in someone's inn brought instant fame and good fortune to the place. News spread ahead of her, and people waited for Rose on the side of the road to offer her good cheer and long health. Dressed as a peasant though she was, with her silly straw hat and her piece of grass for a pipe, she always stopped and cheered the citizens, her father 's subjects, with words of respect and wishes of good health.

The day came, though, when Rose could no longer ignore the bigger cities. Ten days' walk north of her father 's castle she arrived at Teemingdale, situated in the lands of Lord Pilinger. Pilinger was a boatmaker, with a vast fleet he leased out from his port city, Moon Angel Bay. And while the port was nothing but a massive dockyard, the lumber and fineries that graced most of his ships came from Teemingdale, to the south.

Lord Pilinger was an avid boot-licker of her father 's, but he could be a kind man all the same, and a sincere man. Her father would joke that Pilinger was probably a pirate and kept up his groveling just to stop the baron from taking a closer look at Pilinger's operations. And now that Rose was entering his city, having made such a stir with her pilgrimage, and rumors of her being of right mind — finally — Lord Pilinger rose to the spirit of the occasion and announced to his subjects that he would bring the saintly Lady Rose to the town center to honor her quest, and her father for allowing it.

The people cheered him on, although a few questioned why he was making such a big deal out of it. And anyway, they asked, how were they to meet the kind lady who traveled like a peasant if the Nobles got involved and nosed about in her business?

Lord Pilinger turned a deaf ear to them and rode out ceremoniously with an honor guard.

He nearly rode her down before he realized that only a royal lady wouldn't think to get out of his way. Rose and her party had been strolling along unperturbed, conversing and laughing, when the horses came thundering out of nowhere. The riders' uniforms were clean, the armor polished to gleam brightly in the sun. The horse's hooves cast sparks upon the cobbled stones.

Rose, clothed like a man, with her ladies dressed for comfort in mismatched attire; her guards, their uniforms packed away and weapons slung carelessly over their shoulders, promenaded down the middle of the road as if they owned it. And indeed, they did own it, or as close as anyone could come to owning it, and at any rate, certainly closer than this Lord Pilinger.

She saw the thirty or so galloping horses with their pompous standards and ridiculous plumes upon the helmets. Those feathers must have been such a misery to wear, (and were definitely a misery just to look at). But they simply forgot that she did not look anything like a lady. She groaned, "So much for my brief interlude with sanity," then walked on to meet this banner-man of her father's.

Rose came inches from death that day. But at the last moment, Pilinger had a flash of memory about Rose and reined his horse sharply. The animal screamed as it reared on his hind legs, a mere pace before her. The other riders, seeing their lord desperately control his beast, scrambled to do the same; like dominoes, the ranks collided with each other. A banner was dropped; a soldier scurried to retrieve it, and an uneasy silence settled over Pilinger's men.

Rose glanced briefly at her people, then up at a man who could only be Pilinger.

"My Lady Rose Tresville, daughter of Baron Jason Tresville, my trusted Liege Lord And Master?" Although his words were subservient, Pilinger looked as though he had quite purposely nearly ridden her down.

"Do you always run over people?" Rose asked him.

His compliant countenance began to crack. "Most people get out of the way," he retorted.

"That is not what I asked!" Rose snapped. Her thoughts were for her father's people. "What of those that don't get out of your way?" The irate tone in Rose's voice made even her own companions wince.

Lord Pilinger was silenced and snapped to attention. Things were definitely not going according to plan. When Rose made no move to continue he finally answered, "Only a few, my lady; it is unfortunate, but that is why the roads must be kept cleared. My men are well accustomed to it though; have no fear. Distasteful tasks do not break their discipline."

"Distasteful tasks do not break their discipline?" Rose's voice rose dangerously.

Galadin placed a hand on his lady's arm. "My lady, think of the politics," he mumbled under his breath so as not to be overheard.

"Soldiers!" Pilinger bawled. "Remove that man's hand!"

Immediately, every man-at-arms had his weapon out, Rose's guards included.

"Lord Pilinger!" Rose bellowed, her roar loud enough to be a war cry over a battlefield. "Hear my wishes!"

He motioned to his men, who lowered their arms. "Yes, my lady. I am yours to command," he simpered.

She signaled Pilinger to wait a moment, and turned to confer with her people. Presently they produced a scroll, and Rose in turn passed it up to Pilinger. He examined it, not daring to read its contents, for Lady Rose had not permitted him to.

"This is a letter to my parents," she told him. "It is very person - al, very private, for it talks of my madness and the reprieve this pilgrimage has had on it. As you can see, I'm lacking the resources to get it to them quickly."

"Of course, my lady. My fastest horse." He snapped his fingers and one of the riders came forward. "Take this to Baron Tresville." He handed the message over. "See that no one breaks the seal upon it but Lord Tresville himself."

Rose grinned, for that was her seal. "My father might be away hunting," she added as an afterthought, "but my mother may read it as well."

The soldier saluted them both. "If that will be all, then?"

Pilinger waved him off. "Away to it, then."

The courier whirled his horse and galloped away in a cloud of dust.

"I have two other wishes," Rose said to Pilinger

"Anything, Lady, and I will grant them to you."

"One: don't bother me this trip. I am under strict orders from my healer not to do anything that taxes my mental health. And playing politics to my father's nobles taxes my mental health. Don't offer me your hospitality. Don't demand I not be allowed to pay for anything. Don't even come find me unless you're ready to act like a regular human being instead of some polished ass in a fancy metal suit."

Pilinger blinked his surprise.

"Two: and this is the most important one. Dismount, you and your men." There was a moment's hesitation before she waved her arms at them. "Dismount. Come on. You're keeping a lady waiting."

They scurried to do what they were told, and when they were settled, Rose said, "Good, now stand at the side of the road, this side, over here." She herded them and their horses off the road, and when they were all positioned to her liking, ignoring the strange looks that passed between them, she said, "Good. Now stand at attention." They all snapped to it. "Now stand there until one of you passes out."

Galadin and Tremel guffawed while her servants chuckled and giggled surreptitiously from behind their hands.

Rose glared at the frozen, despondent face of Lord Pilinger as she took the arm of her protector and led the way into Teemingdale.

"Put your swords away, Tremel."

"Yes My Lady," Tremel said as they passed the line of motion-less soldiers.

Galadin reversed the grip of his sword with his free hand and slid it into its sheath without so much as disturbing the lady upon his other arm. He glanced over at the soldiers waiting at attention as he passed.

Not one of them dared to look him in the eye.

It seemed to Rose that even the horses were laughing as she left Lord Pilinger and his soldiers behind.

"Oh, My Lord!" she called out over her shoulder, "that message requested my father's personal presence. He'll be inspecting every facet of your operations just as soon as he can get here!"

ഇരുന

Teemingdale was happy to see them, and happier still when stories of what she'd done reached their ears. The celebration of Rose's visit took place regardless of Lord Pilinger's absence. In fact, many more people were relieved than otherwise that he wasn't in attendance. Lady Rose and her group were met warmly. Soldiers approached her to swear their loyalty to her, thanking her for the lesson she had taught their haughty, pretentious lord.

She greeted them all equally cordially, although briefly, letting it be known she and her people were eager to leave Lord Pilinger's lands behind. And the people understood, snubbing their lord for the way he had behaved to such a kind and gentile lady.

There was a great procession that turned out to follow Rose to the boundary of Teemingdale that day, everyone wishing her well and good luck, and Godspeed on her quest to find peace. Such a plague of the mind could not have happened to a less deserving woman, they all agreed. And surely she would find the respite she so longed for.

"If not, Rose would be very welcome to come live in disguise amongst us until the monsters that tormented her in her royal life gave up and left her alone," they said as she left. Their compassion and kind words brought many a tear to Rose's eyes; it was a day she would not soon forget.

Once Teemingdale was out of sight, Rose's group promptly turned west. "Once this healer has been found, we can head directly south," Tremel told her. "There's no need to return through one of Pilinger's cities.

"By then my father will be keeping him more than busy enough," she reminded them. "We'll not be in any danger of crossing Pilinger's path. But still, your words have wisdom."

ೞೞ

Two more days of travel; of good company; of simple yet delicious fare roasted over a spit and washed down with hard brown ale. Two more days of tanning under the sun while her muscles grew lean and taut from the rigors of life on the road. Rose was laughing with her companions, when suddenly she stopped short and all mirth washed from her. The others grew quiet, stunned by the frightened way she stood, poised in the center of the road. She was like a deer on the verge of flight, frozen as if to camouflage herself amongst the company of her friends and loyal companions.

He stood at a distance in the shade of a tall glen. He was tall and blonde, clad in a tunic and forest green trousers. A black belt girded his tunic. A drawstring pouch hung about his neck, a small, functional dagger at his side, and his pack was slung carelessly over his shoulder. He stood with a disarming smile on his face, eyes glittering with wisdom in the sunlight.

But to Rose it was as if he'd brought the pitch of night with him, and that he stood before her, heralding her doom. The air about him shivered, as though he'd stepped out of the heat waves. It radiated from him, virtually sizzling with his presence. And if Rose stared at him too intensely, she could see in him every demon-phantom-creature that had ever haunted her; every monster from the otherworld who had plagued her steps in the dark; and every shade from her nightmares who'd followed her back to awakening, to take up residence in her tower.

"My lady?" Tremel asked, glancing from one to the other. His hand moved to his sword as Galadin moved to stand beside her.

"No," she said, placing an arm on each of them. "I must face him alone. He startled me, is all. I had almost forgotten why we

193

came." Then she stopped and looked around at her people. "You can see him too?"

"Of course they can!" the man called across the distance. "Come, Lady Rose. Let us speak together. You have traveled too far to be frightened off by the mere sight of me."

Rose bristled, but kept her thoughts to herself. He was right, of course, so with the safety of numbers she approached with her cluster of people, representatives from House Tresville.

When they were close enough not to need to shout to be heard, the man said, "Come forward, child; I would see into your eyes."

"Who addresses the heiress of Tresville as a child?" Galadin asked gruffly.

The man grinned. "Pardon my manners." He bowed. "I am Nivien, an Aigelendai of Light. I am the healer you have jour-neyed to find."

"The healer that was too good for the Lady to come to her cas-tle," Galadin reminded him.

"Hush, Galadin," Rose said quickly. "I would not have traded these days for my birthright. If this is the man who commanded such a remedy of me, then he is no enemy of mine." She moved forward and curtsied before the healer. "I am the Lady Rose, of House Tresville. I am at your service."

"Please, Lady, drop your courtesies. I have the misfortune of arriving at court from time to time. Please don't force me to play at that game here, not on such a glorious afternoon." He spread his arms to the horizons. "Let this be our page, our rules of eti-quette." He lowered his arms to his sides. "Besides, I frighten you. Your gentile manners will not hide that from me."

Rose sensed her people stirring indignantly, but held up a hand to silence them before the rebuke could come. "You see well, healer. Do you then know the cause of why I fear so?"

He glanced over at her entourage. "I must request your court leave us for a time." To them directly he said, "I must talk to Lady Rose of what troubles her, and I cannot do that with your ears upon our words."

Rose grew truly afraid then, but Nivien held out his hand. "Peace, child. I truly am of the Light. See." He pulled a shining green stone out of his pocket, a large piece that glowed with its own inner light. "Green for growth and green for regrowth; see how it would banish the darkness with its light?"

She was mesmerized by its beauty, the way it captivated her attention and soothed her at the same time. Rose was mute. She could only stare and nod her head in wonderment.

"I trust all of you will keep what you have seen this day the utmost secret," the Aigelendai warned. "For there are many who would silence your tongues at the price of your lives for witness-ing such a stone as this." He stared at all of them in turn, and then, convinced that Rose's servants understood the gravity of the situation, he replaced the stone in his pocket, to Rose's disap-pointment. "I must talk to her of what troubles her," the healer repeated.

Rose nodded to her companions and watched in silence as they withdrew to a discreet distance. Then she turned to the healer. "Aigelendai, is that some kind of healer's guild?"

Nivien grinned. "Of sorts. You cannot imagine how great you are, Lady Rose, how precious and sought after you are. There is so much I wish to say to you, yet I dare not reveal too much before its time."

"Before its time! If you have something to say, then say it, old man!" Rose hissed through her teeth.

Instead, Nivien seized her hand in both of his and kissed it. Then he pressed her hand to his forehead with such devotion that she could only watch in mute puzzlement as the Aigelendai paid

homage to her. He released her hand slowly and somewhat reluc -
tantly, and said earnestly, "Believe me when I say I am your heal -
er. I say what I must, I do what I must, to bring upon you such a
state of well-being that all that is in my power to do I do now,
before you, at my own selfish loss."

Rose was stunned. "You are a man of many surprises Nivien of
the Aigelendai," she declared. "Tell me, what must I do, then?"

"Tell me of your tormentors."

Something in the way he asked, the way he strangely reminded
Rose so much of the specters; and of the way he had shown her
the mysterious and wonderful stone, left no room for Rose to
believe Nivien could not understand what troubled her so.
Perhaps he too had been singled out by an unbelievable evil once.
But real or imaginary, Rose was sure the healer was familiar with
that which she spoke of, although she couldn't have explained the
reason for her certainty. So Rose told him everything, from the
time she was a little girl to the time she fled the forest and passed
out in Galadin's arms. And the telling of it took all afternoon.

The two made themselves comfortable in the shade of the trees
while they talked, Nivien interjecting with a question now and
again; but mostly Rose talked, growing more comfortable and
more hopeful at the possibility that maybe this man could finally
offer her real help.

At some point during the afternoon she remembered her people
and jumped to her feet, alarmed that they had been left standing
on the side of the road in the summer heat. But she had no need
for concern; they had settled in and made camp off to one side.
Her companions were laughing and relaxing, resting in the shade
of their tents, and there was no need for her to worry about them.

Galadin waved at her as soon as she rose to her feet, and she
waved back, reassured, before settling back onto the grass and
finishing her tale.

When she was finished, dusk was setting in, the heat was diminishing, and Rose suddenly realized she was hungry, and her throat was parched from speaking for so long. Nivien pulled a waterskin from his pack and handed it to her. "Drink," he said.

"It's not some drug that'll do something weird to me, is it?" Rose teased with a grin.

He returned the grin. "No My Lady. It's just water, just pure and simple water."

"I thank you sir," she said impishly. Nivien winced, and Rose ignored that as she drank long and deeply. She handed the skin back to him, asking, "Why do you hate being called, Sir?"

"You're very perceptive too," he replied. "Where I come from my people are divided into two extremes, good and evil. There is no middle ground, no neutrality or compromise with us. In the camp of evil they have such titles — kings and queens, and barons and lords. And sirs. And unfortunately, the most common of all is the designation, slave."

Now it was Rose's turn to wince.

"But in the camp of good there is only one title, which we all proudly bear."

"And what is that?"

"There is only servant."

Rose nodded. "I understand that," she said. "After travelling on the road, after being away from the castle and all its regalia, I do understand that."

"I knew you would." Nivien added mysteriously. "I had no doubt that you would." He stirred and rose to his feet, then helped her to her own, although Rose needed no assistance. Courtesy was a habit hard to be rid of, and each played the role of nobility as flawlessly as the other. That was something Rose would remember.

"There is something I would give to you," Nivien continued, offering her his arm. Rose took it and he led her out of her body - guard's line of view. He waved to Galadin and the guard stopped following, although he looked none too pleased with having his charge disappear from his sight once again. The glen where they were resting was a small one though, and Galadin could just make out their silhouettes through the trees. Satisfied, he crouched down to watch as best he could.

Content with their small measure of privacy, Nivien reached around his neck for the pouch and emptied the contents into his hand.

Rose gasped at the beauty he held. Seven glowing stones, each one a different color of the rainbow, were clustered in the palm of Nivien's hand. They radiated light much as the larger green one had; and together they combined to emit a pure white light that looked like a miniature star held in the palm of the healer 's hand.

"They are all equally special," Nivien said to her. "And although each one is different, for our purpose they are all the same. Please. Chose one for yourself. Although I recommend you not take the purple one. Something tells me you will soon come in to many such stones."

Rose glanced at him, confused. "I don't understand."

"This is your treatment, my lady." The healer gestured towards her. "Please, my gift to you, though small it truly is."

"I cannot," Rose protested.

"You must!" Nivien rasped. There was desperation in his voice. "You cannot turn your back on your gifts, or upon your experi - ences, for you teeter on the brink of madness and will fall unless you fight the shadows. But let it be known that when you return to your tormentors, that with this stone you will have light amid the deepest darkness." Then he reached forward and placed his hand on her head. He leaned towards Rose and whispered, "You will not be alone, for I send a friend to guide you. She will stay with you until you have the strength to stand on your own against the darkness."

With a wink, he added, "Even then, she may be difficult to get rid of!"

Rose gazed into the healer's eyes for a long moment, weighing his words.

"You see to the truth in ways that escape even me," Nivien murmured.

"I shall chose the yellow one, then." She reached forward and plucked the stone from his hand, and the healer closed his fist over the remainder. The light diminished and he replaced the stones in the pouch, then the pouch around his neck.

"All is well, then," Nivien said quietly. Abruptly, he turned his back to her and headed off into the distance.

"That's it?" Rose called after the healer. "Won't you stay – please – and share a meal with us?"

Without turning around, Nivien called back,"I cannot, My Lady! There is much sickness in this world, many lives to touch and to heal."

"Without even a goodbye?" Rose begged, close to tears.

Nivien stopped and turned to face her, his eyes filled with compassion and something else that Rose couldn't identify. "Didn't you know, Lady Rose? The Aigelendai don't believe in goodbyes."

"Will I see you again?" Her voice trembled with emotion.

The healer simply grinned and waved. "Until we meet again, My Lady! And we will, you have my promise." This time, when he turned towards the road, Rose knew she could not coax him to turn back.

She waved anyway, knowing that he would not see her gesture farewell. "Goodbye, Nivien the Healer!" she called after him, letting her bittersweet tears flow freely. "You always have a place of honor at Castle Tresville!"

Nivien roared out in laughter, glanced over his shoulder at Rose, laughed again and slapped his knee in amusement, then continued on his way, chortling until the sound faded from her ears.

Only when the healer was a mere speck on the horizon did Rose look long and hard at her stone before finally pocketing it and hurrying to meet her friends for dinner.

ဆာလ

That night, as the moon hung low on the horizon and her friends were fast asleep in their bedrolls about her, Rose lay slumbering in a world of her own. Vivid memories clung to her senses, filling her mind with a multitude of scents and sensations; once again awakening the visions, the horror.

Rose was in her bed chamber in the castle, sitting up in her bed with her knees pulled tightly to her chest. Her eyes were huge orbs as she stared out at the shadows on the circular stone wall, shadows held back merely by the light of a single candle. Nervous, she chewed absently on a lock of midnight- black hair as her eyes remained unblinking, waiting, waiting for the horror to creep up and overtake her.

When they came, hideous and malicious monsters, they some-how resembled the fair-featured healer Nivien, with their eyes and their complexion, their build. They poured out of the shadows like sewage from a drain hole, to pollute Rose's room with their foul, hateful breaths, their raucous laughs and their taunts. "Lady Rose! Lady Rose! Today is the day, Lady Rose!" they jeered through giant fangs or from under doglike snouts. Then they would swagger towards her and slap her in the face.

Rose would shriek, cover her stinging cheek, and then they would strike the other, or rake her back with their claws, or pinch and twist her flesh cruelly between their icy fingers. One brute, the skeleton Sir Ridney had appeared to her as, stalked towards Rose, grabbed her roughly by the hair and forced her to look into his sunken eye sockets. He grasped her hair more firmly, and through gritted teeth hissed as he mocked her. "Do you like what you see, my lady?" He sneered. "Do you like your servants to appear this way!"

Rose sobbed, although it was hard with her neck distended as it was.

The specter flung her face down upon the bed and lashed her viciously across the back with a length of leather.

She cried out at each sting of the whip, but he ignored Rose's pleas for mercy, as did the rest of the castle. Finally the phantom stood back, pleased with his handiwork. He turned to his cohorts. "What else should we do to her this night?" he asked.

Weakly, Rose lifted her head in time to see the ghouls leering as they crowded towards her.

Abruptly Rose sat up and shuddered, memories of the horror fresh in her mind.

Shivering, her eyes flashed around her, but the atmosphere was calm and soothing, void of the demons such that had plagued her life with torture and anguish. Galadin watched Rose with concern from where he had been dozing on the other side of the firepit.

"Just another nightmare," she whispered quietly, lest she awaken the others. She threw back her bedroll, pulled on her boots, and brought out the yellow stone from her pack. Shielding the light of the stone with her left hand, she crept over to where Galadin lay and unsheathed a long dagger from the plethora of arms he kept on his weapons' belt. "Go back to sleep," Rose murmured. "I will be fine." She hefted his dagger, more a short sword than anything, a copy of the weapon of her choice. Galadin was reassured; afterall, he had seen the way she fought with the weapon, had in fact, helped teach her how to use it.

He nodded. "Don't go far."

Rose pointed to a quiet spot away from the others, where a stream had cut a wide swathe through the fields. "I'll be down there."

Galadin nodded again. "I will stay awake until you return," he vowed. Then he rested his head against his balled-up cloak and stared up at the stars. "I will think of my wife and children." He grinned.

Rose chuckled and crept away silently. Crouching low to the ground, she made her way stealthily across the moonlit field and slid down the bank to the creek, out of sight of the camp and her friends.

Safely alone, she sat down on the stony beach of the bank, lowered her head into her hands, and began to weep, softly, so as not to alert the others to her anguish.

Rose remained like that for some time, in the silence of the night, quietly sobbing her grief away. But the palm of her hand became warm with the inner heat of the extraordinary stone she held, which eventually distracted her from her tears. Intrigued, she lifted her head and opened her hand. A yellow light engulfed her in a cocoon, as if she were totally contained within a golden teardrop.

She felt the comfort, the closeness of the light, like a warm cloak on a winter's day, and realized that no tormentor from the shadow world of her mind could penetrate this shield of safety, or pierce through its revealing light, its smoldering warmth. Her soul felt sheltered and safe; and Rose rested her head against the bank of the creek, closed her eyes and basked in its healing effect. Galadin's short blade slipped to the ground at her side. But

Rose remained motionless, eternally grateful to and amazed with the healer Nivien.

Sounds of someone shuffling down the bank alerted her. Instinctively, Rose picked up the dagger and jumped to her feet, holding the stone high over her head for light.

A girl-woman stood before her. The style of her apparel suggested she was a peasant, yet the quality of the clothing bespoke royalty. She wore a vivid green tunic and matching boots, with a girdle seemingly spun from silver thread. The tunic was much too long, coming down to her knees, and she wore it like a dress. A pair of matching green leggings completed her outfit. Her hair was blonde, like Priscilla's, although much longer, caught up in a ponytail and fastened with a silver ribbon that shimmered in the moonlight. At her side was a short sword much like the one Rose held up before her, only this one was infinitely better crafted. The hilt glowed in the darkness, the same yellow hue as the stone Rose held. The sheath was also made of the yellow stone, and Rose's attention was drawn towards the exquisite blade, fascinated by its rugged beauty.

Rose forced herself to stay focused on the girl-woman's eyes. She had strong cheekbones, and a proud, flawless bearing. Young, perhaps in her mid-teens, with chest and hips that were only beginning to develop into a woman's, her eyes in comparison were old and wise and shrewd, perhaps even a little angry. Her manner of authority and maturity belied her age, far beyond the years of one so youthful.

Their eyes locked for a moment before the intruder spoke. "Nivien sent me."

Rose did not believe her. This girl-woman had the look of Nivien, which meant she also bore a resemblance to the creatures at the castle. "Why did you wait to catch me alone?" she demanded.

The girl-woman shrugged. "The others you are with may not be able to see me," she replied.

Rose snarled and lunged, thrusting her sword straight towards the intruder's heart.

The girl-woman danced back, leaned away, and by the time Rose had withdrawn her sword for another strike, had her own blade out and in her hand in one fluid motion. Their swords clashed once, twice, then a third time as Rose drove the offensive. Then Rose reversed her tactics and brought her blade stabbing upward under the intruder's guard. But where the blade should have pierced her midsection, she had vanished into thin air! But no, thought Rose, not quite. The girl-woman had simply become a glowing green speck of light, suspended in the air before Rose.

Convinced this creature was a simply a phantom of her own mind, Rose growled. But enveloped in the light of the stone, she felt fearless, confident. If Rose could not escape her nightmares, perhaps she could win herself free of them.

Fearlessly, she leaned forward and peered at the green fleck of light. Only half as tall as Rose's thumb, there floated the girl-woman, tiny wings fluttering to keep her buoyant in the air. She still grasped her yellow sword, although the expression in her eyes told Rose she knew it was useless at her present size. But she also knew that Rose could not touch her either and so she held her ground, glaring at Rose angrily.

"What are you?" Rose inquired, blinking rapidly a couple of times, wide-eyed with wonder.

The miniaturized girl sheathed her sword. "I am Penia," she said. Then, in a blur of green and yellow light, she rematerialized into a more human form. She was as large as Rose now, and slightly transparent with green butterfly wings. She floated effortlessly, as though suspended in water. "I am an Aigelendai of Light." Her transparency and wings faded away, and a very solid

204

young woman stepped forward and curtsied. "I am at your serv-ice, Lady Rose."

Rose reversed her grip on Galadin's dagger. Penia remained motionless before her, and after a moment, Rose lowered the weapon and returned the curtsy. Then her composure fell away and Rose collapsed into the otherworldly creature's arms and sobbed. "I've been alone for so long," she cried softly. "I could not believe that you were actually here to help me!"

Penia held her at arms' length. The sword at her side and the stone in Rose's hand illuminated the smile on the ethereal being's face. "Let us change that," she said. "The others can see me like this. Perhaps it is time to bring them one step closer to your world."

"My world … my world is one of nightmares and demons, and unspeakable horror and shame," wept Rose.

Penia's smile never left her face but her eyes glinted dangerous-ly. She repeated, "We shall have to change that as well."

The two young women turned to look across the fields as the sun began to rise.

"Come," smiled Penia. "Introduce me to your other servants." She turned towards the bank, and together she and Rose climbed up onto the field and headed back to camp.

ℰꙄꙄ

Galadin rose to his feet when he saw them, illuminated by the light of the rising sun, the sword and the yellow stone. He stepped carefully over his sleeping companions, his eyes never leaving Penia. "My Lady," he protested to Rose, "I do not advise … "

"Hush Galadin, she is here as a guide." She handed his dagger back. "I do not need this, not with Penia by my side."

He stiffened as if insulted. "Lady Rose, if you would allow me to … "

Rose touched her guard's arm gently. "Galadin," she hastened to reassure him, "all is not as it seems." She glanced at Penia. "She is not human."

Penia grinned at Galadin while he stared fiercely back at her.

"She comes from the world within my head."

"I do not see how that is possible, my lady." His eyes never left the intruder. And as his voice rose, the others began to stir from their sleep.

"That is because the world does not come from your lady's head," Penia said boldly, raising her chin as she spoke.

Their conversation brought the others awake and they moved to rise, rubbing their eyes and stretching their arms and yawning. All eyes were on Penia.

She turned and addressed the group. "There are greater things at work here than anything you could possibly imagine." She looked over at Rose. "And more is at stake now than just one noble - woman.

"You all have been made privy to some of the greatest secrets in the kingdom." She held out her sword. "This sword, this stone, our Lady's apparent 'madness'. These speak of things beyond what we are meant to hear. But here we are, and here she is." Penia paused and gazed intently at Rose. "As impossible as it seems, here she is."

"I am not here to harm you," Penia looked around as she contin - ued, "nor to frighten you in any way. But as you give our Lady strength in this world, I am here to give her strength in another one. For as you are of this world … " She closed her eyes, crossed her arms over her chest, and stepped back with a bow. Suddenly Penia faded before their very eyes into nothingness, reappearing moments later as Rose had seen her earlier, hovering in the air, her green wings fluttering delicately. This time though, she was as tall as the length of Galadin's arm. Penia opened her eyes and stared at Rose's people, daring them to see her. "I am most definitely of another world," she announced.

Then she vanished altogether.

There was a long silence while everyone stared at the space Penia had inhabited and digested her words. "My Lady, you are not crazy!" one of Rose's ladies-in-waiting finally declared.

"Thank you, Kamania. I needed to hear that."

"The healer has sent you an angel!" Tremel announced.

"Where did she go!" another asked.

"Why, she is right here!" Rose asserted. Then she remembered what Penia had told her and turned her head. "They can not see you, Penia. Why?"

"I exist between the worlds now, My Lady. Nor can they hear me, for I am neither here nor there, and only one who belongs in both worlds may see me as I am when I am."

"Why me? Why do I see you?"

"There is a time for all questions to be answered, My Lady. Here is not the time for that one." She stepped forward and uncrossed her arms, and instantly reappeared in solid form. "Now I am in this world." Then her transparency returned. "Now I am in neither."

"Where is this other world?" Rose asked.

Penia re-emerged so the companions could see her. "It is all around us, My Lady. It is far away and close at hand. It is … I do not know, My Lady. It is here and there at the same time. In truth, it is not another world but another realm, the Fire Realm, it is called. And like fire, it is both substantial and not. I have not been there for many, many years. I am here now to help put right the damage the dark Tenlenesse have done to this realm when they were driven from mine."

"Dark Tenlenesse?"

"The evil ones, My Lady, the shadows in your mind; that is what they are called." She eyed Rose carefully. "They are the ones that cannot look you in the eyes for long when they disguise themselves in human form. And they are the ones who take hideous forms when they travel between the two realms, as I do."

Rose growled. "They are not."

"I am sorry to say it, My Lady, but they are one and the same. The nobles, the guards, the cooks, the servants, the slaves; who - ever they may appear to be in your household, they are tormen - tors, jailers, rapists and torturers."

"How dare you speak such filth!" one of Rose's servants cried. "In the company of such fine nobility at that!"

Rose looked at her servant, long and hard, but the woman did not flinch or look away. "Why do you think I brought you along?" she asked.

"It's like that? Truly, it is that terrible?" Tremel asked, shock evident in his expression.

Rose looked at him. "Truly. It is much more terrible than that."

"Then let us dally on our way back," he told her. "Let us take our time and let you learn all you may from this ... " he motioned towards Penia, at a loss for words.

"Aigelendai," Penia told him. "It is a world, like human. It means 'stolen angelism.'"

"Stolen?" Rose asked. "Why stolen?"

"My ancestors were once human like yours, My Lady, but from a time when all humans were immortal. Twenty people stole immortality for themselves, and their offspring became the children of twenty new races that inhabited the five realms of Mishard. Out of all of them, the Aiglendai were the most like angels, although the Trilians are perhaps truer in their likeness."

Galadin stepped closer to Penia. "She makes light of your situation, Lady Rose, talking about inconsequential things when terrible people have been tormenting you all of your life."

Penia glared at him and her hand moved instinctively to her short sword. "You have no idea what she's been through," she spat. "You have no idea what lives between the fire and the surface realm, what manner of nightmare takes asylum from the eyes of both realms. In all other realms the divider between there and here is definite and sudden. You are in the water, or you are not. You are in the air, or you are not. You are in the earth, in a cave, or you are not. But with the fire, it takes a moment before the flames catch you. And what a terrible place it is when everyone around you thinks its not even real." She unsheathed her weapon and held it out before him, to let him study the glowing yellow stone. "And when this is around it is often a crowded place indeed. This stone is what allows the Netherlands to exist. This stone is what keeps it alive, and it is this stone that attracts those greedy creatures to our Lady's household."

She sheathed her sword in a graceful motion that impressed even Galadin. "Let it be known to this group of people that there is much of this stone underneath your master's castle. He knows it is there, and he forges weapons with it such as this one. It is as purple as our Lady's stone is yellow. And it is the greatest secret amongst the human nobles." Her gaze swept across them all. "Do not let this secret be known, even to your own families. By doing so, you endanger the life of your Lady Rose." She turned and bowed towards Rose. "To my Lady Rose."

Turning back to look at the companions, Penia continued, "and a hundred times again, do not let it be known about the fire realm, or any of the others, for that matter. Do not speak of it, even to each other, nor shall I remind you of the place by show-ing off my inhuman qualities." She smiled.

"From this moment on, I am simply the nurse, Penia, come along to serve in the Tresville household as Lady Rose's personal caregiver." Penia stopped talking and gave a little shrug before adding, "I hope that didn't sound too rehearsed."

Galadin guffawed and clapped the lithe Penia on her shoulder, almost knocking her over. She recovered quickly though, and stuffed her hands into her tunic pockets. "I am Galadin," he intro-duced himself, nodding towards Rose. "Her protector."

"And friend," Rose added, taking him by the arm. "All those here are my closest friends and companions in this life. We are a very informal team when we are alone. Let not our undisciplined ways fool you, though. Everyone knows his or her part when we are in public. I can be quite the dictator when I have to be, and he the … um … boot-licker. In truth though, we are equals; and the roles we play are nothing between us, like actors who need a reprieve from rehearsal to share a tankard of ale amongst them-selves following a performance."

Penia nodded. "It is much the same in the … in the other place. I shall get along fine in your company, if you would have me. For I too know the play you are at."

"I'm sure you know more than one role," Rose commented drily.

Penia gave her a tight smile and shrugged. "Warrior, maid, nurse, lady: what are they all if not — "

"Servant," Rose cut her off. "Nivien explained it to me. Come, join us for some food. Let us get to know our otherworldly com-panion, and she us." Rose turned Galadin around and gently pushed him towards the now-dead fire, where her other friends were still staring in silence.

"Please, Lady Rose," protested Penia. "Let us not speak of those things. I am simply your nursemaid, Penia. It is better to put all else from our minds altogether, better to preserve the secrets we must keep."

"But there is much I must learn."

"Indeed there is," Penia agreed. "And much that you must see for yourself, for you have greatness in you, a greatness that will not lie dormant much longer, I should think. But all that will come in time, in its appointed time and its appointed form. I am a bit of a healer myself. Let me be your guide in this."

Rose nodded. "As you wish… My Lady."

Penia chuckled and rolled her eyes. "Starting now."

"Yes, Penia." Rose struggled not to giggle.

"Thank you."

ॐ

On the journey home Penia worked to strengthen the illusion that she was human. At first she would slip-up and grow hazy around the edges, or some of her mannerisms were much too refined for a simple nursemaid. But everyone was quick to point out when she went invisible, or acted like a Royal. Eventually Penia grew accustomed to her role as a member of Rose's entourage. The one thing she did not part with was her gleaming sword, although she wrapped it carefully in coarse linen and concealed it under her tunic.

Neither did she give up her sword work. While the others raised and dismantled camp, Penia spent the time drilling herself with one of Galadin's short swords. At first the others were disgruntled by her behavior, thinking she was shirking her share of the work. But Galadin and Tremel were quick to quiet any protests.

"My Lady?" Tremel asked Rose one night. "I realize this may be inappropriate, and normally I would not dare to ask such a boon of you." The companions, upset by Penia's lack of assistance with regular chores, looked from where she was drawing Galadin's blade back to Tremel. "Please Lady Rose," Tremel requested, "shoulder mine and Galadin's weight this night, as you have already borne the chores that rightfully belong to your nursemaid. Allow us instead to study her movements with the blade. There is much we need to learn in her footwork and in her form."

Galadin stepped in with his plea. "We ask leave to watch the — to watch the nurse. Please, Lady Rose, just leave our share of the work here, and let us accomplish it once she is finished."

Rose glanced towards Penia. "Go," she said. "She has just start - ed. I will see the work gets done."

"Thank you My Lady," Tremel said, and darted off towards Penia.

"My lady," Galadin added, with a nod. Then he too was gone.

"Just teach me all you can!" Rose called after them.

After that the others did not begrudge Penia her practice. "She always does what is best for our Lady," the women commented while chatting among themselves one afternoon.

"Even though it's definitely different than whatever we could do," another one of them added.

And it was true. One night, after a long, enjoyable day of walk - ing and conversing with each other, Galadin — ever alert when it came to Rose's safety — suddenly stirred and awoke to find Penia hunched over Rose's sleeping form. She looked up at him and put a finger to her lips and he sat back to watch what she was doing. He had not a long wait before Rose woke up with a start. She was sweating and there was a terror in her eyes as she sat up and looked around wildly.

Penia handed her a wineskin. "Drink slowly," she instructed. "It is laced with herbs that help to relax."

"I do not want to be drugged."

"Do not worry, my lady. It is only a mild relaxant. It will wear off before the sun rises. But it will also make your head spin if you drink it too fast."

Rose took the wine. "Thank you, Penia. How did you know?"

"You forgot the horror today. When it comes back, it comes back suddenly."

"And how long have you been sitting there?"

"Since you fell asleep. I knew when you went to sleep that you had not remembered the darkness. So I had to take up vigilance and be here when you woke. Do you wish to sit in the light of the sword and the stone?"

Rose shook her head as she drank. "I am not alone. That is enough." She glanced over at Galadin and gave him a brave smile. "And besides, she added, "I have two protectors this night."

Galadin smiled back, then lay down and left the two women to each other's company while he fell asleep.

꙳

By the time they reached Castle Tresville, Penia had been inte-grated into Rose's inner circle so thoroughly and completely, so comfortably, that the others could not imagine what it must be like without her. In truth, the journey had changed them as much as it had Rose. They all seemed much more formal and ceremoni-al when they came face-to-face with the Baron and Baroness. Tremel and Galadin saluted and stood at attention with more crispness and discipline. The ladies curtsied low, their words and manners oozing sincerity. The servants and maidservants knew their places and their duties, and jumped to do Rose's bidding before she even asked anything of them. And Lady Rose held her head high and proud. She did not flinch, nor did she cringe from her parents. And gone, too, was the mad urgency in her eyes, the desperation that had been evident for so long.

She leveled her parents with a calm, unblinking gaze, and curt-sied with all the formality that was due their position. "Mother, father," Rose announced. "I have returned from my pilgrimage. I believe the healer Nivien has cured me of my madness."

"How can that be?" Baron Tresville began.

Feonna placed a hand on Jason's arm. "Daughter, who is this who stands at your side, dressed in the garb of a man, with the hair of a noblewoman, and one of Galadin's swords strapped to her side?"

Penia kept her head lowered like a servant, waiting for Rose to speak for her.

"This is my maidservant, mother. Nivien appointed her to me. She is a nurse and specializes in my condition. She is here to assure I remain sane in… " She looked around the crowded halls. "Under these conditions."

Jason nodded and sighed. "And this sanity can withstand these walls the way they are?"

"I believe it can, father. You have no need to be alarmed. I can perform my social duty as your heiress now; more so, in fact, for I know the burden that duty entails."

The Baron swallowed his discomfort. "That is good then, daughter. Welcome home." He held his arms out to her and embraced her while his household looked on.

"Father, I have a request."

He pulled away and looked down at her. "Anything, daughter. What is it?"

"I ask that the maidservant's belongings be brought to my tower, and that a place be made for her in the chamber above my own."

"In the chamber above your own!" There was one room in the tower higher than Rose's own room. She would have taken it, as her station permitted, but Rose had always been too afraid to be cut off in the tower, with no place to run. This way, at least her nightmares had to barricade both flights of stairs, and so divide their strength while assaulting her. Yet it was an honored place to be awarded, at the top of a tower, with the peaked and vaulted ceiling overhead.

"Yes father. My nurse has many things that must be closely guarded, many secrets that keep my disorder in check. I would not have her room accidentally invaded by a cleaning maid, or overrun by servants and ladies on their way to my own chambers. Let her instead take shelter behind my chambers, for there are many confidences that must be kept and all those who enter my chambers would respect the gravity of such." Rose stepped back and her eyes turned to meet Dalia's.

The stewardess was taken off guard, caught in the act of raising her voice to protest. She nervously cleared her throat and said, "My Lord, My Lady, I protest such an act. It is improper to put a servant, a lowly nursemaid, in such grand quarters. Let her instead be placed at the base of the tower, where there are many rooms for the woman to lock her things in."

Rose snarled and heaved herself away from her father. Her fingers flexed as they itched to take a sword in hand. She pushed straight through the crowd, never taking her eyes from Dalia, who began to look around wildly for a place to retreat.

Rose grabbed the stewardess by the throat and pressed her up against the wall, glaring straight into Dalia's terrified eyes. "If you ever question my authority again, I'll have your tongue removed!" She forced her hand deeper against Dalia's throat, thrusting the woman's head against the stones to emphasize each word. "And if I ever catch you in my tower again I'll kill you myself." She leaned closer to Dalia's ear and whispered hoarsely, "Tenlenesse. I mark you, witch."

Lady Rose straightened and turned to address the court. "Penia is no normal servant! Her wealth is beyond measure, her manner-isms beyond refined. She is a maid because she makes herself a maid, not because she was born one. She deserves the honor, and she will have it. She is here as an ambassador to ensure the House Of Tresville remains stable during my reign, until the time my children may prove to be free of the condition that has plagued me for so long."

"To question her will is to question the integrity of House Tresville, our banner. Do you understand me?" Rose's voice rang out clearly with new-found authority.

"Rose!" Feonna rebuked, shocked at her elder daughter's almost ferocious air of command. "Mind your manners!"

"DO YOU UNDERSTAND!" Rose screeched at her servants, in particularly at those who could not look directly at her, as others did, in amazement.

Surprisingly, one by one, they kneeled before Lady Rose as a sign of obedience. The Baron and Baroness and their younger daughter watched with awe-struck wonder this newly-improved heiress of the barony.

"We understand you, daughter," Feonna murmured, speaking for them all.

Rose shot Dalia one last murderous glance, then turned back to her mother, spread her arms wide and a smile beamed on her face. "Mother!" she cried. "It is so good to be home!"

∞∞∞

Penia could make herself invisible without actually turning invisible. What she struggled to do around Rose's friends she reveled in when amongst people who cared nothing about her, or with those who Rose had no qualms against misleading. Lady Feonna came to understand that Penia knew of the mines beneath Castle Tresville, but the young woman was a mouse. She rarely spoke, and rarely gave any indications of needing to speak. The few times that Lady Feonna had tried to reach out to her and make sure the girl was comfortable with her new role, Penia had answered with cold formality that she genuinely was at peace with her lot in life and that Lady Feonna need not worry.

Finally, Lady Feonna put to rest her fears when she caught Rose and Penia alone in a hallway, for the two never went anywhere except together. "Daughter," said Lady Feonna, "I believe it is time I show you what makes you so ill." Neither Penia nor Rose looked at all surprised by this declaration, so she continued. "I would have a few words alone with your nursemaid, though."

Rose glanced at Penia, who nodded assent, then said, "As you wish, mother. I'll wait down the hall." She and Penia nodded to each other — as equals, it seemed to Feonna — and then Rose was gone, to wait a discreet distance down the hall.

Lady Feonna did not know where to begin, but Penia seemed to drop her charade as nursemaid and looked boldly into the Baroness's eyes, seeming to look right through her. "Your fears and doubts are carefully hidden, My Lady," Penia said coolly, "but I understand them. I myself am daughter to one such as you."

"One such as I?"

"Of station, whose daughter is plagued by terrible nightmares. I became a healer once I was healed myself, to repay the kindness to others like me."

"These are words, just words," Lady Feonna replied. "Can you at least tell me of the house you come from? Or of that which drove you mad?"

Penia shook her head. "I cannot, as you know. I cannot speak of what would endanger my family, for it is not in my authority to go against the vows of secrecy I have kept. But I can show you that which is mine." She reached behind her and unfastened a cord under her tunic. Her sword dropped into her hand and she pulled it out in front of Feonna and unwrapped it.

Lady Feonna's eyes opened wide when she saw the sword. "It's yellow!"

"Penia!" Rose cried. "No!" She raced towards them.

"Hush sister," soothed Penia. "She has seen much more than this, I assure you."

"But she — "

"Rose!" Penia warned, looking up at her Lady. Rose skidded to a halt. "She is your mother! She does not know foe from friend, but she is your greatest ally in this place. This I have seen!"

Rose was cowed into silence and reluctantly bowed her head. "It is as you wish, then."

Lady Feonna stared at her daughter. "Come then, daughter," she sighed. "There is nothing more I need hide from either of you."

Rose stood by Penia's side and said, "I don't know how she knows, but Penia knows what is built below the vaults of Castle Tresville."

The Baroness touched the sword in Penia's hand. "I am not at all surprised by this, only by the yellow stone it's made from. For I have only ever seen green, purple and dark blue. I have heard of the sky blue stone and dreamt of the red ones and pray red exists."

Penia nodded and set to work concealing her magnificent weapon. "It is that way with our yellow."

"Our yellow?"

"I swear you to secrecy, mother, as you have trusted me with it." Rose showed her the yellow stone. "It is what keeps me sane. Nivien said I cannot escape what makes me ill, but I must have light to face the darkness. So he gave me this."

"He gave it to you!"

"What is it you want from us, Lady Feonna?" Penia crossed her arms.

"It seems my daughter has made some powerful allies, and I am very proud of her for that."

"My lady, do not speak of what you do not understand," Penia warned.

Lady Feonna bridled. "I understand a mother's love all too well," she said. "I understand my daughter stands here proud and brave, where once she cowered in the corner and wept. I under-stand that her servants, a small group of you, surround and pro-tect her throughout all hours of the watch. I understand that never is she anywhere without two or three of you, from the lowliest washerwoman to the noblest lady-in-waiting; from the timid woodcutter to the captain of the guard and the champion of my husband's men. And I understand that she inspires such loyalty, such trust, such an unusual love amongst you chosen few, that the inhabitants of the castle dare not speak ill of her, nor challenge anything she may say, either openly or behind closed doors." Lady Feonna glanced briefly at her daughter before turning back to Penia.

"I have never inspired such devotion amongst my own servants, nor has anyone I've ever known. Rumors still drift back to us from her pilgrimage on the road. People talk about Rose, and her ability to see into the heart of a matter and speak justice into that place. If there is something more I have not yet grasped, I do not intend to speak of it, Lady Penia. But I will do what I can to guard its secrets, even from mine own husband the Baron, if need be. The Lady Rose is my daughter, and I am still her greatest ally, although perhaps not the most powerful."

Penia bowed her head. "Forgive my words, Baroness. It is just that I am on guard around so much spectral stone, being worked and forged as it is. It is powerful enough when it is left alone. But brought alive and aggravated like this … " She shook her head. "It is enough to make me start swinging my sword."

Rose turned to Penia. "I know exactly what you mean!"

"Would it matter, then, if I showed it to the two of you?"

"Not at all, Lady."

"Then come with me. Let me show you the secret that you both know more about than I."

§০৫

Lady Feonna led them through courtyards and barns, through kitchens and storehouses, through basements Rose had never thought to explore, and through a maze of tunnels with secret passages. Rose was thoroughly lost long before they came to their journey's end, and she clutched Penia's arm for comfort. The three women kept silent until they finally stopped before a narrow stone door at the end of one of the tunnels. Lady Feonna pushed firmly against it, and it opened under her weight. A gust of warm air blew across their faces and Penia stiffened and clung to Rose as fearfully as Rose had clung to her earlier.

"Guard your eyes," Penia whispered fiercely. "Nothing else matters but your eyes. Don't let them see your eyes."

Feonna turned back to them, slightly amused at the looks of fear she saw on their faces. "It is not all that bad," she murmured. "It's just a mine, after all." Penia looked at Rose and shook her head. It wasn't just a mine.

"This way." The Baroness ducked under the doorway, and Rose and Penia followed.

They entered a normal-sized room with a table and chairs in it. One of the guards was at the table, adding figures with ink and a quill. When he saw Rose and Penia, he glowered and rose to his feet. Lady Rose glanced at him. It was Ridly, the guard who had seemingly turned into a skeleton that time when she had gone without sleep; the phantom nightmare that had beaten her so many times in the night.

Rose averted her eyes immediately as she was led from the room through a door on the other side. This one opened into a vast pit, a huge chamber supported by giant archways that spanned the length and width of the castle. Rose stared up at the architecture in amazement, at the sheer magnitude of it.

"That is the great hall," Lady Feonna pointed it out to them with pride. "The walls of the hall run parallel with the sides of the pit, so as not to put extra weight on the arches."

The pit was a crevice with pathways cut into its sides, and was crawling with people, miners. There was no torch in the room, yet it gleamed with a purple light, from the tiny flecks of stone in the rocks along its sides and scattered along the floor far below. Even Penia seemed impressed by the extent of the operations.

"This way, then," Feonna said lightly, and virtually skipped away along the side of the pit, secure in the safety of the makeshift rope handrail.

They followed and were escorted along a stone tunnel. Glimmers of purple stone glittered from its walls. Rose and Penia were greatly relieved to be well away from that vast empty space of the pit. Their initial fear of being tossed over the side by a

guard or other entity subsided the further they distanced themselves from its edge.

But that fear came rushing back when Lady Nimway suddenly
stepped into their path, a cruel smile distorting her face. She
stood in front of a vast forge. Huge gusts of steam and billows of
smoke rolled along the ceiling and then disappeared up the vents
above their heads.

"The smoke!" Rose cried, recognizing the source of the darkness that hung about her tower on cold days.

"Your eyes!" Penia hissed, and Rose abruptly quieted, her eyes
downcast.

"So, Lady Feonna! You have brought the little one and her pet
into the very heart of it all!"

The Baroness seemed oblivious to the anger that edged Lady
Nimway's voice, or her obvious sarcasm. But to Rose and Penia it
was as if Lady Nimway had just declared open warfare. "How
delightful!" she crooned.

Rose's grip on Penia's arm did not slacken as Lady Feonna
turned to regard her elder daughter with pride. "I thought it was
time, Lady Nimway. Lady Rose has proven her strength, her command of the 'above'. She's earned her right to the 'below', I
believe."

"Has she indeed!" Lady Nimway mocked with an exaggerated
smile. She snapped her fingers and Dalia came forward with a
large clay bowl. Inside were nuggets of the purple stone. "Here
children," Nimway insisted, shoving the bowl towards Rose and
Penia. "Let this be a day of celebration. Take a piece of the stone,
each of you. Let it serve to remind you of the first day you saw
this place and the feelings it inspired." It was obvious that both
young women were terrified, but Dalia came forward and knelt in
front of Rose and Penia.

"My Lady and her maidservant may take any stone they choose," Dalia said. She glanced over at the Baroness to be sure she wasn't watching, then hissed at Penia. "Aigelendai! You little insect! You filth! May this stone always keep you near the Netherworld, where shadow and darkness rule!"

Lady Feonna remained oblivious as she conversed with Lady Nimway.

Penia lifted her head in defiance and took a stone at random. Rose followed her friend's lead and also chose one indiscriminately. "I will keep this stone with pride," Penia pledged, "for it is the second of seven that mark me a healer of the spectral realms. And not just because it keeps me close to the place where your kind have fled to. It also keeps me close to the heart of the Fire Realm, that clean, bright world of laughter and moonfire, where none lock their doors and all carry arms against the memory of injustice and deceit, of wickedness and self-servitude." She stared at Dalia, unflinching, and such a look of horror came over the stewardess's face, that Rose could only watch the confrontation in amazement.

"You would never dare such words in the Netherlands!" Dalia spat.

"I am an Aigelendai, remember? I always have one foot in the Netherlands. I pass in and out of that place daily, a shadow on your wall, a gust of wind against your face."

Dalia gasped and spun around as she sprang to her feet.

"What was that about?" Rose whispered to Penia.

"The place between the realms is where I go when I turn invisible. To me it is a glove I put on, but to them it is like a vast ocean they must plunge into. They stay in groups so as not to grow separate and lose their way for huge stretches of time. Where I go to rest, they go only when their strength is at their greatest, never daring to roam far into it, lest they be burned by what awaits on the other side. I love the Fire Realm, and restrain myself from going there often only because I grow stronger by staying here."

"And the stone?"

"The stone opens the portal between the two realms and the Netherlands. Without the stone, one can not bridge the distance between the two realms, although they may travel halfway into the Netherlands if they know how."

The Baroness had stopped talking to Lady Nimway and turned with satisfaction to look at her daughter. Rose stood watching, her new spectral stone cupped in her hand. "Do you wish to see more?" asked Lady Feonna.

"No mother. I don't." She hefted the stone in her hand and glanced briefly towards Lady Nimway and Dalia. "Thank you for this, though. It will be a light in the darkness of my mind, a place of refuge when madness threatens me again," she added silkily.

Feonna beamed, but Lady Nimway and Dalia scowled.

"May I too know the blessings of this stone, and the realms of possibility it opens up to me!" continued Lady Rose. "Still, so much industry makes me edgy, and without my nursemaid's constant treatment, I am afraid this place would drive me quite out of my mind." She nodded towards the smoke. "It is the smoke, you see. So much of it, and I grow afraid of the memories."

Lady Feonna inclined her head. "As you wish, daughter. Come, then. Let us leave this place and toast to your initiation."

As the Baroness passed, Rose withdrew the cloth bag she kept her yellow stone in and dropped the purple one into it as well. "Thank you for this," she said sweetly to Lady Nimway and Dalia.

Dalia gave Rose a venomous smile, but Lady Nimway merely said, "It is customary. And it changes nothing."

Penia, too, hid the stone on her person. "The lines are drawn, then," she replied. "We'll expect you to make the first move."

"We are Tenlenesse, flea. We will strike and you will never see us. We will destroy you, and then torment the two of you, just as we always have. For you are nothing, less than nothing. The sight of this girl disgusts me, and you," she shook her head. "I have nothing but contempt for your entire race, but especially for one of the Light … You're pathetic."

"Show your true self, then," Penia said menacingly.

Lady Nimway was unaffected. "Another time, little fly. One day I'll tear those wings right off your back."

Rose glared at Lady Nimway, and watched as she grew infinite - ly uncomfortable with having Rose's eyes on her. Rose waited until Lady Nimway was about to flee, then said, "Penia is not alone, Lady Nimway. What are you going to do about me?"

"What we've always done," the older woman spat. "You think it was bad before! Your time is finished here, Lady Rose." Still, she could not look at her, and Rose knew if she ran at Lady Nimway, the creature would flee from her presence — and return later in a different form to exact punishment.

"Come, Lady Rose," Penia said gently, turning Rose around. "Let us not keep your mother waiting."

They caught up with a joyful Feonna just before she passed into the counting room with Sir Ridley. "I'm so happy to see you get - ting along with the inner circle so well," the Baroness said. Elated, she hugged her daughter, then grabbed Penia and dragged her into the embrace as well.

"Come," she said. There is much to prepare for." Then she released them and disappeared through the door.

Rose could only shake her head as she and Penia followed. Neither turned to look at Ridley as they passed.

"Dear noble Priscilla," Lady Nimway purred as the two stood looking over Priscilla's father's holdings. "Such a sad end to such a bright future."

"It was never my future," Priscilla reminded Lady Nimway. "We only thought it might become my future considering how unstable my sister used to be."

"And now she's normal, in strength, so it seems."

"And it is her right," Priscilla said firmly, turning to regard Lady Nimway.

Lady Nimway stiffened and turned her head the other way. "Only by birth. But what would happen if she were to have a relapse? What then? Why would we trust the future of Tresville to someone with a history of being untrustworthy?"

Priscilla looked over the endless fields. "I will not have my sis‐ter assassinated," she stated flatly.

"Oh, no, dear one. I was not thinking of something as gruesome as all that!" Lady Nimway was silent for a moment as she collect‐ed her words – or rather, changed her tactics. "Think of it like this, then. Your would-be husband is going to marry your sister instead. Have you given thought to that? No matter how he feels about you, his obligation will always be to his wife, your sister. His love will always belong to her."

"Thank you of reminding me of that, Lady Nimway." There were tears in Priscilla's eyes, and her voice trembled.

"Oh dear one!" Nimway put an arm around Priscilla's shoulders and gave her a hard squeeze. "The lives we live as nobles need not be the lives we live as women. Why should he love only her, even if he must only love her in public? Why should his every thought be of her, when you two have been such fine friends for all these many years?"

"He loves me," Priscilla stated.

"With his heart only, right?"

Priscilla was silent.

"Am I right?" Lady Nimway questioned, turning the younger lady around to look hard at her. "You've never given your body to the young lord?"

It was Priscilla who turned away, flushing. "No. My flower remains with me."

Lady Nimway released the child and was silent for a moment. "Why should it be like that?" she asked thoughtfully.

Priscilla was horrified. "How could you even suggest such a thing? I would bring disgrace to my house! Why, I would dishonor myself!"

"Only if the two of you were caught."

"How could you — "

"What would you rather have," Lady Nimway interrupted Priscilla. "The memory of one night shared between you when there was nothing of obligation to keep your love apart; or the haunting emptiness that will stay with you as long as your love for him remains? And even then, what of the nagging 'What if?' questions that will haunt you the whole of your life?"

"He is your best friend!" Lady Nimway said earnestly. "Would it be so wrong to go with a convoy to the Lebanath holdings to wish the young Lord your blessing as he marries your sister? None would think it inappropriate to make such a gesture. It would only strengthen your position as an ally in the years that follow, when you'll have your own husband to tend to." She eyed Priscilla shrewdly.

"But when you are there," she continued, "see for yourself how he looks at you, how he's so grateful to be in your company, how he cherishes the short time the two of you will have before your relationship comes to an end. And it will end, you must know that. Nothing will ever be the same once he sleeps with your sis - ter. And he'll ask those, 'What if?' questions himself, even as he distances himself from you; for the mere sight of you will remind him of what a fool he's been not to take what he truly wanted, to let you slip from his hands and be replaced by that madwoman! Who knows what she'll do to him when her madness returns? What happiness will he know then?"

Lady Nimway pushed home the final thrust.

"But you, Priscilla, can at least bring him one night of perfec - tion; one night, that's all I'm suggesting. Don't let your sister steal every part of your life."

Priscilla nodded thoughtfully. "One night free of the rule of Rose."

"Exactly."

"I must think on this."

෨෬

That night at dinner Priscilla proposed a plan to her father. "I would go to the Lebinath Estates."

It took her father a while to chew his food, and the small house - hold silently waited for the Baron's reply. Rose glanced at her sis - ter quickly, then at Lady Nimway, who shrugged innocently. Rose was certain she knew more than she let on. Penia, who stood against a wall to tend to her lady, had an understanding of what was happening, but kept her emotions hidden and continued to play her part.

"Why would you want to do that?" the baron finally asked.

"Kinan is a long-time friend of mine, father. Who better to wel- come him into Rose's family than his dearest friend?"

228

"His dearest friend? You are a woman. How could a woman be his dearest friend and not be his wife?"

Rose knew what was happening then.

"It wasn't always so," Priscilla observed.

"What wasn't always so?"

"I always wasn't a woman. And he wasn't always a man. For heaven's sake, father! We've bathed together!"

"You were children, very small, very young children. And you were supervised."

Priscilla rolled her eyes. "I'm not suggesting I go alone."

"Oh. And who would go with you, to supervise you?"

"I would go, my lord," Lady Nimway offered. "If it is your daughter's honor you fear, My Lord, I will watch over her vigilantly."

Jason suspended his fork in midair. "You would go and watch over my daughter, Lady Nimway?"

Lady Nimway reached over and squeezed Priscilla's hand affectionately. "I am her confidant, My Lord. She has spoken of this matter in great length and I see no reason to deny her request."

Jason glanced at Rose, then back at Priscilla. "Yet she acted so outrageously when she was told of Rose's marriage plans."

"Would it not calm the girl's spirit to see that nothing needs to change between her and her 'dearest friend'?" soothed Lady Nimway. "Her friendship with Kinan Lebinath does not offend Lady Rose."

"That's true," Rose affirmed. It's you that bothers me, she mused inwardly. To be fair though, Rose had to admit that Lady Nimway and her cohorts had not dared to show themselves in Rose's tower since her return. Perhaps the danger had passed and

Lady Nimway knew her place at last. Besides, Rose was still try-ing to find a way to back out of this political joining. If things evolved the way she dared hope, and with Nimway involved, it certainly looked that way, Rose would be free of House Tresville and its cursed mine after all. "Look at it this way, Father," she added. "My jaunt out of the castle with my servants did a world of good for me. What's to say that Priscilla couldn't use a similar respite with her servants and her friends?"

Her father glanced at Penia, who stood motionless, although near at hand. "It's funny how sometimes servant and friend can be one and the same," he said thoughtfully.

You have no idea, Penia thought, feeling the weight of her hid-den sword. Yet she did not flinch under the baron's piercing gaze.

Jason turned back to the table and patted his younger daughter's hand benevolently. "Okay," he said. "You may go. At least you will be in the company of a noblewoman."

Penia smiled and when the baron glanced at her, she continued to smile, and shook her head ever so slightly. The Baron knew there were secrets there; he had been told of her yellow stone sword and her mannerisms by his wife in the privacy of his bed-chamber. Penia suspected he was trying to bait her, hoping that this mysterious noblewoman could be drawn into revealing her allegiances and origins.

"How long will you be gone?" Lady Feonna asked her daughter, drawing her husband's attention away from Penia.

"A month, perhaps," Priscilla said with a shrug. "I have a desire to see these new grounds he's going to inherit."

The Baron grinned. He'd been itching to have a peek at the place himself. But they were off bounds to him for deeply politi-cal reasons and he had respected those reasons. But certainly there was no harm in having his daughter trampling all over the place. She knew nothing of the deeper intrigues that governed her family, and so could be no threat to the hidden allegiances within those intrigues. "Take notes," was all he said, thinking of the first hunting season he'd be allowed on those grounds.

They all laughed at that. Penia's face was a mask of calm, hid-ing a sense of dread. She dared not look at Lady Nimway for fear of revealing what she felt. And Lady Nimway, knowing that only Penia and Rose could see it, flaunted her success silently.

જીભ

It happened as both Rose and Lady Nimway had expected. And Kinan became obsessive as he realized his true feelings for the Lady Priscilla. He became angered, and before Priscilla even returned home he sent a messenger to the Baron.

Lady Rose and Penia were in the courtyard watching the guards practice their swordsmanship when the messenger, wearing the Lebinath colors, rode into the courtyard. He dismounted quickly, and marched off towards the castle and the great hall.

"Well, she seduced him," Penia said glumly.

Rose pretended offense and hit her friend on the shoulder.

"This will not turn out well," Penia predicted.

They went back to watching the guards, and were still sitting there when a servant approached them at a dead run. "The Baron demands your presence, My Lady," he gasped breathlessly.

Rose and Penia glanced at each other, then rose from their stone bench and followed the servant back into the castle.

As soon as they entered the great hall the baron motioned for the servants to leave them alone. The one who had summoned them fled gratefully with the messenger from Lebinath, and when Penia moved to leave, Rose grabbed her arm and said, "I don't think so."

231

The Baron glared at Rose, and as soon as the doors to the great hall closed, he waved the paper in front of them. "He has stolen my daughter's honor!" he fumed.

"It would seem, father, that she has stolen his."

"You knew about this!" he raged, growing angrier by the moment.

Rose shrugged. "Think about it for a moment, father. Of course I knew. Don't I always know the heart of every matter? It's a symptom of my condition, a part of who I am."

Her father glared at her. "Why are you not angry? It is your husband who's been disgraced in the eyes of the Court!"

"My future husband, My Lord; I barely know the man," Rose corrected him.

"But you grew up together! All those years you were at his castle, what were you doing?"

"Trying to hide from the demons that live at home, father; it seems wherever the stone is I'm kept very busy fighting for my life. I had little time to get to know the boy. And we had years that separated us. Besides, he was closer to Priscilla's age. Those two monopolized each other's time; in fact, there was scarce time to learn his name before he was off and running through the forests with his playmate."

"It seems they are playmates, still."

"Father!" Rose chuckled.

"I cannot bring this scandal to light, daughter! Lebinath and I would be the laughing stock of the nobility! We'd be disgraced. You'd be disgraced. The son chooses the younger of the two daughters as his wife, in fact demands it, begs it, is actually willing to fight for it. He rejects his claim to you and your inheritance!"

Rose grinned. "He demands a wedding, then?"

"There will be civil war if I don't comply."

Her grin turned into a full, beaming smile. Rose raised her hands into the air and laughed with glee. "I know just the wed - ding present!" she cried in victory, then embraced a very tense Penia at her side. "I'm free!"

"You would give away your inheritance to Priscilla?" The very thought was inconceivable to the baron.

"Father, I am tortured to within an inch of my life by this place, time and time again. You think it is all eccentric, some kind of a game I play for attention perhaps. I don't know what you think about it, and I don't really care anymore. Your opinion is eclipsed by the very real struggle I'm in for my very life." Rose glanced down at her soft hands and frowned.

"Left to me I would take a handful of servants and establish some quiet, small trade route on the corner of your lands and do much for your political relationships. But leave me alone with this rotting mine and these haunted stones, and I will very likely lose my mind and throw myself out of my tower some day . Give me a husband and expect me to fulfill my duty as his wife while all about us I see my phantom tormentors leering at me and worse? I don't think I will make a very good wife, do you? Do you think I'll bring any honor to your name when you are gone if you put me in My Lady Mother's place? Do you think the Tresville lands will continue to grow, to spread under my stew - ardship; or do you think I'll run off and hide in the kingdom somewhere, disguised as a peasant?"

"You'll never be able to hide your royal bearing from the peas - ants," her father retorted.

Rose laughed bitterly. "Father, the peasants would hide me themselves, if I asked them to. Don't think they won't! Remember the stories you've heard about me? Think of the way I see the peasants, the way I treat them! I would make the greatest queen, if not for this damned stone!" She stamped her foot on the floor of the hall to remind Lord Jason of what lay below it. "I have the power to accomplish things you could only imagine. But I have not the power to rule this Barony, or the spirit for it!"

When she finished her outburst, Rose stood glaring at her father, waiting for him to respond. She could tell, the way she could always tell, that he was considering the truth of her words. Finally though he admitted defeat. "You would give up your place?" he asked.

"I would."

"One daughter disgraces me by taking my title, the other dis - graces me by refusing it."

Rose shook her head and rolled her eyes. "Why does there need to be any disgrace at all?"

The Baron waved the letter in front of him, his fist clenched. "Because he slept with one daughter and cheated on the other! He roared. "And they both wanted it!"

"Perhaps I should retire to my tower," suggested Rose.

The Baron turned his back on her and waved her away. "Go," he commanded. "I go on a field exercise tonight with my men. You have until I get back to think of a way to resolve this."

Rose froze and stared at Penia. She shook her head slightly to warn her of the danger they were in. "I would request you give Tremel or Galadin leave to stay behind, father. I do not trust any others with my safety."

"I know," he said with a sigh. "Your paranoia; I grant your request if it stops you from throwing yourself from your tower."

She and Penia glanced at each other as he turned to face her, to hear her answer. "It might, father. It just might."

"Then go." He turned his back on her and set to making preparations for his training campaign.

ഇറൡ

So far inland, Lord Tresville had no need to directly oversee the
navy. He left that to his vassals. But for holdsteads inland it was
with great pride that Jason set a high tax of fighting men from his
banner-men. At first they had begrudged him the demand, com-
plaining that the tax would drain them of their own men. But
once it had been in force for a few years, no one wanted things
back the way they had been in the time of Jason's father's rule.

With a centralized and active army, the other lords were forced
to rely on their liege lord to govern the peace. Not only did this
allow them more time to worry about the rest of their holdings,
but it also forced them to get along with each other, allowing for
trade increases along all borders.

Jason prided himself on the fighting condition of his men. Not
only did they take on a larger portion of the peacekeeping, they
were also the most physically fit. But more importantly they were
loyal; they were loyal to the death.

The Baron achieved this through his training exercises. Every
now and then, once new recruits had been brought in for the season, he arranged for an outing that lasted several days or more,
depending on the stamina of the Baron and his men. And then he
would push them, physically, emotionally, and mentally; and
marches into the nearly overgrown tracks through the forest were
a common drill.

They left that night and jogged into the forest until they reached
a certain pastured valley. There they set torches out and marched
up and down the grassy slopes. As the torches burned down, they
were replaced by fresh ones and still Jason and his men, dressed
in full battle array, marched on. The crescent shape of the moon
climbed into the sky and then began its slow descent back
towards the far horizon. The men fought fatigue and kept their

pace through gritted teeth. In the morning only a few men clam-bered up the hillside in a loose cluster, each keeping time with the others' footfalls. The majority retched and panted, doubled over from the exertion, or simply stared at the hill in bitter defeat.

Jason Tresville was never among the group that stopped.

With a signal to the men still around him, he had them turn towards those watching and jog down the slope, where he com-manded them to catch their breath and take some water.

"Everyone comfortable?" he asked moments later, although he himself swayed on his feet.

The veterans knew what was coming next, and groaned as they climbed to their feet once more.

"In formation and back up the hill." He was too weary to bark the command with any kind of authority.

The greenies couldn't believe it! But they weren't left behind this time, as the drill began anew. Slowly, the men who hadn't quit earlier began to give out. Pushed past the point of breaking, it was not uncommon for one to stop and vomit, or to collapse in a heap of weapons and armor. Jason himself gave out finally, sank to his knees and began to weep. All the burdens of his reign, of his daughters, of the young Lord Kinan, came rushing out of him in a surge of exhausted emotion, and he was too drained to hold them back.

His men were endeared to him in that moment, seeing the Baron as a fellow man, rather than a lord. They accepted that he would die for them, so they in turn were willing to die for him. The green soldiers were in awe at the man's fortitude, they being too confused by the mix of emotions within themselves to do any-thing but fight the hill with renewed effort, determined to die before they quit a second time. And one by one the other veterans who had lasted through the night dropped as Jason had. Some simply fainted, falling into a deep sleep, and had to be carried over to where their Lord still battled with his own personal demons.

Knowing that his share of the campaign had been brought to an end, Ridley knelt before the Baron. "My Lord." When Jason looked up at him he said, "It is no secret amongst those of us here that it is your daughter that causes you so much grief."

"My daughters, Ridley. Not just Rose, but Priscilla is playing her own games now."

Ridley nodded thoughtfully while the others lent their ear to their lord. "Would it be such a dishonor to announce Lady Rose is unfit to rule?"

Jason was silent for a bit. "Would it?" he asked his men. "She is my daughter, my eldest. I can raise armies and manage the largest parcel of the king's lands, but apparently I cannot raise an heiress fit for marriage. Would it be a terrible dishonor to admit defeat in the face of the rest of the court?"

The others shared his grief. "Yet, My Lord," Ridley began. "Her condition is not inherited from you or your wife."

Jason glanced around to be sure of the company he was in. "Her condition is of the enterprise I keep a secret. She is allergic to the smoke that comes from the forge underneath the castle, the steam from the water."

"So send her somewhere where there is none of that," Galadin, her protector announced.

"I would, Galadin, even if it meant losing you and Tremel and a few others. But I can't! Castle Tresville has been our family's seat of power since the mine was first discovered. I won't change tradition now!"

"Then you have no choice, My Lord," Ridley announced.

"Yes," Jason reasoned. "I must pass rule of the Barony to Priscilla and her husband. I must give them both what they want."

"It's only a small change of tradition, Lord," Galadin said honestly. "The court is a fickle place. The other nobles will forget about it as soon as they come visit the new Tresville Barony."

"Plus, Lord," Ridley added, placing his hand on the Baron's shoulder, "your daughter's ailment is more widely known than you'd like it to be. With each year that passes news of her soft mind spreads. People will see your decision as a wise one"

"It is the only decision," Jason finally declared. Something in the look in his eye made Ridley withdraw his hand. He looked around at his closest friends. "Who amongst you has it in him to make it back to the castle with the news? I would have the men go through some mock battles before I let them collapse for good, and I would have this ugly business with Rose finished and done with as soon as possible."

Ridley rocked back onto the balls of his feet. "I would go, my lord. I've tasted enough battle to benefit more from a march back."

"That you have," Jason admitted. "Then go with all the speed you have, knowing you've put your Lord's mind to rest."

Ridley nodded and rose to his feet. "As My Lord commands," he declared as he crisply saluted. Then he began the long trip back to the castle.

A forced march alone! Baron Tresville would know how long it took Ridley to reach the castle. He could not delay, nor relax. He must push himself as hard as the others behind him, yet he would not have the comfort in numbers that the others had. Ridley's face darkened into a mask of rage. He would have Lady Rose and Lady Rose alone to thank for that.

སོ૦ક

The Lady Feonna sat in her chair in the great hall, listening to Ridley's report. Her hands were in front of her, fingertips touching each other, forefingers resting against her lips. She remained wordless, not daring to look over at where Rose and Penia stood in rapt silence, hardly daring to breathe.

When he was finished she knew her duty and regarded her daughters long and hard. Ridley swayed on his feet and she turned her attention back to him. "You are dismissed, Sir Knight. Go find rest from my husband's fierce training."

"But the other men, My Lady – "

"Go Ridley. I'm sure Jason has allowed them some rest by now. Have no fear. My husband will hear that I received your summons in a timely fashion."

Ridley bowed to her. "As it pleases you, My Lady."

"It does. Now go find your bed."

"Yes My Lady." Ridley bowed again, turned and marched out of the hall. Not once did he look at either Rose or Penia.

Rose's heart was pounding in her chest. She was on the brink of tears, yet fought to maintain composure so as not to give away her true feelings. To be free of this place at last! She could scarcely dare to hope. But for the disappointment she knew her parents were feeling and the pride they were sacrificing at her expense, she felt some remorse.

"This must be exciting news for you!" her mother said at last, watching the war of emotions rage in her daughter.

Rose gave a slight nod of her head. "You know of the horrors I suffer in this place, because of those mines. Mother. And the terror does go away when I'm away from this place! I would be free of it all! Priscilla and Kinan will take good care of the lands. They will bring honor to the Tresville banner."

Her mother nodded. All that was true. "I wish you well, then, Rose. You've been absolved from your title as heiress of the Barony of Tresville."

Penia jumped into the air and clapped her hands together as she giggled. The humans stared at the healer, yet their grave manner did little to dampen her spirits. If the Lady Feonna hadn't been present, Penia would have gone into her natural form and spun amid the rafters of the hall, glowing like a green star.

"Forgive my maidservant, Mother," Rose spoke. "Where she comes from, emotions are more open."

Lady Feonna smiled. "I think I understand her reason," she said. "Just think, no more terrible treatments."

Rose grinned back at her. "No more nightmares!"

"May I ask when you are leaving?"

"Tomorrow; as soon as I can get everyone together and packed."

"Where will you go?"

"Not far, Mother. I have no desire to abandon my family. My title does not bother me all that much either. But that smoke, those mines... ever since you've shown me the place my nights have been filled with images of that purple glow."

"I thought Penia here has been able to cure you."

Rose glanced at Penia, who had composed herself and remembered her place once again.

"There is no cure, Mother. I have only managed to suppress the terrors. It seems with two of us together we are able to intimidate the horrors with the light of our own stones."

"Why is that?" Rose, in need of that answer also, turned to Penia, who chewed her lower lip as she thought.

"That is complicated, My Lady," she finally said. "But it is easiest to say our stones come from different places, and give off different smoke than here. It is a breath of fresh air to our minds, and keeps the terrors unsure of themselves."

"But light is light."

Penia nodded. "And dark is dark. And the two get along not at all."

"If that will be all, Mother?" Rose asked.

Lady Feonna turned to Rose and nodded. "I am happy for you, daughter. You should know that."

"Thank you Mother." She and Penia curtsied and left.

"Can it be true?" Penia's voice rose with excitement once they were away from the great hall.

"Hush Penia," Rose pleaded. "Wait until we reach the safety of our tower."

Penia saw the wisdom in that and nodded, although the grin never left her face.

They remained silent as they strode through the halls together. But once the door to her tower was closed behind her, Rose spun around and clasped Penia by her hands. "I am free!" she exclaimed, as loudly as she dared.

Penia laughed with delight, and her joy was contagious. In a move to express the depth of her happiness Penia disappeared into a glittering spark of light, suspended in the air before Rose. She twirled in the air with her arms spread out before her, then headed up the tower with Rose chasing after her.

It was a great time for Rose. She sent word for her inner circle to come to her tower and waited for them all before she told them the good news. Relief swept through her friends and many were reduced to tears of joy as they extended their congratulations and offered vows of loyalty all over again. It mattered not to them that Rose would not become the Baroness of Tresville. What mattered was that their lady would be kept safe in the years to come.

Preparations began to be laid. They would leave as soon as pos-sible. They would take their families with them this time. They would need tools to establish their new homes. But they would have to wait for the soldiers to come back before those loyal to Rose could supply her with safety in arms.

For all their seriousness, the discussions held an air of celebra-tion that had Penia flitting amongst them as a true Aigelendai, taking form perhaps only a hands' width tall, her green wings fluttering about her on winds only she could feel.

Lady Feonna showed up unexpectedly, causing Penia to squeak with fright and dive down behind a tapestry hanging against the far wall. The others subsided into silence as the Baroness grinned, then forced herself into the room. "I suppose the chores have all been attended to," she said, although there was no reprimand in her voice.

"I summoned them here, Mother," Rose confessed.

The room was buzzing with excitement, though they all tried their best to hide it. The silence lasted all of two heartbeats before one of the servants dived to her knees before Lady Feonna. She grabbed her hand and kissed it, over and over again, as though it belonged to the most precious person on the planet. "Oh Lady Feonna! Your grace is matched only by your mercy! Thank you My Lady for setting Lady Rose free of this place. I know not what causes her ailment, but if you have seen the way she was when she was away from here! You would know you were doing the right thing."

Feonna looked across the crowded room at her daughter. "I will see her. I will visit often, as often as I can. Where will you go?"

Rose grinned. "To the eastern border of father's land; I would like to build a bridge across the River Shrine into Lord Keltrapid's lands."

Lady Feonna's eyes widened. "It is said that place is full of ghosts."

Rose shrugged. "What is that to me, mother? I would give the dead the respect they require, bury the bones and raise a shrine to memorialize the battle that took place there. But I would also see the place turned into a trading route, set a toll on the bridge, and contribute something to this Barony."

Lady Feonna nodded. The plan was a good one. And expansion along the eastern border could never be a bad thing. No one had done it before for fear of the local superstitions. Yes, Rose could sweep in and make something of the place, considering the sup-port she had in this room. "And you would take these servants with you?"

"I would ask that of you, Mother, yes."

"It is a small price to pay for what you seek to obtain. Go with the blessing of House Tresville, and with the hand of Almighty upon you." The Baroness glanced around the room. "I'll leave you to it, then," she said. Then she left, closing the door gently behind her.

Penia came out from behind the tapestry in human form, grin-ning and chuckling, and the celebrations began anew.

One by one the servants returned to their duties, offering well wishes and exclamations of excitement one last time. The ladies-in-waiting, too, had tasks to perform, that could not be left wait-ing, and bid their lady farewell until the morning, grinned at Penia and left together.

Finally, only Penia and Rose remained in the tower, in a room beneath Rose's bedchamber. They sat across from each other in lounge chairs, sipping on spiced wine. "I would have us retire to bed soon, My Lady," Penia told her. "An early rise would benefit us far better than a late celebration."

Rose reached over to a nearby tapestry and felt the fibers with her hand. "This will be the last night I spend in this place. No more insanity. No more demons. No more otherworldly ghosts." She looked over at Penia. "I would not even believe the Netherlands were real if I hadn't seen you change your form with my own eyes."

Penia offered a tired smile. "They are not a bad place. It's just that too much of the Fire Realm is now a place of light, and those who prefer darkness would inhabit the between places."

"Tell me about the stones, Penia."

"Ahhh, the stones …. They act as a portal between the two realms. For those who are capable, we may travel along the stones through the Netherlands to the Fire Realm, and from there to here as well. There isn't any difference between ours and the smoke that curls around your tower, but the Tenlenesse are not accustomed to our stones." She pulled her sword out and laid it on her lap so they might bask in its yellow light. "The purple stone spreads shadow, just as the yellow stone spreads light. Those who mean you harm hide in the shadows of the mines underneath us. Those who would like you to be well bask in the light of a different stone, and the two do not mix, although I sup - pose they could easily enough if they were taught how."

"Why me though, Penia? Why would these Tenlenesse seek to do me harm?"

Penia looked saddened. "I cannot answer that, my lady. I have my suspicions, but it is not my place to speak of them. There are greater happenings here than simply the two wheels within wheels you've been exposed to."

"Wheels within wheels, you mean the secrecy of the mine, of the stones, and the secrecy of the Tenlenesse?"

"And of the Aigelendai." Penia nodded. "Yes. There are other possibilities I am not privileged to know, things of the Fire Realm that sing too close to my heart to be mere coincidence. But I dare not say more." She stood and patted Rose's knee. "Arise and go to sleep, and I will do the same!" Under her breath, Penia added, "I might have a flight around the tower before I go, though."

Rose pushed herself wearily to her own feet, but she had one more question to ask before she was willing to let Penia go to her bed. "How is it you can change form and become invisible to others, yet not to me?"

"When I enter the Netherlands I have more than one entrance into this realm which I may pass through. The entrance I take determines which form I take. While I'm invisible, I am in the Netherlands, neither fully here nor fully in the Fire Realm. You can see me, and touch me, and hear me, because you can do the same with the Tenlenesse who haunt this place." Penia gazed at Rose earnestly. "You are special, my lady," she said. "That is why they hate you so. A human who can see into their home, into their lives and see the corruption they live by. Next thing you'll be traveling through the Netherlands yourself."

Rose laughed. "I hope not. I cannot handle one reality. What would I be like with two?"

Penia kept her thoughts to herself. "Good night, Rose."

"Good night, Penia." She watched her friend ascend the stairs that led up into the top levels of the tower and stood there, wondering what it would be like to be away from this place forever – at last.

Moments later a streak of green light sailed down the stairs to buzz around Rose's head. She moved too fast for Rose to focus on her, but Rose clearly heard Penia's command, "Go to bed!" Then the Aigelendai was away again, down the stairs at the far end of the room.

Rose stared at the place where her friend had vanished, shook her head, then headed off to her bed.

That night she felt secure for the first time in ages. Knowing that her freedom would begin in the morning, and knowing that none of those terrible creatures had harassed her since Penia had come to stay with her, Rose felt almost luxuriant as she enjoyed the flourishes of royalty for perhaps the first time. The pillows of her bed, the down filled comforter, even the drapes that hung around the bed, the looking glass and the tallow candles, all of it finally sank in, and she was able to enjoy it. Rose fell into her bed with a sigh and was asleep within moments.

She awoke to utter darkness. Something about the stillness made her skin crawl and her eyes opened wide in an attempt to see through the night. Then she smelled the faint trace of smoke and knew. "Oh no," she moaned, too afraid even to move.

A creak in the floorboard on the other side of the room; a sud - den gust of wind followed by the silent rustling of curtains set - tling; a tiny beam of pale moonlight; a stirring in the darkness, silent as it was, told her. She knew they were upon her. And wearily she sat up to face her terrors.

"The mighty dignitary rises from her beauty rest," came a rasp - ing, repulsive voice. Rose looked towards the sound, yet the dark - ness hid all. "Someone thinks to win free of us: us, her true mas - ters," The hissing came from a different direction. "One would think one has learned her lesson by now," said a distorted femi- nine voice, as hideous and repellent as the others. "But how can she know who owns her soul if she has never learned what pain is?" asked another voice that sounded much like Ridley, the sol- dier. "Oh, she'll learn. We shall show her this night. Won't we?"

They moved towards her simultaneously, gliding soundlessly through the shadows until Rose could see the outlines of their wraithlike bodies, then the faces that were not faces at all, but masks that inspired terror and dread.

"Penia!" she screamed as loud as she could.

The phantoms pounced; and icy, bony, iron-strong hands held her, and all Rose could do was scream.

"Poor, poor princess," another woman's voice mocked. "So distraught she was, leaving her birthright behind." A tuft of hair was torn from her scalp. "She knew the truth about her sickness. She knew there were no ghosts that tormented her." Ever so slowly, Rose's nightgown began to tear. "She knew if she ever left this place she would only have those terrors follow her. So to win free at last — "

" — The guards find her body in the morning." A rough male voice whispered into her ear.

"Penia!" Rose shrieked, terrified.

"What can one tiny insect do to — "

Green and yellow light blazed through the room, and stunned, the creatures yelped and let go of Rose. Exposed, she could see how slender they were, nearly sinew and bone. They wore the clothing of humans, of servants and royalty, yet the clothes hung about their persons loosely, billowing out as they cried out and tried to hide their faces with clawlike hands. They looked no prettier in the light.

Penia rushed from the staircase, herself ablaze and encased in the light of her yellow sword. She was in her human form, yet her wings billowed out behind her, fully visible and magnificent, bil-lowing currents of air through the room. She rushed straight into the group of eight or nine specters, swinging her sword like a madwoman with such a look of rage upon her face that Rose was infused with hope.

Forgetting her fear in the presence of such light, Rose flung herself across her bed to the end table and the yellow stone she kept within. The table crashed to the floor as she grasped the stone and flung it out before her, coming to stand on her bed

247

while the demons fell away from Penia's sword like grass in the wind.

"Away from this place, creatures of the night! You have no place here, not anymore!" Rose commanded.

One stopped and turned to look at her, ever so slowly, ever so fearlessly. He looked at her, then at the stone in her hand, and his look of contempt made her blood run cold. He began to laugh, straightened and threw his grotesque face back, and howled with such mirth that Rose panicked, looking desperately for a place to run. The laughter died abruptly, and the phantom flung his cloak back and drew out a sword with a glowing purple hilt.

The wraiths, as if on cue, drew similar glowing weapons and went on the offensive, shoving Penia back one step at a time. Rose shrieked in anger and threw herself, weaponless, into the fray. Despite her bravery, the phantom who had jeered her grabbed her wrist with his free hand and forced it behind her back. She was pressed tightly against his chest, his putrid breath inches from her face, and Rose turned away in revulsion.

"Never have we played this game with the lights on," he con-fessed. Each breath smelled of rotting graves. Rose gagged and was pushed back a step.

The wraith sheathed his sword with his free hand. "There is no need to take such a measure as that, is there? Too much blood ends it too quickly. No. Tonight, I promise, will be long, and before dawn you will call me master."

"Rose!" Penia raged.

Suddenly an explosion of light struck the wraith holding her, and he was blasted against the far wall. A great torrent of wind sucked through the room, flinging curtains and cushions around like straw in a gale. At Penia's feet was a large vortex of light, perhaps the width of a man. It was as if the cover of a well of light had been removed and Rose looked into a tunnel with walls of liquid fire.

"Go!" Penia commanded. All pretense of servitude was gone.

"I won't leave you!" Rose shouted through the gale.

"Go!" Penia looked at the Tenlenesse, saw that they were recovering and regaining their feet. "I will cover your escape! Otherwise they'll catch up to you on the other side! Go now!" She stood with her feet planted firmly apart, sword blazing in her hands. Her wings, like those of an avenging angel, were billowing in the gale. Such authority did Penia exude that Rose could not help but obey. She dove into the cascade of fire and light.

Suddenly, she was wrapped in light, enveloped by it. Rose felt weightless: as though she were floating under water. Her mind let go of all worry and doubt, leaving her drifting, as peaceful as though asleep, quieted, limp in the light's embrace.

"You've never paid such attention to me." The admonishment was spoken lightheartedly, and Rose felt rather than heard a presence nearby mutter, "Humph!"

The voice laughed long and merrily. "Put her over here, then. I'll clear some space."

The light began to separate, to form miniature Agalendai: an entire multitude of them. Yet unlike Penia's emerald green hue, these were the color of white fire, like sunlight they were, and moonlight, some of them. And they gave off such a brilliant light Rose could not tell where one began and another ended. They were carrying her through the air, a myriad of them cushioning her and holding her up as they flew slowly, gently.

She could not tell where she was, nor how she got there, or even how long she'd been wrapped in light. But there seemed to be something beyond the light, beyond the brightness of the little Aigelendai supporting her. Rose felt weak yet refreshed, as if waking from a terrible nightmare. The room was warm and comforting. She finally decided she must be in the midst of a dream. Yet when the Aigelendai laid her down on what felt like a pile of hay, the itchy intrusion in her hair and against her neck brought her more fully awake.

A clean-shaven, dignified face, its features both fearless and kind, smiled down at her. His hair was silver, and he wore a white high-cut tunic. It was open down the front to reveal a hairless, muscular chest. In the transcendent light of so many Agailendai, he looked like an angel, yet Rose thought there was no denying he was not human. Too fair was his skin and shining hair. Too wondrous were his pale blue eyes, full of ageless energy and wisdom. She knew him then, and marked him. And her thought was met with delight by the Aigelendai and he smiled even more broadly. He was Tenlenesse.

"Welcome to the Fire Realm, Your Highness," he said, offering her his hand. She took it and he helped her to her feet. "Careful now. You'll feel a bit light-headed for a few moments." He let her bear her own weight experimentally, and she swayed slightly as she rubbed her eyes.

"I feel like I am in a dream," she whispered.

The Aigelendai hovering about suddenly darted away, dispersing like fish in the sea.

"They'll tend to scatter like that, especially when there's too many of them in one place. But they like it here, with the heat of the fire and the sparks and the stone. Pesky creatures, for the most part; but I do enjoy their company, even call them friends when they aren't about some mischief."

"Where am I?" Rose asked, looking about her, still somewhat dazed. She was in a forge, a large one, and surrounded everywhere by light.

"You are in the city of Shalese. I am Terrance Leafvein." He bowed to her. "Your humble servant."

"Penia!" Rose cried, suddenly remembering. She grasped at his arm. "I have to go back! Take me back!" she entreated.

The Tenlenesse bit his lip. "Tell me what has happened."

"My friend, Penia, an Aigelendai. She was attacked by... " She eyed him warily. "She was attacked by Tenlenesse."

"Then they will have a time of it trying to catch her." Terrance wasn't at all worried.

"No," Rose beseeched. "You don't understand. She was in human form, with wings. They had her surrounded. Penia opened a portal and sent me away from them. They were clashing swords when I left. I have to go back!"

"My lady, it has occurred to me that you are not from the Fire Realm."

Rose abruptly stopped talking and stared at him.

"These Tenlenesse, they were evil, were they not?"

She nodded.

"And they live in the shadows of darkness, hidden by the night and taking upon themselves hideous forms?"

Rose nodded again.

"And this Aigelendai, this Penia; she was in human form?"

"Why are you repeating everything I said?"

"Forgive me, lady. I do not doubt your words. But only in human form could an Aigelendai and a Tenlenesse cross swords." He motioned for her to walk with him.

Rose sighed and allowed herself to be led out into the most remarkable place she could imagine. Huge trees with silver blue bark and broad silver leaves soared into the sky. Long green grass, unlike any she had ever seen, carpeted her feet, with flow-ers of every color imaginable hemming in the trunks of indescribably huge trees. She saw that the for ge was built at the base of one. The forge was almost as long as the tree was wide, and this tree was but a sapling compared to some of the others. Even the forge's roof was covered in shrubbery. Droopy vines with tiny white flowers dangled from the roof. As Rose looked on in awe, a silvery-blue Aigelendai darted by, blazing like a star come to gaze upon this heavenly place.

"Forgive me," Terrance repeated. "It is just hard for me to believe an Aigelendai would appear in human form. I have not heard of such a thing."

Rose held out her hand and showed him her stone. "Have you heard of this?" It shone just as brightly here as it had in the dark, and yet seemed so appropriate here that she did not think to keep it secret.

"Ah," he said quietly. "A spectral stone; so, you have them where you come from."

She lowered her hand. "I do not understand."

"Forgive me, my lady. I did not catch your name."

"It is Rose, Rose Tresville, heiress to — forgive me. I am the daughter of Baron Tresville, banner- man of the king of Hansurn. My birthright has been stripped from me."

"And why was that, if you don't mind me asking?"

Rose squared her shoulders and looked him straight in the eye. "The reasons are two-fold. One is personal, between myself and my younger sister, Priscilla, and I would rather not share that. The other reason is that the Dark Tenlenesse have chosen to tor - ment me, for whatever motives. None other could see them or would believe my tales, and so my title was taken from me for fear that I had a soft mind.

Terrance nodded gravely. "My Lady, you are fortunate, a gift to your race, to your family. I bow to you." And he did. "Do not let the dark Tenlenesse damage your soul," he added, "for it is resilient and will heal your body, no matter what damage has been done."

She looked down at her nightgown, seeing that it was so torn as to be almost inappropriate.

"Come," Terrance gestured. "I have clothes you may wear. They belong to my sister, but she will not mind. She does not visit this place often; the heat offends her sensitivities."

He led her back into the stifling heat, to a small room at the back of the forge. It was a storage room, and he pointed to a fresh tunic and trousers, both white, like his. "I shall wait outside," he said, then left her alone to change.

The clothing fit perfectly. So delighted was Rose with this hap-penstance, that when she found her host sitting cross-legged in the grass, she told him so.

He smiled. "I suspected it would," was all he said.

"I have to know," Rose said as she sat down next to him. "What will happen to Penia?"

"Your friend lives in three worlds. Here she is one of these pix-ies, these fairies. In your world she can appear as human, or as she is here, or somewhere in between. It is the same with Tenlenesse. We can travel to the surface realm, appear as we truly are, or take on a much more subtle human disguise. In the place between places, the Netherlands, we are not substantial, much like mists. We are practically like fire itself, oblivious to death, impossible to capture.

"Your friend will try to get back here. She will attempt to leave the surface realm and follow you to this place she must know so well, for she was able to send you here to her kindred. I suspect she will not be killed. For that is not the style of the Tenlenesse."

"She will be tortured."

He looked saddened. "That is so. But you cannot know what that torture will be like. I do not know myself. I've never imagined harming an Aigelendai, not until now."

Suddenly, one of the creatures flew at him. It hit him on the center of his brow and wagged a tiny finger at him, then flew away. Terrance smiled wryly as if the mischievous Aigelendai had just proven his point, then shook his head and continued with his story as though he had not been interrupted. "I have no doubt your friend will be fine once you go back and rescue her."

"How can you be so sure?"

He chewed at his lip again. "Let me tell you of our kind," Terrance suggested. He stood up and offered Rose his hand. She took it and he pulled her to her feet.

"Once, long ago, all of mankind was immortal." Terrance led Rose by the arm into the forest away from his forge as he talked. She noticed he neither closed the door to his shop nor locked it before turning his back to it. "Twenty men and women thought to seize immortality for themselves, so they set out to take the secret of immortality, twenty pendulums of power. On their way one man had a change of heart and tried to stop his companions, yet they succeeded and nineteen races were born. And the one man became the father of a race of winged men. His name was Trilian."

"I have not heard of this man."

Terrance bowed his head gently. "He was a great and honorable hero. But his children turned away and became like the other nineteen races, evil.

"Of the Fire Realm, five races were given. The Tenlenesse and the Aigelendai are two of them. It is said that the Aigelendai are the most like the angels. Tenlenesse are most like humans before their fall. We two races have much of what humans and angels used to hold in common. I suppose it is only natural that as rebel lious nations, we were much like the demons and the darkness of mankind, as well.

"The fire realm was a terrible, terrible place for a time, until one Tenlenesse grew tired of tormenting and being tormented. He took a spectral stone and left the Fire Realm to walk amongst the surface realm, disguised as a man. He was gone for a long time, many lifetimes, by your standard. And when he returned he was a changed man.

"He preached about Almighty, the god the Tenlenesse had turned their back on. He preached of the death of Almighty, how he had taken mortal form and sacrificed his life at the bidding of a great and evil snake. But with his death the fangs of the snake were pulled out, and the creature now has no power except that which we give him."

"Hmmmm, I've heard that phrase a lot," Rose commented.

Terrance nodded. "It is a powerful phrase amongst the Tenlenesse. He continued his narration.

"With his death, Almighty managed to take the consequences of all our evil actions with him to the grave. Three days later he rose again to life, that we might live with him anew, our old vile ways forgotten."

"Why, we have the same religion at home," Rose exclaimed.

Terrance grinned. "Don't you see, my lady? It is that which brings the races back together again, which even makes immortal - ity, or at least some form of it, possible again!"

Rose appreciated Terrance's enthusiasm, but had heard this les - son before. And while it was remarkable, she'd long since taken the message to heart and applied its meaning, especially in the face of the dreadful nightmares she had suffered. Rose was more interested in her home, and what was happening there right now.

Terrance nodded absently and continued. "A great many Tenlenesse followed his example and chose a different form, a different truth to live by. We were transformed into this." He gestured at his form, his hair and his clothes. "Others became the unfortunate dark creatures you have known in your life. A great and mighty war broke out amongst our kind.

"But darkness can not abide with light and so was repelled into the shadow realms between my world and yours. They live there now, as insubstantial shades, their wickedness revealed only to those who can see them. When they unearth spectral stones they may enter our worlds." He waved at the scenery around him. "Yet they are wise enough not to come back to this and risk being destroyed. So they disguise themselves as humans and spread their evil far and wide."

"Why can I see them?" Rose asked.

They stopped in front of a tree larger than anything she could have imagined. Its base alone was as wide as her father's castle. Before her was a broad flight of stairs that went straight up into the lowest boughs of the tree. And there, protruding from a hole in the trunk, was its own castle, a wondrous, graceful thing, with bridges spanning the gaps between the branches, and towers that stood tall and straight, and narrow, linking to other branches by even more bridges, like some great and complex web.

"You will find the answers there," he said, and stepped back with a bow.

Rose looked at him, her eyes pleading.

"I must return to my forge. Yet if you have need of me, please summon me. I am at your disposal."

"Then stay, please," she said. "I am humbled and a little frightened. I need a guide."

He bowed again. "Amongst the Tenlenesse there is no rank. We are all servant."

"Yet you are of the light."

"Yes."

She took his arm again. "Then please. I know a thing or two about nobility. None would begrudge me a guide to show me the way through such a place."

Terrance looked at the castle. "As My Lady commands," was all he said before they took the first step up the stairs together.

ℬℭ

Inside was immense, inhumanly so. Rose looked up to see that the tree this castle had been carved into was hollow, and it stretched up and up, as high as she could see. There were balconies and arches spanning the gulf, with castles and towers upon them. Her mouth dropped open in amazement and all she could do was stare.

"It is this way, My Lady," her guide said to her, pulling her gently towards the side.

Rose went reluctantly, for it was difficult to pull her eyes from the scene. More Aigelendai than she could count lit the inside of the tower, all gold and silver and shining with either the noonday sun or the full moon's radiance. "It would take me my entire lifetime and I still would not have discovered everything there is to learn about this place." She stumbled, and hastily turned her eyes towards where she was going.

"Time means little here," Terrance confessed. "I'm sure your lifetime would last accordingly."

"It is beautiful, and I am filled with wonder looking at it all. Still, I worry about my friend."

Terrance looked up at the millions of Aigelendai overhead. "So many of them are here. Would it not be easy to forget about her while amongst this horde?"

257

"It is not the same," she told him. "Here they are intelligent bugs, insects. All of these butterflies with human bodies will not make me forget Penia. She was my friend, my ally and my healer. We had many conversations that lasted long into the night. She is important to me."

"There is much I do not understand," Terrance responded. "Tenlenesse and the Aigelendai live in separate worlds here, though we share the same realm."

He led her through an archway and Rose found herself standing at the beginning of a broad highway, a path marked with gleaming silver cobble stones. At its edges stone walls had been built low enough to act as benches. Every few paces a tree grew straight up out of the wall; but on closer inspection, Rose realized that these were not trees but smaller branches of the same tree that grew from the branch this highway was built on. The road stretched on and on through the canopy of leaves and branches, zigzagging over her head and enveloping her from the sky. In Amazement Rose looked up once more, for the view was unforgettable, and she was content just to stare at it.

But Terrance Leafvein propelled her forward, though Rose's feet dragged a little. "Come," he urged, "it is some ways yet, My Lady."

Rose patted his arm almost affectionately. "Although we have only met, I feel as though I have known you for some time."

Terrance smiled, although it appeared to Rose as though her words had pained him. "It is the trees," he replied. "They know little of time, and bond people together."

She glanced at him. "Bond people, how?"

"Who can say, Lady Rose? For every person to walk this street there are just as many different people to walk it with."

He paused and rubbed his chin thoughtfully before giving Rose an intense look.

"This street has no name," Terrance said, "and must be named by the hearts who walk it together. It is an old street, older than any other, for it was initially walked by His Majesty Armin Derango, the Shadow-Bane, when he first returned from the surface realm."

Rose nodded feeling a growing awareness of Terrance's presence beside her. Her cares for Penia and her own world gradually fell away to be replaced by the scenes of the world around her, and of Terrance, her blacksmith and guide.

"Metalsmith," he corrected when Rose casually mentioned her growing sense of ease about the place, and of him. They had traveled a good distance down the path, and although Penia still remained on Rose's mind, she trusted in her guide to set the pace. "I smith living metal, the leaves from the trees," he added.

"You jest!"

"I do not! The leaves neither wilt nor change color. The trees draw water from the reservoirs of moonfire under the ground and so grow to reflect its influence. I harvest a leaf when I need it, and build tools and jewelry from it. A great many things may be made from moonfire leaves, for the metal is soft and pliable when it is hot. It melts well, and when it has cooled, is hard and incredibly strong."

"All of the leaf is metal?" Rose still couldn't believe it. Staring intently up at the leaves she saw that although they were silver they swayed in the wind and acted just as regular leaves would.

"No, I confess, I led you astray. Only the veins of the leaves are able to be smelted down. The rest burns away in the fire."

"Thus your name!"

He grinned. "Thus my name, Terrance Leafvein."

He led her further along the path, and although they had walked for some time Rose experienced neither hunger nor thirst. She knew no weariness, nor did her feet grow sore, even though they were bare upon the stones. It all seemed natural to her. Rose was in a dream, a wonderful, impossible dream.

Presently another castle came into view, perhaps the size of her father's castle in the surface realm. It was nestled in a fork in the branches. Other branches grew profusely around it, cocooning it in leaves. When Rose saw the castle she skipped, suddenly feel-ing much too light on her feet to trudge along. She took Terrance's hand and urged him to run with her. Laughing, they ran hand-in-hand the rest of the way.

They burst in upon a single cavernous room. Shafts of golden light pierced through the windows, but after being outside, the room felt somehow gloomy. Still, there was a comfortable tran-quility about the place, an atmosphere of reverence almost, of whispers.

Furniture made of white wood, still living branches growing from cracks in the stone floor, glistened in the shadows, seeming-ly giving off their own light. Row upon row of benches, whose ends blossomed with silver leaves, heralded Rose through the center isle between them. Some of the branches grew high into the room, stretching towards the places where light shone through, cultivating a living tapestry in silver and white.

"It's empty," Rose whispered quietly to Terrance, clinging to his arm once again.

"It usually is," he replied. "There is no set time to gather, yet this place is shared by all; no one is turned away." She noticed he spoke as quietly as she did.

"Where are we?"

Terrance smiled. "This is a cathedral, where it all began; where His Majesty convinced the first Tenlenesse to taste moonfire, and experience for ourselves the truth of our race."

"Truth?"

"That while we are birthed from a fall we may live in a climb."

Rose mulled over his words thoughtfully as they walked to the front of the cathedral.

Before them, bathed in a pool of light, was a fountain. It was magnificently carved from the stump of a branch that lived still, and budded around the edge of the perfectly round rim. The water bubbled from the center of the stump, which was perhaps as wide as the length of Rose's arm. The water glowed silver, shimmering its own light into the cathedral.

Instinctively, Rose looked towards the ceiling, searching for the Aigelendai, knowing they would be attracted to such a divine glowing light. There weren't any.

"The little ones know this place is sacred to us." The voice was human, but wiser, wise beyond any years a human can expect to exist. The voice possessed a youthful vitality that Rose suspected could only result from living in such a wondrous place as this. She turned around to see the speaker kneeling on the floor with his elbows propped up on the front bench. When she turned, he pushed himself to his feet and regarded Rose with deep interest. He too had silver hair, and wore a cloak and robe of gleaming white. On his head was a circlet of silver, a simple narrow band with a piece of red spectral stone shining from the center. "The Aigelendai have moonfire by the lake. Such a little splash as this would not be lost upon them, but they respect our wish to not be distracted."

"And all who would not respect it, have they then been driven from here?" The words were out before Rose could stop them.

The man winced. "We begged them to stay, to drink the water. But above all else they detest what we love most." He gazed over the water, and his face reflected the silver sheen.

Something about the speaker reminded Rose of her sister Priscilla, something she couldn't quite place. She shook her head slightly and brought her attention back to what he was saying.

"They could not bear the light, and with each one of us that took the light upon ourselves, light only grew stronger. They tried to stop us. It was a time of great torment and many tears were shed. In the end they left themselves no choice. They retreated into the Netherlands to haunt the other realms."

He took a step closer. "I have never dared to dream of such a day as this." He reached out a hand to touch Rose's hair, then hesitated and withdrew it again. He turned to Terrance, who stood a few paces away. "Did you tell her?"

"Almost, Your Majesty; but I thought it should come from you. It is not my place."

"And yet you walked the nameless street with her."

Terrance pursed his lips together, shook his head and sat down on the closest bench. He put his hands in his lap and stared at the speaker for a moment before he looked at Rose and said, "My Lady, may I present Armin Derango, Father of the Tenlenesse of Light."

"Are you not going to tell me who she is?"

Terrance clamped his mouth shut and looked straight ahead.

"In truth, young lady, I know who you are," declared Armin. "I may not know your name but I could never mistake your line-age."

"Rose, my name is Rose –"

"Tresville, yes I know. You are a Baroness, or close to it. Your grandmother was when I left her so long ago. You see, Rose, that Baroness was my daughter. I am your great- grandfather."

Rose's eyes widened in surprise as she stared from Terrance to Armin. She was astonished, her mind whirling. How can this be? Her great-grandfather? And yet, so many strange things had happened to Rose throughout her young life. Was this any stranger than her being able to communicate with those from other realms when others could not?

"Only one from the Fire Realm may travel here unaided."

Alarmed, Rose sought her yellow stone for comfort, and suddenly realized she had misplaced it.

"Do not worry, little one. What I would give you is far greater than a mere stone." This time he did touch her hair, holding a lock of it gently in his hands before caressing her cheek. "So like your grandmother you are. And yet there is much more of me in you than anything. I see difficulty and pain. I see anguish and torture."

"And I see the same in you, Great-Grandfather." Rose was only speaking the truth, the heart of the matter, as she saw it.

"It is the nature of our dark ones to torment us. To a Tenlenesse only the light can banish the dark. Whereas with humans, a simple gaze can catch a lie."

"I've noticed that," Rose murmured. "There are many who look rather uncomfortable when I stare at them."

"You don't know the half of it, Lady Rose." Armin stepped past her, placed both hands on the rim of the fountain, and gazed deeply into its light. "To be human and Tenlenesse both," he marveled, "to have both parts awakened and living inside you at once; what a great day this is for us!"

"I do not understand."

"My lady." It was Terrance who spoke. "You can gaze into the Netherlands."

"She can do more than that, my silversmith friend. She can enter the Netherlands and purge the shadows of the nightmares that live there. She can clean the pathways between here and there. She can herald our return to the surface realm."

Rose stared into the water, remembering the nights of unspeakable horrors she'd lived through. "You must be mistaken," she said quietly. "I am not that person. I have no defense against those monsters."

Her great-grandfather only smiled. "Let me give you one."

"This is the part I have most looked forward to," Terrance said, grinning.

Rose's eyes flickered from one to the other, then slid back to the water and she waited.

"Would you drink it?"

Her eyes never wavered. "I would."

"Then taste, and know what it is to be a Tenlenesse of the light."

Rose dipped her hands into the glowing water and exhaled all the stress and worry she had for so long been carrying. Merely touching it was draining the tension out of her back and shoulders, renewing her strength. She looked at her great-grandfather, who smiled encouragingly, then cupped her hands to scoop up the liquid and brought them to her lips.

The whole universe exploded in one single moment of transcendent truth. From a single grain of awareness, a single kernel of simplicity far too simple to be comprehended with words, entire worlds were birthed, growing as they split from each other and emerged from this speck of light. They expanded and coalesced, alive and molten, like bubbles splitting apart and merging again in a strange and liberating dance of the cosmos. Heat and light was everywhere. Change was constant and nothing was uncertain.

Yet as beautiful as this universe was, the unchanging swept across this skyscape in a wave. Things became as they were to remain for eternity. Orbits became circles as the stars in the sky settled into their places. Knowledge surged through Rose and she let it come, drinking up the wordlessness with a thirst that was unquenchable, until it pulsed through her very veins with a radiant silver light.

She learned what it was to be human, a fickle, wavering candle flame, easily tossed from one direction to the next in a sea of indecision. She was overcome with how fragile humans were, how lost in the dark and vulnerable they were. But she was also amazed by their beauty. They battle through their lives, demanding that the seas of change cease their waves; how they swim against the current, when they could simply float on the surface, still and at rest even in the midst of a constant torrent of change.

Then she learned what it was to be Tenlenesse. If humans are the flame, then the Tenlenesse are the candleholders. If humans swim through a sea of change, the Tenlenesse are the shore. Where humans are fickle, Tenlenesse are indomitable. Where humans age, Tenlenesse remain young. More, so much more about her ancestry coursed through Rose that all became as long-lost friends whose names had simply escaped her tongue. Rose understood kindred spirits. She understood truth, and what it was to stand for or against it.

And the birth of her kind became clear. Crooked intent seized the ultimate power and horded it selfishly. The Pendulum Of Power, it was called. It was what had been taken by the Father of all Tenlenesse. It had created their race. He had taken it and fled the surface realm into this realm. Yet with all his powers, he could not stop the spread of Armin's teachings. One by one his children, his slaves, his minions, shed themselves of his control and stood upright under the sunlight, with moonfire flowing through their veins. As truth abolishes a lie, so the Tenlenesse of the light abolished their own kindred to the only place left for the dark to exist — to the Netherlands, the world between worlds.

She was Rose. Here she stood, both human and Tenlenesse. She knew what it was to suffer the constant change of humanity, to be tortured and tormented by the worst of the dark places. Yet she had also been given the indomitable spirit of her great-grandfather and his kind. Never again would she be forced to give in to the dark will of another. And never again would she fear a lie when she knew the truth.

There was a great Armageddon raging between the two factors of Tenlenesse, with casualties on both sides. The dark Tenlenesse had been venting their frustration with Rose's ancestry on her personally, savoring every drop of her suffering as a way of justifying the loss of their once splendid home. But never again.

Never again could a dark Tenlenesse conceal himself in a lie and approach her. Beings of the Fire Realm see to the heart of every matter; to lie, or to speak the truth. And if Rose stood for the truth, the lie would be broken upon her like waves upon the shore.

Rose blinked, and the world changed its colors. All things became richer, fuller, brighter. Yet the light did not hurt her eyes. She could see clearly into every corner, every shadow. She could stare up into the sunlight pouring over the fountain and not wince, and still see the distant speck of Aigelendais flying over the cathedral.

She stepped back and gazed at her great-grandfather in wonder. Armin moved forward and they embraced. Her great-grandfather seemed no older than she. "Welcome home, daughter," he said to her.

That jogged her memory, and Rose pulled away. "I must go home," she said, sadly. She chuckled and shook her head, then tried again. "I must go back."

Armin looked at her, his disappointment evident.

"It is true, Your Highness," Terrance spoke up. "Rose is on a mission of some urgency, to save her friend from the dark Tenlenesse."

Armin nodded. "A worthy cause. May I ask the nature of your friendship?"

Before Rose could speak Terrance said, "She is an Aigelendai."

Armin blinked. "You have to go back, then!"

"I know, great-grandfather." Rose's disappointment was just as apparent.

"Rare is a friendship between our races. Only in the surface realm could such a thing happen, and that sanctity must be preserved. But most terrible is the animosity that may exist between one of us and one of them. Your friend, should she be caught, would know an anguish beyond any human suffering. I charge you, Rose, my daughter. Save her, please. You must."

Rose choked back a sob, nodded, and embraced her great-grandfather. "Until I see you again, then."

Armin smiled gently. "You know how to find me."

She returned the smile, then turned and was led back down the aisle by Terrance Leafvein. At the doorway she turned to see Armin watching them still. He had not moved, but stood before the fountain of moonfire, with his white robe and silver hair. For all his advanced age, he could still have been eighteen. He waved, and she returned the gesture, then stumbled into the sunlight onto the street with no name.

267

Her hair attracted her attention as Rose caught her balance, and she took hold of a strand as she righted herself. It had changed to a silver sheen, otherworldly, yet somehow just right. She stared for a moment before releasing it and glanced over at Terrance's own silver hair. She plucked an eyebrow and checked that, too. It had changed color as well. Yet... Rose held it as far away from her as she could. Then she made Terrance take it and took a step back. Still she could see the minute silver strand. Terrance let the hair drop and she watched it fall all the way to the cobblestones at his feet. Then she blinked in surprise and looked up at him again.

Terrance shrugged. "Welcome to what it is to be Tenlenesse." All Rose's senses had been awakened as equally as her sight had been.

"What has happened to me? Am I stronger, invincible?"

Terrance shook his head. "You are in better shape, for sure. You will neither tire, nor grow weary ever again. But you will know when to take rest, and will do so. You will live in a balance with yourself, and those seeking change from you will break them- selves upon you. I know not all the rules of the surface realm, so I cannot say for sure what will be. But I know you will never fear a dark place again."

"I can see in the dark." It wasn't a question.

He nodded. "Others in the dark can also see you, for good or bad. Yet know you have a power over them they can not chal- lenge." Rose and Terrance both knew of whom he spoke.

Rose nodded. "The moonfire showed me this, in the fountain."

Terrance slid his arm through hers. "Then come. Your friend awaits."

They lingered long on the street with no name. For all her talk of hurry, every step they took was like a year. Lifetime after life- time may have passed, but in those moments was a melding of their hearts into one indomitable love that was as strong as their race. They teased and chased each other, pouted and shared words. They made up and tasted each other's kisses. They talked of things not at all important, and of life-changing revelations. They stopped and watched the life of the Fire Realm pass by, and were visited by a flock of Aigelendai, who swarmed about them before darting off amongst the trees.

"Penia!" Rose cried, reminded of her friend. She took Terrance's hand in hers and they rushed the rest of the way back to the immense castle and its endless ceilings.

He guided her through the place to the stairs leading out of the tree. And as they began their descent the spell was broken. Time returned to normal. Yet their love remained strong; bound by an enchantment their hearts had created together. Yet they remained as one, grown into one long, long ago.

"I know now why you didn't want to walk the street of no names with me," Rose said, holding tightly onto his hand.

Terrance sniffed. "It is not such a bad thing to be bonded to you."

"No." She looked at him and grinned. "But you still hesitated."

"I could not know it would be like this. It must be your human blood that makes our love so heated. We may have bonded as brother and sister, or as cousins. Or as dear friends; no one could have known. With pure hearts, with pure intentions, we would do things no differently if we could do them again."

Rose stopped and pulled him into an embrace. She kissed his neck, looked up at him and said, "If I could do things all over again I swear I would do nothing differently, even having known the outcome."

He hesitated a moment then pushed her away and held her at arms' distance. "We must hurry," Terrance urged. "Your friend has been long in the hands of your enemies." He took her hand in his once again and guided her back to his forge.

Along the way Rose glanced at him at intervals, and each time Terrance dared not return her looks. Yet she could tell he was dreading seeing her part from his side. "I can come back?" Halfway between a question and hope, she finally dragged him to a stop and made him look at her.

"You can. But you will see. You are greater than yourself. You are the daughter of a Baron, heiress to a Barony."

"I have been — " He held a finger to her lips.

"But you are so much more than that now. You are a Tenlenesse as well, and that is no small thing. You are of the bloodline of His Majesty, Armin Derango, his great-granddaughter." He bowed to her. "Your Highness, I am your servant, as I know you are mine. But you may find you will have your hands full in your own realm. You will not be able to handle the burdens of this one too."

"I can come back," Rose insisted. "I know how now. I know all things about the spectral stones, about moonfire, about the Netherlands and traveling through them."

"Your Highness, My Lady, you have wisdom as well. What you haven't realized yet is that time does not parallel itself between these two realms of our homes. You will come back for an after-noon and stay for a year. And eventually that will not be enough."

"You can come with me."

Terrance shook his head. "No, My Lady. My enemies would see us enter the Netherlands and flock to my light like moths to the flame. But these insects sting. Where your human side can drive an army of them away, my Tenlenesse blood will allow but one of their kind to slip a dagger into my back and I am undone."

Rose stared at him for a moment, and then her lips began to quiver. "I will find a way," she promised. "I will scourge the Netherlands of them, and I will find a way."

"Then take hope in that. Only you have the power to do so."

They were silent for the remainder of the short journey back to his forge. When they entered the heat of his workshop once again, the Aigelendai inside began to hum with impatience. "They know," she said to him.

He nodded. "Did the moonfire teach you nothing of their kind?"

She shook her head. "It was all of our kind."

"They see our emotions as colors. I suspect they can interpret the meaning of those colors to find out intent, as well. For them the world is all color, with solid objects appearing only as shadows."

"Green for growth and regrowth," Rose remembered Nivien saying. "Penia always shines green."

Terrance nodded again. "I have never heard of such a thing happening. I believe your Penia is a healer in her very nature."

"She is," Rose said, "and I must save her."

"Then take this." Terrance rummaged through his cluttered workbench and retrieved a glass bottle adorned with silver-work, and attached to a silver chain. The bottle had a stopper and was filled with glowing silver moonfire. He hung the chain about her neck, and she was taken aback by the beauty of the workmanship.

"Did you create this?" she asked, holding the vial in her hands.

"It's just a simple thing," Terrance admitted as he smoothed Rose's hair. "I grow thirsty in all this heat, and moonfire serves me better than water." He would not speak more of the bottle. "Your Aigelendai will heal fast with moonfire in her veins once again. It does not take much for one of her kind. Just wet her lips. The Aigeleindai easily choke if they drink too fast."

Rose nodded, committing his advice to memory.

He stood back to gaze at her. "I would not see you leave me empty handed," he told her.

"Yet I wear your sister's clothing, and carry your flask of moon-fire."

He shook his head. "Straw." He stared at her for a time and she basked in his gaze as if under the sun. Suddenly he crossed to a cupboard mounted on the far wall. As he opened it, the glitter of silver shone brightly from within. He was careful in choosing, for long did his hand linger on each piece. But in the end, Terrance returned with two silver earrings and a silver comb, and placed these into her hands before he was off again.

Rose's mind reeled with the beauty and craftsmanship of the jewelry in her hands. Never in all her years in the surface realm had she ever imagined anything as exquisite. She would be the envy of the court when they saw these pieces of jewelry, clamber-ing for the name of the man who made them, out-bidding each other with prices Rose swore she'd never give in to. She would keep these forever, be buried with them in her ears and in her hair — if she ever died.

She looked up with tears in her eyes to see Terrance standing before her holding a large package wrapped in silver linen. The linen itself must have been priceless. "My sister wove this from thread I made. It is to keep my lunch in. More straw. But what is wrapped inside is not, nor is it any simple trinket of fancy."

"I give this to you, not as my heart, but as my queen. I craft all my pieces with love, hoping to be worthy of the lady I've now found. You've inspired all of these, even though you lived in a different realm, and have been separated from me by a sea of darkness. This piece is worthy of our love." Terrance sank to one knee and held it out to her. "Now I pray it may be worthy of your station as well."

Tenderly, Rose pulled away a corner of the linen and the fabric fell away to reveal a delicately beautiful crown of silver, adorned with shining diamonds and frozen moonfire. Her breath caught in her throat and she stared at it, afraid to touch such unearthly splendor. Everything in her wanted to refuse the gift, but she could not refuse anything given to her by this man.

She took him by the wrists and tugged until he rose to his feet.

Gazing up into his eyes, she carefully took the crown and placed it and the linen cloth on a bench nearby, before turning back to him and throwing her arms around his chest in a strong embrace. Terrance exhaled as she listened to his heart beating, then he put his arms around Rose and held her for a long time.

Finally, he nudged against her head with his nose. "You have to leave," he said quietly. "Do not reveal your crown until the right time."

"I will keep it close and keep it a secret. I promise."

Rose stepped back and he re-wrapped the crown as she held her hair back with the comb then fastened the earrings he had given her to her ears. He handed the wrapped cloth to her and smiled as Aigelendai descended around her, obscuring her vision with their glistening light.

80CR

She closed her eyes and gave herself over to the light, allowed it to flow from her veins. Then Rose reached out to the Netherlands and slid into their murky depths. Immediately the Aigelendai let go of her and she was cast into the darkness like a lone comet coursing through the deep vastness of empty space. In the distance her eyes saw a single, solitary sword. She fixed her course upon it and ignored the shadows moving about her.

Some of them came close, inquisitive about this strange Tenlenesse, curious about her audacity to enter their layer arrayed in such revealing light. Yet when they came close they saw the human warrior underneath, the human whose will was resolutely fixed upon her course, and they quivered in fear as they melted before her.

All at once she was standing in her tower with Penia's sword at her bare feet. She bent down and retrieved the delicate yet brutal weapon, then saw the stone Nivien had given her, lying where she had dropped it in the fight. Such a small thing, to have offered hope in such a dark place.

Her eyes rested on her bed, and there was Nivien himself kneeling beside it. Her dear Penia lay on her back, her blonde hair a tangle of knots strewn against Rose's pillows. Nivean had pulled the strands from her face, but had been too afraid to touch her more. She lay under a set of vast and crumpled green wings. Everywhere Rose could see, even the girl's clothing, was veined, with black tendrils reaching out over her pale skin.

Nivien looked up at Rose, not at all surprised to see her standing before him; with a vial of moonfire between her breasts, a sword in one hand, and a shrouded crown in the other. "My Lady," Nivien choked. He turned back to his friend.

Rose rushed to his side, placed the sword and the crown on the bed, and unstoppered the moonfire. Carefully, she touched Penia's lips with the stopper and Nivien sighed. "Thank you, My Lady."

Penia convulsed as the moonfire drizzled into her mouth. She coughed once, twice, then arched her back and shrieked in agonizing pain. Rose flinched as if struck by a physical blow. Penia opened her eyes and looked over at Rose. She was fully alert but too weak to move, although she smiled weakly to see that her friend had returned.

She was unable to speak as a human, so in the way of her kind she told Rose much about what had happened to her during

Rose's absence. To Penia, the pain and even her death would have been worth it to see Rose here before her now, arrayed as a Tenlenesse of Light and as a human woman simultaneously.

"Your pain will be avenged," Rose responded with her human tongue. She gripped Penia's sword as the rage grew stronger inside her.

"Your tower has been boarded up," Nivien told her. "Your people fear it is haunted."

"It is now!" Rose's tone was menacing as she lifted up Penia's sword once again. "Guard my crown!" She spun around and stepped back into the Netherlands. "I won't be long!"

The world of shadows uncurled around her like a spider its legs. Enough of the surface realm remained that the walls of her chamber and her dear friend with her healer remained in Rose's sight. "So this is what it is like to be invisible," she said out loud, hearing her voice echo through the room and knowing another human would have heard the sound.

Two insubstantial shades hovered over Penia. Each had a finger embedded into the girl's chest. As Rose watched, it seemed to her that a great battle was taking place between the phantoms and her friend. From the touch of those foul beings came the tendrils of darkness. Rose could see the darkness pulsing from their touch, spreading ever farther throughout Penia's body.

She hefted the sword and looked deeper into the Netherlands. Two Tenlenesse materialized out of the smoke and both looked up in alarm when they felt Rose's immediate presence. "What are you doing here?" one of them asked while the other just stared on in terrified amazement.

Rose stepped in and severed the hand of the one who had spoken. He cried out and stumbled away from Penia and half the lines on her body vanished. The other Tenlenesse let go of his victim and unsheathed his sword. Rose smiled bitterly when she recognized him, and the other half of the dark veins subsided from Penia.

His face was a skull, the clothing of one of her father's guards. "Hello Ridley," Rose said fearlessly. Ridley turned and vanished into the darkness. No matter, thought Rose, she would deal with Ridley soon enough.

She lunged first at the injured Tenlenesse and drove her sword through the creature's neck. He tried to say something and gur-gled instead, then died and slid free of her sword, dropping to the floor before he disappeared into the eternal depths of the Netherlands.

Then she turned and faced Nivien. "They must have been missed from the castle."

"They took shifts," Nivien told her. "They could not touch me for I dared not enter their realm and be caught."

"And yet they did not attack you in your human form either."

He shrugged. "Penia reached out and lured them to her to save you. I am nothing except emotion and thought. My physical form is just a disguise."

Without taking her eyes off of Nivien, Rose placed a hand on his shoulder. "You are much more than that, my friend." Her touch communicated much and a great blessing was passed to the man.

He lowered his eyes. "Thank you my lady, that means much to me."

Rose nodded as she carefully stepped over Penia's body and advanced on Ridley.

He stared at her for a moment, then when he realized he could not bear her gaze, turned and fled through the walls. Rose chased after him, and everything became a blur as they raced through the upper levels of the castle, over its rooftops and through the smoke that still lingered there.

She caught up with him and grabbed his cloak. With iron-firm resolve, Rose suspended Ridley's form and dragged him back into the physical realm. Caught with his hideous true form revealed to all the world, Ridley tumbled out of the Netherlands some ten paces above the great hall.

He screeched as Rose stepped back into the smoke. She stood motionless with quiet satisfaction as she watched her former tor-mentor plummet through the stained glass windows that were the pride and treasure of her family.

Rose's family, seated at dinner, were showered with glass as Ridley's body slammed into the table and his head landed in her Lord Father's plate. The Baron jumped to his feet, enraged and terrified, as the table gave out under the weight and folded in half.

Ridley stared up at Jason with his monster's skull-for-a-face. "My Lord," he hissed before his head slumped to the side as he died.

By this time everyone was screaming and pointing, and Jason roared, "What is the meaning of this!"

He glared upwards through the windows, but could not see Rose hovering over him. Lady Nimway saw though, and Rose's eyes locked onto hers unmercifully.

Lady Nimway screamed, her eyes widened with terror, and fled from the great hall.

Rose's eyes narrowed as she disappeared from even her own view. Obviously, Lady Nimway was staying completely within the surface realm, for fear of being caught by her. I'll save her for last, Rose told herself before racing back to her tower.

Penia was already being helped to her feet when Rose material-ized in front of her. "My Lady," Penia said with a slight curtsy that made her sway uncertainly.

"Enough of that," Rose chided. "You did not keep such airs when I did not know who I was. Now that I stand before you — "

"A Halfling," Penia added.

"And a royal one, at that," Nivien contributed.

Rose smiled. " — a royal Halfling, I am still your friend, and all that is changed is all that would remain forever the same."

"Spoken like a true Tenlenesse," Penia said with a weak smile.

Rose took the vial of moonfire from around her neck and held it out to Penia. "One who has tasted the common bond of our kind."

Penia accepted it and took a careful sip. She coughed, but kept it down, then altered into a smaller form. The weight of the vial dragged her down, but Rose caught her up in her hand. Penia was only a hand's length tall, and the vial was nearly as large as she. Yet the girl tipped it back with Rose's help and drank long and deeply, although she barely took any from the vial at all.

When she was finished, she looked up at Rose and smiled. Much of her strength was returned. Thank you, sister, she told Rose in the language of her kind.

In answer, Rose took the vial from the Aigelendai and propelled the little creature into the air. Penia immediately reappeared in her human form, and stretched leisurely as she looked from Rose to Nivien. "They will try to hide," she said. "Let us find them for you."

Rose thought for a moment, then nodded, and two tiny specks of green light streaked out of her chamber.

The Tenlesse who had tormented Rose barely saw her guardian spies, Nivien and Penia, before the Aigelendai found Rose's ene-

278

mies. They knew not that they had been discovered, until Rose came striding out of the Netherlands with the flaming sword of light in her hand, to pass swift judgment on those who had tor - tured her for so long. So suddenly did she appear, and so quickly did she act, that none could take steps to stop or question her, and few even had time to recognize her.

But those who trusted and loved Rose were spared a moment and a smile. They saw the look of relief on the silver woman's face, saw tears of healing and understood; while the Dark Tenlenesse simply faded into the Netherlands as they died.

When she'd finished her work in the barracks, Rose gave the room a final looking over, and glanced at the silent and startled guards that stared at her in complete astonishment. "The Avenger!" Tremel shouted with an upraised fist, recognizing Rose for who and what she was. As Rose stepped back into the Netherlands he shouted, "The Avenger of Light!"

None but Galadin knew what he was talking about, but having only seen Rose's back, he had not been able to put it all together. "The Lady?" he asked, rising to his feet. "That was the Lady?"

The look on Tremel's face answered him, and Galadin began to laugh. "It seems you're out of a job!" Tremel teased.

But Galadin was already running from the room past the other guards who seemed equally bewildered. "The Lady of Light is here!" he shouted. "The Lady of Light is returned!"

No one who had been privy to the inner circle's secret misun- derstood Galadin's message, and a wave of excitement raced through the castle as the news spread. None but Rose's selected few even understood who she was. But the veritable bloodbath that followed in her wake caused quite a different shock.

"We're under attack!" a Tenlenesse shouted, and those that had no idea what was going on had the good sense to take up arms and defensive positions. Rose laughed when she saw this, saw how her enemy surrounded itself with human shields, to no avail.

None but the Tenlenesse could see Rose until the final moment of attack, and these could not look at the magnificence of her. She appeared in the midst of them as her sword drove home, then vanished before anyone could react, to move on to her next judg‑ment.

Finally, all had been purged but for the two creatures who had holed themselves up in the great hall with Rose's family and a number of armed men.

Rose stood before the hall's main doors and felt the surface realm close in around her, contain her. She took half a dozen breaths to steady her nerves, then threw the doors open wide and strode into the room.

There was a great eruption of noise, but Rose stood stalwart, waiting for the chaos to subside. A line of guards leveled weapons at her, yet no one attacked or broke rank. They stood guarding her family and Lady Nimway, but their faces bore masks of uncertainty and fear. Rose noticed that Tremel and Galadin had been summoned by her father and stood with the other men. Yet they wept with joy when they saw her.

As the room finally quieted, Tremel sheathed his sword, and Galadin rushed towards her.

"Hold!" the Baron roared.

But Galadin, with his sword outstretched in front of him, ran rashly towards her. "My Lady!" he shouted, and Rose laughed out loud as he caught her up in a rough bear hug and lifted her bare feet off the floor. "You're alive!" he exclaimed. Tears filled his eyes.

Rose's mirth reached the rafters and the broken windows above. "I yield, brother!" she cried. He squeezed her even more. "Yield, you big oaf! You're supposed to protect me, not break my back!" Rose giggled.

Realizing he had her in a bear hug, Galadin remembered his place and eased her down. Embarrassed by his outburst, he dropped to his knees in reverence and placed his sword at her feet. "My Lady," he pledged. "I am yours to command. I would die for you."

"Pick up your sword, Sir Knight."

"I am no knight, My Lady."

Rose smiled. She placed Penia's sword on his shoulder. "I dub thee, Sir Galadin. The Lady Of Light makes it so. Now stand, Sir Knight, for my work is not finished."

Galadin came to his feet with a roar and spun to face his com-rades with his sword held out towards them. Tremel, their captain, strode towards Galadin, unsheathed his sword and spun around to stand at his man's side in front of Rose. Galadin roared a wordless challenge at the other men, who shrank from the blood rage that was upon him. He shifted his sword from one hand to the next, as if daring them to attack.

"My Lord!" Lady Nimway bawled. "This witch has started a revolt! Your men must attack before it spreads farther!"

"HOLD!" Rose shouted, using her new Tenlenesse powers to add weight to the command. The room froze. "I demand the right to speak, Father."

"Who is this creature that she would call me Father?" the Baron challenged, but Lady Feonna came forward and placed a hand on her husband's arm.

"Something of this woman is familiar to me," the Baroness answered for him. "I do not know her, yet something in me would recognize a child of my womb, no matter the change that has taken place."

Priscilla, too, stepped forward. "Rose?"

Rose gazed upon her younger sister, then curtsied. "I humbly bow to the heiress of the Tresville Barony."

"Rose!" Priscilla rushed towards her sister. Rose had barely enough time to hand off her sword to Galadin, who gripped the weapon with a grin and pointed that one at the guards as well.

"Now he has two of them," one of his targets moaned.

But then Priscilla was hugging her sister and crying. "We thought you were dead!"

Rose pulled away and used her skills from the Fire Realm to tell her sister what she knew, and something about Priscilla's own recent adventures as well.

Priscilla flushed and looked away. "I wouldn't … I didn't …. It was her idea. She was always making it hard to be on your side. She made it seem — "

"I know how she made it seem," Rose replied softly. In a louder voice so that the entire room could hear, she turned towards her father and declared, "And now all my jailers, my torturers, my rapists, my nightmares; all my would-be masters are dead, except for two!"

"She lies!" Lady Nimway shrieked.

Priscilla turned and stared at her. "How would you know Rose was talking about you!"

Lady Nimway could not answer, could not even look at her. She grew frantic and tried to cover her face with her arms as she looked everywhere but at Priscilla. "The woman is a witch! She has cursed me somehow!"

"Look at her!" Rose bellowed. "All of you, those who know me and those who do not! Stare at the Lady Nimway and make that a test! I have not bewitched her! It is she who has done wrong to me! Now look at her, and see for yourself that the Lady Rose was never mad!"

All eyes turned to Lady Nimway. She shrieked over and over, and curled into herself, going to her knees and holding her arms over her head. "Get away!" she cried. "I am a lady of the court!"

"You are a thief!" Rose declared. "And an imposter! I expose the truth of you to my household!"

"No!" Lady Nimway protested. She bore up under the scrutiny for another moment, then slowly faded into thin air.

Rose snarled, took up her sword once again, and stepped towards Lady Nimway. She remained in her physical body, that her court could bear witness to all of it. But enough of Rose walked within the Netherlands that she was able to take hold of the hideous creature Lady Nimway had become, and held her there on her knees by her hair. Then she made Nimway come back into the light of the room, forcing her to maintain her true form as she had done with Ridley.

Everyone was shocked and repulsed when they saw the creature for what she was, and Rose looked to those who bore witness. "For years!" she shouted, "this woman, this thing has sought vengeance upon me for who my great-grandfather was! For he became as I am now, and drove this wickedness, this filth, from his home." She forced Lady Nimway's head up and glared into her face. "Now I am back! And I come in his name, with the authority of his kingdom, with the power of his blood."

The creature shrieked, knowing the Avenger of Light had her at last.

Rose looked down at her, watching the apparition wither under her gaze. "This is my judgment to you, Lady Nimway. You will live, but never again will you enter the Netherlands."

Lady Nimway stared at Rose with new horror.

"Never again will you change form, never again will you deceive. I allow you to go forth before me to warn your kind who would dare meddle in affairs that are none of their concern. Tell them, tell them all! The Avenger of Light is here, and she will find your kind and bring an end to your evil, to the sins you commit against humanity!" Rose shook Lady Nimway once, then released her.

The creature wept and cowered.

"Now go! Get out of my home!" Rose commanded.

All eyes watched as Lady Nimway, the dark Tenlenesse, fled from the castle to do as she was bid. There was a thick silence while Rose watched the open doorway and felt a weight finally lift from her chest. She felt free, and safe at last.

There was but one other matter to attend to, and then Rose could rest and be with her people. "Dalia!" she called in a sing-song voice.

"No!" Dalia shrieked. The stewardess tried to flee from the room, but was caught by one of the guards and held fast. He dragged her to where Rose stood and thrust the woman down on the ground.

Rose stood over her, deciding how best to proceed. She could have ended it then and there, but her new Tenlenesse eyes saw something in the stewardess that was worth giving pause for. So she watched and waited in silence to see what Dalia would do.

Dalia, chief over every servant in Castle Tresville, began to cry. Her crying turned to weeping; her weeping became wailing. She struggled to her knees, her head cast down to the floor, and her voice keened throughout the entire room.

And still Rose watched passively.

The wailing continued for some time, undisturbed in the shocked silence of Rose's people. Finally, Dalia crawled over to

Rose's feet and allowed her tears to fall upon them. "Forgive me!" she cried through her tears. She did not dare look up, but continued to weep on Rose's feet. "Forgive me!"

Rose saw it first, with her silver eyes of light. The court stirred in surprise as they watched Dalia's dark hair begin to glow with a silver sheen. But other changes were occurring as well, for Rose watched the innermost core of Dalia's being change from dark to light, then spread throughout the woman's veins like silver mercury.

Dalia dried Rose's feet off with her own hair, crying uncontrollably all the while, no longer able to say the words. But her soul cried them out in the language of the Fire Realm, and Rose herself was moved to tears. She took Dalia by the shoulder and the woman looked up into Rose's eyes.

Those who saw Dalia's face were stunned by the changes wrought there, for the woman looked much as Rose did, with glittering silver eyes, silver eyebrows, and an air of nobility the woman had not possessed a moment before. Yet the tears continued to fall, and when Rose finally lifted her to her feet, she matched each of Dalia's tears with one of her own.

Rose's sword clanged to the stone floor and the women embraced like sisters as they cried in each other's arms. They stayed that way for a long while, long enough that Penia and Nivien came to stand in the doorway – in human form. They also saw the new Tenlenesse of Light, and were themselves moved to tears.

Most watching understood little of what had happened, yet when the two Tenlenesse broke apart and Rose extended her hand to the Aigelendai, the people felt as though they had witnessed a great victory. Penia and Nivien came forward and placed the vial of moonfire into Rose's hand. Rose in turn handed the liquid to Dallia, who looked to Rose for encouragement as she dried her eyes. Rose nodded, and the woman unstoppered the vial and drank.

The effects were instantaneous. It was as if her whole body was revitalized, as though she had been hollow until she tasted the moonfire from her realm. Dalia smiled with pure joy, and handed the vial and stopper back to Rose.

Then she knelt before Rose and lowered her head out of respect. The two Aigelendai sank to their knees as well; then Rose's closest friends, those who had shared her secret. The rest of the household followed their example, too dumfounded to question Rose's authority. Surely they would never be able to forget what they had seen and heard this day!

Priscilla glanced over the bent heads of her father's subjects, and she too went to her knees. As heiress of Tresville, she was offering her loyalty not to the king of Hansurn, but to the Lady Of Light. Their mother, Baroness of Tresville, understood what had happened to her daughter, and she too subjugated herself to her daughter's rule.

The Baron of Tresville stared at his elder daughter in amazement, remembering the years he had thought her soft in the brain, or faking it. The years he'd sworn she was simply vying for attention, and all the times she had made his life miserable and had been punished for her lies and disobedience. He thought of the shame she'd brought to his family, of the immense waste of discipline and resources her behavior had caused to his land, and how she had made it difficult for Jason to serve his king.

But now her father saw his daughter revealed as she truly was. Even more amazing were the two healers kneeling at her feet, who looked at each other and nodded. And then the glowing green wings. Lord Tresville had seen the wondrous green spectral stones before, and these matched that. Growth and Regrowth, a voice inside his head intoned, as the healers stood and revealed a linen cloth made of fine silver strands.

They unveiled a crown of unsurpassed beauty and affixed it upon his daughter's head. Rose already looked uncomfortable with the weight, the responsibility, yet years of being beaten back by his, the Baron's allies, had made his daughter wise and prepared.

Rose's father choked on his tears, and as Rose turned her eyes towards him, Jason realized he was a man standing alone amid a land lost to him, master of nothing but a fool's belief. He too sank slowly to his knees in subjugation to the authority of the Avenger, the Lady of Light.

The silence was complete as Rose felt her power, and her responsibility. "Arise!" she commanded at last. "I have a husband to win!"

⁊❧

The Dark Tenlenesse tried to resist through the strength of their loyal human friends. Though their influence was without ending, and although armies massed at her approach, Rose's tactics always remained the same. Word of her spread far out into the kingdom, as Lady Nimway saw fit to relay it.

Not all who heard of the purge sided with their crooked friends from another world. Rose was quick to give authority of the Barony back to her father, and went herself to the king. She appeared rather suddenly in a blast of light and glory while he was attending to social obligations and offering devotions in front of a great crowd of his subjects during their celebrations.

"My king!" Rose called out, loudly enough for the entire congregation to hear.

The king and his priest looked on mutely, convinced she was an angel of wrath come to end their own hypocrisy.

"I am the Lady Rose Tresville."

"I know who you are," the king retorted, rising indignantly to his feet. "What are you about?" His gruff manner was hiding his fear, and the attempt made her smile.

"Only the liberation of an entire race of mortals equal in splendor and nobility to that of humans."

"Liberation, certainly, but I doubt your words about equality. You are here to take my crown."

Rose laughed. "Your Highness! Look upon my head! My future husband would be most insulted if I traded his gift for dross made by crude human hands! No Sire, keep your crown and the authority it gives you. I come to tell you I am here to purge your kingdom of an evil that seeks to take from you what I have rightly given back."

"I've heard the most impossible rumors," he admitted.

"I'll let you think on that word impossible for a while. May you come to understand why I don't want your kingdom." Then Rose vanished before his eyes and those of the entire mass who waited for her to begin her liberation of the capital city.

It was the same from region to region. Rose would send word of her coming; the Dark Tenlenesse would mass an army to meet her; she would match them with a growing horde of her own, then vanish while the leaders talked terms. Then she would kill every Dark Tenlenesse standing among the enemy ranks. Rose would reappear a span of a few breaths later only to announce that the army standing before her had no one whom she would wish to harm.

At last Rose would wish the Captain or Sergeant, or General (whatever the rank of the leader), along with his retainers, a pleasant afternoon, and disappear for good. Her men would laugh and shake their heads, then disband until the next time they were needed. Finally, Rose and her two healers would go back into that region and scourge the place from top to bottom.

A few of the Dark Tenlenesse changed, as Dalia had, and they were allowed to live; for their repentance was as complete and absolute as Lady Rose was gracious and good. But tragically, it was a time of reckoning for the human kingdom of Hansurn. The streets flowed with invisible blood.

It came to an end one day in the autumn. In the Netherlands, dark shadows hinged the borders of the kingdom, but the king - dom itself was full of empty white light. Her vengeance had been quick and merciful, yet final.

Rose knew that she had done all that was her right to do, and so settled back to enjoy her place at her father's humble court.

ᏕᎥᏇ

One night a Trilian came to Rose, on the heavy wings of a bird. Everything about the man implied an air of strength. His arms were massive; his chest a barrel; the muscles in his great wings were thick and corded. And he was very angry as he seethed at her through the thick mat of his black beard and short curly hair.

"Hello, Trilian," she said mildly. They were standing atop the flat roof of her father's watchtower, with the full moon low on the horizon and clouds floating overhead. "No doubt you come in secret."

"You stand out like a beacon in the dark! All eyes were turned to you. It was difficult to be unseen."

"How would you know where all eyes are turned? You who were once the most righteous of races, whose grandfather was a holy man in the sight of Almighty — now you seem to know everything about what a mere human does in the dark?"

Rose walked to the edge of the parapet and looked across the darkened fields to the near-invisible horizon. "Most are asleep in their beds, with their eyes closed. Those few who are awake are concerned with their own lives, and have come to understand that

I am only mortal, like they are." She turned to look at him. "Like you are."

He clenched his teeth in anger.

"You come from the southwest?"

"Where else would I come from?" he spat.

"The Air Realm. That is the place Almighty prepared for your kind, to live in peace and harmony with mankind and all other races."

He seethed as he clenched his fists.

"Have you come to kill me?" Rose asked quietly.

"I have."

"Because I am a demon?"

"How do you know so much of what I am about?"

"Moonfire," Rose replied. "It teaches me much about the king-dom of Almighty. It spoke droves about the Trilians, and Trilian their father. He repented from his evil to stand as a banner for what is right and he was awarded an angel-like body for his efforts. He continued the fight for what was right and just, but over the years he and his followers became proud and arrogant, trusting in the traditions of their kind, rather than in the truth they once fought for."

The Trilian had nothing to say, for the man was short of words, yet powerful of deed. But Rose could see doubt in his heart, bud-ding forth as he hesitated from his actions to hear more.

"I know that truth, Trilian," Rose replied gently. "And that truth has utterly and completely set me free. Moonfire is the gift Almighty gave my fallen race, and the race of the Aigelendai, and the Mikenans, the Sporaliki, and the Red Drove."

"All the fire demons have this gift?"

"Did I not just say so? And we are no more demons than you. We simply chose a path of evil when we began. Yet it was Almighty's destiny for us that we become these races, that we share in the abundance of moonfire."

"I doubt your words. For what other mighty form could He give the Trilians as punishment, than the form he gave us as a gift?"

Rose laughed. "Why, the form you have, thick skull! Only He would allow you to add pride to the mix the way He allowed the Tenlenesse to add monstrosity to theirs."

"I admit you have not the form of your demonic kindred."

"You use that term so liberally. I have a feeling you know not the truth you so readily speak of."

His eyes narrowed as he glared at Rose.

"Here," she said, unsheathing a purple spectral dagger from her belt. She slapped it down on the stone between them. "If you come with the authority of Almighty, then nothing I do can stop you from killing me. So, here is my weapon. S trike the demon down, Trilian. I am just a weak woman, in whatever form I take, no matter how proficient I am with that blade, no matter how many of my own evil kind I have destroyed. Take it. Strike me dead with the authority you think you have a right to wield."

The Trilian looked at the blade, then picked it up. "You are an abomination," he roared. Then he lunged. And passed right through her. Stunned, he whirled around, and Rose held her hands up by her head.

"Perhaps you are meant to strike me in my back," Rose mocked him. "Mayhap Almighty is sparing you from having to look into my eyes when I die." She looked straight ahead. "Be done with it then."

The Trilian hefted her dagger and lunged again. This time, while he was still off balance, Rose kicked him squarely between the wings, neatly between the shoulder blades. The blow caught him off balance and sent him sailing from the tower. With a flap of his wings he righted himself and spun around to face her anew.

She appeared, cross-legged as though seated on some hard sur-face, right before his eyes. There was no set of wings to hold her up, no tie to the physical world that she might lay a claim to. She rested her arms on her knees and cupped her head in her hands and said, "Now what are we do to?"

"It is by witchcraft that you do these things!" the Trilian spat, although he had more dignity than to attack her again.

"You are an idiot."

His eyes narrowed at the insult.

"Go away Trilian. I have things to do." Quite deliberately, Rose stood up and walked back onto the tower roof.

"How did you do that!"

Rose sighed. He was persistent, she'd give him that much.

She turned to regard him. "How do you fly?" she asked. "How do you sing in two voices? How do you have so much strength?"

"These are all Almighty's gifts to me. I am this way because he would have me be this way."

Rose shrugged. "You have your answer then."

"Your kind stole this right," the Trilian asserted.

"Trilian, that is the first thing you've been able to say all night that I find insulting. Do not doubt for one moment that the serv-ice I have done your ridiculous cause by eradicating filth from this kingdom was done so that I may be considered one of their kind."

"It is true. You are different than the other Tenlenesse."

Rose sighed again with exasperation, and tried again. "What was the single strongest characteristic the Dark Tenlenesse have?"

"They live in darkness."

"And what is the single most obvious characteristic the Tenlenesse of Light have?" She stood back to prove her point, and gestured to the glowing silver and the shining white that she was and that she wore. Rose shone in the darkness like a beacon, as the Trilian had said.

He glared at her, equally frustrated. "Then, Lady of light; if you are of Almighty's bidding; and have taken on such a radical trans - formation from his presence and his gifts; and if I have been mis - led somewhere until I stand outside his grace and don' t even know it, what radical transformation would I have to mark me as one of His?"

"Let me answer your question with a question," Rose said. "What kind of an eagle hops along the ground and calls itself a bird?"

The Trilian hesitated as he thought about that, then glanced up at the dark sky overhead. "There is nothing up there."

"How do you know?" persisted Rose. "Have you ever gone? Have you ever stretched yourself to your limits to explore that which Almighty has given you? I bet you've never even been so far into your own realm that you've lost sight of the ground. And how can you know who you are if you've never tried what you're capable of?"

"It is the way of my kind to regulate the comings and goings of the other races, to make sure their evil does not spread," the Trilian reasoned.

Rose simply shook her head at him. He tried another approach.

"We are here to see that dark members of any of the races don' t intermingle, and in doing so, allow their abomination to grow."

Rose laughed outright, and the Trilian realized how she would perceive such a notion.

He realized he had been a fool, and placed Rose's dagger on the ledge of the tower. He waited for them both to regain their composure, then admitted, "I cannot deny the simplicity of your words, or the evidence of your actions. I do not like the fact that I have not been included in this work of Almighty."

"Pride." Rose shook her head somewhat sadly.

The Trilian continued as if he hadn't heard her. "I admit that you are of Almighty. I will do as you suggest, and seek out the gifts he has in store for the Trilians, for all the air races. I will explore the Air Realm."

"I assure you, the quest will be miserable enough to destroy your pride and bring you back into his grace," Rose commented lightly.

He bowed to her. "I hope so. Thank you, Lady Of Light."

She returned the bow with one of her own. "May I request your name, Trilian?" she asked.

"I am Kasan Thoroughblood. And I swear to you my lady, that my sons, Flaveldon and Kallan will follow the guidance of Almighty, wherever that may lead them." He paused, searched for words, couldn't find any, so nodded, and said, "Good night to you, then. May you continue to shine as a beacon in the dark."

Rose grinned and curtsied. She knew much more of this Trilian than he would ever guess, but she wisely kept her thoughts to herself. "Good night, My Lord Thoroughblood," she replied. "May you be the first to see the sun rise and last to see it set."

Then he turned and flew off into the night.

෨෬

At last, the day came. She was standing outside with her sister Priscilla. A fresh blanket of pure white snow had fallen, and was still falling lightly even now. The flakes were large and soft, and fell in perfect silence. It was a glorious day, and Rose was helping Priscilla see the perfection in it. The younger sister was shivering and kept her hands tucked under her arms.

"Perfection is balanced with misery," Priscilla's teeth chattered. "And in this case, cold."

Rose chuckled. She did not feel the cold. Although she was of the Fire Realm, it seemed that winter had no affect on her. Perhaps because she was from the Fire Realm, she could stand out here in her white slippers and dress, with no coat, and allow the snow to caress her bare shoulders, and melt in her silver hair and run down the back of her neck and dress in droplets. "Moonfire is the balance."

"Why are you so stuck on that stuff?" Priscilla asked curiously.

Rose handed the vial she always kept with her to Priscilla. "Take a sip," she urged.

"Will I turn into you?"

Rose laughed. "No. Your Tenlenesse genes are buried under a mountain of humanity. But your children might."

"Oh, I do hope so," Priscilla exclaimed as, shivering, she took the flask from her sister's hand. They smiled affectionately at each other before Priscilla raised it to her lips and tasted the silver mercury. Her eyes widened with surprise. "Wow!" She handed the flask and its stopper back to her sister. "I see what you mean."

"Are you still cold?"

Priscilla thought for a moment, then she nodded. "But I see what you mean. Cold can be tolerated. But the perfection of this day can never be withstood, only ignored."

"That's incredibly philosophical of you, Pris!" Rose teased.

Priscilla giggled through her chattering teeth. "Blame it on the moonfire."

"I don't think so."

They grinned at each other again, then Priscilla's eye caught movement and she gazed over the nearby fields. "Where did they come from?" she wondered. A great procession of people were emerging from the falling snow. Dressed entirely in white, with silver hair, she had no doubt who they were, yet Priscilla could never quite grasp the entire concept of the Fire Realm and the Netherlands.

Rose turned, saw who was approaching, recognized the two men at the front of the line, then cried out in surprise. She ran out excitedly to meet them. Priscilla remained in the cold air long enough to see Rose throw herself at one of them. He swung her up into the air and spun her around before they settled into a long, shameless kiss.

Priscilla grinned as she went inside to try to make herself pre-sentable for their guests.

৪০০৪

Legend of Quetha

By DJ Ebenal

Clinging to Kenneth's skin like cobwebs from a crypt, the feeling of wrong hung about him, unshakable; there for so long he
could no longer tell which was he or what was a parasite draining
his life.

Crack! Kenneth winced before the whip sliced into his back,
knowing that even such a thought was punishable by the lash.
Still, the Tenlenesse knew it was futile to beat their slaves sense-
less, and so no one continued to punish him when he grimaced.
He shook his head at their senselessness.

"Get back to work!" one of the angrymen, the one who had
stung him, barked.

Kenneth nodded and bent his aching back to hauling boulders
into the back of a cart, letting his thoughts drift until all that
existed was his labored breathing, the steady pounding of his
heart, and the rivulets of sweat that ran down his back. Every
now and again mercy would show him kindness with a gust of

wind, but for the most part he contended with the blistering noon-day sun without respite.

The angryman continued to glare at Kenneth and his three companions, who painstakingly ignored him. They knew if they kept their mouths shut and worked hard, they would be handed a cruel but grudging respect. If they stepped out of line, attempted to revolt, or even had questioning thoughts about their sorcerous masters, they would feel the slaver's whip once more.

But they never punished him brutally enough that he could not work. In the years since the fall of his home to these treacherous fiends – crack! Another wince, another bite – Kenneth had come to realize they beat him merely to remind him that they were present, where no human had a right to be. No whip met that thought and he harrumphed as he glanced at the angryman. The Tenlenesse stared back, a wide, dark grin on his face, the whip already coiled in his hand for another strike.

Kenneth went back to work and listened in silence as the whip sliced into one of the other slaves, and continued to haul rocks until there was barely enough light to return to the castle. Then he was commanded to stop and the four men took up the wooden yoke of the cart, while the angryman climbed into the back and braced himself for the ride, his whip ready, always ready, in his hand.

All the slaves were permitted to endure was to haul the cart into the courtyard, which they did in complete silence that reigned throughout their workday. After that there was no standing on ceremony; the slaves dropped the yoke and the slaver jumped from the cart. He went one way, they went another.

ఎంసారా

Kenneth sighed as he slouched down on the straw pallet on the floor. Startled by the sudden movement, a rat skittered out from behind the mattress and chattered its protest while it scurried across the room to a hole in the wall. Kenneth ignored it while he studied his wife. The same dance. No whip ever accompanied thoughts like those. "Hello, Hannah," he said calmly.

She was sitting in the light of an oil lamp resting on a table above her head. She was sewing a patch onto a tunic, a tunic with more patches than cloth. But it kept her hands busy and her mind occupied, so he did not begrudge either of them for being forced to tend to such chores. "These whips ruin clothing surer than the sun rises every morning," she commented.

"That's why we go without tunics, most of the time."

Hannah gave Kenneth a hard stare. The angrymen had long ago taken the joy out of their marriage, and she hated being reminded of that.

Kenneth simply stared back at her; futile anger had long ago grown cold.

"They are the masters," she mumbled as she returned to her work.

"Do you ever long for a better day," Kenneth asked his wife. "Do you even remember a better day?"

"Such thoughts are meaningless, childish," Hannah retorted.

"We are permitted to think whatever we want when the sun goes down."

She shrugged. "I like my clothing without the patches in them, thank you very much."

"So you have forgotten."

Hannah shrugged, but said nothing.

Kenneth sighed again. "Always the same," he muttered under his breath.

"What was that?" She looked up and lowered her needle until it rested on the work in her lap.

"Do you even remember our daughter?"

Hannah's eyes flared with anger. A snarl distorted her sun-darkened face. "How dare you mention her!" she cried.

"Why?" He hadn't realized that he could still get so angry, so swiftly.

"The child's dead! And you dare throw her in my, her mother's face, in your own wife's face!" The hurt was all for show though; Kenneth knew it, and Hannah knew it. But it was all the shielding she had left, that and her anger.

Kenneth made an effort to calm himself and said, quietly, "You don't know that she is."

"She went into the forest!" Hannah insisted.

Kenneth rolled his eyes and spread his hands out to encompass their tiny cell of a home. "Look around you, wife — the forest has gone into us!"

Hannah shook her head and went back to work on the tunic.

"Her fate couldn't have been any worse than ours," Kenneth said.

"She died, fool!" Hannah hissed the words at him.

"Then her fate was much better than ours." He got to his feet.

"Where are you going?"

"To join my daughter."

She shook her head again, refusing to even look up at her hus - band.

"Coming?"

Hannah's laugh was cold and mirthless, mad even. Kenneth pitied her.

"Then stay here," he said irritable and frustrated. "Let the angrymen take you."

"They already have, lover."

Kenneth left without looking back, and his wife never looked up from her mending.

No one tried to stop him; no one bothered. Slaves were permit-ted to go where they pleased after dark. Kenneth thought it was because the angrymen, the Tenlenesse, went into the night where mankind could not dare to find them. He left without a light, leaving the oil lamp with his querulous wife as some small com-fort, as if it were a kind of victory trophy she could cling to before the angrymen beat even that from her.

But he could do nothing for Hannah unless she accepted his help, unless she asked for it. With his heart full of weariness and grief, Kenneth made his way back to the courtyard in the dark. His feet knew the way; a lifetime of this place had taught them well, yet his heart was no longer here. And so he followed his heart through the northern gate and forced his feet to carry him across the fields to the border of the Dark Forest.

A gentle sigh, a slight stirring of the wind, was all that accom-panied Kenneth as he slipped in amongst the ever green boughs. There was a darkness that reached out to him, but it was only a physical thing, and held no evil that wasn't already enshrouded about him.

Silently he stepped out of the moonlight and took three crunch-ing steps before his searching fingers brushed a branch of a tree. Kenneth realized that he was completely blind under this canopy. He grasped the branch with sure hands and pushed past it, to wade in deeper, one slow step at a time. Underbrush cut at his arms and legs, snagging his clothing and his hair. Yet Kenneth paid it little mind, pushing on even further from the castle, anx-ious lest the angrymen discover him missing.

Unexpectedly, the ground gave way beneath him, the earth tilted and spun about as Kenneth was jostled roughly, then tossed to the ground. He lay there gasping for breath, unable to move, staring out at the darkness. He had never felt quite so alone as he did then. Yet there was no terror here, not anymore, just a feeling of resolution – and wariness – much wariness. Still wheezing, he closed his eyes and decided to lie very still.

ഇരു

Sleep found him then, in a confused, dreamless state where he would waken intermittently to find himself lying in a painful position, still unable to move. This meant little to him, for as Kenneth recognized what was happening, irrational grief mingled with bitter hope swept through him, and he despaired that he would ever see his daughter again.

Yet perhaps in another life they would recognize each other. Perhaps where he was going, the darkness would someday pass to reveal his little Leena once again.

Time passed, although the darkness did not fade, and Kenneth began to fear that perhaps this was it; this was death. Was this then to be his afterlife, caught in this forest, forever lost and crumpled upon its floor?

A light shone. A beacon in the darkness, a shining star that sil-houetted the trees around it. A supernatural thing, it streaked through the trees as if from the heavens themselves and brushed against leaf and branch. Kenneth smiled faintly as he imagined the trees trembling at her touch.

How did he know the light was a she? The question was faint and detached, much like the feeling left in his limbs. What was real, what was upon him – in his face even, was this glorious light radiating through the darkness, coming to rest gently on the earth far, far away.

Leena stood basking in the light, shining in the light, being the light. She was smiling a much grown up version of her silly piercing smiles. The womanly curves of her body told Kenneth that she had aged into maturity, and to look upon his daughter made him realize how very old he had become in her absence.

Oh Father! Another detached thought, this one much more of a feeling, yet it echoed through his mind with a certainty that she had spoken the words. Her mouth hadn't moved and she was still such a long distance away, and yet Kenneth was sure she had spo- ken. She smirked a little, watching in amusement as her father processed this. Her arms were crossed over her breasts.

Another star-form appeared beside Leena. It was Jarel, sheathed in a fiery silver and green light. He glanced first at Kenneth, then at his wife. Again, there was that awareness, that sense of knowl- edge beyond what Kenneth should know. A message passed between Leena and Jarel, one he did not grasp, and then they were both moving towards him at an impossible speed. And yet their legs didn't appear to move as they crossed the distance. They were simply there, and then they were here, growing in pro- portion as they neared.

Get up, silly old man! Leena took Kenneth's hand in both of hers and golden light enveloped his limbs and his bones in shim- mering illumination. Immediately movement was restored and he felt refreshed, strengthened. Jarel reached out and took his other arm, cupping his elbow. And again, as the silvery light touched Kenneth, he was restored and rose all the way to his feet.

What shall we do with him? Jarel sent the question telepathical- ly to Leena.

His daughter looked up and brushed her hand lightly against Kenneth's greying hair. "We won't take you back to the castle," she said, speaking aloud for the first time.

"And yet I can't stay here," Kenneth objected.

She pursed her lips together and blinked a sudden rush of tears from her face.

"Is there a place for me?" her father asked.

Leena's heart ached as she gazed at her father. "So long have I wanted to go back and teach you how to defeat the angrymen," she replied sadly. "So much did I want to show you and momma about the wonders of Mishard, of the spectral stones. And now, here you are, and I cannot keep you."

Unable to respond, Kenneth embraced his daughter, holding her close to his heart as he had in his memories.

Jarel looked from one to the other. "I will go now," he said out loud, "and keep them away as long as I can."

"Can you hold them off until sunrise?" Leena pulled away from her father to regard her husband.

Jarel shook his head. "It'll have to be for much longer than that, I'm afraid," he said. "Take him north, to the far edge of the forest."

She bobbed her head in agreement as she took her father's hand.

Jarel nodded to Kenneth and slipped off into the shadows. Kenneth tried to follow his movements, but it seemed to him that the young man vanished a few paces away, soundlessly blending with the darkness around them while the mysterious silver light vanished with him.

"Where did he go?"

"Come Father. This way."

Wordlessly he let himself be led by his daughter's hand.

The forest seemed to part in front of them. It was as if the trees were cowering from her, exposing their roots and a straight sure path for her feet. Above his head a few stars shone through the canopy of darkness, and Kenneth could only shake his head in amazement. What had seemed like certain death had suddenly become a world of mysteries and wonders.

At first everything seemed a dream. His body was numb, his feet felt wooden. But as the night wore on the stiffness melted from his limbs and his senses awakened to the sounds and stir - rings of the night, to the wind rustling through the trees, to the feel of the soil under foot. And the questions began to rise.

"What are you, Daughter?" It came suddenly, blurting from his mouth as though he'd vomited. He was horrified by his question, by how rudely it had been asked. But she simply looked up at him and squeezed his hand.

"I am a descendant of humanity." She was smiling, not afraid of the truth that was so obvious to her. Kenneth felt something brush lightly against his shoulder, and he turned to see a shimmering golden wing appear, apparently out of thin air. It was attached to his daughter's shoulder.

Panic swept over him, but before his body could even register the reaction, a greater wave of peace and comfort flowed in and crushed the negativity, the insecurity. He sighed, and the wing faded back into the night. Kenneth looked at Leena again, and saw only the daughter he'd raised as his own.

"Momma knew," she said.

"She said nothing to me about it." He paused. "No, wait. There was a time, a few times when you were still very young. She tried to tell me then, I think, but I wouldn't hear of it. She eventually gave up." He looked at her again, a slight frown creasing his brow. "So, you are not human."

"No."

There was silence again, a comfortable, lasting, peaceful silence that was at odds with the dark forest they strolled through.

"What now?" Kenneth asked.

"This forest is no place for humans," Leena said gently.

"There must be a place for us here."

"No, Father. Such a place does not exist, except maybe in our hearts."

"Then what will I do?"

"The same thing I am doing. You'll make a place for yourself."

"It won't be just for me, then," Kenneth vowed. "It'll be for all peoples, human, angel, ogre or elf."

She looked up at him. "There's no such thing as ogres and elves."

He grinned. "You would know."

"You are serious about this, though, aren't you, father?"

"I am. I will accept them all, even the angrymen, if they choose not to be so angry."

"But you are only one man!"

He glanced at Leena, and could see admiration in her eyes.

"You are only one angel, and look how the trees bend to your will. I raised you, did I not? Surely there are other angels out there who might want to live among humanity without hiding," Kenneth persisted.

"I'm not an angel Father. I'm an Aigelendai."

He rolled his eyes. "Pardon me!"

She looked up at him fondly and smiled, squeezing his hand. "Why would you do this, Father? How would you do this?"

Kenneth shrugged. "I would do it because it seems right to do so. How will I do it … I have no idea."

"I do. With help," said Leena

"You would help me, little Aigelendai?"

"My place is here, with these trees." Her light flared even brighter for a moment, casting brilliant hues deeper into the twilight It seemed to Kenneth that the trees tried to shrink away.

"May I stay?" her father asked.

Leena shook her head and continued to lead him down the path. "I'm sorry, Father, you may not. There is nothing here for you, and the axe and plow cannot belong in this place. But what Jarel and I have in mind is not far away. " She would say nothing more.

They walked for as long as Kenneth could. Fatigue finally overtook him, and he pleaded with Leena to allow him to stop and rest.

"Of course, Father." She was not at all alarmed by stopping for the night in this awful place. "Chose a place, Father, and I will keep watch. Then she stepped away from him and vanished. Yet the golden light of her presence remained.

Kenneth looked around before he found her again, a tiny speck of light floating in front of him. His eyes widened and he shook his head in amazement as Leena grew to be about a hand's length in size. She curtsied as she grinned at him, then flew to a perch on the side of the road and sat there with her wings fluttering out behind her.

He could only shake his head and curled up in the grass beneath her. In his exhaustion, sleep overtook him even as he closed his eyes.

"Why is he still here?"

Kenneth opened his eyes. Jarel and Leena were standing over him with the sun glaring down between them. He winced and tried to pretend he was sleeping, but they seemed aware of his every move and grinned at his attempt.

How is it I know what they are saying and thinking? Kenneth asked himself.

"How is it the angrymen know what you are thinking all the time?" Jarel asked in return.

Kenneth looked up at the young man. "Good to see you," he croaked.

The woodsman bowed. "It would have been easier for you to get out at night."

"Jarel! Have you forgotten what it's like to be human?" Leena scolded him, standing before him with her hands on her hips.

Kenneth sat up and looked around. Any sign of a forest path had disappeared. All around them the forest was thick and confusing. The trees were gnarled and fought for sunlight and nourishing earth. There was no path, and no sign that there had ever been one.

Hunger rose up in him as he pushed to his feet.

"In truth, I had forgotten," Jarel admitted. "We must be slipping."

"You must be slipping!" Leena laughed.

"Come Father. Food is not far away." Again she took him by the hand, but this time she led him amongst the trees.

"Where are you taking him?" Jarel asked.

"To the Tenlenesse. They can feed him."

Jarel caught up to them and fell in stride beside Kenneth. "Leena. That is unwise. They would seek to take him back to the Fire Realm with them."

"He would resist."

"Would he? Could you? After all these years, could you? I know I could not."

Leena sniffed. "I was hoping that because he is human they would not enchant him."

"Perhaps they do not have to enchant him, this is true. But with - in this forest, with so much stone beneath their feet, could they not help but be who they are? Have you shown him your wings? Have you used your light to guide him?"

In the morning light neither the wings nor the light he spoke of were evident, but she grew sullen and silent.

"Hush, children," Kenneth cut in. "I have lived a cruel life under my keepers, the angrymen. Hunger is but a small price to pay to win my freedom from them. I will be fine."

Jarel approved and Leena nodded. "I have snares," she said stubbornly. "I can catch us food, and Jarel can make us a fire. We can cook the old fashioned, human way."

Jarel grinned. "That would be worth something, wouldn't it? To eat like a human once again! If I had known, I would have fetched my bow!"

Leena glanced across her father at him. "You should have known? I should have known and made you fetch it!" Then she laughed. "Look at us, Jarel! Look how useless we've become!"

"Having too much fun with shadows and light," he admitted, casting a glare at the trees around them.

Leena grinned but said nothing. She was thinking about where they would stop to build a fire. A picture of a clearing atop a hill, with a creek at the bottom, came to Kenneth's mind.

"How do I know these things?" he asked.

His daughter simply smiled. "I will meet you there," she said. Then she turned into a candleflame, whisked around his head, once, twice, three times, and was gone off amongst the trees.

Jarel said nothing until she was gone, ignoring Leena's obvious theatrics. Then he looked at his father-in-law and said, "There is a war going on, Kenneth. The races are at war with each other and with themselves, in a struggle that has spread over the entire world. But nowhere is the fighting fiercer than here, on this conti-nent. The Island, it is called, though in truth it is the center of attention for all of the rest of Mishard, and much bigger than any other island."

"Why here?" asked Kenneth.

"There is a stone mined from these shores that is more valuable than any other stone in Mishard. Some say it is a magical stone, although I doubt that. But it is a miracle, for sure. It has the power to unite the twenty sub-races with humanity, to make us equals once again – even though I've always believed that we were equals. But this stone, this spectral stone, it is the great equalizer. It is the stone within the veins of these trees that can make us transparent to you. This stone can take you to the Fire Realm. It can lift you into the Sky Realm. It can light your way if you descend into the Earth Realm, and it can keep you safe in the Water Realm.

"The war is being fought over this stone. For whoever controls it has life, and power over those who do not have it."

Kenneth understood, and nodded as he digested Jarel's words.

"Leena and I are taking you to a place hidden deep within thick forests like this one, with huge, rugged mountains that deny easy movement for troops," Jarel continued. "It is a small valley com-paratively, perhaps sixty, maybe seventy leagues long and thirty leagues wide. And it is completely worthless in the eyes of the powerful leaders. Of course, it has gold and silver, iron and bronze. It has coal, clean water, rich pastureland and broad forests. It even has rivers wide enough to travel in a ship, rivers that reach the oceans in the north, and thus all other oceans as well. But it has not one spectral stone within its borders. No one has time for a place like that, utterly void of spectral stone. It is valued for only one thing. Sanctuary."

"So why don't you and Leena live there?"

Jarel grinned. "We are at war with the angrymen, Kenneth. And we are winning. We are quite invincible to them in human form, and untouchable in our natural form. There are many of our kind who live amongst these trees who are slave to their own dark colors. We would see them freed from their rebellious ways, that they may take the pilgrimage to the Fire Realm and taste the moonfire that flows there."

For once, Kenneth had no idea what his son-in-law was talking about, and must have looked as bewildered as he felt.

"It is of no concern," Jarel assured him. "Here, watch your step. Sometimes animals dig holes under these sticks."

Kenneth, about to set his foot down on a pile of brush, froze in mid-air, stepped back, and carefully walked around it instead.

"A traveller could break his leg if he stepped in a hole unawares," Jarel murmured.

Kenneth nodded. "Where is this place we are going?"

"To the north a few leagues. Leena could have had you out on its plains before dawn but as it is we won't arrive until much later after the sunrise, when the trees become less resistant to our will."

"Are all trees like this to you?"

Jarel nodded. "I do not know for sure, but I think so. Perhaps less so because of what runs through their veins, but all trees drink water, and water reflects light. So I would think they would listen to us. But trees with the spectral stone in them are ours to command. That is the way."

They grew silent after that, Kenneth allowing himself to be led, Jarel allowing himself to lead. It was a pleasant morning, despite the gloom under the trees. The way was easy, although it meandered around them in a confusing, invisible path that Kenneth finally gave up trying to follow.

He let his mind instead return to Keeper Fortress, to the other slaves and the angrymen. No one would miss him, for sure. The angrymen though, how would they react?

"They will pretend you are dead, of course," Jarel said quite suddenly. "They won't want to admit you had the power to escape their rule."

"That makes sense," Kenneth replied, before lapsing into silence again.

Suddenly they were out of the forest, on top of a knoll that swept down into a broad, far-reaching plain. A creek indeed flowed through from the north, disappearing into the forest further south. Kenneth let his eyes linger on the scene, following the plain as it stretched into the horizon.

Jarel gave him time to experience the view, but eventually nudged his arm and pointed off to the right, along the edge of the slope. Leena beamed at them from where she stood in front of a tall wood fire. Even in the summer daylight she shone with her own otherworldly golden light, almost like a tongue of fire herself. She stared in their direction for a moment, then waved with exaggerated enthusiasm, stared some more, then breathed deep and spread her arms out towards the plains below. Two golden wings shimmered out of thin air, like heat waves solidifying.

"Now I've seen everything," Kenneth exclaimed, as he watched the way his daughter seemed to embrace the horizon with her outstretched arms.

Jarel chuckled, but kept his thoughts private. Still, the feeling Kenneth got from him was a cross between, "You think so?" and, "We'll see, old man!"

Kenneth snorted and laughed good-naturedly, then led the way to his daughter, his angelic daughter.

Leena looked up at him, beaming, and said, "Hey, Daddy!"

Kenneth rolled his eyes at his daughter, who, while still angelic, was definitely acting like a rather childish angel.

In response, Leena went to him and threw her arms around her father's chest. He hesitated a moment, then embraced her in return. As if they had a life of their own, her wings curled about them, cocooning the pair in shimmering golden silk.

Jarel went to the fire and crouched down to stare into the embers. "Are you going to show him the place?"

Leena broke off her embrace and stepped away from her father to study her husband.

Jarel kept his gaze locked on the coals of the fire.

"Latanya?"

"Latanya."

"I thought I would. Can we at least eat something first?"

Jarel stared up at Leena. "We don't need to eat."

At this, she grinned and put her arms around her father again. "I thought I might bring back some memories, and make some new ones."

Jarel only shrugged. "As you wish. He glanced down at the glowing embers for a moment, then came to his feet. "I'll go check the snares. Where are they?"

She pointed over her shoulder to the forest, then drew a line along where it ended against the fields.

He nodded, and went off on his own.

"Just like that?" Kenneth commented. "That was all you needed to tell him?"

"You always set a snare on a game path." She shrugged. "He can find the paths as easily as I did."

"Oh."

She laughed. "I'll show you the trick to it, if you'd like."

It was his turn to shrug. "It just makes me wonder how I'm to build a sanctuary if I can't even set a snare."

"When you begin to ask questions you've already crossed into that realm of seeking. The secret to that place is to accept answers as they present themselves, with or without asking the question first. The world can never be what we hope it to be, no matter how many questions we ask. But with each answer you accept, let it change you instead. And you'll find you'll perceive the world in a much different manner, in a way that closely resembles what you wanted it to be all along, though infinitely richer than you could have imagined when you first started. And it'll be infinitely richer as each day you are changed by your acceptance of the differences."

Kenneth stared at his daughter for a full moment before he finally replied, "Spoken like a true… what did you say you were again?"

"Aigelendai."

"Aigelendai."

She shrugged, "In truth, Father, it was my humanity that taught me that. It was just my ability to see like an Aigelendai that helped me frame the words."

Kenneth frowned. "You seem so comfortable with this place, with your heritage, your heritages."

Leena smiled, a little sadly it seemed to him, then held her empty hand, palm up, towards the tree nearest her. As if alive, a branch began to move, and Kenneth jumped back with fright as it bent like a many-jointed arm, until a single finger, the smallest twig, placed a leaf in her palm. Then, with a fluid motion so different from the stiff movements it had used before, the entire tree rustled as if caught in an invisible wind, and the limb returned to its place.

She handed the leaf to her father, teary eyed. "The best part of what I have was given to me by you, you and Mamma. And now the darkness has taken her." It was said as fact, and Kenneth wondered how she knew, although it didn't surprise him.

She shrugged the melancholy away as she gazed out over the plains. "The trees mark where the stone ends. After that it's nothing but regular dirt, nothing that would ever attract warlords."

"And where there are pockets of trees?" He pointed to the horizon, where the leafy canopies were nothing more than shimmering green lines.

She shrugged. "That's the beauty of it. They're just trees. The lakes and rivers are just water. The mountains — " she gestured to the rugged peaks hedging the plains in to a wide, flat, valley bottom. "They are a natural barrier that keeps everyone out. They're the perfect place to hide, though, if you need shelter from the skies and the ground." Or the fire and the water, she said without moving her lips.

"What do you mean, fire and water?"

She looked at him. "Oh Father. What have you decided to become?"

All he could do was shrug.

She gestured towards the forest with a tilt of her head. Follow me. I have something to show you.

As Kenneth fell in step beside her she began, "Water is the essence that flows around us. It is substance, but it is not solid. You understand water, for it is all around us, all the time. But fire is different. Who can understand what we can never touch? It is insubstantial, beyond human grasp. And yet it is life. It is in us, giving our skin warmth, our passions heat. I come from the fire realm, Jarel and I, and Latanya. The surface is a place where all our species can co-exist, though for some of us it's like holding our breath. But Almighty has given those people a remarkable ability to hold their breath for a very long time.

"Without the spectral stones around we are inhibited, confined to the rules of the surface realm. So here is a place of weakness, a place to go once defeat has caught up to us, a place of humility. With so much wealth for the taking it's a place that is shunned by everyone who is not scorned. And it is hoped that as a human you can rally the exiled people together under a banner of peace." Leena stopped and looked around.

"Here we are," she announced. They were at the edge of the forest still. But there was a thin game trail leading off into the thickets, and through the gloom Kenneth could see the illuminated outline of a clearing. Leena grinned at him, then transformed into a thumb-sized butterfly, sparkling a golden light as she hovered before her father. This way! And she was off.

He tried to keep up with the speck of light, yet the child seemed unable to contain herself, zigzagging through the trees like they were an endless obstacle course. The light of her passing winked in and out as she streaked through the branches. Yet the pathway was clear and easy to follow and he felt content — if still hungry — to follow along at a mere human's pace.

Soon the clearing opened up before him. It was small, with sheer walls of trees growing up around it. The trees here had been destroyed by fire. Blackened stumps still protruded from old and gnarled roots, charred earth hadn't yet been overgrown with green stalks from the fields. The forest had not grown back to claim this place; rather, it had grown around its borders as if putting up a wall of leaves Kenneth could scarcely see through. Except for the thinned pathway to the plains, there seemed no other way in or out.

A woman stood in the center of the clearing. She was tall and blonde, lithe and graceful in her movements. Dressed in the fine-ly-crafted skins of animals, her woodsman's outfit allowed her to blend seamlessly with either the forest or the plains. She was exquisitely beautiful and utterly mysterious. A paradox, she seemed angry, yet gentle; brutal, yet calm. She was full of what Kenneth called quiet anger, and yet her smile was ready when she saw him enter her domain.

She ignored him, flicked a strand of hair out of her face with a toss of her head, then resumed her attempts to bite the golden Aigelendai that teased her incessantly by flying in and then just out of reach before she could devour the creature.

Kenneth squinted at the golden flame. Was that Leena that was playing with mortality? For this strange lady was snapping time and time again at the air where the tiny pixie had been but a moment earlier.

Another light appeared, a silver one this time, circling out of the trees to draw the woman off and divide her attention. Kenneth assumed it had to be Jarel who was taking the opportunity to fly in and crash against the woman's skull, again and again, like some crazed mosquito.

Distracted by the one, the woman waved at the other absently with her hand, as if to swat the nuisance away.

Cheat! That was definitely Leena's voice, although it echoed wordlessly through the clearing like a gust of wind. You lose! No hands!

Jarel materialized from of the silver glowing flame, hastily step-ping back from the woman, who made a move to snap at him yet again. "Breakfast is cooking anyway," he observed, eyeing her distrustfully. "Game over."

The woman crossed her arms and stared at Jarel, disbelieving.

"Rabbits," he stated. "You remember, cooked meat."

She glared at him then pointedly turned her head away and ignored him to stare at Kenneth, as if he was a potential meal.

Leena took an almost human form beside the woman. "Latanya, meet my father, Kenneth."

With steely, angry eyes, the woman inclined her head in his direction.

There was an awkward silence as Kenneth regarded Latanya, unable to form an opinion of her. Finally, he shook his head and muttered, "I'm hungry." Without looking back, he turned and headed down the path.

"So is Latanya," he heard Jarel laugh behind him.

There was the faint sound of teeth snapping together, a flare of silver and golden light, silent laughter, and then Leena and Jarel were streaking past him, leaving Kenneth alone with this extraordinary woman.

She followed silently, but caught up to Kenneth once they were on the plains, and fell in step beside him amicably enough. After a long pause, he said, "You don't say much, do you?"

Latanya shook her head. "Not much needs to be said." She fell silent again.

"At least you can talk."

She merely shrugged.

Throughout the day Kenneth found this bizarre company easy to keep. His daughter and her husband, and this unreadable, silent, exquisite lady with impeccable manners and an iron edge of inner anger, so much at odds with herself.

There was much laughter, although less so from Latanya, who was silent and removed from the camaraderie, more of an observer, as she sat by the fire with her arms drawn up over her knees. And although he had given up trying to understand her, Kenneth couldn't shake the feeling that she was an ally, a friend even, although perhaps the strangest friend he'd ever met. So he left Latanya alone and enjoyed the time he shared with his long-lost daughter and her husband, instinctively knowing that it would eventually have to end.

And so it wasn't a surprise when, as the sun began to fade, an otherworldly phenomenon occurred. All along the edge of the vast plains, hidden within the trees, tiny lights began to appear. They flickered faintly at first, but grew in intensity as the sky darkened. At first Kenneth ignored this peculiar event, as nothing much in the way of lights could surprise him anymore. But soon it became impossible to deny that he was under the scrutiny of a vast number of Aigelendai. Their eyes weighed him down with great pressure, as if he were under water.

Reluctantly, Kenneth turned to regard his crowd of witnesses, seeing for the first time the pale figures of angrymen standing in the shadows as well. Yet these were not true angrymen, but Tenlenesse of Light, as Leena called them. They no longer served the dark purposes of the mind, but had given themselves over to Almighty and the gift of moonfire.

"Moonfire?" Kenneth tested the word on his tongue, as if sampling some strange delicacy for the first time.

It was Latanya who broke the silence, with loud, rich laughter that brought her to her feet. She grinned as she moved towards him, like an animal stalking its prey, he thought. And he could not help but take a step back from her, before she reached out and took him by the shoulders.

She looked deep into his eyes, disbelief, almost horror playing in hers, then withdrew one of her iron strong grips and held up a waterskin. She released his other shoulder to let him massage the bruises she'd placed there by her touch. She uncorked the water-skin and held it out to him. "Drink."

He took it, touched it to his lips, and sampled the cool liquid inside.

Immediately his senses erupted. Everything became acute; the feeling of the wind, though ever so slight, upon his neck, the rustling of the stalks of grass out in the plains, the vivid colors of the trees and the strange host of silent witnesses. The smells and the sounds, the stars, the distant gurgling of the creek, everything exploded with vibrancy, became clear and detailed.

Yet in a moment the feelings faded, returning his senses to something dull, as if he'd woken up from sleep and was now returning to a state of lethargy. And yet there was an understanding of the balance of nature, of how the sky and the ground accompanied each other the way the branches in the trees not so much fought as shared the fading sunlight.

Latanya watched the moonfire take effect and then diminish and shook her head. "Humans," she muttered. From what Kenneth could see, Latanya was human herself, even if she was the strangest one he'd ever met. At his thought, she turned and stalked off onto the plains in the fading light.

"Father." The gravity in Leena's voice drew his gaze away from Latanya. His daughter looked sad, indescribably so, even though there was a smile on her face; and a great tide of unlimited love radiated from her, tinting her golden wings with streaks of red.

Kenneth watched the change as it continued to deepen, to spread into her clothes and to darken the light that shone from her. "What is happening to you?"

By way of an answer, she stepped forward, placed a hand on his cheek and looked deeply into his eyes. Her lower lip was quiver-ing and a single tear formed at the outer edge of her right eye. Then the pure golden light returned, grew until it enveloped them both, and Kenneth was wrapped in its brilliance. And yet he could not look away from his daughter's eyes.

Understanding passed between them as the golden rays that were hers began to coalesce behind her eyes, changing them from their natural human appearance to shining golden orbs. She poured out her memories, her experiences, her knowledge, the effects moonfire had on her, and all of creation seemed to explode in an array of light and color that poured into his soul, into his spirit, into the very essence of who he was.

He remembered her shedding her human shell to become what she truly was, saw the way the forest exalted her as a herald of a new age of enlightenment, as their matron returned. Then, quite suddenly, Kenneth understood what was happening, for she had kept the most painful knowledge for the last, that the rite of his passage might be as painless as possible.

"Leena, no!" he cried desperately, wrenching his eyes away from hers.

It was too late. The light was fading, from her clothes, from her wings, and from her eyes, most painfully from her eyes. She swooned and he caught her up, lifting her clear off of her feet to cup her limp body in his powerful arms.

"You didn't have to do that," he murmured to her.

Leena did not have the strength to argue. "I will always be with you," she whispered. And with that, the life flowed out of her and she died.

Kenneth stared at his daughter's peaceful, familiar face and the tears came, unbidden and all consuming. "Why!" he cried into the awakening night, into the dim light of the twinkling stars. And yet he knew why. She had shared all of herself with him. She was part of him now, the essence of an Aigelendai, her life's light, now coursed through his veins as she would through the veins of a tree. And yet the price to become part of another living being was to give up her own life, her own being. It was a price, Kenneth now understood, that had to be paid in order to equip him to be the king he needed to be to unite the fractured and war-torn races of Mishard under one banner, a banner of selfless love.

He sank to his knees with her slight weight in his arms and held his beloved daughter to his chest as he wept upon the plains she had given him.

In time, her body grew heavy to hold, and he became aware that he was ruining her wings. So he placed her gently on the ground and rose to his feet to face her widower, his own son-in-law.

Jarel stared back at him, wrapped in his own silver light, his wings blazing into the night. The look in the ageless man's eyes told Kenneth all, and Kenneth stepped away from him, raising a fist in front of him as he did.

"You stay away from me!" Kenneth growled with as much anger as he'd ever possessed.

"As she is within, I will be without."

"No!" Kenneth snarled, and moved to strike the Aigelendai.

Jarel was too fast. The young man stepped past the attack and caught Kenneth's arm. "I have no wish to live past this night!" Jarel howled. The intensity of his own emotions outmatched Kenneth's. Kenneth understood. Leena had taught him how, and his resolve melted.

The two men embraced in a fierce hug, then Jarel pulled away, held Kenneth by his bruised shoulders, and said, "Your Majesty." He bowed before Kenneth, and the light lifted from the woodsman like a cloud to settle about Kenneth's shoulders like a mantle. The ravages of age and hard labor, all his grief, and the lashes from the slaver's whip healed. All pain in his body faded into the night as the silver light settled over his skin.

And then the light was gone, and Jarel slumped to the ground next to his beloved wife.

♋⚮☊

Kenneth awoke next to the stream after the sun was well up. How much time had passed, he couldn't tell. Yet when he moved to sit up, his body flowed with a lithe gracefulness that was not his own, and he wondered which one of his children's essence had given him that. Probably both.

Latanya sat on the ground with her legs pulled up in front of her, the waterskin of moonfire in her hand.

Kenneth stared at her, for once able to understand much of what her body language spoke.

"Nothing great is given until something great is sacrificed," she said dispassionately, handing him the waterskin. "Taste it again."

He took the moonfire as he gazed into the flowing water of the creek. He watched the sunlight dance off of the tiny rapids like liquid fire; and mechanically unstoppered then upended the waterskin into his mouth.

This time he understood. It took him a moment to recover from the explosions behind his eyes. But then he corked the waterskin and handed it back to Latanya. "It doesn't take away the pain."

She did not need to reply as she took the waterskin. "We have a fair way to travel today. Be up with you."

"I must attend to my children," Kenneth countered.

"Their bodies have been taken away, back into the forest to be memorialized somewhere. One of the Tenlenesse said something about a pond and an island, and a grove of flowers."

323

Kenneth nodded. That was what was right. He could not do any more for them but to live and use the power and the life they had given him well.

And so, after a time, he rose to his feet and approached the creek. He waded into it and sank to his knees, letting the cold water wash about him.

His eyes were golden orbs, the pupils shining suns. His hair, on the top of his head and upon his chest and arms, had turned silver.

New tears sprang forth at this discovery, but he washed the grime from his face, dunked his head into the creek. Then he rose determined not to waste the gift that had been bestowed upon him.

Kenneth could not help his eyes from going back to where it began, to the forest, again and again. It surrounded him on all sides, encroaching upon mountains; and meandered through swampland, bordering lakes and even a sea in the far northeast corner, its rugged boundaries disturbed only by the rivers and roads the Aigelendai allowed to remain.

Leena and Jarel had been their queen and king, had inspired a movement of trust and truth, of light and righteousness, and now it seemed they had passed that torch on to Kenneth. He knew without it being said that the forest and its inhabitants now acknowledged his sovereignty.

"What will they do now?" he asked, gesturing towards the trees.

Latanya looked at him, then away at the forest. "They will open their borders," she said with a shrug. "Those who seek peace will be shown the way to this place. Those that seek wealth will be denied."

They were silent for a moment, Kenneth still knee-deep in the creek, she standing upon the shores in her rawhide boots.

It was Latanya who broke the silence. "Come, Majesty. We have a long way to travel before we reach where we are to go."

Understanding came unbidden from the depths of his Aigelendai-cloaked soul. He nodded, then waded to the shore.

He could scarcely keep the pace of his strange, silent companion. Always laboring, he was thankful for this. With no breath to spare for idle conversation, Kenneth had time to internalize all the terrible events that had taken him this far. He came to grips with his grief, or as much as humanly possible in such a short amount of time, and took in the scenery as they jogged through it.

Latanya was untiring, a fount of endless strength and determination. Her eyes never wavered as she trotted over the rolling plains. And her breath never came in the ragged gasps that Kenneth was presently overcome by.

Remembering the words of his daughter, how Leena had informed him that Latanya came from a place not his own, Kenneth was not surprised by her oddities. And yet he dared not ask about them. In truth, he hadn't the ability to speak and keep pace all at once. And it seemed to him that she preferred it that way, glaring at him whenever he thought about her, before lengthening her stride to his silent groans of protest.

Finally, though, as the sun was beginning to set, she came to an abrupt stop. "Here is where we will stop for the night."

Kenneth collapsed, rolled onto his back and wheezed at the sky.

She shook her head. "I will build a fire, catch some game, dress and cook it, do all those things that humans require." Her voice dripped with sarcasm, but Kenneth was too tired to be ashamed by his weakness.

"Thank you, Latanya," he gasped instead.

She tossed her head again and stalked off, and Kenneth finally allowed exhaustion to overcome him.

He awoke well after sundown, suddenly, as though from a bad dream. Sitting up, he couldn't remember what had haunted him, and in a way he was grateful for that. Kenneth looked at the horizon, amazed that his golden eyes could see details along the tree line. Glowing forms and figures cloaked in shadows drifted onto the plains or glided in from overhead. There weren't many of them, but they were there, always accompanied by the glowing, protective forms of Aigelendai or Tenlenesse.

He looked around for Latanya. She stood, basking by the light of the fire, gazing off into the wilderness. Her arms were crossed and her bearing proud as she stood motionless. At her feet was the carcass of a dressed hare. Its skin was already stretched and curing next to that of another hare, a safe distance from the fire.

"You should eat," she said without looking at him. Her eyes never left the figures drifting in from the woods.

His eyes followed to where she looked. "I'm not hungry."

She nodded, understanding, or not caring, Kenneth couldn't be sure which. "In the morning it will be ready for you to eat on the move."

He nodded.

"Sleep," she ordered. Then she moved off into the night, leaving the comfort of the fire behind her.

Kenneth lay back in the grass, convinced he wouldn't be able to rest. But upon closing his eyes, he was aware of nothing until suddenly he bolted upright.

The fire had burned down; all that remained of its comforting light was the gentle glow of the embers. Kenneth was motionless, holding his breath and straining his ears for a hint of what had awakened him. Overhead, the stars were bright, although the moon had already set. It was too dark for even Kenneth's golden eyes to see far into the night.

A cricket chirped close by.

There was nothing. And yet the eerie certainty that something had awakened him kept Kenneth alert, even after he lay down again and curled his arm under his head. Just when he was finally on the verge of sleep, a great and terrible roar thundered from the air. The noise was horrendous, shaking the ground beneath him. Sounds of feet running into the distance stretched back into silence once again.

Kenneth could not say what had made that noise, but from deep within him came a silent assurance. Much of what his daughter and Jarel had passed on to Kenneth was without words, and he was sure his composure came from them. For no human could lie here calmly, staring into the swaying stalks of grass, exposed and vulnerable, and still feel secure.

And yet he did, completely and utterly. He was almost smiling as he closed his eyes.

Kenneth was awake when he heard Latanya stroll back into their camp and lie down across from him by the fire. He could tell by the way she breathed, she was gazing up into the sky, into the stars. "We will have company tomorrow."

He didn't bother to reply and promptly fell back asleep.

§ଔଔ

Theodin, Baron of Caton, sat upon his warhorse as he stared out across the vast expanse of the ruined desolation of what once were his estates. He floundered in the disgrace. His people dis-liked him, scorning him as they threw offal from starving hands.

Too weary to lift his hand, unsure if his few guards were loyal enough to chase off the rioters, he set his back to them instead. The four that remained wheeled their own mounts around, and kept to their lord's heels.

Theodin was unsure what to do, where to go. He knew his life would be forfeit if he turned his back on his 'masters'. And yet, heartsick by what had become of his Barony, he no longer cared. They rode throughout the day, through the majority of his lands. And everywhere he looked Theodin saw death, disease, famine, plague, rioting; all the decaying symptoms of war.

What was left of his keep lay as he had left it before going on an inspection of his lands. A lone archer upon a crumbling tower waved as they entered a courtyard surrounded by a matching crumbling wall. He dismounted in silence, as did his men, handed off the reins of his mount, and walked alone into what was left of his great hall. The main doors had been torn off. Every window had been widened, until all that remained to hold the roof in place were the main support pillars and a great network of wooden arches overhead.

The furniture had long since been removed, either taken for firewood, to be used in siege weapons, or had simply vanished by way of theft. What awaited him now stood upon two legs each, looking grim and hostile, with arms crossed or hands on their weapons. There were nine of them, all standing in silence at different points in the room. They looked like proud warriors themselves. And all had wings whose great feathers touched the stone floor.

"I have had enough, Medigon." For the first time in Theodin's life, there was no fear in his voice when he faced the creatures. "I cannot continue down this path. My Barony is a haunted place now. There is nothing left."

One of the wingmen, a fierce, terrible Trilian with anger glinting in his eyes, stepped forward to face the impudent human. "There is plenty of stone left," he grated fiercely.

"Then take it. I go into exile."

"You know it is forbidden for the Trilians to interfere with the lives of men," the warrior retorted.

328

Theodin's laughter was without mirth, full of bitterness, even hate. His men waiting in the courtyard cringed to hear it, thinking their lord had just sealed his own death sentence. "And so, you interfere through me!" This fact was undisputed. "The puppet cuts his own strings! Rule this place yourselves! I go!" He turned to leave, but the Trilian caught him by the arm.

Theodin kept his anger in check. He turned and regarded the Trilian.

"I cannot allow this" the Trilian growled.

Theodin pulled his arm free. "All you can do to me you've already done, you and your meddling kind. My family, my wife and daughters are gone. My sons have been destroyed, caught up in some war you started while you peddled that ugly orange stone! I curse the day I ever saw it!" Theodin loosened a money-bag from his belt and threw it at the Trilian's feet. Then he spat at the wingman's chest. "Kill me," he said. "Or let me go. It makes no difference to me. Where I go," he pointed at the mountains in the far distance, "there is no stone. And where there is no stone, there is no war."

"In all my years of serving you, Medigon," Theodin said, "I've learned one thing. Peace is better than profit." And with that he stormed out of his hall, leaving it forever.

Medigon, the wingman, bent down and retrieved the small pouch of stones.

"What will they do, My Lord?" Theodin's men asked him as he remounted his war-horse.

"They will find another puppet to dance for them."

"And our men?"

He looked over at his man. "Sound the retreat. They'll know what it means."

Theodin could not know that the Trilians were sensitive to noise in ways no human could ever be. To hear the anguish and loss in that trumpet call struck a blow that spoken words could never do. The wingmen were weakened physically when they heard what they had done to the humans, forced to acknowledge their part in the devastation that lay about them. One Trilian's knees buckled and he sat down heavily upon the floor, while several leaned against pillars or on their weapons for the strength to stand.

To Medigon, it was as if the entire world was crashing down around his ears. All that he ever strove to achieve, all the wealth he'd sought to control amounted to nothing in that moment when he realized he had been instrumental in the destruction of Theodin's Barony. He grasped the stones Theodin had tossed aside in a fist that shook as he listened to the trumpet sound.

"The stone is all that is important," one of his companions reminded them all. "In the name of Almighty, the stones are all that matters."

"And do you think Almighty would justify what we've done to obtain such a reward?" Medigon asked bitterly. He cast the stones in his hand down upon the ground and stormed from the great hall. Without looking back, he took to the wing and soared over the heads of Theodin and his retreating men. He could scarce look at them, such was his shame. But he knew that where they went he would have to face them sooner or later.

For he too had heard the call of the Aigelendai of Light, and longed for a day of peace.

∞∞∞

Peaceful silence. The vast expanse of nothingness existing as long as he remained utterly still. Stone-Ash was good at remaining utterly still. Even his thoughts and emotions remained quiet. Although his awareness remained sharp, his being was but a deep shadow in this world of darkness.

He wanted it no other way.

Suddenly the stillness was broken by a presence.

Stone-Ash turned and caught the faintest glint of a child shining with a white light, before the light blinked out and the child was gone. Yet a moment later the same light appeared on the horizon, from a point far off in the darkness. Stone-Ash's eyes narrowed and yet his mind remained still, save for a flicker of annoyance.

Who disturbs my rest in this place? The thought escaped him and he regretted releasing it as soon as it was done. Movement brought movement. Only stillness was pure. But there it was, and the child, still from its great distance, shrugged.

Stone-Ash drew breath in an aggravated sigh. You are no child, human though you may appear.

No. The creature was an Aigelendai, hovering in the darkness only a few paces away. I thought you would prefer it if I seemed small in your presence.

Illusions: what difference does one make over the other?

All is illusion here, illusion and dream. And yet here is where you remain until time has no more meaning.

I like it here. It's quiet. Or it was.

Is quiet peace?

Peace is when the thoughts stop.

There is another way.

You are an Aigelendai of Light. It wasn't a question.

A Rame is not so different from the fire races.

No. But I am of the air.

Air and fire.

What of it?

The Aigelendai regarded the Rame for a long moment before she spoke. Moonfire would open your senses.

It would not remain and then I would be saddened? I would know disquiet? No. I like it in the dark, in the oblivion.

And yet you have no fear of the light. To prove her point she radiated all the brighter.

Should I have cause to fear a bug? Stone-Ash asked.

You fear your thoughts,and so you live here. I come alive with my thoughts and so I live wherever I wish; even out here in the darkness. For I am no longer part of the darkness, the oblivion. I am master over it.

The Rame kept silent for a moment, his thoughts and feelings well guarded, but there was a storm building inside him. Has all the Dark Forest been given over to this freedom?

Mostly. There are a few I fear will never turn from their desolation. But… there has been a great sacrifice made that peace might be the way.

"Peace." He uttered the word with his tongue, the sound echoing with a physical blast that blew the Aigelendai back a few paces. If only he might find peace. Peace comes with a price.

It has been paid.

Stone-Ash stared at the Aigelendai for a long, long time. Finally he said, Thank you, little bug.

She bowed respectfully, then was gone.

Stone-Ash bent his will to waking up. It was a long process, one that was complicated and hideous to behold for anyone witnessing it from the outside. But before the sun began to rise, his eyes opened, and Stone-Ash had to use the whole of his might to break from a cocoon that had mummified his body.

He was in a cave with a sand floor, a cave that smelled of dust and age, and contained not a drop of moisture. This meant little to him as he bent his head and strode from the alcove into the pre-dawn light. He stretched his senses out to greet any of his kind, and the quiet voices of his hive came back to him on the gentle breeze. Welcome awake, Stone-Ash. Much of our hive sleeps or ranges deep into the south. Most have gone south.

Why?

Another war fuels our rage.

Stone-Ash shook his head.

Will you go to war, brother? You were always one for such diversions.

I go to seek another path.

Another path?

I go to seek the way of peace. And with that he took to the skies. His leathery wings were a blur behind him as he lifted off of the ground. Goodbye, brothers. Seek me out, if you can.

Silence met him as he flew away.

Kenneth grabbed Latanya's sleeve, though he knew how much she disliked being touched. When she glared at him, he pointed into the distance. Her eyes followed, and grew still.

"I can't believe you didn't see that!"

"It is not in my nature to be drawn to such a thing."

They were silent for a moment as they stared, he in awe, she in some kind of sullen irritation.

"What is it?"

"I cannot believe you don't know what that creature is?" She came almost close to smiling.

"Well?"

"It is a unicorn, Majesty. A symbol of purity."

"And of peace?" Kenneth added.

"Yes, and of peace."

The magical creature appeared in every way to be the finest horse Kenneth had ever seen, and yet none could mistake it for one. For upon its brow was a single horn about as long as an arm, spiraling out to a point that brushed the grass as the animal fed. It was pure white, and to look upon it took Kenneth's breath away.

"We must preserve this place," Kenneth whispered.

"There is no need to be quiet, Majesty. The creature was well aware we were here long before we were aware of it. If it didn't want to be seen, it wouldn't have been seen."

The unicorn grazed upon a wide, flat area of land, some half a league from where they stood. Empty plains stretched out around it far in any direction.

Kenneth moved to approach the unicorn, but now it was Latanya's turn to grab him. "Where do you go?"

He looked at her. "You can come with me."

She looked hurt and looked away into the far distance. She let go of his arm.

"Humans cannot approach a unicorn."

"I'm not entirely human anymore, am I?" He was silent for a moment. "Will you come with me?"

"I will not." She refused to look at him, or the unicorn. "I will remain here."

He set off, never taking his eyes from the amazing creature. Strangely, he felt no fear. He thought perhaps he should, but fascination for the beast drove away his sense of fright, and perhaps the better part of his common sense.

The unicorn did not move.

Surely, I am not pure enough to touch such a creature!

As if it had heard, the unicorn raised his head and regarded Kenneth. Such a wave of human sorrow streamed from the animal that Kenneth almost stumbled with surprise. Somehow he kept his footing and pace, and the creature did not look away. The enchanted blood in Kenneth considered the unicorn as an old wise man, one that had seen many pains and sorrows. But it also knew the days of frolicking and freedom the animal had experienced, the joys and the wonders it had beheld.

Kenneth smiled and walked gently towards the beast, more con-fident now.

The unicorn waited until he was a few yards away, then turned and galloped some distance from him. Kenneth stopped, discour-aged. But the creature reared onto its legs and whinnied. Then, it stamped its fore-hoofs and snorted, shaking its magnificent, snowy mane.

Kenneth tried again, and this time the animal did not move until he was a mere hands' width from running his fingers through the horse's flawless mane. Yet it did not go far, and stamped the ground again. Then it moved forward slowly, and Kenneth heard the distinct sound of hoof hitting stone through the long grass.

"What have you found?" Kenneth asked, feeling not at all ridiculous for talking to the regal animal.

As he knelt, the creature backed away. Kenneth parted the grass and gasped when he saw an immense spectral stone. Perhaps the size of a small cart, it contained every color of the rainbow. Kenneth had never seen such perfection before, and the sight of it made him forget about the unicorn entirely. So this is what the big deal was about. This is what people were fighting and dying over.

Suddenly, the unicorn brushed its head against Kenneth's arm. Without taking his eyes from the stone he patted the bold creature's neck and conveyed his gratitude for the gift. Somehow Kenneth knew that this was the only stone of its kind within the borders of this strange and hidden land.

He glanced at the unicorn's horn and noticed for the first time how it seemed to shimmer with a deep blue electricity, as though a lightning bolt was contained within it.

"Where am I?" he asked the creature, once again dumfounded by the enchantment of this place.

Again, that silent communication that needed no words filled Kenneth with certainty.

"Quetha," he said quietly. "This place is called Quetha."

The unicorn tossed its mane, and Kenneth pushed to his feet. He turned and looked across the distance to Latanya, who stared at him, her face pale. She hadn't moved.

"Here!" he shouted. He sensed the unicorn's unease and patted the creature on the flank in way of farewell, then turned back to his guide as the animal galloped towards a copse of trees to the west. Kenneth watched it run until it vanished and then he turned back to Latanya. "Here is where we build!'

And so they came, from all over the island and beyond. The Aigelendai and Tenlenesse of Light were fabled creatures, even among creatures of legend themselves. So when they left their borders of the Dark Forest to spread word of the invitation, they were met with much interest and also some bitter resistance. But the dwellers of the Fire Realm could disappear and reappear at will, remaining out of reach of harm. The few instances where their enemies sought to end the sanctuary offered to all the races were quelled quickly and bitterly, with much blood flowing under the boughs of the Dark Forest. They tried fire, and yet the wood would not burn. They tried axes, and the branches came alive and struck back with the grace and fluidity of vipers. They tried to fly above and were shot down by wooden darts propelled from the enchanted trees. And they tried burrowing underground, only to discover living roots that were just as terrifying, sometimes more.

But to all those who sought refuge from the violent way of greed, pathways opened up before them. Streams flowed with healing, thirst-quenching water. Sunlight lit their way by day, and the moon and stars lulled them to sleep as they took shelter under protective canopies of leaves while the breezes played lullabies through the branches.

They were shown through the forests peacefully, respectfully, and were permitted to find sanctuary in the rolling plains of a place Kenneth called Quetha.

ಬಿಞ

They came first to Kenneth. Broken and beaten, ashamed and disgraced within their own communities, they came for sanctuary, for a new life. Kenneth knew the blessings of keeping busy, and so put them to work, that they might use their unique gifts con - structively and be united with a feeling of purpose with those that had been their enemies for so long.

No one could have predicted what could be accomplished with cooperation.

They bent all of their will into a single building. Some say it was a castle, some a tower. Others said it was simply unlike any - thing that had ever been built before or since. Surrounded by a vast dry moat quarried for its stone, the castle was accessible by four bridges, one facing each direction. It climbed straight into the sky, a network of delicate towers joined and rejoined with bridges and balconies, each bigger and grander than the last.

It was a marvel to behold, indeed, a wonder throughout all the lands. And it inspired in the Quethans a level of awe that left many speechless. In the few short years that it had taken to con - struct it, Kenneth had come to revere the races with a respect that was only matched by the reverence his citizens felt towards him. Humbly, they served him, and he them, until the day came when the great construction was finished.

There was a great celebration. Everyone assembled in the largest of the great halls on the main floor. Such was its size that all were able to crowd into it to hear the words that would be spo - ken.

"We are united in purpose with bonds stronger than those of the nations outside Quetha!" Stone-Ash shouted towards the bal- conies of the coliseum-like hall. A great roar of agreement swept down upon him and he stood triumphantly, his arms spread wide and his wings curving behind him, glorying in his people. Stone- Ash was a muscular creature, ten times as strong as a man. His face was more like the face of a bat, with two narrow vertical slits to pass as a nose and two outrageously large ears on top of his head. He was of a race called the Rames, desert-dwelling creatures possessing the power of telepathy that made it unneces - sary for them to speak aloud to others of their kind. Rather, they acted as one, like bees of the same hive. There were a few Rames within this hall, and they had adapted to the ways of the other races remarkably well, choosing often to speak with sound rather than thought, and learning to respect the privacy of their country - men's thoughts.

Other sub-races were drawn to Stone-Ash and the other Rames, heralding them as the pride of their new country, knowing full well that past the forested borders of this small refuge, the Rames were feared as demons.

"What is it you say, Stone-Ash?" Kenneth asked, rising from his throne and walking down from his elevated dais until he stood on the same level with the Rame, although the creature towered over him a good two feet.

"What I am saying, My Liege, is that nothing can stand in our way from seizing control over all of it."

Kenneth cried out in despair, clutched his hair with both hands and said, "Never say such a thing! We would become just as they are now, what we once were!"

The crowd exploded, shouting and waving him down. Such was the strength of their opposition that Kenneth glanced at Latanya, who met his eye quickly. This outburst had been planned, their thoughts said across the room to each other. She looked as though she was prepared to bring her inhuman strength to bear against the Rame for conspiring behind their king's back. And yet very little could be done as the roar of sound pounded down upon them. The terrible tragedy had begun – the transformation of good into devastation through greed. Now they must play it out, to whatever end.

It was a Trilian named Feedimon that finally stepped forward and silenced the crowd with upraised hands.

"My fellow countrymen!" he cried. "Hear me now!" He paused and looked around to ensure he was being listened to. "Let us not be too cruel to our lord king. It was Kenneth who united us, who gave us a place to recover from our losses, to grow strong once again!" A shout of approval reverberated from the rafters over-head. "I say, if King Kenneth wishes to advocate for peace, let him do it somewhere else." A hush fell over the assembly as they comprehended his words. "I say let the man be exiled peacefully. Let him take only what he can carry, let him turn his back on this castle, and let him never look back."

Another roar went up, but Kenneth was quick to raise his hand.

"Silence!" Medigon roared with his two voices. "Let the man speak in his defense!"

The place quickly grew quiet under the Trilian Medigon's doggedness.

"I hear your words, Feedimon, and I concede that if this is the choice you wish to make, this place is no longer my home. It was I who conceived of Quetha, who brought her to reality, who worked to see her dream come alive. It was my family that sacri - ficed their lives to ensure I had the ability to do this thing. It was I who led you to build this castle as a monument to peace. But if you choose to rob this monument of its meaning; if you seek to take peace and cast her from your heart, then know it is you who do not belong in Quetha. For she is first and foremost, a kingdom of the heart. And she cannot be overthrown by tyrants.

"I will leave, graciously. I only ask that you permit those who still believe in peace, as I do, to leave with me, that we may find a place to coexist as we have done here."

"Your words are wise, King," Feedimon returned. "Let none of your followers infiltrate and undermine our course in your absence. Take your agents and be gone from here."

Kenneth's eyes swept the congregation once, silently asking them all to choose one or the other. Some nodded and stepped forward boldly, yet many looked away in shame. Still others stared back defiantly, with crossed arms and contempt written on their faces.

"This is your last chance!" Kenneth warned.

"Be gone from here!" someone shouted from the masses. Kenneth nodded, sighed, and grew resolute. Then he turned his back on the people who had rejected him and led his followers, a small group, out of the great chamber and into the rest of the cas - tle.

They were silent as they walked on, not sure of their fate, yet confident they had made the wise choice. Nothing around them could not be replaced or rebuilt and so they said their goodbyes to family and friends that remained behind, in their hearts and in their minds.

At the western bridge Kenneth paused to let his people pass, encouraging them with a smile or a squeeze of their shoulder . They returned his affections with smiles of their own, a great host of wings and limbs and pointed ears, a mis-match of forlorn crea - tures that once thought of themselves as demons, but who now embraced the common thread of humanity that united them all as kindred.

Medigon brought up the rear with Latanya. "We are the last of them," he said to Kenneth. "None follow behind."

"Are you sure?"

Latanya nodded and took Kenneth's hand.

"I must fly, my king. All this walking has weighed my wings down."

Kenneth nodded. "Go. And thank you."

"Not such a small mob," Medigon commented. "It could have been worse."

"Much worse," Latanya said with a smile. Then she paused and looked back at Kenneth. "Now is the time?"

He nodded.

"I'll leave you to it," Medigon said, jumping into the sky.

Together and alone, silent yet with understanding flowing through them, they walked the distance across the bridge.

"Thank you for doing this," he said to her.

"It must be done."

He could only nod. He took a chain from around his neck. Fastened to the chain was a key and for the key was a lock in a pillar. The pillar rose chest high from where it protruded from the ground at the edge of the precipice that was the dry moat of the castle.

He turned the key and there was a snick and then nothing for a moment. But then the bridges began to shake with a terrible rumble that caused those Quethans who had followed him to turn and stare in mute wonder. A moment later and the bridges were collapsing and crumbling into the vast space below them. A Rame roared his disapproval from the castle and Kenneth and Latanya looked at each other quickly.

"Now is the time," she said. Then she dived into the chasm.

"Latanya, no!" a woman cried.

Kenneth turned to see the human held at bay by a Rame woman. Her wings beat to keep them both locked in place against the woman's struggles and she was muttering something into her friend's ear.

"I don't believe you," the woman cried, and then collapsed to the ground.

"Wait and see," the Rame said kindly, quietly. "Wait and see." She held the woman in her arms, rocking her back and forth as she cocooned them both with her wings.

They waited and there was a roar and a shudder from the castle. Deep down in its roots an immense blast of fire erupted. And from that blast a thin film of air ballooned out over the castle's roots towards the precipices that were her towers. The shuddering continued as this strange multi-hued film expanded up along the cliffs around the castle. Then it crested its edges and a bubble grew up to envelope the castle, encasing and imprisoning it.

The shuddering and the roaring stopped and as the Quethans watched from safety, the filmy air solidified. Some stared in wonder. Others smiled and nodded or shouted victoriously with fists held high.

"Latanya?" someone asked.

A moment later a plume of fire shot out from the side of the giant bubble. This was followed by the lithe form of a young fire dragon. She was perhaps only four times lar ger than a human, with scales of red and brown. But even as the others watched she came to land before them and her scales started to shine as though a sun was dawning from underneath them. They were changing color, gaining sheen, from dull to metallic, and finally, to golden.

And then the image of the dragon began to shimmer and Latanya stood in its midst. The human image wept unashamed as the image of the dragon slowly faded, growing continuously transparent until it faded from view all together. But the process was slow and gave the others time to see the Golden Dragon be reborn in splendor.

They watched with amazement as Latanya continued to cry. "It's so beautiful!" she finally managed, looking up with a face of raw amazement. Her self-loathing was gone, replaced by a love and a wisdom as great as any could have.

Peace was triumphant.

And the Legend of Quetha was born.

ഇരു

Fall of Devia

D.J. Ebenal

A myriad of frozen water droplets hung suspended in the air, reflecting countless rainbows into the surrounding clouds as prisms under the golden sunlight. They were frozen in place; the beauty of this delicate miracle remained steady, as changing winds blew massive clouds across the endless, empty sky-scape.

A section of earth floated in the midst of the mist and light. It appeared to have been caused by a crater, the way exposed rock jutted down to a rough point underneath the surface, like a tooth ripped from a giant's mouth and flung into space. Wondrously, this island was teeming with life, with robust vegetation and colorful birds that flew around and underneath the land mass, shattering motionless raindrops then singing happily when they landed to preen the damp moisture from their feathers.

There were many asteroids like this one floating within the sky realm of Mishard. The cause of such miracles was the Spectral Stone, the Fifth Element. This phenomenal substance could take on the form of any of the other four elements, creating new and fantastic realms, such as this sky realm. The mists that encased the island were of this spectral element, called Skystone by those who harvested it, for it eventually reverted to stone once it was contained, although those who appropriated the element would be hard pressed to be free of the mist that would cling to it.

There was more Spectral Stone buried inside the rocks deep within the center of the island. It illuminated the interior of a cave, a lair dug by some creature of past legend as a sanctuary for its young. With the colors of the rainbow shimmering through the dark, the cave's interior was lit to reveal a panorama of horror scattered over the cave floor.

Dragon eggs had been shattered, their shells crushed and scat - tered to every corner of the room. Macabre ooze dripped from the rugged shards, discarded bodies of mutilated dragons similarly lay in grisly death poses of destruction and ruin. It was impossi - ble to count their numbers; the indistinct tangle of limbs and beaks, and sightless unborn dragon eyes was enough for even the most adamant dragon-slayer to turn from in revulsion.

She knew that for fact, for she sat with her back to the carnage, preening herself clean of the gore that had collected on her body. Just in time, she thought to herself, stripping her feathers free of the embryonic remains. The little demons were about to hatch. Divine Providence, it must be. Almighty has sent me here to unleash his wrath against this lot, this abomination. The thought made her feel better about how young they had been, and she hardened her heart to her guilt as she turned to survey her handi - work.

The bile didn't rise quite so high in her throat the second time she looked at it.

When she was finished scouring the filth from her, she climbed out of the cave and stretched as if to embrace the whole, exquisite sky. The prisms shone down on her like rainbows cast by stars.

The sunlight enveloped her in its warmth and golden rays. Thank Almighty none of that plague escaped into this! Surely something as evil as a dragon has no right to look upon such beauty!

Devia made up her mind right then and there to rid the world of the monstrosities that polluted the skies with their foul breath, hideous reptilian bodies, and their bat-like wings. Evil creatures, all of them; they would all share the same fate as the young hatchlings behind her.

Her resolution made, Devia jumped into the air and soared through the rainbows, laughing as she felt the tiny ice beads burst against her skin. Had not Almighty given her these wings that she might track the demons through the air? She looked at her hands and the smile on her face widened. And these knives, these dagger-sharp nails growing right from her fingertips! Such a gift could only be bestowed upon her for one purpose: the tearing and rending of dragon flesh.

Full of purpose and deadly intent, she knew her mission had been blessed from above, and the hunt began in earnest as she soared farther away from the dragon lair. Below her the sky opened up into an infinite sea of clouds in every direction. There was no ground here, no bottom to this ocean of air. All in sight was blue or white. She craned her neck to the left and to the right; then rolled over onto her back, and found endlessness there as well.

"This is my hunting ground!" she roared with arrogance. "All of this before me is mine to stalk!" She was an avenging angel and Almighty had given her a grand task – such glory would it bring!

She righted herself and shot across the expanse of sky, using her keen eyes to search amongst the clouds, confident it wouldn't take her long to claim her next kill.

But as the hours wore on and her wings started to cramp, Devia's confidence began to waver. She spent less time thinking about the hunt, and more time about a place to rest.

She was about to venture into one of the motionless clouds that surrounded her and search for respite, but the prospect only served to anger her. To give up, even if only for a moment, would be to admit failure. Instead, she allowed her wings to cease their beating and glided down between the clouds, resting in flight but still searching as she dropped.

Devia grew worried. If she was seen from above by a dragon, it would be able to escape her before she could regain the height she would need to plunge down on it. So it was with tears of grat-itude that she found the thermal. A warm gust of wind, an updraft, halted her descent and filled her wings with wind.

She began to rise, slowly, little by little. By flying in tight cir-cles, Devia found she could stay within the blessed current, ascending higher and higher into the air and able to rest at the same time.

Hours passed and her gratitude changed to boredom.

Still, she would not give up her hunt. Dragons needed to die, and Devia needed to find them. In order to do that she needed altitude to dive and kill. So she waited, growing angrier with every rotation.

When she at last saw the dragon below her, she propelled the full force of her anger towards the creature. She held the beast with the red and black scales, the elongated neck, and the lizard-like tail responsible her discomfort; and she, Devia, would make it pay for her troubles!

She glided out of the thermal, never letting the dragon out of her sight. She was going to enjoy this. This was her destiny, her fulfillment. The avenging angel was about to strike, to set some-thing right by destroying an evil that had escaped into her pure and clean universe of sky.

Devia had to force herself to remain silent, but her heart screamed out a battle cry as she folded her wings and extended

her claws. A moment later she plummeted, plunging into the dragon, sinking her claws into its back.

The dragon screamed and thrashed, but Devia held on. Planted
solidly between its wings, the monster's attempts only deepened
the gouges she'd started. Devia shouted in triumph. Almighty was
going to grant her this kill!

The dragon stopped trying to dislodge her, straightened its flight
and grew very still.

She looked up at the back of its head hopefully. This was too
easy! All she had to do was plunge one claw deep into the creature's new wounds, and it would bleed to death.

She reached her hand back behind her head to deliver the
killing blow when the dragon's head twisted around towards her
and unleashed a stream of molten fire. She lost her balance. Her
grasp slipped, and she clung to one of the dragon's wings to stop
from losing her prey.

The maneuver probably saved her life. The dragon's breath
blasted past Devia, inches from her face, while its own wing took
the brunt of the attack. The dragon screamed in fury and anguish.
Desperately it curled itself into a ball to seek retribution.

She was within easy reach now, and Devia wrestled to ward off
its grasping talons with her free claw. After a brief struggle, she
was able to grab its carpus and hold one talon at bay while she
clung to the dragon's wing with the other. The dragon lunged at
her again and again, yet each time the creature grappled for
Devia's exposed side, it simply came away with a handful of
white feathers for its efforts.

Her feathers! She had forgotten the feathers, the armor God had
given her against such a creature as this. Of course! Plate-mail or
chain-link would heat up until they were unbearable; fur would
burn, and scales could be pulled off. But feathers, if they were
charred, or seized the way this fire-spewing demon was undertak-

348

ing to do, would simply fall out, leaving Devia no worse off than before.

She laughed in the dragon's face, reveling in her certain victory.

The creature paused, as if to rethink its strategy; and when it reared its head to release another stream of fire, Devia was ready. She released the dragon's wing and immediately lunged forward to take hold of the demon's neck. It struggled for a few precious moments, scrambling to find purchase as it frantically pulled tufts of feathers out of her wings.

Then it understood what the fates had sealed, and the dragon grew still.

Devia let go of the dragon's carpus and adjusted her grip on its neck. Then she roared her victory call and killed the beast.

Only after the dragon was dead did Devia realize that she was descending, that she had been falling since the onset of the battle.

Alarmed now, Devia thrust the carcass away from her, and it spun crazily into the air. With frantically beating wings, she fought urgently against the currents that were dragging her downwards towards certain death.

Her panic subsided when the dragon's body suddenly dropped away from her and Devia was able to recover her balance. Curious, she watched it plummet through the clouds, and followed it inquisitively, able now to fly at a safer speed.

Presently the clouds parted, and Devia was amazed by what lay before her.

As mighty as the sky above, so was the land below. Mountains and oceans and forests, deserts and fields and winding rivers, a whole universe of diversity and change, so different from the realm she'd left behind.

Devia ignored the dragon's carcass and let it plunge through the air to crash into the forest floor below. Her sights were set on the snow-covered mountain peaks, the only familiar thing in sight. Her breast thudded in anticipation. If dragons existed in this strange land, they would be found there, in the mountains.

She made one pass over the craggy peaks. One was all it took. A dragon's lair was nestled at the base of a glacier, surrounded by massive boulders, some as large as the beasts themselves.

Devia circled again and landed among the rocks, confident she still had the element of surprise. After all, weren't her wings the color of the snow around her? Wasn't she an angel of Almighty, sent to free the world of these despicable creatures? She was without fear as she stalked her way around the towering boulders, towards a cave that lay just beyond.

"It took you long enough to get here." The deep bass voice rumbled as though it came from the mountain itself.

Devia's heart pounded. She looked up and around, her eyes lifting towards the skies above her, where she could be vulnerable to attack. There was nothing there; she was alone.

Summoning her courage, she marched forward. She rounded a larger boulder and saw where – or what – the voice had come from. Devia stopped in her tracks, and her mouth gaped.

"I saw you fly overhead." It was immense. At first she thought she was looking at another sun. Golden scales reflected the light from a mountain of dragon flesh. Huge wings lay stretched out across the rising slope of the mountain, revealing golden feathers, each the length of her arms. The dragon lay on its back, unafraid, propped up against the mountain, sunning itself.

In spite of herself, Devia was awed by the majesty of the creature, by it's sheer size as well as its beauty. She gulped and forced herself to harden her heart, and reminded herself what a kill this could make. Almighty would be so pleased with her greatness!

The dragon rose, using its wings to stand upright like a human, like an avenging angel – like her. It regarded her for a long moment, studying the look in her eye, as if he could read her innermost thoughts. "You have traveled far in such a short time."

Devia kept her tongue, steeling herself to the task at hand.

"Now, what am I supposed to do with you?" He stretched his wings towards the sun briefly before they folded against his body and he sat down to await her answer. His tail wrapped around him as he stared down at her.

Still, she did not answer, too amazed by his magnificent scales to be able to speak, and already coveting the trophies she would take once the deed was done.

"You wonder how my scales came to be golden, how I came to be a Golden Dragon?"

Still enthralled, Devia simply nodded.

"That's as good a place as any to start, I suppose," the dragon said. Then he grew thoughtful, as he collected his thoughts and carefully chose his words. "Let me ask you a question." He wait - ed for her to nod again. "How do you feel about dragons?"

This time there was no hesitation. "They are the bane of the sky realm, and of this earth. They are evil, and despicable, and cow - ardly. They are dirty creatures, wicked, dishonest. I despise drag - ons, every last one of them!"

"Even me?"

"You are by far the fairest and oldest and wisest dragon I have ever seen. But you are still a dragon, and therefore deserve my hate. You must die."

"And what of you?"

"I am an avenging angel. I am the scourge of dragons. Almighty himself has equipped me with a body that cannot be defeated by dragons, one meant to hunt them in the air with wing and claw and teeth – if need be. And my feathers, my white. pure feathers, come free when a dragon attacks. I am protected from anything you might use to escape or to attempt to use to defeat me."

The dragon looked around and picked up a nearby boulder. It was perhaps the size of a small horse. "What if I decide to throw this at you?"

Devia tensed. "I will get out of the way, for I can move faster than anything else."

The dragon regarded her for a moment and then with consider-able restraint, put the rock down. He shook his head, and said calmly, "It always amazes me when I find one of your kind."

"You lie!" Devia hissed. "I am the only one of my kind! In all the world, I am unique!"

"I'd expect such a response from a hatchling." She drew breath for an indignant reply, but the dragon held up a talon to halt her rebuke. "Please, I know what you would say. I've heard such things before, and I grow tired of it all."

"What would I say?" She was angry now, and embraced the anger, fueling it for the strength to attack.

"You would tell me how insulted you are at being compared to a dragon, to a hatchling, at that. You would say it's beneath you, that you are so much more than that, and that Almighty himself has ordained you to be a holy vessel, an instrument of his will."

Devia paused. For once, she had nothing to say.

"But I'm not comparing you to just any dragon," he continued. "I'm comparing you to a sky dragon, one who is hatched from her egg with the strength and wisdom of a fully developed human. Although she is born at the same time as the rest of the dragons in her nest, she is possessed with the fiercest anger, the utmost passion, the most impatience, but above all, unsurpassed pride.

She hatches first, covered with white feathers that will protect her and secrete her in the air realm, giving her time to get used to the body she inhabits."

"She will kill the rest of the hatchlings, breaking open their eggs and scattering their bodies in her delusional abhorrence of all dragons. She will gain much strength from the yokes her feathers will absorb during the massacre. In a sense, she takes the nourishment from her siblings, and she will grow strong and haughty from the sustenance they provide her with."

"Then she will strike out on her own into the air realm, away from the shelter and safety of her nest to pursue other dragons, to hunt and be hunted in turn. If she is wise, she will stay in the air realm, high in the air where most of the spectral islands are found. There a dragon can find food, water, and shelter, along with peace and safety. But then, a young dragon isn't really known for her wisdom, is she?"

He looked at her expectantly, but Devia had nothing to say.

"So," he nodded sagely and continued, "a young dragon attacks other dragons, or is attacked by them. Either way, the white feathers you regard so highly don't grow back, not for a long, long time. Once they're gone, a young hatchling becomes a fledgling and must learn what it is to be the hunted; to learn cunning and patience; to learn when to stay hidden and to attack with speed."

"And still the young dragon will despise all other dragons, believing herself to be something other than what she is; certain that she is special, sent from the God Almighty. She may live long enough to find her way back to the islands in the sky. And if she does, she will possibly find a mate, and she might find a lair to lay her own eggs, for the cycle to begin again."

The Golden Dragon eyed Devia knowingly, and a warning note crept into his voice. Devia shuddered slightly in spite of herself.

"But a dragon will never breathe fire until she admits she is a dragon. She will loathe them as much as ever, but she will have obliterated the pride and lies that mask her from the detestable truth of what she is. And that realization will free her to use the gifts Almighty has given only to dragons."

Before Devia could interject, he plowed on relentlessly. "But the cycle of hate and violence can be broken. A Golden Dragon is no different from any other dragon, except that a Golden Dragon has turned his cleansing fire unto himself. Some dragons get weary of their own arrogance. They get tired of the violence, deception and the skulking, the killing and the anger. They get tired of the burden, the weight that their lives place on their souls. So instead of presuming themselves to be avenging angels of the Almighty, they ultimately face their real selves, and come before Him in their hearts."

"Forgive me for my evil nature and all the evil I have commit - ted in your name." they plead. "Please accept me as I am, and change what I am to suit your glory."

"When this happens a dragon feels as though he cannot bear to exist in the body of such a miscreation any longer. So he turns the fire onto himself, and the Almighty purifies him and transforms his scales to the color of the sun, that all dragons may know that this one dragon truly is of the Almighty."

He stopped speaking and waited for Devia to respond.

"I am not a dragon."

The Golden Dragon reached forward and slowly plucked a feather from her shoulder. He gazed at it pensively for a moment before plucking one of his own from his wing. He passed them both to her. Devia could not dispute that, other than in color and size, the two feathers were exactly the same.

"I am not a dragon," she repeated.

354

He extended his wings out behind him, then folded one around in front of himself so he could examine it. He placed his fore-talon on top of the wing and nodded towards Devia to do the same.

She glared at him and, to prove him wrong, mimicked his movements and brought a miniature version of his own wing in front of herself. He stretched out his fore-talon and held his claws up before her eyes. Then he closed and opened his hand a few times and twisted his wrist to show her the shape and range of movement in his carpus. She held her own claws up to her face, and her eyes widened. Even then, Devia continued to cling to her stubbornness and reiterated firmly, "I am not a dragon."

The Golden Dragon sighed, and then patted his tail suggestively against the earth.

She stared at it and then at him.

"I dare you," was all he said with a nod.

Devia had to focus all her strength to concentrate, but in a moment, her own tail swung around to the front of her. Her eyes narrowed hatefully.

"No dragon is of Almighty until she offers willingly to Him the dragon she is," he reminded her.

She felt her lips curl in a silent snarl. "I-am-not-" Then surprisingly, as only a dragon could, fire spewed from her mouth and engulfed the Golden Dragon so that he was obscured from her view. Through the torrent of her hypocrisy she shouted "A DRAGON!"

The inferno that answered her outburst was a torrent, like a rushing wave crashing over her. When she saw it coming, she cried out in horror and cringed into a ball, warding off the blow with her claws held over her head, fully expecting instant death.

Yet, the raging heat and terror gradually subsided, and eventual-ly Devia had the courage to open her eyes. The Golden Dragon was glaring at her, his face close to her own comparatively tiny features. He did not look at all impressed. "Be gone from my presence, hatchling," he spat. "May you live a long and hated existence if you will not repent. But know that you have no right, none at all, to claim self-worth above your kin. You are as despi-cable as they are, as despicable as I once was."

He turned his back to her in contempt, as if Devia no longer existed, and returned to sunning himself on the mountain. Then, abruptly, he fell asleep.

Realizing with dismay that she was doomed, knowing she could say or do nothing that would change the Golden Dragon's pro-nouncement, Devia turned despondently and slunk from his pres-ence. Nothing was left to her but the realization she was every-thing she despised.

ഓരു

Stars and Shadows

D.J. Ebenal

The Heavens revealed their glory as an infinite Cosmos of light and variety. Stars and planets and gaseous clouds of dust and asteroids opened up before Sheana, ruthlessly tantalizing her with their near-ness. There was a point in the atmosphere she could not cross, an invisible barrier she could not penetrate. It had something to do with the air, that much she knew. Some technical gibberish, about oxygen and uplift. It had been explained to her once, callously and matter-of-factly; but she had paid little attention, for those words meant nothing to Sheana.

What mattered was that the universe was out there, revealing its secrets to life forms that could only narrowly be considered mortal. And yet Sheana was here, bound to Mishard like a dog on a leash.

The knowledge debased her, infuriated her, and filled her with despair. Yes, she was a dragon, capable of navigating the threshold between this life and the next. And yes, all other corporeal creatures were below her, subject only to the limited exposure the planet could offer, while she basked in the magnitude and inspiration of space. Even so, Sheana envied the lowlies their ignorance. To see and be denied entry was a terrible burden. To not see and walk around in blissful unawareness, what a great gift that would be!

And yet Sheana returned again and again, feeling the aura of the universe cascade over her, bringing tears to her eyes and strength to her wings. Not all dragons were cursed with this compulsion. Fire dragons existed to savor the shores of moonfire, to toy with the one substance that could burn them like a lover seduced into dangerous, forbidden foreplay. Earth dragons burrowed into the heart of the planet until they were lost in its darkness and depth. And water dragons dove fruitlessly into the abyss, until even the fires of hell were denied them. They were all exalted by their exertions to transcend the limits of their boundaries. But, humbled by what they found there, they came back vengeful and resentful, yet driven by an obsession to return repeatedly to the very thing that reminded them of their own shortcomings.

With a shake of her head, Sheana banished such thoughts and angled away from the top of the world. As she descended and the sky was restored to its usual cerulean hue; the magnificent colours and glory of the Beyond dimmed, and eventually faded altogether. All the wonder of the Cosmos was concealed once again.

She sighed, too weary to hold on to her resentment, and headed towards the nearest cluster of floating islands. According to legend, about sixty years ago exploitation of the enchanted power of the Spectral Stones, Mishard's true wealth, had brought about a great cataclysm, an event that had shaken the planet to its foundations. As prophecy had foretold, the cataclysm had ripped Mishard apart, creating the four spectral realms.

The Spectral Stones, created from substance that could change from mist to water, to solid to fire, sped up evolution. And as they were connected to the fabric of the surface realm, they tore asunder the surface, spewing great mountains of rock into the skies and exposing horrendous caverns in the earth. The mysterious fire realm cast its shadow over all, while the water realm flourished with giant reefs and strange new lands under the surface of the deep.

These same floating mountains, these 'Sky Islands', provided rest and solitude for Sheana, permitting her to stay nearer to the outer edge of the world, closer to the source of her curse and her fixation. It was as if Almighty enjoyed tormenting her by allowing Sheana tanta-lizing glimpses of that which she could never possess.

Sky Island. She hated that name. It was unoriginal and lacked cre-ativity. It seemed though, that so much of the world below the cerulean sky was like that, drab and mundane. Sheana supposed the name suited.

She flew among the islands now. Lush green mountain peaks, sur-rounded by floating water droplets caught in the enchantment of the spectral mists, hanging suspended in the air like a multitude of prisms. The roar of waterfalls plummeting into the cavernous open, dissipating into cloud or rain; accompanied by the sight of ancient statues carved into the face of the cliffs. A glittering rainbow of color shone from the exposed Spectral Stones. Paradise. Yet to Sheana, it meant nothing, less than nothing. It was disgraceful, a detestable reminder that beauty came from above to filter into the planet while ugliness rose from below, wafting up into the skies. It created an equilibrium known as this painful, burdensome existence, an exis-tence shared by all mortals.

Filled with malice, Sheana set the place aflame, not stopping until all was ashes and dust. The rivers and streams became mere trickles. Stone was hidden beneath a layer of soot, forests reduced to a rubble of burnt sticks. What forests still stood looked like the gnarled, black-ened arms of dead giants, but reaching towards that hateful place above even in death. The statues were degraded to slag, their beauty forever destroyed by her wrath.

Sheana crashed down in the middle of a charred wooded area, sending fragments of smoldering kindling splintering into the air. She was
gratified by her outburst. A cloud of gray-white dust rose up to choke
out the sun until it was little more than an orange haze trapped within
the dirty smog. Satisfied with the results of the destruction, Sheana
settled her wings about her and curled into herself, resting her head
on the still smoldering ruins of the vanquished paradise.

"Much better," she said to herself. Then she closed her eyes and fell
asleep.

Dragons sleep. They sleep deeply and for long stretches of time.
And Sheana was drained after her successful rampage of total
destruction. She slept for ages.

When she awoke it was to the sound of running water. She sighed,
resigned to what she knew she would find when she opened her eyes.
And when she did, she saw that the island was blanketed under a
layer of green grasses spotted with vividly colored wild flowers.
Saplings were already sprouting throughout the fields, young trees to
replace the old forests she had destroyed.

Sheana snorted with frustration and pushed herself wearily to her
feet, roving through the fields on all fours, grazing on the tender dan-
delions as she ambled along.

The land was rugged, its secrets barred from her since she'd consumed the place with her fire. And though there were many places –
deep gorges and wide lakes – that had survived Sheana's wrath, any
living creatures had either perished in the blaze, or fled.

"Pity," she thought, scouring the island with her keen eyesight. She
was hungry.

Sheana took to the air and propelled herself across the open space
to another cluster of islands, searching for food. This time, however,
she restrained herself from turning the land to ash, setting down
almost daintily amid the crags and forests.

Some birds were disturbed by Sheana's arrival and took flight, rising into the air. She snapped them up in quick succession, crunching through bone and blood only after she'd caught them all. Then, with her belly only slightly satisfied, Sheana burned the feathers from her mouth and moved onwards to explore.

It was a large island, mostly flat, but with a magnificent rise of rock protruding from the northeast corner of the forested plateau. It was toward this crag Sheana headed, moving lightly, keeping to the rivers and fields and avoiding the dense forest. She was hunting, gliding along the ground with the same silence she used on the wing.

Her prey always heard her too late. She caught sight of a faun grazing at the edge of the forest, and with a rush of wings, took to the skies. The deer must have heard or sensed a disturbance, for it turned its head in the direction she had been only seconds before. Sheana was faster though, already swooping down on the faun, her claws extended for the kill.

Too late, the creature sensed the danger. It tensed, prepared to bolt, but Sheana's claws were already sinking into its flanks. The faun screamed as she lifted it into the air and, with a swift jerk of her wings, broke its back. Food should never be tortured.

Something about the lonely mountain attracted Sheana's attention. For a moment she could not place it; it only seemed somehow different. But then she realized – not a single green thing grew on the black and gray slopes.

Curious, Sheana grasped the carcass tightly and gained altitude. The mountain drew closer, revealing another plateau within its heights. And as she flew nearer she saw that the place had been torched, again and again. Scorch marks caused by concentrated blasts still etched across the barren field, darker valleys amidst the layers of settled ash.

Instinctively, Sheana shuddered and glanced around in fear, but she was alone. The ash had grown cold. She giggled, relieved, and landed on the edge of the plateau, where the mountain rose up beside her.

Her descent caused a plume of ash to rise up around her, and she reveled in the cleanliness, the purity of the fire's scar.

Sheana settled down to enjoy her meal in peace and solitude, almost forgetting the longing in her bones, the ache for Heaven and the experiences denied her.

It was a quick meal. Being a small dragon, she needed less to eat than most. Sheana had realized at a very early age that size was a disadvantage in the thermals, and being able to climb the thermals was everything – everything it took to reach Heaven's walls.

Immediately, she banished the train of thought and breathed a gust of fire to cleanse her mouth. Then she set out to luxuriate in the ashes of someone else's fury. And yet, even as she purposefully kicked up billows of dust, she wondered why only the mountain had been damaged. The forests and fields below had been spared. They look almost – cherished, Sheana mused.

Her misgiving caused her to falter and glance around again, a little more nervously than before. The only thing worse than stumbling across a dragon was encountering a Golden one. However, there seemed to be no place here where a Golden lair could exist.

Most dragons survived by running and hiding, or by stalking and killing. Golden Dragons, however, were territorial although incredibly kind; a strange breed, especially considering how formidable they were, capable of mass devastation and destruction that could ruin even the most powerful adversary.

Still, Sheana reasoned, they were dragons. And she loathed them just the same, perhaps all the more because she envied them too.

She picked her footsteps cautiously now, waiting eagerly but relieved when she left the ash clouds behind. At least now she could watch the skies and flee if another dragon appeared. And she felt it would be best to wait for any monster to show itself first, lest she unknowingly fly towards it.

For the next few hours, none did. Sheana had moved steadily across the plateau, following the edge of the mountain on her left, stalking the hidden viewpoint the mountain produced.

What she discovered instead was something entirely new, and intense curiosity drew her toward it. An immense dome, easily a hundred times larger than herself, rested like a giant dragon's egg against the base of the crag.

"What is that?" she wondered aloud. Forgetting her stealth, Sheana moved towards it.

At first, she approached with trepidation, as though she feared it was alive, this strange sphere half buried by rock and soot. She even stretched her neck out as if to sniff it before truly trusting it to be inanimate.

Movement.

She froze and blinked, then coiled her body under her head, prepar- ing for flight. Yet as she watched she realized that the movement came from within the innermost nucleus of the sphere.

Sheana was surprised. The dome was semitransparent and shim- mered with a faint metallic luster, although the figures that the orb appeared to contain were somewhat indistinct. They seemed unable to see her, for they moved about apparently unconcerned and unaware of her presence.

The figures appeared to be human, for they walked upright and wore the clothes of a surface dweller. And although Sheana could only see partially into the sphere, past the oily, shifting substance of its periphery that hampered her vision, she could tell there was an air of great bustle about them. They rushed back and forth as if absorbed in some urgent, monumental undertaking.

Sheana was amused. She took to the air, and when she rose above the sphere she discovered that she could see much more clearly from overhead than from its base. In fact, it seemed that the buildings inside grew to the apex of the dome. She could see their roofs clearly, and actually, one building even protruded through the pinnacle of the dome itself. It was a curious structure with a peaked roof; housing a square tower with the face of a broken clock half submerged within the dome.

More curious than ever, Sheana hovered in the air beside the clock tower, and gingerly tested her weight against the dome. Mercifully, it held. More confident now, she perched atop the dome and curled herself around the tower.

Feeling settled and comfortable, she peered downwards into the dome to watch its inhabitants scurry around with the hustle and bustle of their lives.

Dragons watch. The passage of time is meaningless to dragons; so for them, whatever they can accomplish sitting still is something they can do for a long, long time.

How like ants these humans are, pondered Sheana, rushing hither and yon, back and forth, hunkering down in their dwellings when it grows dark, then racing madly about again throughout the day – only to do the exact same thing, day in and day out.

Of course, Sheana could not comprehend such lunacy, but in the days that followed and as she studied them more, she slowly came to realize that these beings took immense satisfaction in their routines, some apparently more than others. To Sheana, such aimless activity bespoke of, for lack of a better word - penance, But no matter, it seemed to give them a sense of worth.

Obviously, the inhabitants had no knowledge of just how close they were to the Cosmos, no awareness of their own insignificance. To Sheana, they appeared to be puffed up with arrogance and self-pride, blinding themselves from the reality that they were in actual fact, prisoners within an impenetrable dome.

Yet there was one human that gave the impression of being different. He never seemed to be in a hurry, but moved slowly and deliberately. He would often stop and observe the others rush by, absorbed in scrutinizing the expressions on their faces. The man carried an easel and canvas with him everywhere. And wherever he happened to be seemed to be his destination.

He would spend hours standing on a street corner or in a park, sketching, always scratching busily on paper with a stick of charcoal. Occasionally he would raise his head and gaze almost wistfully, perhaps even with a twinge of regret, at the domed ceiling that marked the boundaries of his world.

As the days progressed, Sheana became conscious that they had much in common, this human and she – his watcher. For as the man evidently recognized the prison in which he existed, Sheana, too, understood the boundaries of her own world.

As time passed, unmarked by the clock, her incessant curiosity eventually over-rode Sheana's caution.

ഹരു

Aidan strolled through the crowded streets. He clung to his tools to ensure no one inadvertently knocked them from his hands. But he wore a smile on his face and was well content, in spite of the pressing dominance of the sky overhead. His art was selling, and selling well. Each piece he created sold for more coin than the previous one. And he'd recently been able to move out of his hovel near the edge of the dome to a decent studio above a shop in the Guild district. He could entertain guests in the evening, when the light dimmed and the streets quieted down enough for the people to take some leisure time. Aidan could do a lot of things now that he was becoming respected as an artist. He imagined that the scornful looks he used to see as people passed by had decreased, and occasionally thought he saw looks of envy, and even respect. All in all, Aidan supposed that he enjoyed a good life, despite the knowledge that this place was virtually a prison.

Still reflecting on the advantages and blessings of his life, Aidan reached his favourite park. It was a quiet alcove of trees and bushes, where a spring bubbled up from the earth to feed a stream that eventually meandered through the city. He liked it here. It was less popu-

365

lated than elsewhere, and it gave him a panoramic view of the lofty buildings, so tall they were dwarfed only by the dome. But few ever admitted to the presence of the orb. It was a truth no one really want - ed to acknowledge.

Because of this, Aidan knew that if he included the dome in his sketches, the pieces would never sell, and he would be ridiculed as an oddball. However, if he focused on drawing only the buildings, creat - ing one structure per drawing, and leaving the space around the edi - fice blank, all who lived in that building would vie for the opportuni - ty to hang his artwork on their wall.

A woman was seated on a bench nearby, content, it seemed, to sit and watch Aidan as he set up his easel for his next project. He ignored her at first, thinking she was either an eccentric, or that she was scorning him. But the constant pressure of her gaze became a distraction as he tried to focus on his sketch.

Finally, Aidan looked over at her and smiled. "Hi, I'm Aidan. I haven't seen you before."

"My name is Sheana," she replied. "I live on the far side of the city."

"Then what are you doing over here?" He had not meant to sound rude, and grimaced as the words escaped him.

She simply smiled back at him. "I grew tired of working, so I took the day off."

"Your employers must have blown a gasket!" Aiden grinned rogu- ishly.

She shrugged nonchalantly. "I would rather watch you work."

"Is that so?" Aidan was not accustomed to this kind of attention, and knew it would be impossible to accomplish anything today if he was being studied like a bug under a microscope. "Then perhaps you wouldn't mind if I drew your portrait?"

She shrugged again. "Perhaps." She wore a tan tunic and trousers, with a pair of worn leather boots. One knee was pulled up against her chest with her elbow propped on it, while the other leg stretched out comfortably to the ground. Her other hand was pressed against the bench behind her, slightly to the side of her back, holding her weight. Golden hair cascaded over one shoulder and disappeared behind her bent knee. The smile on her face was fixed. Aidan grinned. Her charming pose would make a fine portrait.

Later that day, while the light dimmed from a setting sun, Aidan and Sheana laughed and lingered side by side on the bench, comfort - able in the companionship they had found. This was such a mad world they lived in that to just sit and talk, to enjoy a deep conversa - tion rather than rehearsed lines spoken without truth or significance, which was the norm here, was a pleasant change for both of them.

When dusk began to settle Aidan and Sheana knew it was time to return to their own lives. They stood in unison, both a little regretful that the day had passed so quickly. "Will I see you again?" Aidan asked.

Sheana smiled and nodded. "I will meet you here tomorrow."

"But I must work," Aidan admonished. "I cannot draw portraits of you day after day, although I have no doubt that they would all sell. In truth, you are a bit of a distraction."

"Then I will not look at you."

Aidan laughed. He could not refuse her, even though he did not trust Sheana to hold to her end of the bar gain. "But what about work?" he asked.

She shrugged her shoulders casually. "I have an inheritance. I won't be missed."

Aidan nodded, strangely relieved that he would see her after all. "Which way are you going?"

She pointed towards the city.

"May I walk with you?"

Her grin was genuine. "Of course."

They chattered non-stop, and Sheana walked with him until the fork in the road on the outskirts of the city. This was where she knew they had to part ways, and yet Aidan seemed reluctant to do so. He knew his reluctance was obvious, but Sheana made no comment of it as she said, "Good night, Aidan."

"Good night, Sheana."

₞)ₓ

"Have you ever wondered about venturing beyond the dome?"

They were lounging on cushions in his studio, enjoying the refresh-ing night air that wafted through the expansive windows that opened onto the city. Sheana and Aidan had spent nearly every day together the last few weeks, enjoying the companionship they had found. When they were together they felt far removed from the pointless grind of life everyone seemed to be caught up in. Aidan's art had flourished rather than diminished, and now he had excess pieces to sell off. He could enjoy his time with her.

When Sheana asked him about venturing beyond the dome, he was a little surprised. It was prohibited to be so forthright about their imprisonment. And yet, Aidan supposed, nothing should surprise him where Sheana was concerned, so he shrugged off a vague feeling of discomfort and replied, "I pass beyond it every day."

"You do not!"

" Yes I do, in my heart," he insisted. "Sometimes I imagine that I can feel amazing sensations, things I can't express, phenomena that I have no words to describe. That's why I draw. All my inspiration comes from the other side of the dome, I'm sure of it. But rather than just let everything simply bounce off me, I accept this amazing stuff, as a gift. I know that I could never be worthy enough to take it. It has to be given as a gift, and accepted as a gift, and that's what I do. For there's nothing I could do to ever earn a reward like that, but for some reason, I've been bestowed with it anyway."

Sheana leaned towards him. "And?"

"And I feel as if I've been born all over again," Aidan replied. "I am not just a mirror for the dome's beauty to rebound from. The dome is a mirror reflecting the beauty it's taught me – the beauty I've received from Almighty, I suppose."

She sat back and stared at him. "Huh!" After a moment, Sheana stood and announced, "I have to go. It's getting late."

Aidan rose to stand with her. "Let me walk you home. The streets aren't always safe."

She smiled, almost sadly. "They are always safe for me."

He believed her. Somehow, even though she'd never seemed intimidating to him, Aidan believed her. "Will I see you tomorrow?"

"Of course." And then she was out the door, melting into the night.

ՖՈՑ

In the sky, where night and day are one, where dark and light both pale to the incomprehensible splendor and brilliance of space, Sheana stretched her wings to their limit. She hovered on the edge, caught between a world of ash and a reality so great and wonderful that her heart ached to transcend the boundary that held her prisoner.

The words of her artist friend drummed in her head, repeating over and over again, while bitter, sulfuric tears streamed from her eyes. To contain such wonder inside her soul, would not her soul become a field for something greater still, something which would itself be incomprehensible? As it was, what consumed her was a self-loathing, a hatred for all dragons, and a desire to kill as many of them as she could before one of them killed her.

Her only diversion from the drudgery of this life was the strange the man named Aidan. A human, imprisoned in a prison inside a prison,

369

he was nonetheless content to live out his simple life, although surely he perceived the captivity he'd been born to.

Discontent filling her heart, envy of Aidan and his simple ways permeating her mind, she turned back towards the dome, deciding to rest on the currents for a few hours before returning to the simple but agreeable make-believe life she had created for herself. What was the solution? Could this human furnish her with answers, with a way out?

Sheana did not know, although she realized cynically that, having gone this far already, she had little choice but to seek the answers regardless.

Days passed. Life under the dome continued unchanged, although Sheana realized that to continue her charade with a measure of success, she would have to part from Aidan's side and allow him to do his work. Under the guise that her own duties could not be put off anymore, she made her temporary farewells and explored the city from a fresh perspective. She remembered every person under the dome from the days she had spent as their watcher. But this time something was new to her – now she was watching them from the perception of belonging.

Sheana slipped in and out of each shop unimpeded, exploring the industry and tasks that kept people's eyes cast downwards rather than up towards the dome. She passed through the streets unnoticed, for she had chosen her illusion well, blending her guise and clothing so as not to appear either poverty stricken or as overly wealthy. She was simply a commoner, invisible in the throng of other commoners, although perhaps she carried herself with a bit more confidence. The fire in her blood was much harder to disguise than her appearance.

ఴღ

One day, she discovered a place called, The Dragon's Eyes. Normally such bold effrontery would have gone unnoticed, but the sign hanging over the front door caught Sheana's attention and she stopped to stare, frozen in her tracks by a premonition of dread. The sign was wide and short, with the words written in blood-red calligraphy across the bottom. Above the text were two eyes, and by their placement and shape, and by the alien emotions that emanated from them, Sheana knew she was looking at a portion of a portrait.

Both curious and filled with a sense of foreboding, she spun on her heels and went to find Aidan. As usual, he was sketching in his favourite park.

"Do you believe in dragons?" she asked, sounding as casual as possible.

He glanced at her before returning to his drawing. "I wouldn't know. I haven't actually physically been beyond the dome."

"Has anyone?"

He shrugged. "Rumor says that some have, although none have returned to tell about it."

Sheana could believe that. Out on the plain of ash, a human would be easy sport for a passing predator. "But you've heard of them – dragons, I mean?"

"I have." His charcoal continued to fill in the blank places on his paper. He was silent as he worked, mulling her words over in his mind. After a moment he said, carefully, "Sheana, I don't know who you've been talking to, but dragons are as much forbidden here as discussion of the dome; more so, in fact."

She shrugged. "I saw something today. That's all."

The hand holding the piece of charcoal froze and he stared at her. "What is it?"

"Finish your sketch."

Aidan's hand dropped to his side. "Show me now. The sketch can wait. I don't need to look at the view to finish it."

Sheana nodded. "All right." She helped him collapse his easel and led him to The Dragon's Eyes.

Every muscle in Aidan's body tensed when he saw the sign. "This place," he said, his voice deliberately flat.

"You've been here?"

He stared at Sheana. "I'm not as bound to routine as most people under the dome," he replied. His words drew scowls from some people nearby, but they dared not challenge Aidan as they scurried past.

She shrugged again. "I've only recently been freed from my schedule and wanted to see the sights. I didn't find this place until today."

"Have you been in it?"

"I wanted to show you first. I thought we'd explore it together."

He nodded and then his gaze swiveled to the door in front of him. "That was wise."

Did he think her some kind of naive schoolgirl? What would he think if he knew the truth? Sheana shrank a little from that thought. But outwardly calm, she took him by the arm and led him towards the door of the small shop. And wordlessly, albeit rather uncomfortably, Aidan let himself be led into the gloom behind it.

There was nothing spectacular about the place. Aisles of low shelves lined the room. A design on the floor depicted a mosaic of the outer Cosmos, the Heavens that Sheana herself was so painfully addicted to. And to Aidan's surprise, or horror – she wasn't sure which – some of his sketches were framed and hung on the walls.

At first Sheana couldn't tell what had upset Aidan. But as she looked more closely she realized that every sketch included a depiction of the dome, rather accurately, she thought, in all its hideous truth. "There is only one other," he mumbled to himself as a woman glided into their presence from a room to their left.

The woman glanced at Aidan, then at the pictures over her shoulder, then back at Aidan again. "I thought I had them all," she confessed with a smile. She was aged, though not old, slender but not brittle. The woman had a grace about her, but Sheana could see through her

372

disguise immediately. She had to restrain herself from hissing at her and tensed, longing to reach over and rip the woman's throat out. The woman looked at Sheana, her expression bland. No actual physical change came over her to give her real identity away; but she did look amused, much too amused for Sheana's liking.

"How are you enjoying your stay inside the Dragon's Egg – or the dome, I guess you'd call it?" she asked.

Sheana glared at her. Only a dragon would ruin the time she was having with Aidan by revealing her true identity. She hated the woman on sight. "Fine," she snapped. "I'm liking it just fine."

Luckily, Aidan was too awestruck by the discovery of the presence of these particular works of his to notice the exchange between the two women. "I thought these had all been destroyed," he murmured as he crossed the room towards a larger drawing, so that he might look at it more closely.

The woman, who apparently owned the shop, shrugged and folded her arms. "I saved them from the mob," she said, her voice matter-of-fact. "It wasn't hard to do. The truth is, no one wanted to acknowledge these drawings. By taking them I did your patrons a favor, it seems to me. Here they are free to enjoy your work without having to acknowledge there is actual truth in it."

"And what is the truth?" Aidan asked as he turned to look at her.

"That you see things as they are, not as you wish them to be."

He looked over at Sheana. "I don't know about that."

For some reason, his glance caused her to blush, and mercifully, he turned to examine another drawing.

"What brings you to The Dragon's Eyes?" the woman asked.

Aidan, still scrutinizing his artwork, pointed absently towards Sheana.

"I saw the sign outside," Sheana admitted.

"I see." The woman, elegantly outfitted in an ankle-length black dress, her hair pulled up behind her head and tied with a leather cord, looked directly at Sheana, her eyes piercing through her façade; and similarly, Sheana saw through the woman's masquerade. There was no doubt that in another place, outside the dome, the two would have killed each other. But for the sake of maintaining their disguises they put all that aside – for the moment.

Aidan seemed unaware of the confrontation between the women as they each fought to control their emotions. He was too engrossed in looking at his drawings. Presently he looked over at the shopkeeper and remarked, "The last one is under my bed in a case."

That was enough for the woman to push the situation of Sheana's presence to the back of her mind. Her eyes glittered and she almost rubbed her hands together in her eagerness. "Would you sell it?"

Aidan shrugged and then shook his head. "Let me think about it."

The woman nodded. "I have something to show you," she said. Her eyes swiveled to Sheana. "Both of you."

She guided them to the counter at the front of the room, where she walked around to the back and stooped over to produce two melon sized oval-shaped spheres. Sheana gasped and stepped back in horror. But Aidan was fascinated and moved forward to take a closer look. Sheana caught his shoulder to prevent him from touching them.

The spheres were glossy black with yellow cat irises, slits that stared out into the world as if they could still perceive. The sight of them unnerved Sheana completely. She fully expected them to swivel of their own accord and stare up at her with the intelligence and cunning of a dragon.

"How did you – " she could not finish without giving herself away, so Sheana bit her tongue and looked up at the shopkeeper.

"Some illusions are illusion. Others are a reality none want to see. Still others, my young fledgling, are whatever we would make of them." The woman put the spheres away, setting them, to Sheana's great relief, out of sight.

"I must go," Sheana announced, to Aidan's disappointment.

"But what about – "

"No, Aidan. I can't stand to be in this place."

The almost desperate urgency in her voice was obvious. He gave the shopkeeper an apologetic smile and she nodded as if to let him know it was okay. "We'll talk later of that picture," she reassured him.

He returned the nod, then hurried to catch up to Sheana as the door slammed shut behind her.

"I need to go home," she said after he'd fallen in step with her fierce pace.

Aidan was silent, trying not to take that as a rejection. "May I come?" he finally asked.

"I don't think you could see what I have to show you if you don't."

"I can see the dome."

Sheana sniggered cynically. "That you can." After a pause, she declared, "This isn't wise," but took Aidan by the arm and led him towards the heart of the city. She could tell he was growing uncom-fortable in the crowded streets; but he kept his thoughts to himself, simply commenting, "Prices must be horrendous."

She shrugged. "I wouldn't know. I never pay for anything."

"Wait."

She held on and continued to guide him onwards.

"Wait!"

Still, she did not relent.

"Wait, Sheana!" Aidan exclaimed, and wrenched himself free of her grasp.

She stopped and stared at him.

"You never pay? For anything? How is that possible?"

"Things that are forbidden in this city can reap huge profits for those without superstition."

"Except when you start drawing pictures of the dome."

She smiled and shrugged. "Except for that."

"So where do you live?"

She turned around and pointed towards the clock tower, rearing its head through the dome's underside. "At the top of that."

Aidan paled. "At the top?"

She nodded. "It doesn't go too far above the dome, about a story or so. At night, you can see the stars."

"The what?"

Her smile was sad. "I have to go, Aidan. Are you coming, or not?"

Aidan thought for a moment, glanced at the throngs of people plod-ding through their drudgery, then made up his mind and looked back at Sheana. "This is unwise," he said.

"That's what I said." She took his arm once again and they contin-ued in silence.

As curious as he was, at the door of the tower, at its very threshold, Aidan pulled away and gazed at the masses of people rushing around the city streets. He was silent and Sheana gave him time, watching his back with complete understanding, aware of her own feelings of misgiving.

Finally, he spoke. "Help me Sheana." He clutched his easel and his artwork as if he could pull strength from them.

Sheana reached for his elbow and gently turned him around. "It's all right, Aidan. Nothing will hurt you."

He looked as though he didn't believe her, but braved the dreaded tower and stepped into its shadows.

All about them was a vast open space and a set of rickety stairs built along the walls, spiraling upwards through the gloom. The door slammed behind them with a bang and Aidan jumped at the sound. Sheana smiled as he gaped at the dizzying height. "That's a long walk. Will the stairs hold?"

"I don't know," she admitted, stepping into the center of the room. "I've never used them." And her metamorphosis began.

At first, Aidan stared in rapt puzzlement. But then, as it became clear who, and what, Sheana was, his expression changed to black hatred. "No!" he bellowed, the ferocity in his intonation shaking the stone and mortar around him.

Sheana turned to look at him, already realizing she had made a mistake.

Aidan dropped his tools and his sketch, heedless of them now in his wrath, and sprinted towards the stairs that he had feared only a moment ago. He took them three at a time, shouting unintelligible words of fury as he ran, and Sheana, bewildered, followed his steps with her keen, unblinking dragon's eyes.

He reached behind his back. Undetectable before now, his hand gripped very real, very evident cold steel, and drew out a flaming golden long sword.

"Some illusions are illusions," Sheana whispered, quoting the shopkeeper's words.

"And some none want to see!" Aidan shouted in his rage. But then he was at eye level with her, leaping from the staircase with his sword raised above his head.

Sheana was too startled to react quickly in the confines of the tower, and so his enraged flight carried him straight at her face. Within seconds, with twin downward strokes of his fearsome blade,

Aidan gashed at her eyes. Sheana cried out in pain as her sight exploded into a crimson haze, before all went black.

Aidan stood at her feet, the ooze from Sheana's wounded eyes dripping like the juice from pulverized grapes. He bowed his head and his sword lowered to the ground. His anger dissipated; only sorrow remained, and Aidan ignored her as she staggered into the open air, causing a draft of wind to kick up the dust about the base of the tower.

Aidan let her go. After a moment he adjusted his grip on the sword and slid it back into its invisible sheath. As he fought for control and regained his disguise as a simple artist, he wiped the gore from his eyes and face and inspected his discarded artist's tools. Knowing that he could not go out into the city covered in filth as he was, Aidan sat down at the foot of the stairs and began to sketch a depiction of a dragon within a hollow tower that reached into a mighty dome above her head.

ഇറൻ

Sheana stumbled from the tower. Her claws scraped for purchase as she clung desperately to the unrelenting surface of the spectral dome. She whimpered from pain and from her broken heart, berating herself for believing it was possible that things could have turned out differently. Yet exposed and blinded at the top of this dome upon these plains of ash was not a safe place for Sheana to be. If she wanted to die she simply had to remain where she was, and death, in the form of another dragon, would find her. Tempting as it was to surrender herself to fate, Sheana forced down her sobs and concentrated on focusing her other senses and her memory for guidance.

It took a moment to get her bearings, but Sheana's memory served her well, and she was able to draw a map of this sky island in her mind. And on it she visualized the forests left unmolested by her kind. There she would be safe.

With one final sob, Sheana hurled herself into the sky and plummeted in a straight line towards the cover of the forest. Despite her pain she was able to bank before she crashed into the trees, and lowered herself amongst them, heedless of how her wings were caught up in the branches. She was snagged. The dense forest was able to hold her weight up, her wings spread out over the treetops.

Her composure fled, and Sheana cried out in anguish as her wings melted into thin air. She once again transformed her appearance to that of a young woman clothed as a simple traveler. Sheana dropped to the ground, blinded, landing heavily upon the forest floor. The force of the fall expelled the breath from her lungs, and Sheana lay there panting and weeping while her hands made claws in front of her eyes, gritting her teeth against the effort it took not to touch them.

Sheana was unsure how much time passed, but eventually her breathing became less laboured and she was able to make it to the base of a tree and wearily rested her back against it. Still her tears fell. She was overcome with anguish as she recalled the course of events that had befallen her and had brought her here to an uncertain fate. Every now and again Sheana thumped the back of her head against the tree, exclaiming, "Stupid, stupid, stupid!" through her clenched teeth.

Hands reached out to her from the dark abyss of her blindness, startling Sheana and she panicked, thrashing out as she tried to escape their reach.

"Hush, child!" The woman's voice was soothing; kind and inviting, safe and warm. "I'll do you no harm."

Sheana quieted. Until you discover what I am, she wanted to say, but she kept the thought to herself.

"There now," the voice said. "You're safe now." Hands reached for her again, this time holding Sheana in a motherly embrace with a tenderness that Sheana had never known before.

Sheana wept, believing the words for the first time in her life. Eventually her tears were exhausted, but still she sat there, clinging to the stranger she couldn't even see. After a time, the woman helped

Sheana to her feet, gently took her arm and guided her, stumbling and blind, through the forest.

At first, her enigmatic escort was quiet, speaking only when she thought necessary, and Sheana was unwilling to break the silence that penetrated the gloom of her own thoughts. But eventually, the repetitive warnings of, "watch your step, there's a branch here. Go to your right. Careful, a bush," lengthened to – "that branch had a leaf in bud on it, right at the tip, as if the branch was stretching further than it could reach and grew longer while trying." Or, "here's a rough spot, best go around. Watch your footing, there's no need to pull us both to the dirt." The warm laughter that followed these good-natured exchanges left Sheana puzzled.

Still, she kept silent. The pain in her eyes permeated all of Sheana's senses and dulled her attention anyway. But eventually she heard the sound of a gate opening and was alarmed at the prospect of being so exposed as they emerged from the safety of the trees.

"No need to worry about the skies," the mysterious woman said quietly. "Dragons can't find us here. There are too many cliffs surrounding us, and so many stray Golds roam about these parts that few such as yourself dare to venture down here."

"You know what I am?" Sheana was incredulous.

"You don't live long in the sky realm without picking up a thing or two along the way," the woman responded.

"And you still help me?"

"Of course I do!" she replied firmly. "What harm can you do me now, in this form, in this condition? And besides, what kind of a servant of Almighty would I be not to help one of His creations in need?"

"One of His most pitiful, most evil creations!"

The woman chuckled and closed the gate behind them. Warm sunlight and delicate flower scents washed over Sheana on a slight breeze. "The most majestic, if you ask me."

Sheana was in too much pain to argue, but she wondered if this mysterious woman had ever actually seen a dragon eat. She kept the thought to herself though, and as Sheana was led down a stone walk-way the woman cautioned her about a step. Then another door opened and Sheana was issued through it into a room where she sensed both shadows and stillness.

"Welcome to my home. My name is Entualla ThoroughBlood. I am a spear sister for the clan ThoroughBlood, and an out-flyer. This is my outpost, on the border of my family's territory."

None of this made much sense to Sheana, but she was in too much pain do much more than mumble, "I am Sheana." Then with a slight shrug, she added, "I am a sky dragon."

"You look a beat up wreck!" Entualla laughed, and it lightened Sheana's heart to hear the fearlessness in the woman's voice. "Come. I keep a first aid closet for just such emer gencies."

This time, Sheana found the strength to comment, rather dryly, "I'm sure you never expected to need your closet to heal a love-sick drag-on with her eyes cut in half by her lover's invisible golden sword."

Entualla laughed again. Sheana was beginning to realize she did this a lot. "Oh, you'd be surprised." Then she was pushing Sheana gently down onto a hard wooden bench. "I need you to open your eyes."

Sheana complied.

"I need you to open your eyes, please," Entualla repeated.

"I thought I did."

"No, you didn't."

Again Sheana opened her eyes.

"I see," Entualla murmured.

Sheana's heart thudded. "What is it?" she asked, her voice trembling faintly.

"Illusions within illusions, that's all."

"What do you mean?" The sound of commotion made Sheana cock her head to the side as Entualla rifled through her supplies.

Entualla ignored her. "Here," she replied. "This is a gauze that will soothe the sting, and hopefully make you a little tired so you can get some rest. I don't dare say it will work. There's nothing made from plants strong enough that will knock out a dragon, but perhaps in your human disguise it will have some effect." The touch of Entualla's fingertips applying a cool paste to her face made Sheana groan with relief.

"Thank you."

"And this bandage is golden," Entualla continued. "May it become a symbol to you that not all of your kind are as despicable as you say they are."

Sheana gingerly touched the linen strip as it was wound several times around her head. "Will I be able to ever see again?" she asked hesitantly.

"That is up to you. But don't worry about it now. Please rest. I would offer you a softer place to sleep, but … you're a dragon."

Sheana felt the bench with her hand. It was hard and unyielding. "No," she replied, "This will be comfortable enough. Thank you."

"Do you require a pillow, covers?"

As Sheana stretched out on her back with a weary sigh, she answered, "There's no need. Thank you Entualla. For everything."

She sensed rather than saw the woman bow before retreating into the depths of the out-post. A few minutes later, as Sheana hovered on the edge of sleep, she heard her hostess slip quietly out the door and close it softly behind her. After that, Sheana slumbered, and dreamed fanciful dreams of fiery swords, and prisons made of spectral domes.

ഇരുന്ന

"You're awake."

"Dragons don't sleep the same as other people do." There was a long pause. "How did you know I was awake?"

There was an awkward silence as Sheana imagined Entualla reason-ing out in her mind how to explain to her. "I could see it on your face," she settled with at last.

"The simplest rationalization is usually the best," Sheana comment-ed wryly.

Entualla laughed at that. "How long do you think you slept?"

"How long were you gone?"

The woman shrugged. "A time, I guess."

"I did not hear you come in."

"I guess that answers my question."

"Is it night or day?"

Sheana heard the faint rustling sound of Entualla standing up and of curtains being pushed back. "Morning. The beginning of the day. You slept for a good twelve hours, I'd say."

"And you," Sheana asked her. Do you sleep?" Nothing could be taken for granted within the sky realm.

Again, she sensed the woman's shrug. "Not much. But I do. I am vulnerable when I sleep, though. And while this place is safer than many, it is sometimes difficult within the sky realm to find a good night's sleep."

Sheana's quiet chortle was cynical. "I know that."

"Why is that, do you think?"

383

Sheana sat up.

"I mean, everywhere I go I carry my spear with me. Every time I close my eyes I strain my ears to listen for a possible approach. And an approach is usually very probable, and is almost always a bad thing."

"I will never gain my sight, will I, Entualla?"

Entualla stared at Sheana in puzzlement. "What does that have to do with what we're talking about?" she asked.

"Why else would you help me unless you wanted to make an ally of me," Sheana retorted. "What's to say I don't eat you as soon as I get better?"

Entualla's mirth was sincere and heartening. "You couldn't catch me," she grinned.

"What!"

"You couldn't," she insisted. "You're bigger than me."

"I'm a sky dragon!"

"And I'm a swallow," Entualla said. "There are tunnels through these rocks that I can traverse, where your fire cannot reach. And … other things protect me from your kind. Besides, none have ever bothered. And as I said before, there are too many Golds around for dragons like you to be common enough for real concern."

"Dragons like me." Sheana spoke the words with bitterness, as the honesty of what she was filled her with self-loathing once again. Her recent rejection by Aidan and his violent reaction to her true identity, along with the agonizing pain afterwards, both of the body and the heart, had stolen her strength. "Why can't I be something else!" Sheana cried, almost shocked by her own honesty.

Entualla sat down beside her and Sheana felt feathers brush against her neck and down her back. The woman's arm went across the drag-on's shoulders and they held each other as Sheana wept unashamedly.

The feathers enveloped Sheana's shoulders, blanketing her in warmth and comfort as she cried.

Eventually, Entualla led the dragon outside into the warmth of the sunlight. Sheana had ceased her weeping at last, and felt rejuvenated from the warmth of the sun upon her face. "I've never really noticed before," she admitted.

"Open your other senses." Sheana couldn't see, but Entualla's head was tilted back as well, and her eyes were closed, mimicking the dragon. "Let the sensations come to you."

After obeying for a time, Sheana exclaimed, "It's like being against the Cosmos."

There was an uncomfortable silence from her newfound, mysterious friend.

"I'm sorry," Sheana apologized. "I spoke without thinking. That was cruel of me."

"I have never heard of this Cosmos you speak of," the woman divulged.

"It is where the sky meets the Heavens. I cannot cross into the Heavens, the Cosmos. But I can almost touch them, I get as close as I possibly can. It is a bitter thing to do, but I am addicted and can only gaze within it. Such a breathtaking place it is – the sounds, the colors! It is … there are no words to explain it. But it is not gloomy so as long as I am not under the skies of Mishard, which darkens things, takes them away and makes them corrupt; or reduces them to a mere food source. There is nothing that can compare to what is above and beyond. Nothing."

"I think the sky realm is pretty good."

"Things are more beautiful the closer to the Heavens we come. And uglier the closer we get to the oceans."

"I see." Entualla allowed the ensuing silence to grow until Sheana could bear it no more.

"I've offended you," Sheana said.

"No," Entualla lied. "You are a sky dragon. I would expect you to have that point of view. But I would have to wonder what a water dragon would say about that."

"That's easy." Sheana still had her head tilted towards the sun. "Water dragons are all about strength. To fight the currents, to surge against the surf, to dive into the abyss and bullet back from it, to wrestle with the leviathans that live there, these are the things that a water dragon values. For me it is about beauty. There is no shame in admitting that a water dragon could tear my wings off, if I allowed one to catch me."

"Strength." Entualla's voice sounded far away, as if she was talking to herself. "Strength and beauty."

"Strength and beauty," Sheana echoed.

"So can you feel the breeze, smell the flowers, hear the wind in the trees?"

Sheana smiled. "I can even hear water running in the distance."

"Oh, yes," Entualla nodded. "I will take you there one day. But first we must fix your eyes."

"I will never heal, Entualla. I told you that."

"Why do you say that?"

A look of intense pain crossed Sheana's face. "My eyes were cut open by a sword!"

"The woman under the dome, she had her eyes removed and she can still see!"

"How do you know about her?" Sheana asked, curious in spite of herself.

"I am friends with the illusionists that live amongst the humans there. Every now and again one will leave the dome to visit with me, and to see that our lands are not pillaged by another 's wrath."

"There are more than one!"

Entualla laughed again. "I would say that you know of at least two!" she said.

"I suppose."

"And yet you will not take control of your own illusionist gifts, even at the cost of your sight."

"And without my sight I am dead," Sheana agreed softly.

Entualla shrugged. "No," she replied. "You could learn to live here. There are things you could do, snare meat, grow vegetables. In time you would not feel so helpless."

"But I'll never again see the Cosmos."

A whisper of wings rustling suggested to Sheana that Entualla had shrugged once more. "Is it such a bad thing not to continuously look upon that which you deny yourself?"

"Deny myself?" Sheana's expression was incredulous. "None can cross into the expanse!"

"Are you sure?"

"Of course!" But for the first time, Sheana experienced a pang of doubt. She shook it off abruptly. "You've never even seen it, much less heard of it!" she accused Entualla.

"It is but a mirror," Entualla declared.

"I've heard that before," Sheana replied, her voice somewhat sub-dued.

"There is nothing without that I cannot embrace from within," Sheana's new friend told her. "My creator lives, and He lives within and without," she continued. "I can embrace Him from within and in so doing, He embraces me from within and from without. He shows me beauty where ever I am as He coaxes me to give up the ugliness that is me."

"The ugliness that is me." Sheana was on the verge of tears once more. "You can not understand what you say when you say those words to a dragon."

"I can and I do," Entualla chided her gently. "For we are all descendents of humanity, cousin. Your origins are the same as mine, and not so old, at that. We are just – different, you and I. But not unlike."

"The ugliness that is me." Sheana turned in a circle, feeling the wind and the sun, hearing the water and the trees, smelling the flowers. "So how do I let go of the ugliness that is me?" she asked.

Entualla touched her breastbone. "Let go, fall back and trust. Embrace Almighty."

For some reason, those words made sense to Sheana, and even knowing that Entualla was simply being metaphorical, the dragon nonetheless took her hostess's words literally and let herself fall back. She crashed to the ground, her head bouncing off the paving stones.

Entualla winced, but the dragon only laughed. And then Sheana experienced something that had never happened to her before, an epiphany, a spiritual flash that would forever change her. In a burst of revelation, comprehension of the essence of the Cosmos dawned in her heart. Sheana laughed with exhilaration as a gust of wind rushed through her to sweep away the shadows within her soul. Tears of joy she'd never been able to imagine before streamed down her face. Again the inexplicable spiritual current overcame her, driving away her bitterness, conceit, anger, lust; destroying her need for violence and destruction. In mere moments, Sheana intuitively understood forgiveness and trust.

And finally, it purged her addiction to gaze upon the Cosmos as Sheana at last realized what others had been saying all along. The Cosmos, and all that it contained, were within her. Her negativity had simply gotten in the way of letting her realize what she truly was, but now Sheana felt the ecstasy of true freedom. Laughter merged with euphoric tears. Entualla, inspired by witnessing Sheana's elation, left her to her newfound bliss and slipped away to take pleasure in her own expressions of freedom.

॰)૦(॰

Air creatures are solitary, so it was not disturbing that the two, in their joyfulness, did not seek out each other's company for the remainder of the day. And honestly, it was a long, glorious day for both, a day of inner revelation and celebration. But finally, when the shadows began to stretch, Sheana, almost reluctantly, pushed herself to her feet, her keen ears detecting Entualla trudging through the forest towards her. She grinned to herself.

"Why don't you just fly!" she called out to Entualla.

"Holy! You have good ears!" the woman shouted back carelessly, heedless of the possible dangers so often prevalent in the sky realm.

"Well?"

"My legs cramp if I don't use them!"

Sheana thought about that for a moment. "What kind of sky creature gets cramps in her legs?" she finally asked.

"I'd show you if you were to open your eyes!" Entualla retorted. And then, before Sheana could respond, she commanded, "Open your eyes!"

Sheana laughed with bravado, and yet she was afraid. The pain was still there. The memory of Aidan's rejection still cut her deeper than his sword had. She and Entualla had formed a bond, but would that change? Could Sheana risk even the possibility of further rejection?

"You'll stay blind until you do!" Entualla's pronouncement roared through the forest, as though she could sense the dragon's thoughts.

Sheana nodded. Entualla's words made sense, and it wasn't as if she had anything to lose. And so, tentatively and with much trepidation, Sheana unwound the bandage from around her head and used it to wipe the salve from her eyes. Then, knowing she could not put it off any longer, she sighed and strained her eyes to bring her surroundings into focus.

At first everything was blurry. She dabbed at her eyes a couple of times and realized that the haziness was caused by the salve. Slowly Sheana looked around her, expecting to see the repulsive ugliness she had always seen. She spied a spider sucking the blood from an insect on the leaf of a plant beside her, and for an instant Sheana was horrified, her suspicions verified by this violence.

She was distracted from the gory scene when a waft of tantalizing perfume from a flower drifted towards her. On closer inspection, Sheana saw that the oval-shaped petals were an exquisite, luminous midnight-blue. She reached out timidly to touch them. They were velvety-soft, almost comforting. A tiny ruby-throated hummingbird hovered above the flower uncertainly, and Sheana pulled her hand back shyly, waiting breathlessly to see what it would do. The minute bird darted hungrily towards the center of the flower, and drank thirstily from the delicate blossom, and then, suspended before her, hummed a greeting softly to Sheana in its own language.

She was still, her heart beating firmly but comfortably in her chest while she listened to the creature, and to her own rhythmic, calm breathing. Suddenly, surprisingly, Sheana found herself humming also.

In that moment Sheana's mind grasped the wonder of sounds and colors and shapes and shades that made up the world. Glancing around in astonishment she saw the vitality and fragility of life – and it's tenacity – wherever she looked. The very atmosphere encircling Sheana bespoke a freshness that she had never realized existed before.

Sheana's eyes flickered back to her immediate surroundings. She was seated in a small garden strewn with brightly coloured flowers bunching together to form paths and resting places amid patches of shade and sunlight. A wooden fence painted a dull terra cotta enclosed the garden. Jagged stones in shades of ochre and chestnut formed an arched gate, from which a small footpath led to a modest stone cabin with a peaked roof of canary-yellow tiles, charming circular windows, a russet wooden door and a tiny porch. The structure looked ancient, yet under Entualla's feminine touch, it had blossomed with an understated beauty that was striking.

Sheana immediately felt at home here, and wanted nothing more than to stay.

She turned suddenly as she felt eyes upon her, and there was her hostess, an auburn-haired Trilian with an engaging crooked grin and a spear held casually over her shoulder. Her wings, not the typical dove or pigeon-shaped ones of a Trilian, were fashioned like a sparrow's, smaller and more streamlined, emerging over her shoulders and disappearing down her back in the shape of a giant heart. They were the color of the earth, a natural defense to conceal her from predators hunting from above. Her garment, a dazzling white dress, billowed to the ground, hiding her feet. And at the moment it was soaked through, plastering itself closely to her figure. Her entire body was dripping.

"You see!" Entualla exclaimed.

"You swim!" Sheana declared simultaneously.

Entualla shrugged imperturbably, and said again, "You see!"

"I do!" Sheana laughed, and still basking in the glow of the budding enchantment she was experiencing, opened her arms to Entualla.

Entualla pushed through the gate, jubilant, and ran to the dragon. The two woman embraced like sisters, tears mingling with their laughter.

"You got me wet!' Sheana giggled.

This set the Trilian off on another fit of laughter as they pulled apart slightly, their arms still entwined. "Come," Entualla urged. "Let me show you!" She clutched the dragon's arm and tugged her back towards the forest.

She kept up a fast pace, although to Sheana it was nothing to trot along beside her, especially now that she could see properly. Still, she asked curiously, "What's the big hurry?"

Entualla smiled mysteriously as she glanced at her. "You'll see."

It had rained recently and the rock-strewn paths were dangerously slippery. It took all Entualla's attention just to place one foot safely in front of the other, and Sheana allowed her to concentrate. However, since a dragon's motor skills were far superior to those of other life-forms, Sheana was able to relax. She took her time to observe the huge, stately trees as they passed, the full lushness of the shrubbery, the abundance and variety of verdant grasses and plants, and the impressive brilliance of the setting sun as it penetrated through the trees. "It must rain a lot here," she commented.

"All the time," Entualla confessed. "But it's not bad. The oils from my wings keep me warm, so that I don't really notice the rain while I'm outside, looking after my responsibilities. And the rest of the time it doesn't matter. Now, allow me to pay attention to my footing, please, lest I fall flat on my face."

Sheana chuckled and loped ahead of her new friend, running easily over the rugged terrain. She heard the low murmur of rushing water and followed the sound, racing towards it with greater and greater speed until suddenly she came upon a large pond and practically fell in before she could stop her momentum. Perched precariously on the edge, she stared in amazement at the beauty of the place. At the base of an enormous cliff a waterfall gushed about the distance of ten air dragons, tip of tail to nose, into a sheltered pool of water. It was protected from the air by jagged mountains and massive cliffs. No dragon would comfortably fly into this ravine, thought Sheana, although one might torch it from above. Yet if everything Entualla had told her about Golden Dragons was true, this refuge was definitely paradise found. And Sheana was enchanted with it.

Entualla bustled up beside her, slightly out of breath, grinned mischievously, and then removed her skirts without ceremony, exposing her womanhood.

"Entualla!" With her new, pristine heart and consciousness, Sheana, scandalized, turned beet-red.

But the other woman was oblivious, already wading into the cool water until she was waist deep, the water concealing her nakedness. Only then did she turn and face Sheana, with that lopsided grin on her face. "It's uncomfortable to sleep in that thing while it's wet. And I need to be ready to take to the skies in an instant."

Still vaguely taken aback, Sheana stammered, "you … you're not now!"

Another grin was Entualla's only answer. The Trilian lowered herself into the water until her face disappeared. One moment, and then another, as she rubbed her hands over her legs, and then she stood upright again, dripping and smiling. Sheana's eyes widened with surprise. "Beauty and strength, you said so yourself!"

The dragon gasped.

Gills had appeared on Entualla's cheekbones, opening and closing at frantic intervals as they gasped for want of water. Then, with a powerful thrust of her wings, Entualla burst out of the water. A tail the color of the russet paint used at her cabin had replaced Entualla's legs. She dived backwards with her back arched, up and over, into the center of the pool, disappearing with hardly a splash into its depths.

Sheana stumbled back, wide-eyed with apprehension. Although she hadn't gone into the water, she instinctively checked her feet to make sure they weren't wet, as if their being so would somehow put her in danger.

The Siren-Trilian must have been watching her from the water, because Entualla's head emerged a moment later. Her smile had been replaced with a guarded expression.

Sheana stared at her, her senses recoiling instinctively. "I cannot go into the water!" she whispered.

"Why not?"

"I'm better off protecting us here, where I can get to the air in a hurry."

"Your face says you lie."

Sheana's eyes narrowed. "No Trilian would know that."

In answer, the tip of a tail floated up out of the water. "Silence is spoken amidst the deep," Entualla responded enigmatically.

"What are you?" There was repugnance in Sheana's voice.

"Is it not enough to acknowledge the difference but accept the similarities?"

"What similarities?"

"Our love for Almighty."

Her response made Sheana stop and think. Entualla had never shown her anything but kindness. Many had been the opportunities for Entualla to thrust a knife into her vulnerable dragon's neck and be done with it. Yet, for her to bring Sheana here, to her inner sanctuary; to reveal her true self, was to risk Sheana's wrath, and could possibly even precipitate Entualla's own ruin.

There was something all too familiar about this. Sheana thoughts turned to Aidan. Was not her reaction to Entualla the same as Aidan's had been towards her, Sheana, when he discovered the truth about her? The instant pang in her heart reminded Sheana of how grievous- ly she had been judged, how utterly repulsed Aidan had been by her, and how completely grief-stricken Sheana had been at his attack. She was confused. It had never been her nature to think these things before, but after today, her old way of thinking now seemed somehow foreign to her.

Suddenly, the tension drained from her and, unexpectedly weary, Sheana plopped herself down on the rocks along the shore. She set Entualla's skirts beside her, taking her time to smooth out the voluminous fabric while, under the shield of her lashes, her eyes guardedly scrutinized the mermaid-thing, who was studying her silently in return.

At last Sheana sighed deeply. "I did not know there was such a thing as a Mermaid-Trilian," she began. "I'm sorry I show so much discomfort. It's just that, well, you know how I have felt about those who dwell in the depths of the sea. You are a freak."

Entualla raised her hands into the air and began to float towards her out of the water, only to fall back onto her wings and sink back down. "I'm a freak, you think. And you're not?" she challenged. "You – You're a dragon. Who else is as despised as dragons, even by each other?"

Sheana snorted. "Especially by each other."

"So whom do you loathe more then, an interbreed, or a dragon?"

"An interbreed. No, wait." She stopped herself and thought for a moment before speaking again, more honestly. "I have to say a dragon. I loathe dragons more." Sheana stopped again, her brow furrowed as she reflected again. She looked at Entualla with more than a little surprise as she said, "But I don't. Not any more."

"When I look for that hatred it's no longer there, not even for myself. I don't really understand … " her voice trailed off.

"Me either," Entualla replied. "I mean, I did at one time; loathe myself, I mean. But not anymore."

Sheana nodded her head in agreement, a look of bewilderment lingering on her face.

395

Entualla smiled at her then, and said, gently, "Then could it not be said that I've been forgiven for being me?"

Sheana swallowed the lump in her throat and nodded again. "It is hard to hold on to my prejudice after all that you have done for me, all that you've shown me and allowed me to become."

"Then won't you come into the water with me?" Entualla held out her arms invitingly.

Sheana stared at her, uncomprehending at first. But then the warm feeling she had experienced earlier was renewed; and as it grew stronger and more powerful, Sheana felt as if she would burst with happiness.

She grinned, then suddenly leapt to her feet and bounded into the air. It seemed to Entualla that her dragon's form unfolded in a matter of seconds before the immense leviathan was poised over the water and collapsed with a mighty splash, right at the spot Entualla had only just vacated. Laughing as she darted under the water, Entualla swam far enough away to avoid being crushed by the giant lizard and her folded wings.

৪৩৫৪

"I must go back to him."

They'd grown close in the days that followed, their friendship blos-soming with a shared trust and sense of kinship. Entualla and Sheana were bonded by mutual love for their invisible Creator. Now, Entualla did not have to ask who Sheana was referring to, for they had spoken of him often.

"What do you think he'll do?"

"I cannot say. He might kill me, I suppose."

Entualla shrugged. "He might try."

"But that sword, Ent." Sheana shuddered at the memory. "You didn't see that sword."

"You were startled. You were afraid. And you were trapped in a tower. No, Sheana. You should be worried about much more than the death of just one dragon. If you go back there the two of you might destroy all that shelters under the dome."

Sheana sighed. "I still have to try. I need to make him really see the new me. I know I am risking a lot, but I think the risk is worthwhile, even for those lemmings who live under the dome." She gazed wistfully at Entualla. "I wish you could come with me."

Entualla looked at her friend and shook her head. "One sub-race is bad enough. Imagine what he would think of two." She smiled. "Perhaps you could bring him here."

"Perhaps," Sheana nodded, her eyes clouded in painful remembrance.

"When will you leave?"

"Now, I suppose. There's no point in putting it off." She looked miserable at the prospect.

"Before you, go, there is something else I would have you know."

Sheana stared at her friend.

"Come outside with me." Entualla rose from her seat and walked out of the cabin, leaving Sheana to follow after her. She directed her to a clearing among the trees and commanded, "Now, change into your natural form."

"What?"

"Give up your human guise for a moment. I noticed this when we were swimming. I think you should see it too."

Sheana shrugged and complied with her friend's demand.

"Now," Entualla instructed, "look at your scales."

Sheana swiveled her head and blinked in surprise when she saw the sun reflecting radiantly off her body. It cannot be! Entualla closed the distance between them with one step and hugged Sheana's leg to show her support. The dragon in turn, delicately so as not to cause unintentional harm to her friend, placed one of her claws gently against Entualla's back."

I'm a Gold!" Sheana whispered in amazement. "I'm a Gold!"

"Entualla, look at me," Sheana exclaimed more loudly. "I'm a Golden Dragon!" She was shouting, yet there was no anger, only exhilaration in her voice. "Look how beautiful I am! Look what Almighty has given me!"

Entualla stepped back and gazed up at her friend. Tears of joy shone in her golden eyes. "If your friend knows better," she said, "he won't be in such a hurry to cut those beautiful eyes out a second time. Besides, it is the Law of Almighty – Gold cannot cleave Gold."

Sheana bowed her head. "Thank you, Entualla," she whispered. She raised her head regally and with a new confidence. "Now I'm ready to return. Will you come with me as far as the dome?"

Entualla nodded her consent and fetched her spear. "Let's be off, then."

೫ා౧

A Golden Dragon, and a Trilian with a tail, friends and companions. Stranger things had happened – and then, perhaps not. It mattered not that the two were in the sky realm, or that Sheana's scales were golden. It was of no importance that Entualla's tail was somehow hidden from view and that her legs were concealed beneath a flowing white dress. To Sheana, this entire experience was surreal. She felt as though they were somehow breaking new ground, in a whole new era, an age that could be of peace or of war, of re-growth or of death. It was simply fantastic.

Yet most of all, what made this whole event bizarre, what made it incredible, was that the duo were flying towards a city of humans, in an attempt to win the favor of a human.

"I'll wait here," Entualla said as they alighted beside the tower and Sheana transformed back into her human masquerade. "I have no wish to be trapped inside that sphere."

Sheana concurred. "There is a platform inside the tower, should you wish to get out from under the sky. You should be safe there." At Entualla's nod, she slipped noiselessly into the building and disap - peared.

She chose to walk down the stairs, testing their weight and making sure Aidan would not fall through a rotten board if he were to return with her to the outside world. The notion was silly, she knew, and it caused Sheana pain she could not possibly understand, even with her dragon's insight. But at the very least it gave her time to think, to try to formulate the words she would speak.

He was waiting for her, sitting calmly on the bottom step.

She was surprised when she saw Aidan. Her heart thudded at the sight of him, and by the time she reached the bottom Sheana had already convinced herself that Aidan was guarding the city from her. He rose and walked to the far side of the tower, where he turned and watched her descend. A stack of paper lying on the floor was filled with drawings. Aidan had obviously been busy in her absence.

He saw Sheana staring at the sketches and said, "It helps me to think." At her surprised look he shrugged and added, "I had a lot to think about."

"I fly." Her words seemed trite, even to Sheana, but she suddenly could not remember one word of her carefully rehearsed speech.

Aidan continued to stare at her, his eyes boring into hers.

"Why didn't you kill me?" she asked.

"I have no wish to harm you."

"And yet you cut my eyes!" Sheana accused.

"I didn't want you to fuel your addiction any longer," Aidan replied.

"That is not true!" Sheana spat at him. "I don't believe that for a moment! I think you enjoyed mutilating and humiliating me!" She paused to catch her breath, chest heaving and heart pounding, and then stopped short as she grasped the significance of his words. "My addiction?" she repeated.

"You are a sky dragon, are you not?" Aidan asked her.

"You know of such things!"

Aidan shrugged and glanced around at the tower walls. Turning back to Sheana he said, "Illusions cannot always be taken at face value."

"Who are you?" She asked.

"More importantly, Sheana. Who are you?" Aidan was not angry, only protective of his city, his home. "I cannot allow a dragon to roam through these streets unchecked. I will not allow it, Sheana, not even from you."

"There is no reason for me to stay, then." Eyes downcast, Sheana bowed her head in desolation. "Forgive me for what I am," she whis - pered. "Know that I would much rather be with you, than to be who I once was." She turned and began walking up the stairs, her footsteps heavy and heart melancholy.

"Who you were?"

Sheana stopped and turned to face him.

"I see, finally," she said quietly. "And I have no obsession save one. And it is not a desire to see through my old eyes, nor to enter the Heavens, but simply a need to be connected to that which the Heavens speak of. I speak of Almighty.

"You may despise me still," Sheana continued, "you may even kill me; but even so, I forgive you, Aidan, even if you cannot forgive me for what I have been in the past."

Aidan's eyes widened as the full impact of Sheana's words hit him. He staggered with the force of it; and as the truth penetrated his consciousness, he began to weep. He sank to the floor with his head in his hands and his back to the wall, and wept. At first Sheana did not know what to do. Should she leave him here, as Aidan had indicated was his wish? Would he be repulsed by her if she approached him? She hesitated, uncertain. In the end though, compassion won and Sheana went to him. Aidan was still her beloved. She knelt beside him and caressed his back gently, and he turned and reached for her. Sheana clung to him and he to her and they cried together, their tears merging to pool upon their shoulders and in their clothing.

After a time, exhausted, their weeping ceased and they disengaged themselves. Sheana stared into his eyes and knew she was forgiven, and Aidan in turn understood that the city was safe. They knelt before each other, gazing wordlessly into each other's eyes, until Sheana grew discomfited at the intensity of emotion she was experiencing. She looked away, torn between reluctance and relief. She felt somehow bereft, but at least now she could breathe more freely.

"I would show you the sky, at least," she said, "and an angel in physical form, though she would deny the truth of that."

Aidan nodded assent and rose to his feet, reaching out to Sheana. Suddenly shy, she blushed and took his hand.

"It looks like a long walk," he commented, his neck straining towards the vast reaches of the tower.

"It's not so very long," Sheana demurred softly. "Wait until you see outside. You will know endlessness."

Aidan said nothing, and they began their ascent together.

He did not speak; nor did she. Mounting the steep staircase together, feeling the exquisite touch of each other's fingers and the thrilling proximity of their bodies was enough.

Aidan showed little fear as he stepped through the aperture onto the roof of the dome. Sheana wondered a bit at that, but reminded herself there was much more to this man than was immediately evident, so she followed him through the opening unquestioningly.

Aidan and Entualla stood there staring at each other. Entualla turned to Sheana. "That didn't take you long," she said

"He was waiting for me at the bottom of the steps."

The Trilian nodded and glanced back at Aidan.

"You know him." Sheana's voice was accusing as she glared at Entualla. Aidan turned towards Sheana then, and she rounded on him. "And you know her!"

"I know most of the scouts for the ThoroughBloods," he replied quietly. "They are my friends."

Sheana was mystified, and a little angry with both of them. "What is this? Who are you?" She demanded as she turned towards Entualla again. "And why didn't you tell me you knew him?"

"It wasn't my place," her friend replied with a slight lift of her shoulders. "He needed to reveal himself to you in his own time."

Sheana turned back to Aidan, understanding dawning in her eyes. "You are as I am," she said flatly.

By way of an answer, he threw off his disguise and immediately morphed into a Golden Dragon. "I would show you something, Sheana, if that is all right with you?"

Sheana's eyes narrowed slightly. "It is."

Aidan's head coiled downwards until he faced Entualla, his huge form mere feet from her slender body. "Goodbye little one," he said gently. "Fair thee well, and protect my dome while I'm gone."

Entualla stepped forward and threw her arms about the dragon's nose. "You won't be gone that long, Aidan," she whispered. "You can never stay away from your art."

"Things might be different this time." Aidan grinned. They stepped apart and he turned and chuckled at the shocked expression on Sheana's face. "You ready?" he asked.

She shrugged and bobbed her head. "As ready as ready gets," She replied flippantly. She was still a little perturbed that Aidan and Entualla had kept this knowledge from her, not quite ready to let either of them off the hook. And yet Sheana acknowledged that she guessed Golden Dragons had their own reasons to hide from sky dragons, as much as sky dragons had their reasons to hide from humans. Then Sheana too morphed into a dragon, her gold scales flashing vividly. She glanced at Entualla, who simply waved and gave Sheana that lopsided, engaging grin that was so unique to her.

The Golds shot effortlessly into the air. "Which way?" Sheana asked Aidan.

"Any way, as long as it's up."

She raised an eyebrow at that, but followed Aidan's lead and rocketed past him, flying higher and higher, towards the Cosmos. He caught up to her as she reached the edge of Mishard. Sheana spread her wings and soared along the periphery of the world, exploring the infinite multitude of colors and lights, feeling an infusion of waves of many lifetimes of experiences as they washed through her to ignite her insides with revelation in ways of acceptance she'd never encoun-tered before.

The miracle of the Heavens taught her everything she could possi-bly want to learn about their Creator. They showed her how they rejoiced in His ways, celebrated in His plans. And Sheana's beautiful, golden spirit exulted and frolicked with the comprehension that had always been denied her and which she was now forever blessed with.

Aidan, too, gazed at the vast expanse of wonder that lay before them, but only briefly before he grinned mischievously, tilted his head away from Mishard, banked and shot upwards through the barrier of the world.

Sheana laughed and cried simultaneously. Then, feeling as though she'd come home for the very first time, she smiled, her heart full, and followed Aidan, the artist, her beloved, into the Heavens.

$\infty$$\propto$

About the Author

Mark S. Roberts was born into a military family and followed in his father's footsteps. He served in the United States Air Force as a security policeman for 20 years and is a Desert Storm veteran. Mark holds a bachelor's degree in administration in criminal justice. He and his wife, Lori (also a USAF veteran) lived in Charlotte, North Carolina, after his retirement for many years before moving to a small town just outside Green Bay, Wisconsin, where they currently reside.

Mark was raised in Jacksonville, Florida, and has lived and served in locations around the world. He and Lori travel whenever possible and have visited all fifty states. They enjoy the national parks and many historical places throughout the lands, including many civil war sites. In addition to travelling, he likes to golf, woodwork, hike, and attend the occasional Jacksonville Jaguars game.

www.ingramcontent.com/pod-product-compliance
Lightning Source LLC
Chambersburg PA
CBHW071143020726
47502CB00002B/252